Shroud of the Scion

Watchers of the Land ~ Book 1

DARREN BRETT KING

To my wife, for her tireless support of this particular project, and her endless enthusiasm for all things creative.

FOREWARD

When it comes to digesting fiction, it has been said that there are two kinds of readers. One kind prefers to have a few contextual cues in place from the get-go, some landmarks for the journey, so to speak. The other kind actually prefers to uncover those contextual cues within the narrative itself, in what we might call "real-time". If you fall into that second group, you may very well prefer to skip the remainder of this introduction, and move on directly to the Prologue. We'll pause to let you do that now...

But for those of you who'd appreciate a little bit of backdrop to begin this tale, read on...

This story takes place on a planet called Eiasa – pronounced [Ee – AY – sa]. Eiasa is a world still slowly recovering from the effects of a mysterious, destabilizing event, or rather – series of events, collectively known as *the Disintegration*. During the height of the destabilizing period this world was seemingly coming apart at the seams, in a way that the peoples of that world could not comprehend.

Explanations were plentiful, though usually nothing more than fanciful grasps at matters far beyond the collective understanding of the time. Blame was even more common – one nation blaming another; one religious group blaming another; many sure their fate was nothing short of a judgment from the gods.

Following the Disintegration, a series of brutal, costly wars were fought over these divergent interpretations, no nation being spared from the revolving door of blame, attack, and revenge. In the end, when the wars finally fizzled out, Eiasa's population was half of what it had been only two decades previous, and many formerly prosperous states lay in ruins, some ceasing to exist altogether.

Isolation, not peace, then became the norm, with each people group still wary of the others. Eventually though, after a generation or more, that pervading sense of mistrust began to gradually ease.

It is in this period of gradual easing that our story takes place.

Of these various people groups, our story is particularly interested in a peculiar, wandering clan known as the Vaidas. For the record, the word Vaida is pronounced (v – EYE – da). The Vaidas are few in number and mysterious in nature. To their contemporaries, their origin is as opaque as is their mission. While some see them as nothing more than a vagabond order of eccentric mystics, we will learn that there is much more to them than meets the eye. Above all, they are guarding a secret knowledge; the very knowledge at the heart of the Disintegration.

For generations the Vaidas (also known as the Watchers) have sought to protect the world from a recurrence of the Disintegration, by guarding the secret knowledge that initiated it.

And thus begins the drama of this tale. For as we soon find out, one thing is clear: strange things are happening again in the world. And to the Vaidas chagrin, their secret... is out.

PROLOGUE

As the rain drove relentlessly upon the drenched wooden deck, the ship's stern rose towards the sky before crashing down again into the raging surf. Seconds later the process repeated itself, the ship seesawing upon the massive waves. Nervous deck hands did all they could to keep the vessel upright, but it was beginning to feel like a losing battle. The ship was taking on water now, faster than the crew could disperse of it.

From the navigation deck that first mate looked on, shaking his head. Rather than seeing the clouds begin to clear, as the captain had promised would happen, the horizon looked more ominous than ever. He turned and marched down the steps, intent on speaking with the captain. As he approached the door that would lead him down into the belly of the ship, he caught sight of several of the crew, huddled together under minimal shelter. As he approached he slowed, ducked behind a mast to hear the conversation.

"It's not wise, I tell you. The captain's not thinking straight."

"Not wise?" another man blurted out, sounding exasperated. "It's madness is what it is! It's a suicide mission is what it is! Every one of us knows what comes of ships looking to find the Isle of Shroud."

"Demise," a third man offered. "Either slow or quick, it matter none. Death and destruction be the result, every time, as near as I can tell."

"As near as *you* can tell?" spoke the first mate, suddenly stepping out to confront the others. "And what, pray tell, do *you* know about such things, Canderson? Hmm? Rumors? Old wives' tales? You with your world-class education, do tell, what *do* you know of such things?"

"Well I..." the man stumbled.

"Rhetorical, Canderson. *Rhetorical!* The point being, you don't know *anything* about such matters. So best you keep to sweeping the deck, rigging the mast, cleaning the latrine – things you do know a thing or two about!

"Besides, you weren't so afraid of this mission when first we took sail. Are you spooked now simply because the water's grown a little rough? *Hmmm?*"

"Sir, when first we set sail we didn't know our destination. We were only told–"

"Silence, man! That wasn't an invitation to carry on with your complaining! The point is, you agreed to the mission because you were promised to be handsomely paid at the end of it. So I expect you to follow through with that commitment, *without* any more bellyaching!

"Now, listen up, every one of you. I don't want to hear any more talk of such matters. It's *just* a storm. We've been through such before, and we'll be through such again. Stop acting like frightened children spooked by fairytales. And if any of you succumbs again to such whims, I will have him court-martialed right quick, and then off the plank you go. Is that understood?"

The group mumbled their ascent.

"*Is it understood?*" the first mate repeated, louder and more pronounced.

"Yes, sir. Tis understood," they chimed in together, in almost perfect unison.

"Right! Then back to work, all of you, lest we succumb to this storm out of your sheer neglect of duty."

More mumbles of assent and the group went their separate ways. The first mate watched them for a moment, following with his eyes as they returned to their stations. Then he turned abruptly and yanked open the cabin door, sending his feet drumming down the stairs to the cabin below.

The captain, dressed in full regalia, sat before a large oak table, studying a crinkled map. He smoothed out a section and peered more closely, pulling on his long jet black goatee as he did so.

There was a rap at the door.

"Captain, a word?"

"Hmmm?" the captain replied, distractedly, turning from the map and looking in the direction of the door. "Oh, Maynard... If you must, I suppose. What is it now?"

The first mate cleared his throat, stepped forward, peering down at the map upon the table.

"Sir, it is the crew, and the storm, it seems–"

"Well, which one is it, Maynard? The crew, or the storm?"

Maynard took a deep breath, removed his drenched hat, noticing the captain's eyes trace the water that fell upon his dry polished floor.

"Sir, the last time we spoke of such matters you said we were within three days of finding the island."

"So, what of it?"

"Well, sir, that was four days ago."

The captain snickered. "Maynard, my young yip, these things are not exactly a science you understand. After all, there is a reason why it's called the *Isle of Shroud.* Tis a tad difficult to locate."

"Well, yes, Captain... of course. My concern, however, is with the morale of the crew."

"*Morale?* What of it? Each man has been promised his weight in gold at the end of this voyage. What better moral-booster is there than that?"

Maynard smiled awkwardly, then, seeing the look on the captain's face, grew concerned that the captain took the smirk to be something akin to insubordination. He cleared his throat again.

"Sir, they grow restless."

"They grow restless?" the captain parroted, "Well, how quaint. Well then, Maynard, *settle them down again.* That's your concern, not mine. And if you want your share of the gold you best get to it."

"If I may speak plainly, sir, my role is also to make you aware of any potential for mutiny."

"Potential?" the captain mocked. "*Potential?* Maynard, the moment a ship pushes off from shore there is *potential* for mutiny. It goes without saying. And that's what you're here for. To make sure the *potential* is never realized."

The first mate paused, his eyes studying the floorboards, before deciding to change course.

"Sir, in addition, the ship is taking on water."

"Indeed, Maynard, ships at sea are known to do that. That's what the buckets are for. I suggest–"

"Sir, what I mean to say," Maynard interrupted, growing impatient with the delicate game he was forced to play between captain and crew, "is that at this rate we have only a few days before this situation comes to a head. I'm not sure what will crack first, the ship itself, or the crew that mans it. But it is coming. I pledge all my seafaring years upon it."

The captain met Maynard's eye and held his stare. For a moment Maynard feared he had crossed a line the captain would not forgive. But then the captain waved a hand in the air, dismissively, before turning back to his map.

"Within a few days? Well then, we have nothing to be concerned about."

"Sir?" the first mate said, not understanding.

"Maynard, my eager young yip, a few days is more than we need. I've been studying this map and we're within a day of spotting land. The Isle of Shroud's famed shore is almost within our grasp. So fear not."

Maynard nodded slowly, clearing his throat yet again. "Very good, sir. But if by chance–"

"*No!* No more, Maynard! I've said what I've said and that's that. Now be gone, I have work to do."

With that the captain turned his attention back to the crinkled map. Maynard paused only a moment longer.

"Yes, Captain," he said, before turning and marching out the same way he came.

1

Gursa was a simple game – in theory. A team, comprised usually of four players, move a ball (actually a thoroughly steamed, purplish fruit from a guriya tree) down the beach, by passing it from player to player, with the aim of depositing it in a weaved basket in the opponents' end. Do so and your team scores a point.

In practice, however, the game was not so simple. Because each player could only move from his spot when he wasn't in possession of the gursa ball. And when he received it from a teammate, he could not hold it in his hand, nor let it drop to the sandy ground. Rather, he would use a combination of his head, shoulders, chest, and, most of all, legs and feet, to keep the ball in constant motion. So, in reality, it was a very difficult game to master.

However, these boys playing on the beach today *had* mastered it. After all, they had been playing it since they were barely old enough to walk. It was really the only game played on the island. And, as such, it was played often.

Presently one of the boys, feeling an opponent at

his heal, struck the gursa ball with a little more gusto than was required. The ball soared so high it cleared the beach altogether, and came down on the roof of one of the huts at the edge of the village.

"Oh boy, Frisa," one of the boys called out, "you really pick your places. Aim much?"

The boys laughed and one of them, an olive-skinned, wavy-haired young man named Ademo, scrambled up onto the thatched roof.

"Oh swicka," he called out, shaking his head, "the ball actually went through the skylight."

Looking down, Ademo saw that the ball had landed on the stomach of a man who lay motionless on a floor mat below.

"Not possible!" he exclaimed, with disbelief. "The ball landed right on top of Huriso!"

Shouts of surprise, laughter, and some dismay rang out amongst the boys. For while this man may have looked like he was sleeping, in reality he was in a comatose state. He was breathing. But he had remained still, his eyes closed to the world, for more than a decade now.

On top of that he wasn't just any average village member. He was in fact the senior elder – the man who's authority was trumped only by the chief himself.

"Hold on, I'll go get it," Ademo called out, beginning to lower himself down through the rudimentary skylight.

Just then a hand grasped firmly onto his forearm.

"Not so fast, Asterling. You should show more respect for Elder Huriso. Not just anyone should go climbing into his hut."

Ademo, seeing the chief's eldest son glaring at him, thought about saying something in retort, but then relented.

"Suit yourself, Tyaso," he said, shaking his arm free, backing out to allow Tyaso access.

Moments later the ball had been retrieved.

While the others were ready to start up the game again, Tyaso demanding they join him, with heads bowed, in a prayer of well-being for the comatose elder who was clearly oblivious to anything that had just transpired.

The others acquiesced to Tyaso's demand. After all, he was the chief's eldest son. But truth be told, they would have been just as happy to go on without a word. Did Huriso really mind either way?

A young man named Frisa dropped the ball to his foot, before flipping it nimbly to his other foot and kicking it diagonally across the field to Ademo.

With dexterity Ademo cushioned the ball with his thigh, letting it drop to his opposite ankle, before kicking it back up to his head (just barely keeping the ball from Tyaso's outstretched foot), then back down to his left foot – which he then used to send the ball sailing over the heads of two opposing players.

The ball came down close to the basket, where a teammate simply nodded at it, sending it right into the center of the basket.

Ademo and his teammates roared in triumph, backhand-slapping shoulders in celebration, as was custom. That point brought the team's total to 10 – and thus, to victory.

"Nice pass, Ademo!" said the boy who had nodded the ball into the basket.

"Nice nod!" Ademo responded in kind.

Tyaso's teammates walked over to the chief's first-born and made sure to make note of Tyaso's near interception. But he shook them off, clearly frustrated that he hadn't taken the ball away from Ademo when he'd had the chance.

Just then the clear sound of a wialoe horn rang out strong and true, as it did three times a day on the island, signaling the start of the community meal.

"Perfect timing! I could eat a whale right about now," one of the boys (who's waistline suggested perhaps he already had, on occasion) said.

The boys ran up the short path through the tropical shrubbery and palm trees. At the edge of the village they crowded around a pump to wash off before dinner.

Once clean, they darted around the clay and straw buildings into the very center of the village, where a clearing revealed the long, rectangular community table.

Many of the village folk were already seated, families sitting side by side. Ademo spotted his mother, Siya, seated somewhere near the middle. When he reached her he leaned down to kiss her before taking his seat.

Moments later the village chief, Fyoma, stood up from his place at the end of the table. He held his hands up to the sky, said a prayer, and then clapped – signaling the meal had begun.

In the middle of the table, and running end to end, steaming fish sat on racks next to wooden bowls full of pineapples, guriya, and coconut. The villagers now eagerly reached in, the children and youth (for the most part) patiently letting their parents and elders serve themselves first.

As the feast began, a slim teenage girl dressed in a straw skirt made her way around the table, pouring coconut milk into wooden mugs for each member of the village.

Siya couldn't help but notice her son's eyes tracing the steps of Jania as she made her way towards them.

When it came their turn to receive the drink, Jania, with her dark hair and almond eyes, smiled down at Ademo.

"Hi, 'Demo. How'd the gursa game go?"

"Not bad," he replied, smiling back. "I think I managed to make a decent play or two" he said, with false modesty.

The boys around him rolled their eyes. It was common knowledge that Ademo was one of the better players, though he didn't always show it – preferring to use his skill sporadically. Some called that humility. Others, including a few of the village elders, thought it more likely attributable to laziness.

The boy is skilled, in both joint and jinto (joint referring to athletic prowess, and jinto the old word for intelligence), *but not so much with tria* (wisdom), they would often say.

"Your fish is getting cold, floaty-eyes," Siya said to her son, noticing with humor his interest in the blossoming Jania.

Ademo felt blood flush to his face, and presently got down to pulling his fish apart and stuffing it into his mouth. But his mother, spying him from the corner of her eye, couldn't help but notice his eyes frequently rise to watch Jania as she continued to serve drink to the rest of the table.

Siya also noticed Tyaso, the chief's eldest, watching Ademo watching Jania. *That Tyaso, born with so much, yet with so much to prove – in his own mind, anyway.*

Looking towards her son, Siya saw that he'd already finished his first piece of fish, and was presently reaching for another. He's grown up so fast, Siya thought to herself. It feels like just yesterday that I was praising his first steps, and look at him now, looking more and more like a man every day. Looking more and more like his father; the one he's never really known.

In fact, he was almost the spitting image of his father, were it not for the thick, wavy hair and strikingly large, blue, penetrating eyes – which came from her side. Those eyes had drawn plenty of notice throughout the village. For they were unique to Siya and Ademo. Some, including this girl Jania, Siya assumed, thought it made Ademo exotically handsome. Others seemed only to notice that those eyes branded him an outsider.

Still watching him from the corner of her eye, Siya sighed. Yes, he was on the cusp of manhood. In fact, the very next morning he was due to make his Placca – his journey into self; his pilgrimage into adulthood. Siya wished Ademo would have spent the day before such an iconic event meditating, preparing for the mental strain that would come a day later. But he, in his usual manner, had brushed such concerns off, saying that he'd had eighteen years to prepare for such a day. If he wasn't ready by now, what difference would one more day make?

She knew that wasn't exactly the point. But convincing her hardheaded son of that was another matter entirely.

So he'd spent the final afternoon before his Placca playing gursa with his friends. Well, if nothing else, at least he would enter in with a light spirit and a clear conscience. And perhaps that would be enough. She hoped so. But she didn't really know much about such matters.

Later that evening, as the village lay mostly silent, Siya entered Ademo's room, found him sitting cross-legged on the floor, reading a scroll. *Ah, he is studying the ways of the elders. So perhaps he isn't quite as carefree as he would have me believe.*

Hearing her shuffling footsteps, Ademo turned, rolling the scroll up as he did so.

"Hello, Mother."

"Hello, Darling. Are you enriched by your reading?"

He nodded. "I am."

"Good. And how do you feel?"

He looked at her for a moment, shrugged. "Alright, I guess."

Siya noticed the doubtful look in his eyes, a rare event to be sure.

As Ademo turned to look towards the open window, a silence ensued, with only the sound of the swishing palms trees to fill the void.

"I *so* wish your father were here to speak to you now. I have prepared you as best I know how. But the Placca is something best described from father to son."

Ademo looked at her briefly, then back outside again. She knew he felt it: the lack of a father. Of course he felt it, especially in a moment such as this one. He rarely spoke of his father, but sometimes, in his vacant stare, she sensed the longing all the same.

"Chief Fyoma spoke to me some."

"Did he?" she said, trying to sound pleased.

Ademo nodded. "Drico's father, too."

"Oh yes?"

He nodded again.

"Mother, did my father... did he ever speak to you about his Placca?" Ademo asked, almost sounding embarrassed.

Siya bit her lip, joined her son's gaze towards the swaying palms in the moonlight.

"No, Ademo. I can't say that he did."

Even though saying so was only a half-truth, she let it stand. How could she tell her son that his father never went through the Placca – when every other man he'd ever known had? She didn't know how to tell him more. And she wasn't sure knowing more would help him anyway. Not with the life they had here on the island.

He nodded slowly. "I suppose it's something most men keep to themselves," Ademo said, not wanting his mother to feel his loss.

Her eyes grew watery. This son of hers: hardheaded and sporadic he may be, but also so aware and considerate of others' feelings. He had been careful to never let her feel responsible for his lack of a father. Never.

"What time do you plan on leaving in the morning?" she asked.

"Before first light."

"Then you best be getting to sleep, Son. The moon is already high in the sky."

He nodded.

"Be sure to eat a hearty breakfast before you make for the trail," she said.

"I will," he said, smiling at her.

"Son," she said, feeling her eyes water again, "you know that I am so proud of you, as would your father be."

He nodded, meeting her eyes.

As he stood, she moved towards him, stood on her toes to reach his shoulders, then put her arms around him and held him tight. She wanted to talk to him more about his Placca, but she knew it would only embarrass him. This, again, was the place for a father.

"And when will you be back?" she asked, already dreading the waiting.

"Not sure. Chief said the sign almost always appears by the second day. That those who don't see it by then aren't really looking."

Siya nodded, trying not to betray her concern.

"Good night, my darling," she said, embracing him again. "Sleep you well."

"And you, Mother," he said, giving her another of his reassuring smiles.

Even now, he worries for my concern as much as for himself – perhaps more, she thought to herself. My sweet boy, now nearly a man, but no less sweet as a result.

And in that way perhaps he was a little less like his father, and she was glad for it.

2

Ademo slept restlessly and awoke with his eyes feeling heavy. Today was in important day though.

And as adrenaline did its trick he quickly revived. As much as he had played down the Placca experience in recent days, he knew it was a momentous occasion; a rite of passage into manhood; a time to receive his calling from the seven winds at the Whispering Cliffs.

But what if no such call came? Ademo had wondered this on various occasions lately, but felt afraid to voice the thought to others. As far as he knew no one had ever returned from their pilgrimage having not received a call.

But then again, he wasn't quite like the others. At least that was how he felt. He couldn't help but wonder if others felt the same way when their Placca came due. Perhaps it was a common fear he was having. Perhaps it was part of the experience itself.

This rationalization made him feel better, for a moment or two.

With so much on his mind, Ademo didn't feel particularly hungry, but knew he'd promised his mother he'd eat a good breakfast. Once he had left the village it would be up to him to forage for food. He was to bring no provisions with him. He was even forbidden from bringing a common hunting knife or throwing disc. That was the way of the Placca.

In the kitchen he found a basket of boiled mapaui eggs with bread and coconut milk already laid out for him. He smiled. This was probably difficult for his mother, standing back and letting her son venture into this passage alone. No doubt the nurturer in her would rather have made the journey with him. But

23

that was strictly forbidden. Village life was generally easygoing and lighthearted. But not when it came to the great traditions. These were treated with real gravity, lest a curse fall upon the entire village, as had been rumored to have happened many generations before.

With a last slug of milk, Ademo quietly exited the hut. He looked up at the sky and saw a hint of color behind the silhouetted palm trees. It was later in the day than he thought. He knew he'd better get moving. He had a long hike ahead of him.

Now feeling energy in his bones, Ademo quickly moved through the haphazardly organized huts of the village and then out onto the beach trail.

He followed along the shoreline, comforted by the soft lapping of waves, for nearly an hour. And then he turned onto a narrow trail, barely visible amidst the dense brush.

Soon the trail began ascending towards the hills at the center of the island, looping back and forth in wide turns. If he moved quickly enough, Ademo hoped to make the summit of Mt. Uduri by noon.

By the time he emerged onto the Uduri summit plateau, where a full panoramic view of the island was available, he figured by the position of the sun that it was probably already an hour or more past midday.

Though he didn't really want to admit it to himself, Ademo had dragged his feet a little on the trail that morning. It was nerves. He wasn't sure what awaited him on the other side of the island. And on

SHROUD OF THE SCION

such occasions Ademo tended to greet the unknown
with reluctance, trepidation and delay.

He picked from the vindu berry bushes that
littered the top of the mountain, while stealing glances
down towards the village. It looked startlingly small
from this height. The island itself was not a large one.
One could leave in the morning from one point and
return to that same point two days later, assuming a
brisk walk and only minimal rest throughout. Not that
Ademo had any real perspective on the size of the
island. He had known nothing else. It was to him the
sum total of the inhabitable world.

Even with the island not being a large one, the
tribe rarely ventured far beyond the village. Rabbit,
fish, and a deer-like creature known as kinta were
plentiful on the island. The tribe grew fruit and
vegetables nearby as well. So venturing far wasn't
usually necessary.

And then there was the strange way the elders
sometimes spoke about the far side of the island.
Ademo had never been able to quite put his finger on
it, but he sensed unease in their voices on such
occasions.

Speaking of the far side of the island, what was it
the chief had said about his Placca pilgrimage? *Keep to
the trail, due east, all the way to the Whispering Cliffs
on the other side of the island.*

Ademo had nodded, trying to look resolved and
confident before the chief. But ever since then he'd
wondered what on earth those words meant. So he

was supposed to hear messages in the breeze? It all sounded bizarre to him. Again he felt pangs of longing for his long since departed father. The chief had done what he could to prepare Ademo. But the chief was a man of few words, and many demands. His availability was limited.

When he'd had his fill of berries, Ademo rose to his feet, stood looking farther outward, to the surrounding waterscape. He admired the crystal blue aquamarine, and how the sunlight danced upon it.

Lifting his gaze further still, his eyes looked upon the ring of mist, known to the villagers as the *Lord's Shield*, that encircled the entire island. As always, Ademo's mind pondered what was beyond the mist – if anything. Such matters generally weren't spoken about. When asked, the adults usually told the young ones that only the old had time for such considerations; that the young should concern themselves with learning skills to help the village.

All Ademo knew was that, in his lifetime, no one from the island had ever launched a craft beyond that fog line. Nor had any outside craft visited them from beyond. It was for all intents and purposes, the end of the world.

His mother had always behaved rather peculiarly when such topics were discussed – which again, was rarely. She would smile awkwardly, excuse herself or tend to some errand that suddenly seemed important when it had only a moment before seemed not to be so. The one time he had particularly pestered her for more information, sensing she wasn't telling him all she knew, she had said something about a terrible accident that had happened in the wider world; killing off whole populations, leaving the areas beyond the Lord's Shield hopelessly contaminated.

When Ademo asked her for more details, she had looked at him long and hard before responding.

"There will come a time to discuss such things, Ademo. But not yet. You have other things to dwell on for now."

Not the least of which was, of course, his Placca. Speaking of which, he decided it was time to move on; he should delay no longer. He spat berry seeds into the bush and moved towards the trail that picked up on the other side of the plateau.

The trail that had been firm and clearly marked on the other side of the mountain, quickly deteriorated into one that was obscure and overgrown with tall weeds. As he followed the trail he began descending into a narrow canyon, sheer cliffs rising up to his left and right, looking treacherous and too steep to climb.

Before long the ground beneath Ademo's feet grew soggy, and more than once he almost lost a shoe. Since this side of the island received the majority of the rainfall, he supposed soggy ground was to be expected. But still, he felt a little frustrated that no one had told him to expect such terrain, or how best to transverse it. After all, what good was a trail that led you into a bog?

To make matters worse, the horizon now revealed dark, swirling clouds moving in quickly. This wasn't rainy season; that wasn't due for weeks yet. And still, those clouds were no illusion. They were packed full of moisture, and they were headed his way.

Before long Ademo's feet were plunging into soggy mud. This time he did lose a shoe when trying to ply his foot from the mucky ground. He cursed and dug deep with his hand to pull the shoe up again.

One thing was clear: he needed to change course. He could see that he was still on the trail, because it was still discernable (just barely) from the surroundings. But, evidently, it was also not passable. If anything, the ground seemed to be getting soggier as he descended, not less so.

As steep as the cliff walls looked, he decided he could perhaps make his way along the bottom of one of them – holding onto the wall face for support.

He shuffled left, as best he could, till he came close to the sheer face of the cliff wall. He put on his shoe, trying to ignore the sickly wet feeling that came with it, and attempted to resume the general direction of the trail. Here by the rock wall he was on marginally higher ground, that offered slightly drier footholds. As he walked he tried to ignore the squishy, sucking sounds his feet now made as he moved slowly through the tall reeds.

Ademo assumed nearly two hours had passed by the time he finally found himself leaving the boggy terrain and entering into a dense rainforest. By now the clouds that had been on the horizon were rolling overhead. A stiff breeze had picked up as well.

Ademo was barely one hundred feet into the dense undergrowth, where ferns rapped against his arms and face, when he heard a loud crack overhead. He turned his face skyward and almost immediately began to feel large water droplets stinging his face. Even with the tree canopy, he knew the downpour from these storm clouds would have him drenched in no time.

With the dark clouds was coming early evening. Light was fading fast on this day, to his great dismay. Making it to the Whispering Cliffs before nightfall now seemed impossible. Ademo decided he had best find what shelter he could and batten down for the night.

He pushed on through the vegetation, getting wetter by the minute. He tried to keep to the same general direction. But, in weaving to the left and right - as he was forced to do in the dense undergrowth – that was proving difficult to do.

It was more than an hour later that Ademo came upon the section of the island that was home to the largest trees of all: the massive, thick-stumped guima palms. Here there was a little more shelter from the rain.

Eventually, when the light was growing truly dim, he came across one such tree with a tall, hollowed out trunk. Ademo decided this was as good a camping place as he was likely to find with the light quickly failing.

He entered the overhang and immediately collapsed to the ground, which proved relatively soft with a padding of old palm leaves. Ademo was exhausted. Beyond exhausted. He was also hungry, but what would he find to eat here now that it was near dark?

He decided he didn't have the energy to even attempt a search. Instead, he lay down on the ground, listened to the soft pelting of rain drops for a few minutes, and then fell directly into a deep slumber.

3

Even before morning light broke over the village, Siya was awakened by a voice at the door. She bolted upright, taking only a moment to gather her bearings. Ademo! She thought to herself. Was something wrong? Have they come to bring me bad news?

The village huts were small and the walls thin. From where she lay Siya called out.

"Yes, what is it?"

A voice – that she immediately recognized as belonging to Kwanti, one of the chief's sons – replied: "Uma Siya, forgive the intrusion, but Chief requests your presence in the Skytent. There is a conference being held as we speak."

Siya took a moment to process the strange news. A conference? Now? At this hour? This was no scheduled event. And that could mean only one thing: an emergency.

Feeling her chest tighten, Siya rose from her bed and began dressing quickly. She tried to assure herself that it likely had nothing to do with Ademo. Even if something had happened on his Placca, why would they convene a conference over such a matter? No, it was unlikely to be related. And still, she had to remind herself to breathe as she ran from the hut only moments later.

As Siya neared the Skytent, which was a large structure built with large log polls reaching towards the sky, with a small opening at the top, Truji, another of Fyoma's sons, opened the door to receive her.

"Light of the morning, Uma Siya. They're waiting for you inside," he said.

Siya mumbled her thanks and rushed inside.

The six elders, comprised of three women and three men, as was custom, were seated at the center round table. Siya couldn't help but notice the strains on all their faces. And that made her nervous. The elders were seldom shaken by events. They were counted upon to be the "unchanging stones" of village life.

As she approached, Muina, a grey haired women who was the oldest of the six, motioned for her to take a seat beside her.

Siya crossed her heart and bowed slightly, as was custom, before taking a seat.

Fyoma, the chief, looked in her direction. "Light of the morning, Siya. Thank you for coming."

"Of course, Chief. I came as quickly as I could. What news?"

She knew it was a little presumptuous to ask such a question out of turn. Usually the chief would be the one to raise a matter, when he deemed it appropriate. But the concern in the eyes around her, and the fact that her only son was out wandering somewhere on the other side of the island, got the best of her.

"Siya, we have convened the council because of the Storm Sign," he said, with a sense of great import.

Siya glanced around the table, trying to read the expressions. She didn't share their knowledge of the island's deep traditions. And on another occasion she would have perhaps been embarrassed by her lack of understanding. But this morning her concern was too grave.

"Chief, apologies, the Storm Sign?"

Gela, the chief's wife, seated to his right, spoke up.

"Siya, the Storm Sign is foretold in our lore. As you know, the rainy season begins every year, within a day or two of the autumn santo. The greatest deviation of that timeline came seventeen years ago, when the first rains of the season fell three days after santo."

Siya began to understand. Today was the 17th of August. More than a month before santo.

"I see," she said, not knowing what else to say.

"But yesterday afternoon a storm rolled in," Gela continued, "and this was no lost cloud. It was a true autumn thundercloud. A series of them to speak true. And in our lore this event is said to mark grave danger. Indeed it is a warning sign sent by the gods."

Siya nodded, trying to be patient as Gela paused and cleared her throat. Siya couldn't help but notice those around the table exchanging glances. An elder named Kuio shifted in his seat.

"Your son," Kuio began.

"Yes, what of him?" Siya asked, trying not to sound alarmed or fearful. Kuio was a quiet, serious man, who always seemed to Siya to be primarily interested in installing order to the usually carefree goings-on of the village folk. And she had never really trusted him. It was something about the way he looked at Ademo.

"He embarks on his Placca, does he not?" Kuio continued.

"He does," she responded, wondering why she was being asked to confirm something they all well knew.

Kuio nodded, then frowned. "And yet, he is not a native."

There was a slight shuffling and more stolen glances from around the table.

From the silence Siya gathered she was to respond to Kuio's statement.

"Spoken true, Dali Kuio. But what has this to do

33

with your Storm Sign?"

Kuio's eyes rose to meet hers. There was not only a seriousness there, but elements of anger as well.

"As you may remember, when the matter of the boy's future in the village was first considered – when he turned ten – some of us questioned the wisdom of letting him take on the path of a native."

"I remember it well," Siya responded evenly, meeting his gaze, determined not to shy away.

Fyoma placed a hand on Kuio's shoulder, a sign that he would speak. "Siya, the council fears for the safety of the village. While it was decided, those years ago, that Ademo should be granted the way of the Path, this recent turn of events... well, it gives us pause."

Siya nodded, taking notice of the Chief's vague conclusion. It was not his custom to speak in such a manner. And that made her more nervous still.

"You feel this Storm Sign is the gods' way of expressing their displeasure at Ademo's pilgrimage?" Siya asked, not able to disguise the rising tone of her voice.

The chief frowned. "Siya, you must understand, you and your son are well liked. You have become like two of our own. You know that."

"I know that is true for some," Siya said evenly, shifting her stare to Kuio, who met her gaze only for a moment, before looking away.

Silence ensued. When no one else spoke up, Gela turned to her husband, mumbled something unintelligible. He frowned, as if distraught, and then spoke.

"You will be provided with a craft of the finest timber, to be constructed by Hiola, who is the greatest craftsman we have," spoke Fyoma, trying to sound conciliatory.

For a moment Siya stared uncomprehendingly towards the chief. Then reality hit home.

"You're *banishing* us? Because of an early rain?" she exclaimed, rising from her seat.

She looked from face to face, taking note of the expressions. She noted fear, compassion, and in Kuio's case, a barely concealed rage.

"Even now she mocks our traditions, even the Great Lore!" Kuio said, shaking his head, pointing in her vague direction with his long, narrow finger.

Fyoma placed a hand on Kuio's shoulder – again. "I am sorry, Siya. Again, we have embraced you and your son like native-born. But this is a commandment from the gods. We know no other way of reading the Sign. And to ignore the warning; even to delay, may mean a worse fate for the entire village. And we cannot risk that. We have convened. We have considered. We have found unison. It is thus pronounced."

With that he clapped his hands together in front of him, signaling that the decision was now law. *Law.* There was nothing else to be said.

Siya remained still, dumbfounded, staring blankly ahead, while the others rose slowly from the table.

4

Ademo awoke from his slumber when he felt something moving across his lower leg. His hand immediately brushed at whatever it was, but found nothing. He looked down and saw a small lizard scampering away from him. Ademo sighed. It could have been worse. He was imagining a snake.

Once he'd stood and stretched, he moved out from under the hollowed out trunk. Beams of sunlight were piercing through to the jungle floor, and Ademo thought the scene a much friendlier one than the night before.

His next thought was of his stomach. It was growling. He hadn't eaten since the previous afternoon, when he'd munched on berries at the summit of Mt. Uduri.

In preparation for this very journey he'd taken the time to learn from some of his elders about what was edible along the path to the Whispering Cliffs. And he remembered being told that when it came to the jungle, he could usually find Flowershrooms in plentiful supply. The key – and it really was key – was to make sure they were Flowershrooms, clearly marked by their two color appearance. A near relative, known as Mirrorflocks, looked almost identical, except that they typically came in single colors (usually grey or a dull green). These plants were not exactly poisonous, but they'd leave you with nasty bouts of diarrhea.

Ademo marched on, keeping his eyes pealed to the foliage all about him. He'd been walking for what felt like a long while – and was beginning to think he'd been lied to, or had somehow ended up in the wrong part of the jungle – when he spotted a swatch of them not ten feet from the trail.

He bent down and inspected closely. Sure enough, two colored – purple and yellow, and distinctly flowery in appearance. He picked one from its stem and sampled a bit from the end. Its texture left something to be desired, but the slightly nutty flavor was likeable enough. Soon he was finishing off that Flowershroom and reaching down for more.

When he'd had his fill, Ademo picked several more for good measure, and tucked them into his clothes. Now he needed water. He knew the path would eventually crisscross a stream, or so he was told. So for now he tried to put what was becoming a rather insatiable thirst aside, and marched on.

It was difficult to keep track of time while the sun was hidden high above the jungle canopy. The guima palms really were massive, and their leaf-tops, some two to three hundred feet over his head, created a near roof-like effect.

It was probably an hour or so later that Ademo

began to finally hear the unmistakable trickle of a stream. His dry mouth ached at the sound. He figured his mouth would have watered if only it had a drop to spare. He picked up his pace now, pushing large shrub leafs aside as he followed the meandering trail. Finally, fifteen minutes after first hearing the trickling sounds, he came across the stream bed.

The rushing waters rose in a crescendoing sound as he bent down at the stream's edge and dipped his hand in. The water was cool and fresh. He thought he'd never drunk anything so delicious in his life. After scooping water into his mouth with his hands, he leaned farther down and dunked his entire head into the cold, rushing stream. He took several large gulps and rose back up feeling fully refreshed.

With food and water in his belly, he now felt ready to continue on in relative strength. It would be noon within about an hour – or so he surmised as best he could – and, if so, he hoped to make it through the jungle and out onto the plains that would lead him to the Whispering Cliffs by early afternoon.

Just when he thought the jungle had no end, or that perhaps the trail was a trick that looped around in a giant circle, Ademo spotted blotches of sunlight through the tree line ahead. Soon after the palms around him became more sparse. And then he was out of the jungle altogether, walking directly into bright sunlight.

He followed the trail, more clearly visible out here in the open, for half an hour more, before the path began to rise up again, not steeply, but noticeable. Rocky crags began to appear to the left and right. From what he'd been told, the cliffs were now within reach.

And then, as he turned a corner and moved around a large, craggy column, there it was: the sheer face of a cliff wall. The cliffs rose like a tower at the end of the plain – in both impressive and intimidating fashion; intimidating because he knew the last part of his journey would involve climbing that rock face, with nothing but his hands and feet as tools.

As Ademo continued on the path, his eyes gazing up at the growing enormity of the cliff face in front of him, he began to feel a strange sensation – almost as if someone were watching him off to his left. He stopped in his tracks when the feeling became almost overwhelming.

As he turned and looked in that direction, he could have sworn he felt the direction of the wind, which was considerable, turn with him. And the wind created a strange effect: it blew strong through a corridor of boulders and rocky crags, almost seeming to highlight a trail as it bent over the knee high grass.

Two hundred feet or so away was another line of trees, densely packed together. And yet, through that thicket, Ademo thought he could see a flickering of light coming from somewhere within, like light reflecting off a shiny surface. He also sensed that there was water in that direction, thought he could almost hear it flowing – though that seemed unlikely at this distance.

But south was not his compass bearing. He was headed for the Whispering Cliffs. And after all his journeying over the last day and a half, here they were at last. So he turned again, made his feet move one in front of the other, even as his mind seemed to be gripped by some misgiving in doing so. Is this fear? he wondered. Is this my mind's way of avoiding the inevitable climb I must make at the end of this trail? He didn't know, but decided that over-thinking would get him nowhere. So he focused on plodding along, keeping his eyes facing straight ahead as the cliff face reared up in front of him.

5

The skies above the warship had stayed so dark, and the seas so turbulent, and the rains so relentless, for so long, that it was almost as if the crew had accepted their fate. The gloom amongst the crew was worn heavy like winter coats. But it was a dutiful gloom. The sheer relentlessness of their oppressive surroundings had robbed them of any daring ideas; including mutiny.

Alas, if there was to be death – as it seemed almost certain there would be – it would be a collective one. Either it would be a sudden end, perhaps when one of the rogue waves – that commonly rose up from time to time in this part of the world – crashed overboard. Or perhaps it would come with a giant whirlpool, again, also fairly common on these waters, if the tales were to be believed. Others thought that perhaps no such end would come, but that they would eventually succumb to either madness or starvation, as they trolled aimlessly, and endlessly, though this never-ending, drenching darkness.

Then, rather abruptly it seemed at the time, no more than a day and a half from when First Mate Maynard had last spoken with the captain, the skies began to clear. Not completely mind you. There was no blue sky to admire at last. But a canopy of high cloud was a good deal better than the claustrophobic, murky mist they had been crawling through for days on end. There was still a light layer of fog over the water, but not nearly so thick.

That night the crew (those who were not on active duty anyway) retired in much better spirits, thinking that perhaps disaster wasn't so inevitable, after all.

And then came a shout, early the next morning, loud enough to wake them from their deep slumbers.

"Land!" came the cry from above deck.

They herded like hungry cattle up the steps and out into bright sunlight. At first they sheltered their eyes, taking a few moments to adjust to the brightness of a cloudless sky. Then they looked across the waters, their eyes straining.

And there it was, unmistakable: an island. The *Isle of Shroud*. Kiraboa, as some called it. And never had dry land looked so welcoming.

And then each member of the warship's crew turned his mind to the bounty that had been promised, now within their grasp. *Gold*! A near fortune for each of them. And greedy smiles were now draped across the deck. And the gloom that had seemed so thick only a day before, was nowhere to be found.

At the stern, for the first time on the entire voyage, stood Captain Prigg. As usual he was stroking the point of his jet black goatee. But this morning there was a gleam in his eye like none had ever seen. For he knew what this discovery meant. Not only riches – no, it meant something far more important than that. It meant fame. He was about to become the most famous seafaring captain in all of Eiasa. As it should be, he thought to himself. As it should be.

6

Ademo stood at the base of the cliff, his hands on his hips, staring up at the seemingly sheer rock face that rose up like a tower in front of him. He had spent the past fifteen minutes walking back and forth in front of the cliff wall, trying to spot the handholds that would lead him up to the top. But, no matter how many times he moved along the semi-circular base, he just couldn't find a clear climbing line.

What about all the others who had done this before him? This was a tradition that went back generations and generations. And yet for all he could tell, the cliff showed no signs of wear at all.

To make matters worse, it was clear that the sandstone material the cliff was comprised of was still wet from yesterday's storm. That would make any attempt at an ascent even more treacherous.

But what choice did he have? As far as he could tell, no one had ever turned his back on his Placca. Never. Darned if he was going to be the first. What if he died in the attempt? Well, that was preferable to the shame he would bring on himself and his mother if he were to return to the village never having made the attempt. No, come what may, his destiny lay at the top of this cliff, or at least in an attempt at getting there.

He moved back to his left one more time, stopping before the only spot that looked slightly less dangerous than the rest of the smooth, yet chalky wall face.

"All right, you seven winds, if you would be so kind as to help me with a gust in the right direction from time to time, I'd be most grateful."

Ademo stood a moment longer, tracing with his eyes the climb-line he would attempt to keep to. Then, with a deep breath and a quick hand to his heart, he dug his hand into a shallow cleft in the rock face. To his relief, it seemed relatively solid. If there were enough of these divots, perhaps this wouldn't be so impossible after all.

He lifted his leg, was able to find purchase in another, more shallow divot. He pulled himself up, staying close to the cliff face. His other foot found purchase. And he reached up yet again, searching for the next handhold.

Thirty minutes later, an exhausted Ademo looked down and found that he'd managed to ascend three quarters of the cliff face. On a couple of occasions he thought for sure he'd come to a place where farther ascent was impossible. And in those moments he'd paused, considering his options. But those options had been few. And in the end he'd had no choice but to reach up, clinging to the shallowest of clefts, and hoist himself up yet again. And, somehow, he'd managed to keep going. Just barely.

And now the summit was more than just a pipe-dream. It seemed almost attainable, as unlikely as that had seemed only minutes ago.

Looking up he spotted two more handholds, one on top of the other, only a few feet apart. And suddenly his hope soared. Now those did look like real climbing points. No doubt he had chosen the same line as his predecessors, after all. And with that Ademo felt a surge of pride. Perhaps he was different than the others in some ways he could never quite put his finger on. But on this day he was one of them. Today he would become a man. He would complete this ascent and then wait for the seven winds to speak of his destiny.

Smiling, Ademo reached up for the next handhold. And just that moment the light breeze about him suddenly gave way to a westerly gust. And as his weight shifted Ademo felt a crumbling underneath his left foot.

He scrambled to shift his weight to the other foot, only to feel that foothold crumble into nothingness in process. Ademo let loose a muted scream, slamming his other hand into the cliff and scratching for purchase. He found one, barely an inch deep. He hung on with both hands, his legs dangling beneath him in the open, blustery air.

Only by twisting his back in an unnatural way was he able to swing one leg to the right, where he found solid footing. The muscles in his back screamed in protest. But Ademo didn't care. He was, for the moment, not plunging to his death. And that was more than he had expected only a moment before.

Just when he thought his back would spasm he caught sight of another potential foothold. He swung his other leg over, found purchase. Ademo let himself relax, for just a moment. He breathed deep and stared straight ahead. He wouldn't allow himself to look down. Not again. Not when he was this close to the top.

After a few moments rest he began to feel the winds kick up again. And he decided resting here was not a wise choice. So he looked up, scanning back and forth for the next handhold.

Then he saw it, two in fact. He reached up, found a firm lip to hold to. He reached up with the other hand and found the next lip, hoisting himself up. He was almost there. He could hear the howling of the wind now, coming off the summit that was only a few feet above him.

He tentatively swung out his right leg, scrambled against the sheer face for a moment, before finding purchase against a small clove of moss. It wasn't much, but it was all he would need. He reached up again, landing his forearm over the top ledge.

He pulled with all his might, using his arm as leverage. It felt like the muscles he didn't even know existed in that part of his arm would explode, but they held firm. His other arm reached the lip of the summit, and he pulled for all he was worth. Then, with one last gasp, he swung his other leg up and over the ledge, rolled over against the flat ground.

And there he lay for a long time, content to let the winds howl all around him, as they came in gusts from every direction. They could do nothing to him now.

7

When his breathing had returned to normal, Ademo rolled over several times, till he lay in the approximate center of the nearly flat, circular summit. He sat up and reached over to a column of rock that rose up almost like a miniature replica of the rock tower itself. He held to it, thankful for its solid feeling.

To his great surprise, not to mention relief, Ademo saw a small fountain of water spurting from the top of the rock column. He reached out his hand, let it be wet, and then touched it to his dry tongue. Even that small taste was delicious.

He scrambled onto his knees, leaned forward, and took several long draughts from the cold, clean, water. When his body finally felt rehydrated, he collapsed back down into a sitting position, his back to the rock column.

The winds at this height really were relentless. He was thankful for the rock fountain, not just because it offered the water that he so sorely needed. But because it gave him something to brace against as the gusts slammed into him from all directions.

Moments later, feeling much more rested and at ease, a troubling thought occurred to Ademo. The seven winds: what did they have to say to him? For it was from them, the Great Lore suggested, that he would receive his calling.

And yet, all he heard was wind. Wind like it always sounded. There were no voices. No whisperings. Nothing out of the ordinary at all. And then Ademo began to wonder if the Lore about the winds was all a rouse. Perhaps the task was just in getting here? Perhaps that was the point? To prove your manhood by a feat of bravery?

And as he pondered these things, Ademo began to feel a great weariness overtake him. Moments later he fell fast asleep.

The woman scrambled down the steep embankment, doing her best to keep upright while holding tightly to the babe wrapped up in her arms. The baby was crying, and she was doing her best to console him. But the infant seemed to sense the contradiction. One moment his mother made calming cooing sounds, the next she would gasp as the embankment underneath her almost gave way. And she was breathing in gasps, and frequently looking over her shoulder. No, despite what she said, "It's alright, sweet one, it's alright," the baby instinctively knew it wasn't.

Finally the slope became more shallow and the woman let gravity take her into a full-out sprint. She ran alongside a creek-bed that widened into a narrow river, searching for something, her eyes dancing left and right. The child was quiet now, merely studying her, as if the speed of their motion helped him to relax.

Suddenly there was a shout from somewhere above them, somewhere up near the top of the embankment.

"There!" a tall man, clad in mail and bearing a large sword called out. "She's down by the river!"

The woman cried out: "No! No, it must be here. It must be here. He showed it to me once. If only I'd paid closer attention!"

The woman's expression grew tense as she glanced up the embankment and saw a group of armed men scrambling down after her.

And then she spotted something, brown and green, almost the same color as the underbrush.

She stopped in her tracks, stepped off the trail to pull back a pile of branches and ferns. The small boat hidden underneath was a sight for sore eyes. She did her best to pull the boat towards her with one hand, while holding on to the baby with the other. But it just wouldn't budge. The rains had made the ground muddy, and the bottom of the boat lay wedged in, the ground now half dry.

The woman glanced up, but was unable to see her pursuers. And that was bad news. That meant they'd already reached the bottom of the steep incline – that they were now only moments from reaching her.

The woman leaned down and placed the baby, still wrapped in linen, onto the floor of the boat. She then held to the front edge of the craft and gave a swift tug. Nothing. It wouldn't budge.

"Oh, please. Please!" she cried out. This time she pulled for all she was worth, and felt a stabbing pain in her back as a result. But this time the boat came loose from the half-dry mud. In fact it moved so quickly after jarring loose that it knocked her over. The baby rolled over and started crying. The woman was focused. She scrambled to her feet and pulled at the boat, pulled with all her might, through twigs and underbrush, ignoring the scratches she suffered as a result.

Seconds later the boat splashed into the water. She gave the craft one long push and then leaped in herself, almost capsizing it in the process. The baby was wailing now. But the woman couldn't tend to him. Instead, seeing with a quick glance of her eye that he was in no immediate danger, she grabbed the oar from along the wall of the boat. She plunged it into the water and pulled for all she was worth. Again, that same spot in the small of her back roared in protest. But she pulled again, hard, before switching the oar to the other side and pulling twice there.

Just then she heard shouting and then a loud splash behind them, as one of her pursuers leapt full on into the water. She didn't turn to look, knowing that would only slow her down. Had she looked she would have seen that just as the man leapt from the trail, in a spread out dive formation, his feet had caught in the muddy ground. As such his leap fell short of his aim. And only the top half of his body landed in the shallow of the water's edge. The rest of him thumped into rocks. He screamed out in agony, as a jagged bone tore through his pant leg.

The woman pulled the oar in one long stroke, then another, then switched to the other side. Seconds later the small craft entered the center of the river, and found a swifter current. Suddenly she found herself hurtling along with some speed. She now used the oar to control their course. She dug the oar into the water and used it as leverage to steer clear, just by inches, of a boulder that veered up in the very center of the river.

Once past the boulder she stole a look behind her. She caught site of movement: several men, running full speed along the path beside the river. They were fast, but they were no longer gaining on her – not at the speed the swift, churning water now carried them along at.

The woman then glanced down between her legs, saw the baby lying peacefully now, wrapped warmly, staring up adoringly at his mother. The baby saw that she had seen him and gurgled delightedly. She gave him a smile in return. "See, sweet one? Tis alright. Alright, after all."

The small craft then wove around a bend in the river, the woman deftly using the oar to keep their course true. The baby continued to gaze up contentedly at her.

And then he saw her demeanor change. Her face bore an expression of shock, and then worry. Even at this tender age, the baby knew that look.

If the woman would have turned around she would have seen her pursuers slow and then give up the chase altogether, pointing towards the very sight her eyes now beheld. Up ahead of them, seemingly unavoidable, the fast moving river disappeared over a foaming drop-off. They were headed straight for it, with no hope of slowing or reaching shore.

The woman pulled the oar back into the boat, reached down and snatched the baby into her arms. She rocked him back and forth, in an attempt to sooth herself as much as him. And then she closed her eyes as a churning roar filled her ears, and the river fell out from underneath them.

Ademo gasped and was awake. He felt and heard the wind swirling all about him, and for a moment confused it with the furry of a waterfall. Then he looked around and remembered where he was.

He felt so peculiar. The dream had felt so vivid, unlike any other he could quite remember. And yet, now that he was awake again, he didn't feel an ounce of fatigue. It was almost as if he hadn't been asleep at all.

And what a strange dream it was! The woman, who's face he never did see, was running from men dressed in strange garb, through an alien forest full of tall, triangular trees with narrow, pointed leaves.

He sensed the men in the dream meant to do her great harm, she and the baby she held to her breast. And her escape had seemed so fortuitous, so valiant, right up until the point that she sailed straight over a waterfall, no doubt to her and her baby's death. Though, graciously, he had awoken before that matter was complete.

Ademo rested his head against the stone, could hear the gurgle of the fountain, and thought about another drink. And yet now, strangely enough, he wasn't thirsty. Not even a little bit. It was as if the idea of a drink from the fountain now repulsed him.

He sat there perplexed, for a moment. And then something dawned on him.

This was no ordinary fountain. That was no ordinary dream. And somehow, the two were connected. The water had brought on the dream. And now that he'd had the dream, the water had served its purpose. He somehow instinctively knew that he was not to drink again.

But what of the Placca? What of hearing of his destiny from the seven winds?

Somehow he knew it was all connected. The dream contained the message. Of that much Ademo was now sure. Although, how he could be so sure seemed a mystery in itself.

But if the dream contained the message, then what was it? What did this woman's escape – and then subsequent demise – have to do with him? How was he supposed to glean a destiny from *that*?

He sat there for an hour, perhaps two, thinking on such things. But understanding eluded him. He was replaying the dream in his mind, yet another time, when he noticed the sun's glare in his eyes. The giant fiery orb was now significantly lower in the sky, and turning the purplish-orange color of a yupi fruit. He realized he needed to get moving. The prospect of spending the night at the top of this cliff tower was not at all appealing.

Ademo lay down on his stomach, and pulled himself up to the cliff edge. He looked over, trying to locate the route he'd ascended. He found it soon enough, but one thing was evident: getting up was one thing, getting back down another one entirely. He scanned back and forth with his eyes for a few minutes more, but found no route any more appealing.

He pulled himself to his feet, turned and walked

to the opposite edge, looking down to the ocean so far below. And far below it was. The cliff was probably a hundred feet tall from where he had begun his climb. But the sea below on this side was probably four times that height. Ademo felt a strong sense of vertigo in looking over and trying to eyeball the distance.

He backed away, then sat down cross-legged on the smooth, flat rock.

Something else came clear to him in that moment. No one returned the same way they came here. It was simply impossible. No, the only way down was a long dive into the ocean below.

Ademo was not a fan of heights, on the best of days. And despite being a strong swimmer, the thought of leaping hundreds of feet into those watery depths gave him real pause. From that height, hitting the water wrong, in any number of ways, could mean serious injury, even death.

He took a deep breath, walked again to the cliff edge, glancing over. He tried to imagine the arc of his dive at different launch speeds. Should he simply drop over – since the cliff face was nearly vertical, all the way to the water? Or should he take a run at it? And if so, how much of a run? He didn't want to tip head over heels mid-flight – doing so could be disastrous.

Ademo sighed out loud, let his shoulders slouch. It was no use over-thinking this. Best to just get it over with. He reminded himself, for moral support, that others – plenty of others in fact – had done this before him. If only heights weren't the particular phobia he was plagued with, this would be so much easier.

He stepped back a few paces, decided he would jump like any other time he'd leapt from a high place – even if he knew full well he'd never leapt from even half this height before.

He took off running and leapt one foot in front of the other over that daunting precipice.

It was a long fall to the water below. Feeling himself pitching forward, Ademo used his arms and legs to fan himself back into his preferred posture.

It only worked so well. When he hit the water his forehead took the brunt of the slamming sensation.

Ademo was seeing stars and his head was throbbing. The rest of his entire body was tingling uncomfortably. And then he drank in water, and felt himself gag.

That kicked his instincts into gear. Despite his body's protests, he forced his arms and legs to pump through the water.

He swam for all he was worth. Still, it felt like a long way to the surface, and Ademo felt his lungs would burst at any moment. He was anticipating that moment when his head would rise out of the water. And yet, he didn't feel it. Knowing drinking in more water could be disastrous at this point, he kept his mouth shut, kept pumping, legs and arms, despite the burning in his chest.

Then, finally, his head emerged from the watery depths and he gulped in from the precious late afternoon air.

He tread water where he was for a couple of minutes, taking in air, letting his muscles recuperate. When he felt the stars clear way enough for him to have a solid sense of his bearing, he began a gentle swim to shore.

Minutes later he welcomed the sensation of sand beneath his feet. He stumbled forward up onto the shore before collapsing in an exhausted heap.

8

"How can you possibly carry that thing?" Himoa asked, smirking as he watched his friend Supilo walking the trail to the beach, with the strange overlong fishing poll balanced precariously on his shoulders.

"It's no big deal. Just takes a little balance, my friend. Besides, even if it is a little awkward to carry, all the deep sea fish I'll be catching will make the effort of lugging it back and forth to the beach more than worth it. Perhaps I'll cook up some bass tonight for Shayisa," he said, winking at his friend.

Himoa put his hand to his belly, let his head roll back, and laughed heartily. "I'm not sure what's less likely," he said, "you catching a deep sea bass, or Shayisa being served at your table."

Supilo smiled, letting his friend enjoy a little lighthearted fun. The truth was, he really had no idea if the elongated poll would work like he planned. It had seemed like a good idea in his mind. But, even though it was made with light and sturdy fraica wood, as were their valias, it was awkward to carry and would be even more awkward to cast effectively.

Oh well, it was worth a try, he thought to himself. He had attempted other engineering feats before. And, even if only one out of every five seemed to work at all like it was supposed to, progress would never come about if people didn't try. The villagers seemed content to work with the same tools and technology that their ancestors had. But he believed in bettering things, even if the life they had *was* already good.

Himoa stood aside and let Supilo walk in front as they crossed onto the warm sands of the beachfront. Just then Supilo proceeded to drop his gargantuan poll onto the sand, narrowly missing Himoa's foot in the process.

"What, it's too heavy to carry down to the water?" Himoa said with humor. "Need me to carry one end for you?"

When Supilo didn't respond, Himoa looked up and saw that his friend was staring towards the water with a distraught expression. When Himoa let his eyes wander in that direction, he immediately understood.

For the first time in their lives there was something out on the water that had not originated in the village. It was a large, sailing vessel, painted in jet black with deep red and silver trim. A piece of cloth flew in the air above its mast, bearing a strange, crimson encircled insignia.

Neither boy knew this, but it was a fully manned warship – the largest of its kind. And it was headed directly towards them.

9

Ademo, happy to be back on solid ground after his lengthy drop from the cliff top, quickly gathered his strength. Even the piercing pain in his forehead soon faded to a dull ache. He was ready to move on. Ready to trace his steps back up the mountain and down again, to the village where his mother waited with a likely mixture of anticipation and growing dread.

Ademo turned and offered one more fleeting glance towards the towering cliff face, before walking up the short incline that took him back to the trail.

He marched for an hour or so, his mind firmly fixed on the strange dream he'd had at the top of the cliff, when he turned a corner and again came to that same location – an open plain dotted with a few rocky crags – where he'd before felt something strange come over him.

And now he felt it again. Almost like a presence. He turned and looked in the direction the wind had blown before and, just that moment, saw something fly over him, casting a shadow upon the tall, swaying grass. Ademo followed the flight of the creature until it landed in the treetops across the field.

It was a bird, a large one, with a wingspan of six feet or more. Even at some distance it was easy to make out, because it was painted in bright yellow with orange wingtips. Ademo had never seen such a bird on the other side of the island, and couldn't help but wonder what other mysteries this side of the island contained.

Again he considered exploring in the direction the bird had flown. *What lay behind that line of trees?* Just another dense jungle? Or something else? He remembered the glint he'd seen – or thought he'd seen. Had that been water? Or the sun glinting off the eye of some large animal – perhaps a hillcat?

If so, he was in no rush to investigate. Besides, he'd delayed long enough. He was another day's hike from the village, and his mother would grow worried if he didn't show up when expected. He didn't want to add to her concern unnecessarily. He decided he had better push on.

Soon he was back in the dense, lush green of the jungle. Light was now fading, and, as always, the canopied jungle was darker than the open land that surrounded it. But Ademo kept to a brisk pace, intent on reaching his same sleeping spot underneath the hollowed out guia palm.

As he drew near to where he'd slumbered the night before, he could feel his eyes straining to make out definition in the grayed-out terrain. Just when he thought he'd lost his way, he rounded a corner that looked familiar. And then, there it was, hard to make out in the failing light, the hollowed-out guia.

Ademo's mind was too preoccupied to think much of food, though he was hungry. He'd eaten a couple of flowershrooms earlier that day, but nothing since night had begun to fall.

His fatigue growing by the moment, Ademo decided he would look for food again in the morning, and lay down in the spot that still showed an impression of where his body had been before.

For the few moments before sleep overtook him, Ademo thought again of the dream. Who was the fleeing woman? What strange land did she come from? Was it real? And, if so, what bearing did it have on *his* future?

Ademo's next thought was about whether or not Chief Fyoma would expect him to give an accounting of his Placca experience. Was it normal to have a vision with an unclear meaning?

Once again, Ademo felt that nagging sense that he was an outsider; that what he had experienced fell outside the norm. He hoped that the next day would bring some clarity. Preferably before he reached the village.

And then he was too tired to form any additional cogent thought, and lapsed into a deep sleep.

There was an audible snap as the pursuer leapt, only half successfully, into the river. The woman gasped as he screamed out in pain. He had come out of nowhere. She knew they were close, but didn't realize how close. If the man's feet hadn't caught in the mud he would surely have reached them before they had any momentum.

But that extra few moments was all she needed. Now that the boat was out of the brambles and out into the open water, she began rowing for all she was worth.

Her pursuers, of which there were still four, were chasing in parallel along the river trail. And then the boat began to pull away from them, caught in the fast moving waters.

She left herself relax, just a bit, smiled down at her baby. And then, as she looked up again, she saw something very wrong. The river seemed to disappear up ahead, falling over a steep cliff that they were now hurtling towards at an unstoppable pace.

She knew there would be no steering out of this predicament. She dropped the oar, reached down and picked up her baby, who was now noticing the fear in her eyes. She rocked him against her breast for a moment, even as a roar of falling water began to fill her ears.

And then she closed her eyes as the boat tipped over the side of the waterfall.

The two plunged into the deep pool below, fifty feet from the precipice above. Bubbles and gurgling water washed all about them. The woman gasped, took in water and began thrashing with her right arm, her left still clutching to her baby.

The struggle was a loosing one. With only one arm to work with she couldn't create any upward momentum.

A moment later she was sinking again, her airless lungs ready to explode. As she sank she glanced below, and saw only darkness.

Then, quite suddenly, there was a glow, a faint light, emanating from below, and simultaneously she felt her stomach turn, as disorientation set in.

When her mouth instinctively opened to gasp for oxygen, her vision quickly became fuzzy. And then she lapsed into unconsciousness as she and her baby plunged into the depths below.

Ademo sat bolt upright, gasping empathetically for the air that was plentiful all around him, his heart beating mightily in his chest.

Finally, feeling his pulse normalize, he reached up and grasped at the side of the tree, stood up. He brushed off a few of the crumpled leaves that clung to him, and stepped out into the jungle.

It was still very early, but there was just enough light for him to be able to make out the trail. He was anxious to get going. He had thinking to do – about this strange dream that he'd now experienced twice – and he could do that while walking. In fact, he'd always found he did his best thinking out on the open trail.

10

The crew had been given their orders: find and bring back alive a man-child with birthmarks behind both ears. It seemed a strange request. And they were neither aware of what importance this man-child had, nor for whom they would be capturing him. They were simply relayed these orders from the first-mate, Maynard, who had received them from the captain. As to whom the captain received them from... well, no one was the wiser as to that question.

But these were bounty-men, familiar with such arrangements. And as long as they received the gold they'd been promised, they'd be happy to take on an entire island to bring back a lipsticked pig if that's what they were told to do. Besides, the nice thing about this set of orders was that, besides finding this dually-marked man-child, they could do what they liked with the rest. And they commonly enjoyed orders with that kind of leeway.

The first-mate gave the orders and the smaller rafts were lowered into the water, several of them, filled to the brim with ten men each. They'd want to move quickly now, because the element of surprise would soon be lost. Even now there were two figures on the beach, and as the rafts hit the water they turned and ran back into the jungle foliage, no doubt to raise the alarm with the islanders.

Himoa and Supilo darted up the path, Supilo's experimental, deep-sea fishing rod now long since abandoned and forgotten on the sand.

"Where's Chief Fyoma?" Supilo shouted as they entered the village. "Where is he? *Quick!*"

The villagers beheld the boy's strange demeanor with a mixture of surprise and curiosity. No one on the island had been this worked up since a wild boar had destroyed one of the vegetable gardens two years before. Eventually one of the elder ladies pointed towards the Skytent.

"Chief Fyoma!" Supilo shouted, slamming open the Skytent door and rushing inside.

Kuio stood, pointed a long finger at Supilo, and said: "Boy! What insolence! Do you dare to charge in without first being beckoned? You–"

"A ship!" Supilo exclaimed.

"What?" Kuio said, still looking indignant.

Supilo ignored him, turning to Fyoma. "Chief, a ship has come; the Lord's Shield has been breached!"

There were gasps of surprise all around the table of elders, and several of them quickly rose to their feet.

"Where did you see this?" Fyoma asked, a look of dread draped across his face.

"From the south beach! They are launching smaller craft to shore as we speak!"

Kuio slammed his fist to the table. "It is exactly as I had feared! That outsider's Placca; the Storm Sign;

and now *this!* We are doomed! We have betrayed the ways of the elders; we have brought upon ourselves the wrath of the gods!"

As his voice rose to a fevered pitch, those around the table were mobilizing. Fyoma barked out commands to each of the elders, then turned back to Supilo.

"Supilo, go and blow the community horn – four short blasts, then pause and repeat, four times – just like you were taught. And then run and find the others of Placca age or beyond, and gather at the foot of the beach trail with your valias ready!"

Supilo nodded, turned and dashed out the door, Himoa following closely at his heals.

Moments later the village was in a state of mass confusion. The horn blew out for all to hear, in a pattern that could mean only one thing: *invasion.*

It was a pattern none had ever heard. It was a series of sounds to stop hearts. What was happening now hadn't happened in the lifetimes of anyone on the island – not even in the lifetimes of their distant ancestors. While some of the villagers moved with deliberation, others stood in stunned silence, their hands covering their mouths in shock, fear and disbelief.

When he'd blown the horn long enough, Supilo did what the chief had commanded, he called out to his friends who were now crowded around the village square – told them to fetch their valias and meet at the foot of the south beach trail as soon as possible.

Soon a crowd of men and boys at, or nearing, the age of Placca had gathered at the foot of the trail, valias in hand. Fyoma strode to the front of the crowd and turned to them.

"Brethren, today a great omen has befallen us. The Lord's Shield has been breached. I fear those who seek our shores do so with less than friendly intentions. The Storm Sign we received only two days ago bears testimony to this fact. So let us go and protect the valor of this land; protect our way of life; protect our families. For the honor of Kiraboa!" he shouted, holding his valia high in the air.

A great roar arose from the crowd, though some, both younger and older, betrayed looks of grave fear.

The chief then turned and marched down the trailhead, the others in tow.

11

The men and boys were lined up along the beach. Fyoma had hoped such a show of force would give the invaders pause. Making mental note of the numbers of men now dragging their small craft to shore, he took solace in the fact that the men he commanded outnumbered the invaders.

When each of the boats had reached dry land, the visitors lined up in front of them, facing off against the village-folk. Fyoma stepped forward a few paces, lifted his valia and held it with both hands, horizontal above his head.

"Voyagers from beyond the Shield, I am Fyoma, chief of this island. What purpose have you on our shores?" he shouted in a commanding voice.

The villagers stood tall, proud of the brave tone the chief had taken. They couldn't understand the words, for they were foreign, spoken in the common tongue of the outside world. But the tone of the chief's opening was clear enough.

Then their pride turned to a mixture of anger, fear, and bewilderment, when the chief's pronouncement brought a cascade of laughter from the crew who had just made landfall. Supilo and Himoa exchanged nervous glances.

After a moment the laughter died down as one man waved his hands at his sides, indicating that enough was enough. First-mate Maynard stepped forward.

"Fimer, hear me well. If you are a wise leader of your people you will listen closely. We seek a man-child, barely of stubble-age, who bears a birthmark behind both ears. Hand him over to us now and your people and possessions will be spared. We will take him with us and be on our way, right quick."

The men-folk of the village glanced nervously towards each other, wondering what the chief would do with the gibberish coming out of the mouth of their unwanted guest. The chief however, was a different story. He had learned the common tongue from his father, Chief Limi. And he from his father before him, as was tradition. The long line of chiefs had learned the common tongue for just such a moment as this.

"There is no one who matches that description here. We are a native-born people, and have no business with the outside world. If it is a fugitive you seek, he is not to be found here. Now, we ask that you return to your ship, and go back the way you came. We ask for no trouble with outsiders. All we ask is to be left to our own way of life."

The chief paused, wondering if he'd said too much. In the moments leading up to this meeting, he'd thought about the tone he would take in this face-off. He didn't want to be appear hostile, but neither did he want to appear weak and afraid. All he could do was hope he'd struck the right balance.

The man who stood across from him took a few moments to digest what Fyoma had said. Then he smiled, and the other members of the crew mimicked him, clearly enjoying their moment of superiority. The crew had taken account of their opponents, and they were feeling pretty confident about their chances. The natives carried staffs that appeared wholly wooden – except for the sharpened ends that glistened with a dark, green sheen, perhaps jade. Those weapons would do little to hinder them were this to come to battle.

First mate Maynard eyed the chief, legs spread out, arms crossed over his chest. He seemed almost amused with the situation.

"Now, now, Chief Fimer, native-born you may be, as perhaps are the men and boys who stand next to you. But you know full well that is not true of *all* who inhabit this island. The information I have tells me there is a non-native among you. This is the man-child we seek. He is not even one of your own. So, why deny his existence? And why bother resisting us? Tis not wise to do so. For wisdom's sake, Fimer, I suggest you end this charade and deliver this man to us, right quick."

Fyoma studied Maynard, intent on measuring just how sure he was of what he'd said. Was it worth denying the existence of this man-child that Fyoma knew full well *was* on the island?

"Even if such a one were amongst us, what business have you with him?" Fyoma asked, trying to sound non-committal.

Maynard smiled again, while his eyes narrowed to slits above his nose. He chuckled softly.

"Fimer, Fimer... How coy of you. What business we outsiders have with this outsider, now that is outsiders' business. If you'd like us to respect the ways of your people, then you'd best respect ours as well. Again, this doesn't concern any of you. So let's tarry no longer. We'll have the man turned over to us – *now*."

Supilo was incredulous. He may not have been able to understand the precise words of this insolent foreigner, but he gathered the tone well enough. And of that he'd had enough. He had never seen anyone speak to the man of highest honor in such a way.

Supilo stepped forward, driving his valia into the sand in a show of force.

"How dare you speak to most honored Fyoma like that! On your knees swamp-crawler; beg forgiveness for your insolence!"

There was a dead silence that fell over both groups. No one moved a muscle or made a peep.

And then, all at once, the boat crew broke out in roaring laughter, many letting their heads roll back, holding their sides like they were in stitches.

Supilo couldn't conceal the look of shock that spread across his face. And that bewildered expression, not lost on the boat crew, just made them laugh all the more. Several of them pointed at him while bellowing heartedly.

The young man had had enough. Such insult could not stand. Supilo picked up his valia, took two steps forward, was about to drive the staff back into the sand – as was custom when making a point even more pointed – when a loud explosion rocked the ears of the villagers.

Supilo fell to the sand, where he lay unmoving. The shocked islanders looked from the their fallen friend, to the crew of men that stood across from them, noticing the puff of smoke that slowly dissipated from the strange baton tool held by one of the strangers.

Himoa rushed forward and knelt down by Supilo's fallen body, immediately realizing that his friend's spirit was departed. Supilo's empty eyes stared up at nothingness, while a hole in his chest pooled with blood.

Maynard gave the natives a moment to recognize what had happened, to fully take stock of their inferiority, before he raised a hand to silence his mumbling crewmates.

"Chief Fimer, the boy's fate is unfortunate. He would have done well to take note of his proper position before stepping out so boldly.

"But let the bloodshed end here. I understand your desire to protect the non-islander we seek. Tis an honorable act, one might even say. But, as I mentioned earlier, tis not a wise one. You and your people are now fully aware of our weaponry. So I ask again, for the sake of your people's own wellbeing, stop this silliness and turn over the man-child we seek, right quick. As I said, once we have him we will turn and be gone."

Fyoma stood motionless for a moment, staring at a space in the sky just above the invaders' heads. He knew it was his responsibility to protect the island and its people. But now he felt so helpless, so inadequate. He and his people had kept their way of life, largely unchanged, for generations. But those from elsewhere had clearly moved on. The weapons these invaders bore proved that point all too painfully. And that made Fyoma question many things, all in one instant.

But for now such matters were moot. The

situation was what it was. How would he best help his people now?

Maynard shifted his posture, seemingly bored with the delay. He kicked at the sand distractedly with one booted foot. After a moment Fyoma cleared his throat, prepared to speak.

"Outworlders, we understand your terms. And I now ask that you allow me to return to our village and convene my council. I must have their approval before agreeing to your terms. Two hours is all we ask for. After that I will return here with our response."

Maynard eyed the chief, smiled again. "Fair enough, Chief. But make it one hour. That should be plenty of time for your council – if they are sensible – to agree to our demands. We will wait here until then. When you return, bring the branded man-child with you.

"But... I warn you, do *not* attempt anything else. Don't flitter away what little time you have with some hasty plan of resistance. Your fate will be the same as that foolish boy if you do," Maynard said, matter-of-factly nodding towards Supilo's corpse, that lay in a bloody heap on the sand.

The chief, reminded so coldly of Supilo's fate, burned with rage. He knew the boy had died – if foolishly – defending his own honor. He vowed that moment to never let that thought leave his mind. He would avenge Supilo, if any power remained open to him to do so.

These thoughts rolled through his mind, but

outwardly, he merely nodded towards Maynard. Then he turned towards the beach trail, indicating that the islanders should follow suit.

Slowly, almost like zombies, each of Fyoma's compatriots turned and followed.

Even above the gentle rolling of the tide, the islanders heard a shuffling of sorts behind them, and the unfamiliar clinking sound of metal being drawn.

Then, before they had opportunity to register another thought, the beach erupted with the sound of cascading gunfire. Smoke filled the air as the invaders fired their weapons upon the backs of the retreating islanders.

As Fyoma's deafened ears screamed in agony, his mind began to comprehend what was happening. But it took a moment to do so. He could hardly believe he was witnessing such an act of cowardice. He turned, and began to note the growing numbers of brothers now laying motionless on the sand.

And on the explosions went, smoke now clouding his view. And then, at the moment his brain told his arm to raise his valia, a bullet smashed through the space between his eyes, and he contemplated no more. Heaps of bodies, some strewn on top of each other, now lay scattered on the blood-soaked sand.

Only a third of the islanders who had made the march to the shore managed to make it back to the jungle trail. Those who did survive ran for all they were worth, unthinking terror gripping their hearts; fearing that at any moment they would be shot down, like their brothers, by these foul weapons of dark magic.

When Maynard had finished firing he turned to the men on his left, pointing towards the jungle and barking orders to follow and finish them off. Half of his men took off running in pursuit.

Maynard smiled as gunshots erupted again, this time from behind the tree line. "Well," he said, "I think that went rather well."

"I thought you planned on giving them the chance to bring the man-child peacefully first?" a crewman to his left said, looking perplexed.

Maynard shrugged. "I changed my mind. Less opportunity for mess this way. They're not likely to resist us now, are they? Not with two-thirds of their best fighters already out of the picture.

"Leverage, Mieders. Leverage. You watch, when we march into their village later today, they'll hand over this branded man-child like he was a leper."

12

Ademo felt a surge of relief when he emerged from the soggy reeds and stepped foot onto the dry summit plateau of Mt. Uduri. He certainly hadn't pushed his pace over the last few hours. Instead, he had meandered his way back and forth towards the mountaintop, taking time to stop, rest, and meditate on his Placca experience. But still, it felt good to have that part of the journey done with.

In truth, he wanted to get his story straight – if such a thing were possible – before arriving back at the village. He needed to know how he was going to explain the experience, the dream, and what message he had derived from it, before those inevitable questions were asked of him. Alas, for all his meditation, he still didn't really know what to make of it all.

Though he'd hiked rather slowly, he was still famished by the time he stepped foot onto the summit. So he took a few moments to pick from the berries there. With a large pile of them cradled in his shirt, he walked to the summit edge to look down towards the village.

His jaw dropped and suddenly it felt like the air had been sucked from his lungs.

The village was on fire. Above the flames smoke billowed up, before pouring out over the ocean.

Through the smoky haze, Ademo could see the mast of a large seafaring vessel. It only took a moment to put two and two together: the village had been attacked by outsiders. The Lord's Shield – for so long seemingly impenetrable – had been breached.

Ademo's thoughts immediately turned to his mother. Was she alive? From his vantage point he could almost see the part of the village that housed their hut. And that section appeared to be on fire like all the rest. Ademo's heart felt clenched and he was having difficulty breathing.

And then... adrenaline kicked in. He dumped the berries on the ground and tore off towards the trail that would lead him eventually down to the village. He ran at a full out sprint.

After a few moments his feet scrambled on loose scree, and he tumbled to the ground in a heap. But, despite his bleeding arms and legs, he felt no pain; the adrenaline urging him forward, relentlessly. He staggered to his feet, kept running. But no matter how fast he ran, it wasn't fast enough. And with each passing meander of the mountain trail, the village still seemed impossibly far away.

When he finally reached the beach and turned to run down the shoreline to the village trail, his heart sank. There were bodies strewn on the blood-soaked sand. The scene was so horribly wrong; almost unfathomable.

Among the slain were his friends: Supilo, Himoa, and then, to Ademo's great horror, even Chief Fyoma! If the chief was dead, what hope was there for the others?

As he turned to enter the short trail that led to the village, Ademo had difficulty weaving between the corpses. And then he fell, tripped up by an arm that lay at an oblong angle.

Ademo scrambled to his feet again, noticing the blood now smeared on his leg. He told himself not to look, not to stare into the faces of his dead brethren. Instead he turned and chased down the village trail. Along the way more bodies littered the path. He saw that many of the dead were young men of his own age.

He should have been here! His place was by their side, defending the village!

Even as he approached the village, intense waves of heat wafted towards him, distorting the air. Ademo chose to ignore it, and tore into the village square at full speed.

He heard wailing. A woman's voice. And then more than one woman. Fuita, who was Supilo's mother, came rushing out from one of the huts and grabbed Ademo by the shoulders.

"My boy! My boy is gone! Have you seen him, Ademo? Have you seen Supilo? He's nowhere to be found! Where are the others? Were they with you?"

Ademo stared into the woman's frightened eyes and was lost for words. What could he tell her? Nothing to alleviate her pain. The memory of Supilo's open but unseeing eyes was still etched in his mind.

He shook his head, saying nothing, then tore away from Fuita's grip. She stumbled to the ground and called after him.

"My boy! Where is my boy? Ademo – *please*, was he with you?"

Supilo's mother was almost shrieking now, as if the wiser part of her already knew his fate. Had she seen the truth in Ademo's eyes?

Ademo saw that the front entrance of his hut was

wide open. Feeling his heart pound, he charged inside.

"Mother? Mother! Where are you? *Mother!*" Ademo didn't notice that his voice was taking on the same fevered pitch as Fuitia's. His shock sheltered him from that, perhaps mercifully.

He glanced into his mother's room – empty. He turned and ran into his own room. She wasn't there either. The hut was empty. But in looking around, it was clear there had been a struggle here, not long before. Two of the pottery vases his mother had fashioned herself lay cracked in pieces on the ground. And their small eating table was overturned.

And then he heard a crash from his mother's room. He turned and ran in that direction. He saw that, in one fell swoosh, half of the room had been engulfed in flame, as the winds – as if conspiring against him – blew fire from one hut to another.

Ademo had only a moment longer to look around his boyhood home before the flames swooshed into the eating area. Snatching his valia from against the wall, Ademo ran, the intense heat chasing him from the hut.

Outside he turned and looked towards the village square again, saw several women and two of the older men gathering in a crowd in one of the few places still sheltered from flame.

Ademo ran towards them, all the while feeling the oppressive heat wafting over him.

Even before he had time to ask about his mother's whereabouts, the group turned towards him. He recognized them as a group of the village elders. One of the men, the stern Kuio, registered Ademo's presence and pointed directly towards him. "It is him! The outsider! He who has brought this wrath down upon us!"

The man had a berserk expression written across his face, almost maniacal. Ademo had had few encounters with him, but he often caught the old man eyeing him warily. Ademo never knew what to make of it. Perhaps it had to do with the mystery of his father's absence. Perhaps it was something else. When he'd asked his mother about Kuio, she had dismissed the subject, saying he was just a bitter old man. And yet, Ademo was never quite sure that was all there was to it.

One of the other elders, a silver haired woman named Shanita, stepped towards him. "Ademo Asterling, where have you been this long while? Why do you appear only now?"

Ademo looked at her dumbfounded, her question laced with suspicion. "My Placca. I was trekking to the far side of the island."

Kuio stepped forward as well, until he was only inches away from Ademo. Ademo could smell the man's foul breath as he leaned into him.

"And what did you learn, outsider? Anything of value? Or did the seven winds remain silent – knowing full well you are not of this island?"

Ademo blinked, fury mixing with self-doubt. He remembered his dream – but knew full well the meaning remained a mystery to him. He dismissed the thought from his mind, remembering his current plight; his fear for his mother's wellbeing outweighing any personal grievance he had with Kuio.

He turned to one of the women who had remained silent. Her expression told him she was more sympathetic.

"Please, Sada Nuisa, have you seen my mother? She's not in our hut."

The woman looked upon him with sad eyes. "Ademo... they took her."

"Took her? Who took her? Took her where?"

"The outsiders. They took her away with them. On their seafaring vessel."

"They took *only* her? But why?" Ademo's mind was racing; questions begetting more questions.

Kuio made a sarcastic grunt, shook his head. "He plays dumb, even now. Do you think we're fools, boy? They took your cursed mother because of YOU!"

Ademo could stomach some of these accusations, but hearing the old man speak of his mother in such a manner was too much. He rushed at Kuio, blood surging through his veins.

The old man stepped back quickly, his arms flailing above his head. "He attacks us – even now – just like the others of his kind!"

Two of the others intervened, held Ademo back. Feeling more bold, the old man barked at him again.

"Boy, they came for you! *You!* They came asking for one of your age, with birthmarks behind both ears.

Do you dare to pull back that bushy hair of yours, show us what's there?"

Ademo's expression turned to puzzlement. Could it be true? Were these outsiders looking for him? And had they destroyed most of the village, killed the men of battle age, and taken his mother prisoner, all because of him?

Then he remembered that his mother bore the same marks as he. The birth markings behind each ear. That must have been how they identified her.

He pulled himself free from the others' grasp, stumbled backwards.

"Yes!" barked Kuio. "He knows it's true! The guilt is written on him like etchings on stone! You have cursed us, boy! Cursed us all!"

"They raided the village looking for a marked young man, Ademo," Nuisa said, even as her eyes moved towards his neck, though his hair covered the area in question.

"We fought them as best we could," she continued. "But they would have killed us all if they thought the person they were looking for was still here. I think they came to believe that whoever that was had already fled the island. I heard their leader say as much. It was only then that they left, with your mother in tow."

Kuio had heard enough. He turned to the other elders, waving his hands in the air. "I warned you! Warned you all! We never should have permitted the likes of him and his mother into our community. The day we did we cursed ourselves. The wrath was inevitable, only delayed these few years!"

This angered some of the others, and shouting broke out amongst the usually calm elders group. Ademo turned and wandered in the other direction, his eyes darting to and fro amidst the death and destruction all around him.

And then it became too much. Ademo broke out into a sprint, running towards the thickness of the jungle beyond. He let the branches whip him as he pushed through the dense underbrush, seeking to be away. Just to be away.

13

Ademo sat under the stars. The soft sand and gentle lapping of the waves served as a soothing balm for his troubled soul.

How could it have all gone so wrong, so quickly? That's what he kept asking himself. Why, of all possible times, was the Lord's Shield breached, and the village attacked, on the very day he was away on his Placca? How could fate prove so cruel?

And now, so many dead. And his mother, gone. Could he even dare to hope that she was alive? And if so, under what conditions? Was she wishing for death, even now, as he sat comfortably under the stars?

And then, on top of all that, there were the strange ramblings of Kuio; saying it was all because of him. Saying it was because of his status as an outsider. That he had brought a curse on the island. That he had brought down the very wrath of the gods upon them all.

Surely these were the ramblings of a half-mad old man. But... on the other hand, while his mother had never given specifics, Ademo knew there was something different about him. What were the details of his background? How was it possible he had no relatives on the island other than his mother?

And what of his father? How had he died? Ademo's mother would never elaborate, other than to say he had died as a consequence of his own foolishness. But what did that mean? Ademo had always shied away from asking more about that subject; because it seemed particularly painful for his mother. And, truth be told, Ademo didn't really want to know such truth – not if it meant learning that his father had disgraced himself somehow.

He was burdened with so many questions.

As was custom on the island, it would have been his right, as a man, to ask more of these matters after having returned from his Placca. He knew that. And his mother knew that. He'd expected to have that conversation with her soon after returning. She had promised him as much.

And now... Now, that might *never* happen. Again: the timing. It all just seemed so cruel and uncanny.

Just then Ademo heard what sounded like the cracking of a twig. He turned his head back towards the jungle, trying to pick out detail amidst the shrouded trees and brush.

Only the darkness stared back at him.

He decided it was probably just one of the many animals that roamed the jungle, especially at night. He wasn't too concerned though, he knew that the larger predators, like hillcats, rarely if ever roamed down to the shoreline. Their habitat was up on the slopes of Mt. Uduri.

Ademo relaxed, turned his eyes back to the ocean. And then, suddenly, he heard rustling from behind him. He turned and rose to his feet all in one motion.

Three male figures stepped out quickly from the brush. Even in the darkness Ademo quickly recognized them. It was Tyaso, the chief's eldest, and two of his friends: Jasolo and Diavi.

As Ademo fully expected, it was Tyaso who took the lead, stepping forward until his face almost touched Ademo's. The penetrating eyes, so much like Fyoma's, bore down on him. The other two took a position on either side of Ademo.

"What are you doing out here, coward? Running and hiding from danger again, are you?" Tyaso asked.

Ademo felt rage rise like a swell from deep within him. But he remained silent, meeting the taller Tyaso's intense glare with his own.

"I asked you a question, coward," Tyaso continued, spittle flying from his mouth. "And you say nothing. No doubt because you have no defense. Your silence condemns you."

"Tyaso, you fool," Ademo began, doing his best to remain calm, "I am silent because I refuse to dignify your question."

Suddenly there was a blur of movement in Ademo's peripheral vision, and Jasolo's valia rapped across the side of his head. Ademo felt an explosion of pain as he fell to the sand, blood oozing from behind his ear.

"How dare you speak to the heir-apparent in such a manner! Watch your tongue, rogue!" Jasolo barked at him, clutching his valia as if he might swing again at any moment.

Ademo was nauseous and his vision was blurred, but he refused to let Tyaso and his goons know that. He wiped the blood from his ear and onto the sand.

"Is that what you're declaring yourself, Tyaso? The *heir-apparent*? Doesn't that need to be spoken by the elders first?"

Jasolo raised his valia, ready to strike again, when Tyaso held his hand in the air, waving him off.

"As it shall be, soon enough, coward. As my father's eldest son, the chiefdom is rightfully mine. It's merely a matter of time before the elders hold the torch ceremony to make it official.

"And do you know what my first order of business will be? I'll have you condemned as a traitor – and burned in the fires of Uduri."

Despite his dislike for Tyaso, these words stung

Ademo. This was the second time that day that one of the villagers had blamed him for what had befallen the village. To his great chagrin, he was lost for words. He merely stared up at Tyaso, signaling his contempt with his silent glare.

Tyaso knew that he'd gotten to Ademo, and thoroughly enjoyed the experience.

"What do you think, boys," Tyaso began, "how many of those invaders have had their way with this coward's mother by now?"

As the other two laughed on cue, the rage boiling inside Ademo erupted.

He leapt from the sand with lightning speed, taking hold of Tyaso's own valia and ramming it against Tyaso's head before the chief's son even knew what was happening. With Tyaso reeling, Ademo turned to reach for his own valia, laying on the sand a few feet away. He managed to get a hand on it when two blows came over him; one on his lower back, the other on the back of his head. He grunted in pain and collapsed on the ground.

Both Jasolo and Diavi struck him again, for good measure. Ademo lurched in the sand, coughing up blood and gasping for air. The two were ready to strike again, but Tyaso, who had recovered from Ademo's blow, raised his hand.

"Enough!" he barked, leaning over Ademo with a menacing glare. "Take heart, traitor! When we feed you to Uduri's fire your death will be rather quick. Probably less painful than the blows you've experienced here. That is, if we don't make you the goat for our hunt beforehand."

The other two chuckled at that. Again, almost as if on cue. Do these two ever think for themselves? Ademo wondered. Of course not. That's exactly why Tyaso had picked them, for their unwavering, unthinking loyalty.

"Enjoy your last few days on the island, cowardly one. When it's time, we'll come fetch you. And no matter where you hide, we'll find you," Tyaso added, glaring down at him for a moment longer.

"Let's go, boys. We'll leave him to consider his crimes. Perhaps the gods will pity him when he enters the next world. But I doubt it. From fire to fire he will go."

With that the three slipped like shadows into the tree line.

Ademo rolled over, then grimaced as pain stabbed his ribs. He spat up blood one more time, before surrendering to black.

14

Ademo knew staying in the same place wasn't wise. After all, Tyaso and his followers could return at any time. Still, when he first awoke to a swollen ear and badly bruised ribs – realizing that everything he'd experienced over the last couple of days was not a nightmare after all, but all too real – he just couldn't muster up the will to move. So he lay on the sand, moving little, drifting in and out of troubled sleep, as the sun rose and slowly arched across the sky.

It wasn't until high tide came late that afternoon, when the salty waters washed up against him, stinging his bleeding wounds, that Ademo really shook off his daze. It was then that he pulled himself to his feet, now feeling the injury to his bruised left knee cap as well, and managed to stumble farther up onto the shore.

Close by were some berry bushes. Ademo sat there, eating berries until his stomach hurt. He was hungry, but a stomach could only handle so many of these acidic things.

Seeking something to calm his enflamed insides, Ademo managed to stumble into the brush beyond, wandering around until he came across a coconut lying on the ground. It looked to be reasonably fresh. Ademo carried it back out to the shore, found a rock, and proceeded to dig into the coconut shell, his ribs erupting with pain with almost every movement.

It was long, difficult work. But finally, half an hour later, he held the coconut above his head and let its content drain into his open mouth. The liquid was delicious. He just wished there was more of it. He wished he'd taken the time to find another coconut before returning to shore, because now he was too tired to move.

He leaned back, and watched as the sunlight began to diffuse into the horizon of the fogbank they called the Lord's Shield. As the light turned golden, then crimson, then began to fade, Ademo felt fatigue overcoming him once again. He rolled over onto the sand and let sleep take him.

The next morning Ademo awoke at first light. While his ribs were still sore, the rest of him felt somewhat revived. He stood up, rubbed his knee, and stretched. The ribs complained at that, and Ademo cursed himself for trying such a move so quickly.

The next thought was of hunger. It gripped him now. It had been days since he'd had a proper meal, and he could feel it in his slim frame. His meager clothes hung much more loosely now than they had when he'd first embarked on his Placca earlier that week.

He leaned down, picked up his valia, thankful that he'd managed to hold onto it. It had been a gift from his mother. He examined the intricate carvings along the edge, her handiwork. Ademo couldn't understand the strange markings. But apparently they did have a meaning. This was yet again one of the matters he was supposed to receive more illumination on upon his return from the Whispering Cliffs.

And now his mother was gone. So who would decode it for him now? After all, she had hinted once before that she was the only one on the island who understood the strange tongue it was written in.

Ademo sighed and leaned back. Where was she

now – two days on from when she'd been taken by the outsiders? How far could they have traveled by now? Was their destination near or far? Ademo had no idea. As with all of the other islanders, Ademo knew nothing of an outside world. The Lord's Shield had been the beginning and ending of everything. Now he couldn't help but wonder: what else was out there? One land? Two? Many? How large was the expanse of the world?

Later that day Ademo sat crouched low on the ground, silent and still. He'd done this for hours now, waiting on some small game to come by, armed with one of his throwing discs. His valia lay by his side. It was a helpful weapon, but not ideal for work such as this.

Twice already he'd sensed movement nearby, only to have the creature disappear without even getting a good look at it. Whatever they were, they had been small. Probably squirrels or something similar. And even the smallest movements on his part were enough to spook them.

But now his eyes grew wide. For only a dozen yards to his left, a scamper came into view. The creature was about the size of a rabbit, and looked like a cross between a wolverine and an otter. These creatures were known to wander down from the hills to fish by the shore. Still, they were rarely *observed* doing so. They were stealthy.

Ademo waited patiently, his throwing disc in hand. He knew he'd only get once chance. By now his stomach was growling, so loud he was concerned the animal might hear it. But then he put that out of his mind, focusing on the task at hand.

Just then the animal turned its head, so it was facing fully away from him. Ademo raised his arm slowly, silently, then let fly.

The disc slashed through the air in one fluid motion, Ademo willing its path with his eyes. It struck its target quickly and effectively. For the first time in days Ademo smiled, knowing that, at least today, he would enjoy a hearty meal.

He knew it was probably unwise to start a fire in broad daylight. And he certainly had no desire to signal his whereabouts to Tyaso and his goons. But the idea of eating broiled scamper was just too delicious to pass up.

Using the sharp, hard end of his valia, Ademo began the long, tedious work of drawing flame from wood. He spun the shaft of his valia back and forth, in a blur of motion, and waited, and waited, and waited – for the smoke to rise.

When he finally saw the first wisp of smoke, he leaned down to blow on it, and to his relief a flame sprang to life. The breeze off of the ocean was slight, feeding the fire just the right amount of oxygen. He added some larger branches to the fire, and then thrust a stick hung with the scamper over the flame.

The fire was soothing. And Ademo let himself get lost in the dance of the flames.

He turned the scamper over several times until he

felt it was cooked sufficiently. When he finally took a bite he found it delicious, if a little dry. His body responded with enthusiasm to his first protein in days. He had planned to douse the fire before eating his meal, but now that he'd had a taste, he decided the fire could wait. He ate ravenously, taking large bites from the succulent meat.

When he finished the last of what he deemed the edible parts of the scamper, he put his stick down and poured sand over the simmering flames. The fire was quickly doused.

Then he heard a snap.

Ademo froze, listening intently. But all he could hear was the sound of the waves lapping on the shore. His ears strained, listening for the padding of feet, or some other telltale sign he'd been discovered.

After a few moments he concluded it was a false alarm. Still, he'd stayed in this one location for long enough; it was time to move on.

Picking up his valia, with a last gaze towards the ocean, Ademo turned into the dense jungle, doing his best to tread lightly and not leave a trail.

15

Siya's eyes fluttered open, and she took a moment to acquaint herself with her surroundings. She sat up, every bone in her body protesting after hours against the hard floor. Reaching up, she rubbed the back of her neck. The muscles there were sore after that man – Maynard was his name – had twisted her head around to examine behind her ears.

Of course, he'd found what he was looking for. That explained why she was here now, the only captive of the entire village. It was because of something she'd never actually seen other than through certain reflective surfaces. But it was a trait she shared with Ademo. And she had beheld his many times – the birthmarks.

Siya felt anger and frustration, thinking on the cruel nature of their shared trait. A biological branding is what it felt like.

She breathed in deeply, and immediately regretted it, for the smell here in the belly of this massive ship left something to be desired. She wondered what could create such an odor. Perhaps a mixture of fish and human waste?

She forced herself to think on other matters. Immediately, questions rose in her mind. Now that these marauders had her, what would they do with her? No doubt their plan, after finding Ademo absent from the village, was to force her to reveal his whereabouts.

The fact that Ademo had been away on the day of the invasion truly was a kind of miracle. And for that Siya gave thanks. That little bit of serendipity helped to assuage her frustration around the birthmarks.

Her thoughts turned to Ademo's present condition. Assuming all had gone well on his Placca – and for that she could only hope – Ademo likely arrived back at the village not long after she'd been taken aboard the ship.

What was he thinking now? What would he do after finding her missing? How much could the others help him sort this all out? Feeling helpless, Siya let her head sink between he knees.

In reality she knew the villagers could do very little to help Ademo understand their present predicament. In fact, in light of the council meeting she'd attended in the Skytent, they would most likely blame him for the entire series of events that had befallen the village.

Tears welled up in Siya's eyes. She feared for her son. There was so little he knew about his background. She had kept it that way, deliberately, thinking that was the best thing for him. But now she questioned that decision. Because reality had come crashing down on him. And because of her silence he had no compass with which to navigate. That was solely her fault.

Just then she heard the sound of a chain being loosed, followed by the creaking of a door opening. Heavy footfalls rang out as someone descended a set of stairs from above. She expected it would be Maynard, come to interrogate her.

But this man looked nothing like Maynard. No, it was clear – from the regal nature of his clothing – that this man approaching her now, smiling, was likely the captain of the ship.

"I apologize for the rough treatment you've received, madam. The crew can be such brutes at times. Not much going on upstairs, if you know what I mean. But I'm forgetting myself. Let us first be introduced. My name is Captain Prigg," he said, removing his black hat and bowing with flourish.

Here he paused, as if waiting for her to speak. When Siya continued to stare up at him, silently, he continued.

"Now, there's no need for this entire situation to be so... uncomfortable. I hold no enmity towards you. I simply seek your son. He must be quite some fellow, because very important people would like to speak with him. And that's all I'm trying to do here – facilitate a meeting, as it were. Do you follow me?"

Siya kept her silence.

"So... with all that said, why don't we bring this matter to a resolution sooner rather than later? That would be a scenario in everyone's best interest, don't you think?"

Again, silence.

"Now, the crew searched the village high and low, and yet no sign of your son was found. So why don't we talk about where he is. Has he left the island? If so, where was he headed?"

Silent staring, nothing more.

The captain's tongue made a ticking sound against the roof of his mouth, as he did his best to wait – masking patience.

"Madam, I asked you where you son is. Come now, let's not be enemies. Tis not necessary. What awaits your son could be a coronation for all you know. He is a special boy, if I hear it right. But I'm guessing you already knew that, correct?"

Now Siya shifted her gaze from the captain to a random point in space, saying nothing.

For a few moments there was only silence between them. Then Siya sensed the Captain's emotions stirring. It was doubtful he was accustomed to waiting. And in that moment she feared that perhaps he would strike her. She braced herself when he shuffled his feet.

"Very well, have it your way. Play the mute. It bothers me not. We have a long voyage back to the mainland, madam. Long enough for you to starve if you persist in your silence."

Here Prigg paused, letting the threat hang thick in the air between them. Then, seeming unsure of himself, or so Siya sensed, he changed course yet again, softening his offer.

"Now, there's no need for that. We have some very delicious provisions aboard. In my Captain's quarters I have some Busillian wine, an exquisite merlot. I'd be happy to dine with you, share some of these spoils, if you would but simply answer the question as to your son's whereabouts. So, shall we put this matter to rest? Madam?"

Siya almost wanted to laugh. Prigg's tactics seemed pathetic. But she knew that doing so might put what she beheld to be a deeply insecure man over the top – make him fly into a rage. So she kept her lips tightly shut, still staring into empty space.

The captain tapped his large boot against the hard wooden floor, several times. When it was clear Siya had made her decision, he tsked.

"Have it your way then, woman. Let's see how long you can keep this up on an empty belly."

And with that he turned and marched back up the stairwell, the sound of a slamming door following moments later.

16

From the summit of Mt. Uduri Ademo felt relatively safe. Here he was a long way from the village, yet he could see its charred remains from where he stood. And from this vantage point he could also see the mountain trail for a long ways – providing him early warning when Tyaso and his goons came looking for him.

And in Ademo's mind it really was a question not of if, but when. He knew Tyaso had it out from him. Always had. And he knew that Tyaso blamed him for his father's death. In other words, his threat was not an idle one. He would wait only as long as it took for the elders to confirm his chiefdom, and then he would come looking for him.

With Kuio's raving fantasies added to the mix, Ademo had little doubt Tyaso would be appointed chief, and even encouraged in his hunt. After all, even for those of a more moderate mind on the elder council, evidence from recent events would only lead them to conclude that they had angered the gods – and that penance must be paid to prevent further ill from befalling the village. Ademo's death would serve as the perfect sacrifice to that end. And with no relatives left on the island to defend him, who would oppose such an action? He was the ideal scapegoat.

Ademo stood still, contemplating his options. On the one hand, perhaps he could survive by making camp in some hidden location on the far side of the island; at least for a good period of time anyway. But would the others ever forget about him? Would they ever leave him be? Merely banished? Not likely. Tyaso would see to it that he was hunted for as long as it took to find him. No, he might exist like that for a while – weeks, months even. But sooner of later, they would find him.

And that left only one other option: to leave the island.

Ademo had always wondered, but now, with the coming of the invaders, knew for certain, that other lands, other peoples existed – beyond the veil of the Lord's Shield. Despite whatever apocalypse his mother and the elders referred to, there was still a wider world out there. And he was curious to know more of that world, felt it beckoning him.

Besides, somewhere out there his mother was still being held captive. At least he held out some hope that she was – that she was still alive. And as long as that was a possibility he knew he must try to find her. He had no idea how he would do so – because he had no idea what lay beyond the Shield. But try he must, nevertheless.

Two days after he'd stood at the summit of Mt. Uduri making his decision, Ademo pulled the last of the binding vines taut around the log pole, then sliced off the excess with the jade end of his valia. He stepped back, assessing his handiwork.

It looked nothing like the vast seafaring vessel he'd seen from on high, but he was pretty sure it would float. Either way, it was the best he could do. It was a raft, about six feet long by four feet wide, comprised of log poles strung together by jungle vine and buiyala sap. And, as near as he could tell, it was finished.

Ademo sighed, relieved to have the task completed. He sat down on the warm sand and gazed off towards the rim of the foggy shield. What lay beyond there? He would soon find out. For he was confident the raft would carry him that far at least. And after that? Well, time would reveal all. That's what his mother would have said to him. That's what she always said whenever he'd asked about his mysterious past.

And, as much as he yearned to have some of the questions about his background answered, the truth was, for now he'd settle for seeing her patient, loving gaze again. Mysteries could wait. What mattered more was having her with him.

Ademo made note of the sun's position low on the horizon, its bottom edge now obscured in the mists of the Lord's Shield. It was too late in the day to embark on his journey. He would wait till morning, leave at first light. He'd already taken time, in between long hours spent building the raft, to collect provisions for his voyage. Coconuts, berries, and other food items he thought would fair well on the voyage lay in a pile beside the raft. He would spend some time that evening gathering a little more. He hoped that would be enough. He had no idea how much water lay between him and the next land, but, either way, the raft wouldn't hold much more. He would just have to hope it would suffice.

Ademo was deep asleep, dreaming of dancing with Jania at a seasonal feast, when leaves rustled in the jungle brush behind him. Sleeping lightly, with one ear to his surroundings, he immediately opened his eyes, but remained laying perfectly still.

When moments went by, void of any other unusual sounds, he began to relax. He was *so* tired. All he wanted was to rest, to let his aching muscles recuperate.

Ademo's heavy eyes were just beginning to droop again when he heard a second round of rustling, closer this time. Whether it was an animal or something else, it was too close to ignore.

Ademo turned over to look behind him, saw a shadow step out from the brush. But before he could make anything else out, pain tore through him, as something pierced his chest. It was the sharp, jade end of a valia. Ademo gasped as all the air was sucked from his lungs. He tried to breathe, but it was no use. His lung had collapsed.

He let loose a muffled shout, instinctively pressing his hands to his wound to staunch the bleeding that was streaming onto the ground around him.

Looking up towards his attacker, he saw a wide smile carve across Tyaso's shadowed features.

Ademo bolted upright, his breath coming in gasps. His gaze darted left and right, searching for Tyaso. *Where had he gone?*

Then he looked down at his wound, found it was no longer there.

Reality struck: a *dream*. It was only a dream. The jungle was still, and he was alone.

Ademo collapsed onto the ground, where he lay looking up at the starry sky. Dawn was hours away yet. After a few moments he rolled over, forcing his eyes closed, begging that sleep would wash over him yet again. But the adrenaline that continued to surge through him made that a vain wish for quite some time.

When Ademo opened his eyes again the sun was already peering over the edge of the jungle canopy. He sat up, stretched. Remembering his nightmare all too vividly, he was eager to make his departure.

Even though he'd heard not a peep from the villagers since his run-in with Tyaso et al several days earlier, Ademo sensed that they would come for him soon. He didn't want to wait to find out *how* soon.

And yet, as the time for this voyage was now upon him, he felt grave misgivings. Suddenly the question of what lay beyond the Lord's Shield was less a beckoning mystery, and more a troubling unknown. Was this suicide? That morning the seas looked peaceful, inviting. But Ademo had seen those same waters churn during storm season. And what if that was what awaited him beyond the fog line?

Again, as his mother would say, time would reveal all.

For breakfast Ademo drank some coconut milk and enjoyed the meat of some small game he'd hunted the day before. This would perhaps be the last time in a great while that he enjoyed such a delicacy. He certainly hoped it wasn't the *last* time.

When he was done, Ademo pulled the raft out from the underbrush and out onto the cool morning sand. He moved quickly, even now fearing he would be apprehended by Tyaso and his goons at the very last moment.

But as he waded into the warm surf, no one came running from the jungle. This beach was deserted.

When he could no longer touch ground Ademo started swimming, pushing the raft along in front of him. When he was a good ways out, he hopped aboard. The makeshift craft wobbled, but stayed buoyant. He looked over his handiwork again, saw that it was holding together nicely. For now.

He turned to look back at the island one last time. Doing so brought on a bizarre cocktail of emotions. This had been the only home he'd ever known. He recalled treasured memories from his youth, his childhood flashing before his eyes. How happy and carefree he had been.

But these memories were tainted with recent horror and the pain of false accusation and betrayal.

With his mother gone, he had no place here anymore.

Without another backward glance, Ademo took up the oar and began paddling out towards the rim of the Lord's Shield.

17

Ademo rowed in a comfortable rhythm, eyeing the misty horizon as it drew ever closer. Eventually he began to notice the temperature dropping around him, as the wispy edges of the fog line began to enfold him.

He rowed amidst the ominous silence, wondering what may lay hidden in the misty depths of the Shield. What was it that had kept foreign ships out for so long?

When he was a boy, Ademo and his friends used to imagine strange beasts that patrolled the waters, waiting eagerly to devour any craft that came their way. Ademo was quite sure such thoughts were best left to children. He wasn't fearful of huge tentacled arms suddenly reaching overboard to snatch him – not very fearful, anyway. But he was concerned about his sense of direction. Now, as the fog settled in on him more heavily, he began to feel dizzy. And suddenly rowing a straight line seemed immensely more difficult. Was he rowing in circles? How could he know? Ademo did his best to ignore such fears, kept rowing.

He had hoped the fog line was a rather shallow ring that circled the island. When the mists only grew more dark and dense the longer he rowed, that thought was cast aside into the wishful thinking category. Suddenly Ademo began to question his entire plan. Was this the foolishness of youth? Thinking he, Ademo Asterling, could brave a feat no islander had ever before attempted? Suddenly it felt very much that way.

Had he misjudged his fate on the island? Was it possible that some may have opposed Tyaso's intentions? A few faces came to mind: mothers of his friends and such. But none of those particular women were on the elder council. And besides, who would really challenge the commands of the Chief? It was simply forbidden to do so.

A wise chief, like Fyoma had been, would draw advice before making his pronouncements – to ensure justice was truly served. But once those commandments had been given, they were set in stone. Would Tyaso solicit such feedback? Doubtful, at best. And even if Tyaso's commands ultimately proved foolhardy and rash, they would carry that same weight. It was the way of village life; had been that way for generations. It was as old as the Great Lore itself.

No, come what may, this was his path. The only one that offered any real hope; even if that hope was scarce.

As the fog clung to him strangely, Ademo rowed on, even though he could no longer see more than a few feet beyond the edge of the raft. And row on and on he would, for as long as he had strength and sanity to do so.

Just when Ademo thought he may go mad from the sheer mundanity of the endless, silent fog, he began to notice the raft bobbing up and down more frequently. A few minutes later what he would consider a true wave thrust the raft up and down, lifting it two feet or more into the air. As the waves began to grow larger and even more frequent, Ademo cursed himself for complaining of the mundane calm only a few minutes before.

Time was difficult to gauge out here in the dreaded grey, but sometime later on the rains began to fall. And before long, what at first had seemed like extra moisture in the foggy air suddenly became pellets of hurtling raindrops, stinging in their intensity.

Ademo spat water from his mouth, wiped away his wet, wavy hair from his eyes, and pushed ever on, doing his best to pull his oar evenly through the choppy, seesawing waters.

Every few moments a wave would threaten to topple the – what now seemed like a – pitifully weak raft. In those moments Ademo would reach down, grab a hold of the floorboard polls, doing his best to ride out the surge.

The only thing that kept him from succumbing to the fullness of the terror about him, was his resolved sense that this task required every ounce of his strength, every iota of his attention.

So on he rowed, even as the dull grey gave way to the black of night – leaving him to pull his oar along in the storm, without even the aid of a pale light to guide him.

18

With the seas calmer again, the next day passed much like the former. Only this time the claustrophobic fog was with him from morning till night. And even when the sunlight faded the next evening (he never actually saw the sun, just perceived slight changes in the backlight behind the mist), he knew the fog was all around him, as thick as ever; he could feel it on his skin. He lay down to a troubled sleep, as the raft was carried along with the current.

When the black brightened ever so slightly to a dull grey the next morning, Ademo awoke hungry. He uncovered his sack of provisions and found that he was running low. He now second-guessed how much food he'd brought with him. Perhaps he didn't want to bring any more – subconsciously, anyway – because he didn't want to face the idea that he could be out on the open water for this long – for days on end.

At this rate, even if he rationed his food, he would run out of provisions within a day and a half. Ademo tried to put the thought out of his mind; tried to enjoy his breakfast of berries, nuts and coconut milk.

When he was done he wrapped up the food again, and glanced towards the water. It was still difficult to make out through the mist, but it certainly felt as if the current was stronger this morning, carrying him along at a faster pace.

Of course, after this long in this grey expanse of nothingness, he had no idea what direction he was going. Before he'd embarked on his journey he'd counted on being able to navigate by the stars – at least at night. But of course he hadn't seen a single twinkle since he'd left the island.

Either way, there was no use resisting the direction the current was taking him. It would be a foolish expense of energy to attempt it. So he rowed with the current, if for nothing else than to keep from going mad from the mundanity of his surroundings.

When morning rolled around the following day, Ademo stared bleakly at his food supply. He ate two berries, two nuts, and allowed himself only a dash of the coconut milk – which he proceeded to immediately spit overboard. It had turned rancid. Again, he hadn't planned on that – hadn't planned on being out here on the water for so long.

The small ration he'd allowed himself did almost nothing to curb his appetite. And, to make matters worse, he knew that today would see the last of his rations disappear. So what would he do when we awoke the next morning, to find nothing left to eat or drink? He didn't want to think about it. He picked up the oar, started pulling through the water at a steady pace, doing his best to ignore his aching thirst.

As the sunlight began to fade again later that day, Ademo was just contemplating opening up his food bag – for what would be the last time – when he noticed the raft beginning to rock back and forth. The seas had been calm, for so long now, that it caught Ademo by surprise.

It was then that he recalled the choppy waters he faced the first night, and swallowed hard. The lack of nourishment, and days of rowing, had left him feeling weak. At this point it was taking all he had just to keep going. Facing stormy waters now was something that almost terrified him.

Ademo popped the last few of his berries and nuts into his mouth, noticed the parched feeling in his mouth grow even worse. Even as he did so the raft began seesawing more distinctly. Looking into the mist it occurred to him that it seemed to have gotten dark earlier than usual. He had no way of knowing this for sure, just a gut instinct based on his internal clock. Yet he felt quite sure that the early dark was a sign that storm clouds were now rolling overhead, unseen through the thick of the fog.

An hour later the rains began. At first Ademo welcomed them because he was so thirsty. He held up the leather flask that had contained the coconut milk to collect as much of the rain as he could, even using a funnel leaf to gather even more. The water was like an elixir for his dry throat. It was a wonderful, welcome relief for a time, and he was able to chase away his thirst almost entirely.

But then the waves picked up even more, surging toward him and sending the small raft heaving up and down. Before long Ademo dropped down flat upon the raft, his hands and feet wrapped tightly around the log polls.

Now it was all he could do to stay aboard as the raft heaved up and down upon the raging surf. He reached over into the thoroughly soaked provision bag and pulled out the last of the vine. He made fast work of tying his ankles, as best he could, tightly around the round, log polls. Then he did the same to his right wrist, tying it tight to the floor polls so that only his left arm swung freely.

Just when it seemed impossible the rains came even harder, stinging his back and legs as he lay prostrate on the raft.

And as night came on fully, the storm went on and on like this, even intensifying further. Thunder began to roll and lightning strikes lit up the dense fog in brief, furious flashes. Ademo kept clutching to the raft poles, fairly confident the vines he'd tied around his limbs would hold. But as to whether the raft would stay upright, that was another matter entirely.

In the dead of night, when the most massive waves came, it felt as if the raft would tip over entirely on the crest of each wave. And Ademo knew that if that were to happen these ties would become anchors, holding him under the surface in an overturned boat.

But the raft didn't tip, always flattening out just in time as it rode with each massive wave.

Ademo couldn't believe a storm like this could go on for *so* long. How long had it been? It was difficult to gauge in these circumstances. Certainly hours and hours had gone by. Hadn't they?

Ademo scanned the dark horizon, to see if perhaps some hint of dawn could be gleaned. Such a sight would be welcome, even if the storm continued to rage.

And just that moment the wave surge snapped off one of the end poles, sent it hurtling towards him. Ademo didn't see it coming. When it hit him squarely on the forehead he was out before he knew what hit him.

19

Siya crouched uncomfortably against a latticed panel. The overwhelmingly unpleasant odor emanating from within suggested it was connected to a sewage drain coming from the compartment located directly above her. She had come across this opening while walking (check that: pacing) the previous night, long after most of the sounds above deck had ceased.

All but one that is. When she happened to wander by that opening, looking – perhaps foolishly – for some way of escape from her windowless, odorous confines, she had heard a strange rumbling. Moving closer to investigate, she had determined the sound was – unmistakably – snoring.

Putting two and two together she thought there

was a half-decent chance the night rumbling was coming from Captain Prigg himself. After all, who else would have a separate sewage shaft; the main one, being larger and even more revolting smelling, located on the other side of the bellow-decks chamber.

So, perhaps against her better judgment – because it took some degree of crawling and contorting to get into this tight space to really listen well – she had clambered in here, on several occasions since then, hoping to perhaps overhear some morsel of information she might find useful.

If nothing else, it helped to pass the time. Because down here, without a window to the outside world, inundated with the smells of human refuse and rotting remains, finding something somewhat productive to do became near necessary; just for sanity's sake.

In her several previous attempts at listening in she'd been underwhelmed with what she'd gleaned. The first time she'd heard nothing but the throaty, wheezing snoring. The second time she'd heard nothing at all. The third time she'd heard the Captain faintly singing, with his decidedly pitch-challenged voice.

And most recently, about an hour before, she'd heard a slopping sound, and had only just moved away in time, as the Captain's excrement came sloshing down only feet from where she'd been crouching.

As she bent her body awkwardly to listen in for a fifth time, her breath caught, because she could make out voices – two of them, coming from the Captain's chamber.

After a few moments of straining to listen, she grew even more excited when it became clear it was Maynard that the Captain was conversing with. Both were speaking with voices that were distinctly, aggressively raised.

"...listen, Captain," Maynard said, with some clear degree of exasperation, "I followed your orders to a tee when we first sought out this dastardly island, and that in itself nearly got us all killed. Now there's *this* to deal with."

Siya's eyes darted left to right, and she pressed even closer to the grated opening, wondering what "this" referred to. It took only a second for the Captain to respond to Maynard's remark.

"Catch yourself, Maynard. You forget your place. Now, what exactly, pray thee, are you referring to?"

"Our course!" Maynard near shouted, as if the point should be obvious.

"Well, what of it, Maynard? Don't be so obtuse, man!"

"Captain, we. are. *lost*! I've been trying to tell you this for nearly a day now."

"Well, man, consult the maps, look for navigational reference, and get us back on course! Must I do everything myself?"

There was a pause, and Siya couldn't help but imagine Maynard, perhaps now almost lost for words, shaking his head slowly before responding.

"Captain," he began, with deliberate calm, "you

don't seem to understand. This is not an issue of incompetence on the part of myself or the crew. It is this... this dreaded *dead spot* on the sea. Nothing makes any sense out here.

"Beginning yesterday even our compasses – all of them – started giving contradictory information. How can one navigate when one compass says we're headed west, another east, and another south?

"And now that we're back into this blasted fog the men are on edge. They believe there's something supernatural at work. They believe we're cursed. And, the thing is, Captain, even if I try and convince them otherwise, there's still this main issue to deal with: *we. are. lost.* I don't know how else to say it."

Siya pressed even closer, wondering if the Captain was responding in too low a tone for her to make out. But no, he was pausing; thinking. Finally, after several seconds he spoke.

"Maynard, do you know what an optical illusion is?"

"Captain?" Maynard replied, either because he didn't, or perhaps because he didn't know where the Captain was going with this line of thought. The Captain continued:

"It is when your eyes play tricks on you. Tell you something other than what is real. Sometimes this happens. Especially at sea, when the expanse of water runs from horizon to horizon. And when that happens, a *seasoned* navigator knows to carry on, waiting for his senses to come around-"

"But Captain, even the *compasses*-" began Maynard, sounding more exasperated again.

"No! I'll hear no more of this rambling, Maynard. Now *you* are first mate. Your job is to run the crew in my stead. So I suggest you get back to it. Pick a course, and stick to it. And make sure the crew does the same.

"That's your problem, see, you allow too much room for rabble-rousing – letting the crew sound off like a bunch of spooked women, only making the situation worse. Perhaps they don't have enough work to do. So give them more. Once they realize that's what they get for spouting off, well, then they'll quit doing so. And we'll all be the better for it."

Maynard paused, Siya imagined him plotting an alternate approach to get through to the stubborn captain. Eventually, when he did speak, he barely got another word in edgewise.

"Captain, I know how to settle a crew, when dealing with the usual fare. However, we-"

"*Maynard*, I said *no more*! Do the words mean nothing to you? Be gone. Now. *Immediately!*"

This time there was no pause, only the drumming of feet and the sound of a door closing with a bang.

20

Landry was a small, coastal city that sat perched high

atop a sheer cliff, overlooking the Emalderine Ocean. The high perch helped to shelter the townsfolk from the storm surge that was known to come with ferocity in the winter months. Not surprisingly, the people of Landry were of a hardy variety; conditioned over generations to endure the long, grey, wet winters. And, for the record, summers were only slightly less cold, and slightly less wet.

It was a typically moist, grey day, the scent of the salty sea thick in the air, when a tall, slender young man, with high, chiseled cheek bones, and hair so blonde it looked nearly white, was making his way down a steep, rocky trail to the narrow beach line below.

For a large part of the day the shore disappeared altogether, as the foamy sea crashed, wave after wave, right against the steep rock face. But for a short period of time, during low tide, the waters would pull back enough to reveal a narrow band of beach, comprised of small crushed rock and shells.

The young man's name was Banon. And this was his favorite time of day to fish. Others were content to sit perched high above, dangling fishing line over the precipice to the sea below. But Banon liked to feel the scree of the shallow beach between his toes, and would brave the cold water in bare feet to do so. Others would likely think him mad. But then, no one else was ever there to see him do it. He did his best to keep this particular hobby to himself.

Once on the beach, Banon stopped, removed his

boots, and rolled his pant legs up to his knees. He tucked his boots behind one of the rocky outcroppings, where they would be kept relatively dry from the surf, and then wiggled his toes, enjoying the coarse sand that massaged his feet.

He wound his fishing line as he strolled along, preparing for his first cast of the day. Yesterday's catch had left a little to be desired, and today he hoped to do better.

His eyes drifted to the foamy surf, watching as it rolled in towards him. His eyes followed the edge of the waterline as it crawled on towards the rock face, stopping only six feet or so from the sheer face of stone and moss.

And then he spotted something unusual.

Something had washed up on shore. It was difficult to make out from this distance, because it was entwined in seaweed. He walked more quickly, his curiosity peaked. As he grew closer he noticed pieces of wood lying at various points along the beach. Even then a piece came to a rest only a foot from where he was walking, deposited there by the rolling water. He glanced down towards it, but kept walking, his focus on the larger something that lay farther along the shoreline.

As he grew closer still his curiosity turned to shocked surprise. It was a body, laying flat, facedown on the beach. Banon dropped his fishing line and gear and ran towards the figure, ignoring the pain of the rocks beneath his bare feet.

He leaned down to get a closer look. Whoever it was, he definitely wasn't from Landry. It was a young man, of about his age, though his skin was darker than Banon's fair variety. The young man's hair was dark, thick and wavy. Again, like nothing seen in these parts.

The body was dressed in only a thin garment around the waist. The young man would no doubt be shivering in the cool, moist, morning air, if it weren't for the fact that he lay unconscious.

Banon reached down, turned him over, listened by his mouth to perceive breathing.

He sensed nothing.

"Hello? Can you hear me? Are you alright?" Banon shouted, as if shouting would revive the man.

He turned him over again, bent him in half over his knee, hoping gravity would empty any water the young man may have swallowed.

Nothing happened. The body was completely limp against him. Banon frowned. This young man had been in the water for no short amount of time. The skin was cold and clammy to the touch. Not a good sign.

He turned the young man's face towards him, gave it a slap.

Nothing.

"Hello! Can you hear me?" he shouted, directly into the young man's ear.

Again, nothing. This time Banon slapped the other cheek, even harder.

Suddenly the body convulsed in his arms. The

figure gagged and water gushed out of his mouth. Banon's eyes went wide.

He turned him over again, so that he could cough the water up on the rocky sand. And he did so, in great heaving convulsions, one after another, gasping for breath in between.

Banon helped him as much as he could, until the convulsions slowed and then stopped. He turned the young man over again, laid him face up on the ground. The eyes were fluttering now.

"Okay, you're alright. You're alright," Banon said, slightly lost for words.

"Do you speak the common tongue?" he asked, trying to make eye contact as the young man's head rolled left to right, the eyes still fluttering.

Banon wasn't even sure the young man had registered he was there. But then, suddenly, he looked up at Banon for a moment, making eye contact for the first time.

"Hello there. My name's Banon. You're alright now. You're out of the water. But we need to get some clothes on you," he said, as much to himself as to the figure who still seemed only half-conscious.

Banon realized he needed to get him up to warm quarters in the town – fast. But that was a steep hike from here. He considered it, but realized that trying to bound over jagged rocks and up the steep narrow trail to the town, while carrying him, just wasn't feasible.

He grabbed the young man underneath both armpits, pulled him as far up the beach as he could; till the other's head was near touching the rock face. Banon looked out towards the water. The tide was at its lowest now, but it wouldn't be that way for long. He'd have to move fast if he wanted to make it up to the town to get help and get back down to the shore again in time.

Banon leaned over: "Listen, I need to go get help. I can't carry you up the rock face without a stretcher. But I'll be right back, with help. And then we'll get you some place warm to recover. Alright?"

The man's body was limp, and only his head continued to move, rocking back and forth, still not seeming to fully recognize Banon's presence.

"I'll be right back. Hold on, friend. Hold on."

With that Banon turned and darted away as fast as his bare feet would carry him.

21

When Ademo finally fully opened his eyes he thought for a moment that he had lost his mind. Nothing about his surroundings made any sense. He found himself in a basically square room, built with hundreds of strange, grey, rectangular shapes. He lay on a raised platform – which was strange enough in itself, as Ademo was accustomed to sleeping close to the floor. Not far from the foot of this sleeping platform was the strangest feature of all: a raging fire. A fire! Inside the room! It was housed in some sort of stonework – but still, such a structure seemed highly dangerous; likely to burn down the room at any moment.

Ademo considered the fire and thought for a moment that perhaps Tyaso had been right – that he had passed over into the next life, where a fiery pit awaited him. Except...

Except that these surroundings didn't exactly fit that description. A fire inside a room certainly seemed bizarre, but, he had to admit, it made him feel rather cozy. And this was a good thing. He had memories of being cold not long ago. *Very* cold. He remembered being caught up in the fierceness of that never-ending storm, and then... And then what?

He remembered nothing else. It was all a blank slate.

It wasn't until a tall rectangular shape at the edge of the room swung open that Ademo realized it was a door. On the island nothing so solid was ever used to bar an entrance.

And then someone was coming through the doorway and approaching the sleeping platform. The person looked like no one Ademo had ever seen before. His hair was long, but straight as an arrow, and the color of the palest sand. His skin was almost just as fair. And the eyes. *Green*! Emerald green. Once again Ademo wondered if he'd crossed over into some netherworld.

And then the young man smiled.

"Hello, friend! It's good to see you awake. That was quite some slumber you had. But then, I guess you needed the rest. When I found you were in pretty pitiful shape."

He paused, seeing the surprised look cast over Ademo's features. *Did he understand anything I just said?* Banon wondered.

"You speak Faraway," Ademo said, with surprise.

"Sorry?" the man said, tilting his head in the process.

"Your words..." Ademo stuttered, "it's Faraway."

Then the young man seemed to realize what he meant; realized Ademo was referring to language.

"I speak in the common tongue, as clearly, do you – though your accent certainly is... unique. I can't say I've ever heard it referred to as feriway before, but perhaps in different places it's called different things. But here, please have something to drink, you'll be needing it I'm sure."

Ademo took the mug that was offered him with suddenly ravenous eyes, drank down the cool water in one fell swoop.

"My mother taught me Faraway – ah, the common tongue, but it's not my native language. Another, please?" Ademo asked, holding the mug out to the stranger.

"Certainly," he replied, quickly replenishing the mug from a strange jar on a table by the sleeping platform.

When Ademo had drunk three whole cups, the

man handed him a loaf of bread.

"I suspect you'll be wanting something to eat as well. You can start with this, and I'll get you something more substantial later."

Ademo had never tasted bread, but he thought it wonderful. Sweet and substantive. When he'd eaten several pieces, chasing each one down with more water, he appeared to relax.

"Thank you. I thank you..."

"Banon," the man said, pointing his finger to his own chest. "My name's Banon. And you are?"

"Ademo," he replied, smiling.

"Excellent. Well met, Ademo. So, how do you feel?"

"Replenished. Thank you. Replenished, and... confused. Not sure where I am. Can't remember what happened."

"Don't worry. I'm sure it'll come back to you. As to where you are, I can fill you in there. This is the town of Landry."

"Landry?" Ademo repeated, letting the strange sounding word dangle on his tongue.

"Yes, Landry, located on the western coast of Corselva."

Ademo stared up blankly at the young man named Banon, who realized at that moment that Corselva was unknown to this exotic-looking foreigner. And that *was* strange. From where had this young castaway come from to not know the name of one of the continents? Or, had he just lost his memory from the ordeal he'd been through? That seemed entirely possible. Banon had heard of such things before.

"Listen, Ademo, you should rest some more. You've come through Hammer's Cove and back, haven't you?"

Ademo stared back blankly, not recognizing the local idiom. Banon made a mental note to keep his metaphors as general as possible.

"What I mean to say is, you've been through a lot. Now that you've taken some food and water, why don't you rest some more. I'll come back later."

Ademo realized this is exactly what his body was craving. As strange as this new place was to him, his body was sending a clear message: rest... *more*. So Ademo, even with his curiosity peaking, nodded.

"Thank you, Banon. I think that'd be a good idea."

Banon nodded. "Rest well. We'll talk more soon."

With that the fair skinned stranger with the hair like sand turned and left, closing the strange, solid frame door behind him.

Ademo sat up for a moment, marveling that, after all those years, learning what he considered to be a dead language – at his mother's insistence – here he was actually making use of it! It truly was astounding.

And then his thoughts turned inevitably to his mother's predicament. He lay awake worrying about her; wondering where in the world she could be, before exhaustion finally overcame him and he fell mercifully back asleep.

22

This unfamiliar new place only grew stranger when Banon returned to fetch Ademo later that day. The moment they stepped outside onto the wet ground, Ademo understood why Banon had offered him these awkward, fur-laden clothes – two layers thick. It was cold here. A kind of cold he'd never experienced on the island. Bitter, bone cold. It had something to do with the dampness of the air. Looking up, Ademo saw that the sky was an overcast grey, without definition, for as far as the eye could see.

Ademo noticed that the colors of the town were similarly bland. He wondered if it was the light that made them appear that way, or the colors of the materials they were built with. Perhaps both.

Ademo looked closer, marveling at the stone structures. "These buildings, are those stones found rectangular like that?"

Banon wasn't sure what Ademo meant at first. Then he made the connection. "Oh, no, these are bricks. They are fashioned that may. Then glued together with mortar."

Ademo nodded, not really understanding.

The structures here were organized in an orderly manner of neat rows, equidistant from each other. Again, different than what Ademo was used to – where new huts were placed wherever people fancied them.

As they walked along the streets – and even they were made of cobbled stone – Ademo noticed the stares of the other townsfolk. He did some staring of his own. They were all fair-skinned like Banon, with blue and green eyes. Many wore hoods over their heads, but those who didn't had light colored hair, similar to Banon's, though some were tinted with red or a very light brown.

Banon then led Ademo down to the ocean overlook. At the end they came to a small stone lip, no doubt meant to prevent people from plunging over the precipice. On a foggy day Ademo thought that was probably quite possible.

They stopped and looked out over the ocean expanse, a stiff breeze blowing their way. Ademo could see where the water seemed to blend with the sky out on the horizon. Both were shades of grey, almost indistinguishable from each other. Immediately underneath them, through a layer of mist, Ademo could see where large waves crashed against the rock face far below.

"Down there is where I found you," Banon said, pointing just off to the left.

Seeing Ademo's look of confusion, he added: "I found you at low tide, when there's a narrow band of beach before the cliff face."

Ademo nodded. "And when was that?"

"More than two days ago now."

Ademo looked surprised. "You mean... I slept..."

Banon smiled. "Almost a day and a half – yes. I take it you needed it, after what you'd been through."

As Banon said this he felt his curiosity peaking, and decided to ask a question that had been on his mind from the moment of his startling shoreline discovery. "Ademo, did you fall overboard from a ship of some kind? Perhaps a trading vessel or something like that?"

Banon was careful with his words here, remembering what his father had said of the matter when he'd first heard about Ademo. His father seemed to think that perhaps Ademo had been cast overboard, or made to walk the plank as a traitor.

His father's reaction hadn't really surprised Banon. It was common for him to be wary. As the town's mayor he claimed such precaution was necessary. In truth, Banon had hoped his father would congratulate him for saving the stranger. But no such praise came. His father was already too busy being suspicious of the stranger's background.

"Father, he nearly drowned. He needed help. And I provided it."

"Yes, Banon, but what if the man you saved was never meant to be saved? What if he was serving a death sentence? Then those that cast him to sea would not look too kindly on our helping him. They'd likely

consider it akin to harboring a fugitive."

Banon came back to the present moment, noticing that Ademo was taking his time in answering the question. Could it be his father was right?

"No, I didn't fall off any vessel of size, Banon. I was at sea on a small raft I'd fashioned myself."

"A *raft*?" Banon exclaimed, amazed, remembering the bits of wood he'd found littered on the beach the day he found Ademo's limp body. "Out on the open ocean? The waves out there can be enormous. How ever did you–"

"Survive? Well, I almost didn't. But, thanks to you, I managed to scrape out with my life," Ademo said, clapping his new friend on the back.

Having heard about the raft, Banon's mind immediately leapt to the next question. *Why? Why would someone choose to brave the wild seas upon a few pieces of fastened wood?*

Realizing that Ademo wasn't offering any additional details, Banon decided to change the subject; partly out of deference to Ademo, and partly because he didn't want to learn that his father had been right after all; that perhaps Ademo *was* a fugitive.

"Well, I'm sure you've seen enough of the ocean to last you for a lifetime. Let me show you more of the town," Banon said, smiling.

Ademo nodded, thankful for the change in subject. He followed Banon as he stepped between the long, water-soaked fishing benches, and back onto the stone streets.

23

The following day brought more of the same. Banon showed Ademo around the town, this time also taking him through some of the local stores: the blacksmith shop, the butcher shop, the seamstress, the bakery. It was all new to Ademo, and he listened intently as Banon explained the various functions.

As far as the people they came across went, they all seemed rather wary of the olive-skinned stranger. Ademo wondered if they acted that way towards all outsiders, or if there was something particularly disconcerting about himself. These thoughts he kept to himself.

Ademo did notice one particular local who seemed a little more curious than the others. He saw the man watching from a distance when they were lunching in the town square. Ademo thought perhaps he'd seen the same man the day before as well. He wore a long grey robe and, as with many of the locals on this wet, grey day, his head was covered by a hood. But there was one point when Ademo made brief eye contact with him. The man's eyes were a pale green color, but different than Banon's – almost haunted. The man nodded slightly, and Ademo returned the gesture, before the man moved on.

That evening, following a bountiful dinner of beef stew, sourdough bread and a strange, bitter concoction Banon called ale, the two sat on chairs in front of a roaring fire.

"Ademo, you seem to have recovered well. Do you feel any weakness lingering, or do you feel close to full strength?"

Ademo thought the question sounded a little strange, but he smiled nonetheless. "Again, thanks to you, Banon, I do feel fully recovered."

Banon returned the smile, but Ademo thought something about it seemed false; as if it were forced. It seemed that Banon's usually easygoing manner had departed him.

"What is it? Something troubles you?" Ademo asked.

Banon seemed to snap out of his stupor. "No. Well... not exactly. You see, the thing is, my father asked to see you once you were back to full strength."

"I see," Ademo said, nodding slowly, "and that troubles you?"

Banon looked thoughtful. "It only troubles me in that when my father asks to see someone, it's not usually to share ale and bread."

"No?"

"No. You see – him being the mayor and all – he feels it's his duty to know everything he can."

Ademo nodded, slowly understanding Banon's concern. "Banon, do you mean to tell me that your father plans to interrogate me?"

Banon looked as if he were about to shake his head. But then he stopped himself, returning a slight nod instead. "Something like that, yes. The truth is, I don't know exactly what his questions will be. But, Ademo, up until now, even I – who've spent the last two days with you – haven't a clue what brought you here to begin with. I know you washed up on our shore after attempting to cross the high seas in a raft, and that's about it. My father seems to be concerned that you're on the run from something; or someone."

"And you're saying your father, the Mayor, as you call him – which I assume means he's what I understand to be a chief – will expect to know all of that. To know where I come from, my background."

Banon nodded, seemingly relieved to have that out between them.

Ademo drew a long breath, looked out the window (which here was made of glass, unlike on the island), took some time to collect his thoughts.

"My apologies, friend. You're right. I haven't been very forthcoming. The thing is, my recent history was rather... chaotic. And painful. And so, to be honest, I've done my best to keep my mind on other things. And with you as my guide these last two days, that's been rather easy to do. But that wasn't fair to you, and I'm sorry."

Banon waved his hand in front of him. "Think nothing of it. I just didn't want you to go into a meeting with my father... unprepared."

Ademo nodded. "Again, my thanks."

The two sat silently for a moment, and then Ademo thought to add something.

"Banon, I should say, as to your father's fear that I'm running from something or someone?"

Banon nodded, listening intently.

"Well, unfortunately, that part's true. I was on the run."

Banon only stared back at Ademo, not knowing what to say. But suddenly he feared this meeting between Ademo and his father all the more.

24

The ship was largely silent. Eerily so. Normally, even though it was late into the evening, raucous noise could be heard emanating from the off-duty crew.

But not tonight. The ship had been sailing through this never-ending mistscape for days and days and days now. And that had taken its toll. Even on the voyage *to* the island things hadn't been *this* bad.

The stars hadn't been seen for several nights now, and the ship's navigation equipment had gone all haywire; different compasses pointing in different directions simultaneously.

The crew below-deck tried to pass the time with card games and drinking. But the rum was running low. As were the spirits of the men themselves. So instead they spent their time off trying not to fear the worst. Trying to remember what the sun looked like on a clear day.

Above deck only a handful of the crew manned their stations, not speaking with each other, perhaps only mumbling to themselves, as the oppressive, grey fog clung to them like some massive leech.

At the wheel of the large vessel was a young man named Givens; he was one of the youngest aboard. He normally wouldn't have been given such a charge. But everyone else was tired of taking the wheel. For what could they do? How could they navigate? All they had been doing at the wheel was passing the time, with no sense whatsoever as to what direction they were headed.

When Givens had first been charged to take the wheel he had been nervous. But soon he realized what the others were on about. This wasn't really navigating. There was nothing to see – just the grey. And nowhere really to go, just more of this blasted fog hanging over an endless sea.

He remembered being told that he would be relieved of his post by one of the older men shortly after dinner. But that time had come and gone hours ago. No one had come to relieve him. And there really wasn't anyone around to complain to. Most of the men wandered within their own solitary worlds these days.

So Givens kept his hands on the large wheel, even as fatigue began to seep into his bones.

When yet another hour or more had gone by, Givens really had had enough. He turned to look behind him, searching for someone to call to. While he didn't really want to complain – not when Maynard may very well clap him on the ear (at the least) for doing so – it would be even worse if he actually fell asleep at his post. And over the last few minutes that seemed not such a remote possibility.

He finally saw someone emptying a barrel overboard, fifty feet or so away. Givens called out to the man, then became frustrated when the fellow didn't respond. That was the thing with this blasted mist. It swallowed all you could hear *as well* as all you could see.

After feeling his voice grow hoarse, with still no sign of recognition from his crewmate, Givens gave up. His shoulders sagged as he turned round to face forwards again.

And then he shook his head, willing the weariness from his bones. Because now his fatigue was making him see things.

But try as he might, shaking his head didn't make what he was seeing go away. It was a shape; a dark silhouette cast against the grey darkness all about them. Givens leaned forward, trying to make it out; fearful it was some ghastly ghoul arising from the deep, come to drag them into a watery grave.

And then... reality struck.

"Land!" he shouted, even as he began spinning the wheel to the left, as fast as he could.

The large ship began to – ever so slightly – shift in that direction, if only by inches at a time... or so it felt.

Despite Givens shout, no one came running. No one had heard him. Most of them were still below-deck; oblivious to the emerging danger.

He spun the wheel again, swearing now, demanding the vessel turn.

But then came a sound that no one could have missed; a ghastly, bone-rattling scraping. The ship shuddered as it plowed directly into the jagged rocks hidden just below the waterline.

And now Givens *could* make out voices, as the crew began pouring out from below-deck, some shouting, some screaming.

The ones screaming had just seen some of their shipmates drowned, as surging waters had poured in through three gaping holes now located below.

For a moment Givens contemplated what Maynard or Prigg would do to him, and he felt fear like a vice, tightening in his chest. But then, watching the others, his survival instincts kicked into gear. He chased after others, towards the too few life boats stored nearby.

Fistfights soon broke out, as the men clambered for the few spots available on the small, wooden craft.

Others thought better of it, and dove overboard, even as the ship began to groan and lurch suddenly to the left; barrels and other loose material rolling across the deck and splashing overboard.

In the deepest underbelly of the ship, Siya's eyes

looked on in terror as water poured in through a large hole that had torn open on the port side.

Then, as she felt water begin to pool beneath her, she jumped into action. She ran to the stairs and started climbing. As she neared the top of the stairway the door suddenly swung open, almost on cue. *Someone was letting her out!* Even if it was only a temporary reprieve, she was grateful.

But then she caught site of the man who had stepped forward to fill the doorway with his bulky frame. And the expression on his face was of anything but mercy.

It was a look that froze Siya in her tracks, even as the waters sloshed about below, already climbing to the second step.

Seeing her startled expression, the man stepped forward; a sinister grin spreading across his stubbly, square jaw.

Siya's attention dropped to his right hand, which held a sharp, ten inch dagger. She gasped and took a step backwards, only to be greeted by waters that now washed up to her waste-line.

Just then howls from above rang out over the sound of the sloshing water. The sound seemed to bring the bulky figure resolve. Perhaps he had at first intended on taking his time, enjoying this task. Now the pressing nature of their predicament made him pick up his pace.

He moved quickly, drumming his feet down the stairway towards Siya. When he was within a step or two from her, she turned and leapt towards the swirling salty waters.

She had waited a moment too long, even to make that dreaded decision. Because now she felt his weight slamming into her, pushing her down, her mouth instantly filling with the lukewarm, salty water.

Then she felt his large palm clamp down onto the back of her head. He seemed to be toying with her, letting her gasp for air for a moment, before plunging her under again. Perhaps he'd decided he'd enjoy the sport of drowning more than a knifing.

But then, all of a sudden, she felt his hand lift off of her head. She surfaced and gasped for air, looking for something to grab onto.

And then his hand found hers, and he yanked hard. But when she looked at his face, she realized this man wasn't her assailant. It was Maynard. Had she traded one evil for another?

"Come on, woman! Do you want to drown down here?" he said harshly, as he began pulling her behind him, back up the steps and out onto the deck.

Siya chanced one glance behind her, and saw the lifeless body of her assailant floating with the current of the swirling, gathering waters; a red cloud oozing from a hole in his back.

Why had Maynard of all people shown her mercy? His heart had seemed as black as the rest.

But as the first mate scrambled towards the last of the lifeboats, knocking another man aside and overboard as he did so, mercy was the furthest thing from his mind.

He had come all this way to find something – or, more specifically, someone. They hadn't found that person. But they did have the next best thing: the mother. Damned if he was going to let her drown now, when keeping her as leverage was the only thing they had to show for this entire wasted venture.

Siya felt her left side bruise, as she was tossed into the small, wooden craft. Maynard then used the knife he'd killed his crewmate with to slash at the ropes, and suddenly the ship dropped into thin air.

A moment later they crashed hard into the swirling waters below.

Maynard reached for an oar and began pulling hard to escape the bulk of the larger vessel that was now careening in their direction; an ominous groan sounding all about them.

A few of the men were in the water, shouting for aid. But Maynard ignored them. As far as he was concerned they could make it to land under their own steam, or drown. He had a more important task to attend to; keeping their only asset alive.

As the larger ship finally capsized into the swirling waters, crashing, splitting sounds filled the air, as the current and the jagged rocks tore the ship apart, piece by piece. Maynard glanced once around to eyeball the beach line, and then focused again on pulling hard in that direction, his back to the shore.

25

Both Banon and Ademo sat in front of Banon's father's large wooden desk. Ademo thought the desk itself rather intimidating. On the other side of the desk sat one large, empty chair, soon to be occupied by the mayor. Or so they both assumed.

"Sorry, Ademo, he shouldn't be much longer. Apparently he had a meeting with some of the farmers this evening, a problem with wolves or something like that."

"Wolves?" Ademo asked, unfamiliar with the term.

"You don't have wolves where you're from?"

Ademo shook his head.

"Oh, well, they're like large dogs, only wild."

"Dogs?"

Banon went to speak, then stopped himself, unsure how to proceed.

"Ferocious wild animals. They usually keep to themselves, out in the deep woods. But apparently a few sheep have gone missing lately. And the farmers think it's wolves that are to blame."

Ademo nodded, wondering if wolves were anything like Kiraboan hillcats.

Just then the front door swung open and a man, looking much like Banon, only older, thicker, and grey-bearded, strode in from the rain. He put his coat aside and walked over.

"Sorry for the delay, gentlemen. Our meeting went rather longer than I expected," he said, not making eye contact but moving across the room and sliding into the large chair behind the desk.

"Just a moment, if you don't mind..." he said, while retrieving some paper and apparently jotting down a few notes. He still hadn't looked up and, as the seconds ticked by, Ademo began to feel the silence a little awkward. Such manner was decidedly un-Kiraboan.

Without looking up, while still jotting notes on the page, Banon's father said, matter-of-factly, "Banon, you may go. I will speak with him alone."

Banon put his hands on the arms of the chair, and glanced from his father to Ademo, looking surprised. "Sir, didn't you want me to introduce-"

"As I said, Banon, I will speak with him alone. You may go."

Banon bit his lower lip, glanced once more towards Ademo, shrugging his shoulders slightly before rising to leave.

When Banon closed the door behind him the Mayor continued scribbling away, leaving Ademo to stew in the relative silence. The mayor then began shuffling through papers, as if comparing notes of some kind. Finally he put his pen aside and leaned back in his chair, crossing his hands in his lap. He eyed Ademo for a moment before speaking.

"Son, what is your name? Your *full* name?"

"Ademo Asterling, sir."

Ademo swallowed, licking his lips, as the mayor gazed towards him with an eagle eye. Several silent seconds passed.

"And where do you come from, Mr. Asterling?"

"Sir, I come from Kiraboa."

The mayor's eyes narrowed.

"*Kiraboa*? I'm not familiar with that name, Mr. Asterling. Is that a city somewhere on Criesca? Perhaps in the Tulawinso territory?"

Ademo knew as little of the names Criesca and Tulawinso as the mayor apparently knew of Kiraboa.

"Ah, no, sir. That's the name of the island I come from: Kiraboa."

"An island named Kiraboa?" the mayor repeated, almost sounding skeptical.

Already Ademo knew exactly what Banon was getting at in preparing him for this meeting. Still, all preparation aside, Ademo wasn't expecting to feel this uncomfortable.

"Mr. Asterling," (Ademo had never been called by his surname so many times in his life prior to this evening), "my son tells me you claim to have been at sea aboard a... a *raft* of some kind. Is that your contention?"

Ademo nodded.

"I see. And how many days had you been at sea

before you were... before you were shipwrecked here in Landry?"

Ademo fidgeted in his seat, feeling uncomfortable because he knew he didn't have a precise answer for the mayor. He had been knocked unconscious at some point. But he wasn't sure how long after that it was that he washed up on the Landry shoreline.

"Sir, I'm not entirely sure. You see, I was knocked on the head at some point. And I don't remember anything else after that until Banon found me."

"I see. And you miraculously managed to survive? How is it you didn't drown?"

"Sir, I was tied down on the raft, so the waves wouldn't wash me into the ocean."

"Indeed. But surely you can tell me how many days you were at sea before you were struck so unfortunately, can't you?"

Ademo nodded, thinking back.

"Three days, sir. I believe it was three days."

"You *believe* it was three days?"

Again Ademo fidgeted in his seat, and saw the mayor's eyes follow his motion as he did; as if he were making note of Ademo's discomfort, perhaps concluding something from it.

"Sir, I do believe it was three days, give or take. I was in the fog for a long time, and it became difficult to make note of the time of day."

The mayor remained silent, nodding his head slowly up and down.

"And did you have provision for the duration of

your journey?"

"Provision? Sir?"

"Food and water, Mr. Asterling."

"Oh, yes. Three or four day's worth, anyway. I was running out of... provision – right around the time I was struck on the head."

The mayor took a long breath, then let it out slowly.

"Mr. Asterling, I'm having difficulty making sense of your story."

"Sir?" Ademo replied, not sure what the mayor was getting at, but feeling all the more uncomfortable, anyway – if that were possible. Now it felt as if the mayor was accusing him of something unsavory.

"You see, Mr. Asterling, I've sailed west from here before, more than once in my lifetime. And I know for a fact that it is a considerable voyage from here to Criesca; and that's being aboard a full-sized vessel, mind you, not floating along on a few twigs strapped together. And you and I both know that Criesca is the nearest landmass from here. Everything in between is wide open water; and rather nasty, turbulent seas at that.

"*So...*" the mayor continued, "how is it that you could be at sea for that long, on nothing but a raft? Such a journey would be impossible, don't you think? One would die of thirst or starvation within days, even if one really were unconscious for much of the time. Don't you agree?"

"Yes, I suppose that's true, sir. But as I said, I

wasn't at sea for that long. I had been aboard for three, maybe four days before I was struck. And my guess is that it was only a day or two later that I landed here."

"A day or two? And how do you surmise that, considering you were supposedly unconscious the entire time?"

"Well, like you said, sir, if it were much longer than that I would have died of thirst or starvation."

The mayor's eyes narrowed again, as he glared across the large table.

"Mr. Asterling, be that as it may, we are still left with the issue of there *being* no landmass between here and Criesca – which lies on the far side of the Emalderine Ocean. So you see, this tale you weave just doesn't hold water, if you'll pardon the pun."

Ademo had no idea what a pun was, but he discerned from the mayor's words and tone that this recounting of his journey just wasn't to believed.

When Ademo remained silent, unsure what to say, the mayor reached for his paper and pen again, began scribbling a note even as he spoke to Ademo.

"Mr. Asterling, as mayor, it is my concern to know everything of import regarding those who would travel to our fair port. And, as of now, in regards to you, I know almost nothing.

"To be blunt: I don't believe you. I don't believe you're telling me the whole truth as to what brought you here. I will give you leave now to consider the truth you *will* tell me when next we meet.

"I will see you in my office the same time

tomorrow evening. And then I expect to hear the fullness of the truth, and nothing but."

With that the mayor shuffled more papers and jotted some more notes. After a moment his eyes lifted only slightly, while his head remained directed towards his desk.

"That will be all, Mr. Asterling."

Ademo realized he was being dismissed. He rose quickly, reached for the door, and almost ran out into the cold, wet, evening air.

26

When Banon caught up with Ademo he could tell the meeting hadn't gone well.

"What happened? What did he say?" Banon asked, pacing beside Ademo, who seemed intent on not slowing down.

"He asked questions. Just like you said he would."

"Okay, and then?"

"And then your father seemed quite convinced that I was lying to his face; making the whole thing up."

"What whole thing?" Banon asked.

"My journey on the open water. How I came here. How long it took me to get here. Where I came from. Pretty much all of it."

Banon sighed, shook his head, still marching alongside Ademo. This was exactly what he feared would happen. He wasn't sure who he was more frustrated with: his father, for being so suspicious and un-welcoming; or himself, for not helping Ademo better prepare for the meeting.

"Listen, Ademo, my father needs to know certain things. People expect him to find out-"

"I get it, Banon. He's the leader, the native. And I'm the outsider, the unwelcome one. You don't have to explain that to me. I know *exactly* how that goes."

Banon sensed Ademo's words were loaded with more than just the exchange with his father, but now wasn't the time to pursue it.

"Listen, Ademo, maybe we... *Hey*, would you stop for a minute?" Banon said, reaching for Ademo's arm.

Ademo brushed him off.

"No thanks. I'm going to keep walking if that's alright with you. I'll make my way back later tonight, *if that's allowed*. If the outsider can be granted a moment's leave to be alone. Is that too much to ask? Freedom to go for a walk?"

Banon stopped in his tracks, while Ademo kept on marching. Banon didn't know what else to say, and by the time he thought of something, Ademo had already disappeared around the street corner.

Ademo walked on and on, turning only once to head east. He was familiar enough with the layout of Landry to know that the woods lay in that direction. He saw the odd passerby on the way, and couldn't help but notice as they stopped and stared while he strode past. He wasn't exactly dressed for an evening stroll, and that probably drew attention in itself. But for him it just drove home his status as an outsider all the more.

At one point Ademo thought he heard footsteps behind him, and turned to ask Banon to leave him alone. But Banon was nowhere to be seen. All he saw was what might have been the shape of a figure moving into the shadows. Ademo saw the figure for only for a moment, but thought perhaps it was the same robed man he'd noticed twice before. He stood there a moment longer, but perceived no additional movement. He concluded that perhaps it had only been his imagination, after all. Besides, he was in no mood for mysteries, so he strode on.

Ademo reached the edge of Landry's last street, and then scrambled up an embankment through rocks and shrubs, to the tree line of towering, majestic firs. Like everything else here, the shrubs were wet. By the time he reached the forest edge, and pushed through, he was thoroughly drenched. He didn't care, though. Didn't really even notice.

He walked on until he came to a partial clearing, fifteen or so minutes later. He was at the edge of a large pond, and now that the drizzle had finally relented, the moonlight reflected brilliantly upon the now still waters. Ademo sat down, gazing into the calm of the surface, willing it to give up some of its tranquility.

Through the pale moonlight he was able to see the perimeter of the pond, which was encircled by tall evergreen trees. It occurred to Ademo, in that moment, that the trees were the roughly same triangular shape he'd seen in the dream he'd had atop the Whispering Cliffs.

He couldn't help but wonder if that meant he was close to the location where the woman had rushed to escape her captors, only to fall to her apparent death soon after.

For some reason he believed the dream was more than imagination, that it somehow referenced a real event. Ademo wasn't sure why he had started believing that. Perhaps it was the texture of the memory; so unlike other dreams.

The trees did look awfully similar. But then, he hadn't seen much of the outside world. And, for all he knew, perhaps these kinds of trees were commonplace in various locations.

He sighed, realizing how ignorant he was of the world and its ways. He had experienced only a sliver of its true scope; was only now beginning to glimpse the rest. Now it seemed silly that he and his friends had once thought the island the sum total of all there was.

And then he thought of his mother.

Where was she? Was she hurt? Was she even still alive? And what were the marauders intentions in taking her? Was it for sport? Was it to enslave her in some foreign land? Or was it possible that they had taken her as leverage to ultimately lure him? But that thought seemed preposterous. Who was *he* for some marauding band to go to so much trouble for? And yet, hadn't Kuio and the elders hinted at as much?

Ademo remembered his Placca journey. Remembered the first day, when he'd taken his time up the mountain trail. Even on the way back, he hadn't pushed his pace – far from it. What if he had been more deliberate in his journey, not stopping to dilly dally upon every passing interest? Perhaps then he could have made it back in time to help his mother and the others; to help his brothers defend their home.

Brothers? That's certainly not how Kuio and the others had made him feel in the aftermath. Perhaps it was too much to think they saw him like that, as one of their own.

And this only made Ademo feel all the more alone. First, rejected in the land of his youth. And even here in Landry, which had first seemed so welcoming, he was now greeted with suspicion and distrust.

A tear rolled down Ademo's already damp face. And then another. Then he let them flow. The air was damp and growing colder by the minute. But Ademo didn't care. He remained still, long after his tears had dried, staring blankly into the moonscape upon the water.

27

The next morning Ademo awoke feeling stiff but more resolved. He stretched and wondered what time it was. From the light coming in through the window he guessed it was already close to mid-morning.

He pulled on a set of clothes Banon had left for him, opened the door, and walked out into the sitting room. Banon was at the table, drinking a mug of some steaming beverage.

Ademo smiled at his friend. "Morning, Banon."

"Morning. How are you?" Banon asked, almost tentatively.

"Good, thanks," Ademo said, taking a seat across the table from the fair-haired Landrite. "Listen, Banon, sorry about last night. I was... I didn't mean to be that way towards you. You've been nothing but kind since you found me washed up on the shore."

Banon, who almost seemed embarrassed, waved his hand in front of him. "Think nothing of it, Ademo. Listen, I of all people understand how my father can be sometimes."

Ademo nodded and smiled. "I guess so."

"Hey, what do you say we take a hike today? You haven't seen the view from the hills yet. You can see a long way from there."

"I'd like that. I like high places. But just so you know, your father asked to meet with me again this evening in his office."

"I heard. Don't worry, we'll be back in plenty of time."

Ademo nodded. "Great. Sounds like an adventure then."

"I'd hoped you'd say that. I've already packed us some lunch," Banon said, reaching behind him and holding up a backpack. "But first things first, let's get you some breakfast. What'll it be: porridge, or toast and butter?"

Ademo soon realized that Banon was a seasoned trekker, and actually found it difficult to keep up to his brisk pace as they hiked into the hills later that day. Even with a steep incline Banon's pace didn't relent. In fact, at points where the trail would meander back and forth Banon would go off-trail, taking a more vertical path that cut the walking time in half.

It was early afternoon by the time they emerged from the forest and stepped out onto a ledge that offered an impressive, expansive view. From here, as Banon had promised, they could see all round for miles. Ademo quickly realized that this landmass dwarfed his own island. He looked east and saw layers of hills, in shades of green, blue, then grey. And behind them: mountains, stunning even at this distance. And to the west was the grey-green ocean, the one they called the Emalderine. It stretched so far that the curvature of Eiasa was visible. Ademo's eyes were wide. He'd never experienced the world on such a scale.

"They call this the Cloud Dome," Banon said, while he pulled their sandwiches and drinks out of his backpack.

"Why's that?" Ademo asked.

"Because, half the time you're up here you're actually at cloud level."

"Really?"

Banon nodded, munching away at his sandwich.

Ademo did the same, and the two were content to sit silently for a time, admiring the view.

After several minutes the near silent calm came to an abrupt end when Banon suddenly stood, turning to face the bushes behind them, drawing his sword from its sheath in one swift movement.

"Did you hear that?" Banon said, wide-eyed, staring to and fro into the tree line.

"Ah, hear what?" Ademo asked, perplexed.

"Something's moving back there!"

Ademo's eyes danced between his fair friend and the bushes. "Ah, you mean the squirrel-kind-of-creature?"

"What?" Banon said, eyeing Ademo as if he were playing some sort of joke.

"The squirrel," Ademo said, pointing up and to the left.

Banon was having trouble seeing what Ademo was referring to. So, all in one motion, every bit as fast as Banon, Ademo reached behind his back, drew his small throwing disk, and flung it with great speed in the direction he'd been pointing.

The disc missed the creature by inches, embedding itself instead in the trunk of a large pine tree. The strike was close enough to spook the squirrel, and it went scurrying higher up into the lighter tree limbs, making them sway in the process.

"Oh," Banon said, now tracking the path of the squirrel, "you sure that's what was making all that noise?"

"Certain," Ademo said, moving towards the tree and retrieving his disc, though it took a hard tug to take it back.

"Nice shot," Banon said, resheathing his blade. "You didn't miss by much."

"Oh, I wasn't trying to hit it," Ademo said, as if the point should be obvious.

"You weren't?" Banon said, surprised and perhaps a tad suspicious.

"No. What would be the point? We've already eaten a hearty lunch. I was just trying to get it to move, so you'd see it."

Banon eyed his new friend for a moment, trying to discern any hint of being put on. Sensing no duplicity, he decided to relax.

"Can I see that?" Banon asked, reaching for Ademo's disc.

"Sure," Ademo said, handing it over.

"Wow, that's light."

"But strong. It's made from a kind of smooth volcanic rock."

Banon nodded, impressed. "So who taught you to throw like that?"

"One of my friends. He's a couple of years older than me," Ademo said, suddenly realizing, guiltily, that his friend Balio likely died defending the island from the marauders. "What about you? Who taught you to use that sword? Was it your father?"

"My *father*?" Banon exclaimed, as if someone had just said something funny, or ironic. "No. I was trained by the town blacksmith; the man named Frenic – you met him, if you remember. He happens to be a skilled swordsman. I don't think my father has ever handled a sword in his life."

"Oh, I see," Ademo said, nodding.

Banon, feeling as awkward about his background as his friend, decided to return the favor. "What about you? Didn't your father teach you any of your throwing skills?"

Ademo stared off into the distance for a moment, before responding. "No. You see, I never really knew my father."

"Oh... Sorry. He passed on then?"

Ademo nodded. "Yes, though *how* he died is a bit of a mystery to me. It happened when I was very young. And my mother was always very tightlipped about it. Said she'd tell me some day, when I was old enough to understand."

Banon nodded, looking off to the horizon as a quiet unease set in. "You know, my mother died when I was fairly young as well."

Ademo turned to his friend. "She did? Sorry to hear that. I wondered why I hadn't met her. How old were you?"

"Twelve. Not *that* young I guess. I mean, I remember her. I remember everything about her... It was an accident. She was out late one night, down by the cliff-face, and, we're not sure, but we think she slipped on some black ice."

"Black ice?" Ademo said, never having heard of such a thing.

"It's ice that's almost impossible to see, takes on the color of the ground underneath. But it's extremely slippery... Anyway, like I say, we think she may have slipped on a patch, and went over the cliff. That was before we'd built the stone lip at the cliff edge."

Ademo sat in silence, taking in his friend's tragic story. And in that moment he realized it was one thing to lose a father you never knew, quite another to lose a mother you had loved very much.

After a time Ademo, still gazing out towards the distant hills, decided to bridge a subject he knew Banon must have wondered about.

"Banon, I haven't been very fair to you. I know you must have questions about where I'm from, what brought me here. Things went badly for me just before I left my island on that god-forsaken raft. And I've been content to keep it out of my mind – as much as possible. But you deserve to know the story. All of it. Tonight I plan to tell your father the same. But you should hear it first."

Banon nodded, content to let Ademo continue at his own pace.

Ademo told Banon about the island, about his upbringing with his mother. About his strange sense of always being an outsider. He spoke of his Placca journey, and the horror that awaited him when he returned from it.

Banon had been eager to let Ademo tell as much of the tale as he would. And he was glad to have heard it. It helped him understand his friend more, to understand the plight he was in. Now he understood that running was really the only option left open to him.

Looking west, Banon saw that the sun was distinctly lower in the sky, and realized that several hours had passed. In order to make the meeting Ademo had scheduled with Banon's father, they needed to start heading back.

They both took another swig of water, and then started bounding down the trail. And bound they did. Apparently Banon was of the belief that for any hill you walk up, you must inevitably run down twice as fast.

28

When they arrived back in town it was dinner time.

Banon quickly served them up some bread and salted meat, with more of his favorite ale to chase it down. When they finished eating Ademo rose from the table.

"Thanks, Banon. And thanks for the hike, that was great."

"Glad to show you more of our wet wonderland, my friend."

It was wet, Ademo had certainly noticed that. And much too grey for his liking as well, but he kept that to himself.

"Listen, a quick word before your meeting with my father," Banon added. "I know he can be stern. I know he can be serious. But he is not a cold-hearted man. More than anything else, he is just thoroughly pragmatic. But if you tell your story as you told it to me this afternoon, I think you'll find he is not altogether unsympathetic."

Ademo nodded, thanked Banon again, and went to change before the meeting.

Ademo approached the closed door to Banon's father's office and realized he was unsure how to introduce himself. No doubt it was done differently here in Landry than on the island. Unsure what else to do, he simply spoke loudly, announcing himself.

"Hello, Mayor? It's Ademo Asterling, here for our meeting."

There was no sound from within, so Ademo repeated himself, louder this time.

Again, no response. Could it be that the mayor

was late for their meeting a second night in a row?

"Hello! Mayor? It's Ademo Asterling!"

This time there was a shuffling from inside the office, and a moment later the door swung open.

"Mr. Asterling!" the mayor exclaimed, clearly annoyed. "Haven't you ever heard of knocking?"

Ademo hadn't, but he took this as his cue to enter anyway. As he moved towards the chair in front of the mayor's desk, he noticed something off to the corner of the room. Or more specifically, someone.

"Mr. Asterling, may I introduce you to one of our townsfolk: this is Morin," the mayor said, gesturing towards the tall, grey-robed figure seated in the corner.

Morin met his eyes and Ademo was again struck by the piercing nature of the man's gaze. For this was the same mysterious figure he'd noticed on a couple of prior occasions. Now that he saw him with his hood removed, Ademo realized the man was much older than he first had assumed. Morin's head was bald, and his hawk-like features were drawn tight over weathered, leathery skin. Morin nodded slightly towards Ademo, like he had from a distance before. Ademo nodded back and quietly said hello.

"I've asked Morin to join us because he may have council to provide in this matter," the mayor said, matter-of-factly, as he gestured for Ademo to take a seat.

Ademo did so, though it seemed strange to him that Morin remained in the corner of the room, slightly behind him. The mayor slid into his impressive chair and stacked his hands over each other in his lap.

"Now then, Mr. Asterling, tonight I will have your entire tale. Please take your time, and remember what I said last night: I will have the truth. And nothing but. Are we clear?"

Ademo nodded, then stole a glimpse towards Morin, who's head was now bowed and resting on his teepeed hands.

Ademo leaned back in his own chair, gathering his thoughts for a moment, before beginning to speak. As with Banon earlier that day, he spoke for a long while, now feeling more relaxed after having already told the tale once.

But his calm was not just a result of rehearsal. It was actually a relief to get everything off his chest; to bring recent events to light. Ademo had decided that, whatever the mayor decided to do with him, he would have exactly what he'd asked for: the truth, and nothing but.

All Ademo hoped was that Banon wasn't too far off the mark in his assessment of his father's character; "not unsympathetic" is how he'd put it. The mayor's brisk tone was so unlike the demeanor of islanders, so unlike the way even Chief Fyoma had been, that it put Ademo a little ill at ease. But this was a different culture. And there was much Ademo didn't yet understand about it.

When Ademo finished his tale by re-counting the

blame placed on him by Kuio and Tyaso, and how that had led him to his subsequent flight to the open seas, he stopped, took a deep breath, and waited to hear the mayor's response.

The mayor seemed deep in thought. Ademo looked behind and to his left, saw that Morin was sitting in much the same position as before, his head bowed slightly, leaning on his teepeed hands. Ademo wondered if it was some sort of meditative posture; that's what it looked like to him.

Then the mayor shifted in his seat and this brought Ademo's attention back round. The mayor stretched out his arm and drummed his fingers on the table, staring intently across at Ademo.

Ademo couldn't make out if the intensity of the gaze meant the mayor was looking for Ademo to crack, or that he was solemnly considering what it all meant. Ademo hoped for the latter, because it would mean that the mayor had believed him. Still, he just wasn't sure.

"Mr. Asterling, again, that is quite some tale you weave. I would say it is almost too fantastical *not* to be believed."

Ademo shifted in his seat, uncomfortably. He didn't know what to make of the mayor's statement. Their eyes met for several seconds longer. Again, Ademo felt that his mettle was being tested.

Then, very much like the night before, the mayor pulled his chair into the table and began sorting through papers. When he spoke, his eyes were busy with his paperwork, not fixed on Ademo.

"Mr. Asterling, I will take some time to consider what you've shared this evening. I will call for you when I've come to some conclusions."

Ademo paused for a moment, then gathered he was being dismissed for the evening. He rose from his chair, turned and nodded towards Morin – who's head lifted ever so slightly to return the gesture – and then opened the door to the dark, damp night.

29

Ademo was awoken the next morning by a knock at his door. He lifted his groggy head, pulled himself out of bed, and walked over. It was Banon, fully dressed for the day, already looking alert and purposeful.

"Morning. How'd you sleep?"

"Fine, thanks. Something happening?" Ademo asked, knowing that Banon usually waited for him to arise on his own.

"Yes. My father's asked to see you again."

"Now?"

"Yes, and this time he wants me there as well."

"Oh," Ademo said, immediately wondering whether this news bode good or ill.

"Better get dressed quickly. My father doesn't like to be kept waiting. And he's got other matters to attend to after he sees us."

"Right. Okay, I'll be right out."

Banon knocked at the mayor's door, and opened it slightly to announce their presence. The mayor, already seated at his desk, waved them in. As they took their seats in front of the table, he eyed them both.

"Well, best get down to it, then. Mr. Asterling, I said I would need some time to consider what you told us last night."

Ademo nodded, waiting for the mayor to continue, unable to discern from his body language anything regarding his position on the matter.

"Well, to be honest, on my opinion alone, I still find your tale to be highly... unorthodox. I don't want to accuse you of being a liar because... well, because you don't strike me as that kind of fellow. But my common sense also tells me your story sounds preposterous. So, that being said, I'd be in a bit of a quandary, if things were left to my opinion alone."

Banon and Ademo exchanged a glance, neither any the wiser as to where the mayor was headed. Banon knew his father was being straightforward and honest, but he wished he would consider Ademo's feelings in the matter.

"However," the mayor continued, after a lengthy pause, "I have more than my own opinion to consider in this case. Mr. Asterling, as I mentioned to you last night, I asked Morin to sit in on our meeting, because he often has council in these kinds of matters."

Ademo wondered what "these kind of matters" meant, but he let it go, as the mayor continued.

"For Morin's part, he seems to believe you. When I asked him what he would suggest we do about you, assuming you were telling the truth, he suggested – no, better put, he *insisted* – that we refer the matter to Renata Worthing."

Banon's brow furrowed. "Renata Worthing? Who's that?"

The mayor turned to Banon, with an almost amused look. "The *Lady* of the *High Hills*."

Banon's expression turned to surprise and confusion. "*Her*? Is she even still around? We haven't seen her for, what... ten years? I was just a boy the last time she paid the town a visit. And even then she was very old."

"Morin assures me she's still around. Still living in that dwelling of hers, somewhere deep in the Greystone Mountains."

Banon shook his head, still perplexed by this strange turn of events.

"Now, being the case that – as Banon points out – Miss Worthing is now quite old and frail," the Mayor continued, "she cannot very feasibly come to us. Therefore, we must go to her. More specifically, *you* shall go to her. The two of you."

"Us?" Banon said, looking doubtful. "But how would we even find her? I've no idea where her dwelling is. I thought the tale spun round here was that she kept that location secret. That she'd come to town with her strange pronouncements from time to time, but that she allowed no one to follow her back to where she lives."

"True enough," the mayor said. "But apparently that location is not wholly unknown by all."

"Morin?" Banon asked, putting two and two together.

The mayor nodded. "Yes. Morin. He says he knows the location. For a man so quiet, he certainly seems full of strange knowledge at times. Anyway, he's drawn up a map for you. He's asked for my assurance that we will be very careful with it. He doesn't want anyone other than the three of us to know the location of Renata's residence. So I will hand it over to you tomorrow morning."

Banon and Ademo sat silently, contemplating the journey they were to take. After a moment the mayor pulled his chair towards his desk, started shuffling papers, as he was known to do when signaling a meeting was drawing to a close.

"I feel foolish even agreeing to this, but, alas, the entire matter seems too strange to approach via common sense. So, for now, I will follow Morin's council. Regardless, there doesn't seem to be any immediate danger to the town as a result of Mr. Asterling's presence. So we will see what *the Lady in the Hills* would say and take it from there.

"Now, you two best take the rest of the day to prepare for your journey. You are to leave first thing tomorrow morning."

"Father, is there any way we could see Morin before leaving, to ask him some questions ourselves?"

Without looking up from his desk the Mayor responded. "I thought that might be a good idea, too. But it turns out Morin's gone. Apparently he left early this morning. I found the map, wrapped in a sealed envelope, on my doorstep when I arrived."

Later that day, once their gear had been packed and preparations for the next day's journey made, Ademo and Banon sat down in a town pub called *The Thicket*. The bartender brought over two large mugs of ale, slammed them down on the table, letting the froth spill over the tops of the glasses. A barrel-chested, bushy-bearded fellow, several inches taller than the already tall Banon, the bartender nodded towards Banon, and then eyed Ademo warily. Ademo noticed the glare.

"He doesn't like outsiders much, does he?" Ademo asked, already sipping from his mug. He found the strangely bready, bitter taste was growing on him.

Banon shrugged. "Hasserin, you mean? Well, it's just that the last time a group of outsiders came through here they stiffed him for a pretty hefty bill."

Ademo wasn't sure what Banon meant, and his expression betrayed as much.

"They didn't pay what they owed for ale and food before skipping town."

"Oh," Ademo said. "Listen, speaking of that, Banon, you and your father have been very generous, and I feel badly that I don't-"

Banon waved him off. "Not to worry, Ademo. You're an honored guest. It's our pleasure."

"You sure your father feels that way?" Ademo said, smirking while taking another drink from the frothy beer.

"My father? He's actually very generous by nature. It's just that his role as mayor kind of trumps that."

Ademo nodded. "It's a tough job, being mayor I mean."

Banon returned the nod. "Yeah, I suppose it is. But he's been the mayor for so long – since I was very young – that it's hard to imagine him as anything else."

"Since you were very young? Wasn't the mayorship his birthright?" Ademo asked, confused.

Banon titled his head, trying to understand what Ademo was asking. "Oh, no. It's not like being a King or anything. Here in Landry we elect our mayor."

"Elect?"

"We each have one vote regarding who should lead. And whoever gets the most votes gets the job."

Ademo nodded slowly up and down, trying to imagine how different that kind of arrangement would be. It occurred to him that Tyaso probably wouldn't have a chance of leading the village if the people really had a say in the matter.

"So Banon, I'm curious to hear more about this Renata lady. But before that, who is Morin? He doesn't seem like your average Landrite."

Banon took another drink, shaking his head.

"You've got that right. Morin is nothing typical, that's for sure. People say he was once a Vaida."

"A Vaida?" Ademo could hardly keep up with all the new terms he was hearing here in Landry.

"Yes." Banon said, plainly, before realizing that, of course, Ademo had no idea what a Vaida was.

"Sorry," Banon continued, "the Vaidas are a group of meditatives, religious in some way, I guess. They live in retreats far away from populated areas. They're rarely seen, except for certain occasions."

"Such as when?"

"I don't know exactly. Some say they come around when conflict arises, to help restore peace. But who knows, maybe that part's just a fairytale. All I know is that they keep mostly to themselves."

"And Morin used to be a Vaida?"

"Some say so."

"What does *he* say about it?"

Banon laughed. "Morin? He doesn't say anything. See, he's mute."

"Mute?"

"He doesn't speak. *Can't* speak."

"Oh, really? Then how does he communicate?"

"He uses a kind of sign language that some people round here can understand. But mostly he writes things down."

"So that's how he communicated with your father about me... he wrote things down?"

Banon nodded, and Ademo understood more about Morin's demeanor the night before.

"So what happened, did he leave the Vaidas at some point?"

"That I'm not sure about. My understanding is that once-a-Vaida, always-a-Vaida. So I don't quite understand what happened there. And Morin doesn't communicate anything about that time in his life. So all we have are people's idle guesses. And I don't put much credence in those."

"Any idea where Morin ran off to so quickly this morning?"

"No. And the thing is, as far as I can remember, he hasn't left Landry in years. So I'm not sure what would make him pick up and leave all of a sudden. I suppose it might very well have something to do with you, Ademo."

"Me?"

"Yes. You're the only thing that's different around here. And him leaving right after your meeting yesterday evening... well, I don't think that's coincidence."

Ademo nodded, sipping some more from his ale. He felt that strangeness again. That feeling that somehow people had got this all wrong. All this fuss about him. It just didn't make sense. And yet, person after person seemed to keep suggesting it was so; that all these events were connected to him somehow. He just didn't know what to do with it all.

"And Renata? Tell me about her."

"Ah, yes. The *Lady of the High Hills*. Well, there's not much to say there. Like I said, we haven't seen or heard a peep from her in ten years or more. And even back then, her visits were few and far in between; thankfully so. On the few occasions that she did trek down from her shell in the Greystone's, it was usually to warn us."

"Warn you? Of what?"

"Usually of some impending doom. Thing is, she was never very sure about when that doom would arise. And yet she expected people to take her seriously.

"I remember a little bit about the last time she was in town – though I was just a boy then. She stood up on the fountain in the town square, and started ranting and raving at all comers by. It was actually pretty funny at first. But after the first few days it got a little cumbersome. Plus, she got all the more belligerent the longer we ignored her."

"So then what happened?"

"I guess she eventually gave up and left," Banon said, shrugging. "And we haven't seen her since."

"And did any of her warnings pan out?"

"Good question. I'm not sure. Like I said, I was young back then. Maybe my father would know more about that."

"So is she connected to the these Valdas somehow?"

Banon thought long about that question, polishing off the last of his ale, and signaling Hasserin for another.

"Not sure about that. I never used to think so. But

knowing now that Morin – if it is true that he used to be one of the Movadem, one of the Vaidas – referred you to her, then maybe. Maybe there is some kind of connection."

As the bulking figure of Hasserin slammed down another mug in front of Banon, the contents spilling over the side again, Ademo considered these new revelations. Renata with her warnings; Morin and the Vaidas with their role in responding to conflict and peril; the outsiders who had attacked his village. Ademo couldn't help but wonder if all these elements were threads in some larger narrative. And that thought made his pleasant-tasting ale sit rather uncomfortably in his belly.

30

A crescent moon offered minimal light in what was otherwise the dark of night. The beach was strewn with the sleeping bodies of the marauders, who had eventually succumbed to sleep after arguing and debating their location for hours. They knew this land shouldn't be here, nor they on it. They had set a course the same way back that they had come. And so it should have taken them – after a good long while out on the open ocean – to the rolling green shores of Criesca.

But that hadn't happened. Instead, they'd come across this dreaded land – clearly not Criesca, because here it was tropical – only days into their return journey. But there shouldn't have been anything out here. No land at all. Not if they were actually headed west as they assumed.

The young man at the wheel had claimed it was impossible to steer clear of this land; that it had arisen out of nowhere in the blasted fog. And, though they wouldn't say it out loud to each other, many of the men believed him. For they knew these were enchanted waters. Truthfully, though they wouldn't be caught dead voicing this in front of Maynard, they all felt cursed.

One thick-bearded, portly fellow had been assigned guard while the rest of them slept. And he had done that rather faithfully, for the first few hours. But a full hour before he was supposed to wake his replacement, he found himself staring, drowsily, at that crescent moon. And that beautiful sight, along with the gentle lapping of waves along the shore, soon sent him into dreamland.

It was at this time that the action on that particular beach really picked up. The force that lay in wait behind the thick line of brush and palm trees was about to make its move.

The first few of the marauders were picked off in their sleep, as trained warriors hurled spears and daggers that quickly found their mark.

And then the warriors, their faces painted black

like the night, crept farther forward, now taking aim at the next line of men gathered loosely around a central, dying fire pit.

This time one of the spears dealt only a glancing blow to one of the sleeping marauders, and he broke the silence of the night with a loud shout that quickly awoke the entire beach.

Now that the silent part of their operation was done, the warriors raised their spears high above their heads, and screamed one of their maddening hunting cries, crafted specifically to drive fear into their enemy.

The abruptly awoken marauders were in a state of mass confusion; eyes still adjusting to being awake, as movement and sound erupted all about them.

The island warriors began chasing around them, in three counter-directional concentric circles. And this only served to confuse the marauders further, for in this dim light, with all that shouting, it was difficult to know how many of these island warriors there were. Forty? Fifty? More?

More spears and knives were launched, easily finding their mark against the startled, weaponless marauders (for when the gash had opened in the side of the boat, earlier that day, one of the first crates to slide out into the water was the one containing their firearms. And by the time it had been realized, that crate was well out to sea).

The only armed man of the bunch was Maynard. Once he'd managed to clear the fog of confusion at having been awoken so suddenly, he stood up and began firing at will. Several bodies fell, two of which were island warriors; the third being one of his fellow marauders, who, running in fear, had chased directly into the line of gunfire.

Maynard saw when his own man went down, and swore. The last thing they needed to survive this onslaught was to be killing each other. Just then he raised his gun again, taking aim at one of the natives who was presently rushing towards him.

First Mate Maynard was in the process of pulling the trigger, when he suddenly felt a sharp pain in his calf. The gun fired, but the shot flew high and wide of its target, even as the charging man ducked. Crying out in pain, Maynard looked down towards his wound. His face took on an expression of anger mixed with surprise. *Now, that is some nerve!* But that, as it turned out, was his last thought. Because a split second later the charging islander's axe chopped halfway into his skull.

Less than ten minutes after the attack began, it was over. Every single marauder, to a man, lay dead on the blood-soaked sand.

The warriors gathered in a ring around the corpses, spears and axes lifted high, and let out a ferocious, deafening, triumphant battle cry. There were far fewer than the forty or fifty Maynard and crew thought they saw. In reality there were only sixteen of them, warriors comprised of boys, several years younger than typical fighting age, and men, old enough to be their fathers.

And though it was difficult to see in the dim light, several of those fierce warriors had tears in their eyes, for this had been no random siege. This had been an avenging attack, for the memory of their fallen brothers.

Then there was movement amongst the corpses. First appeared an arm, then a leg. Then a woman struggled free from the weight of the two bodies that had collapsed on top of her.

Siya looked up with a mixture of gratitude and surprise as Frisa, who had been a neighbor and a good friend of Ademo's, reached down to offer her a hand. She grimaced when she felt the pain in her side where Maynard had kicked her, right after she'd bitten him. But the immense relief she felt in that moment overcame any pain she may have felt.

As the celebration continued, on into the night, none of those gathered on the warm shore noticed the single pair of eyes gazing their way from amidst the tropical shrubbery, nor the hand tugging thoughtfully on a grey-black goatee.

31

When Ademo awoke early the following morning, he looked out through the windows and shook his head.

It was raining. *Again.* He really had hoped for a brighter, dryer day to begin their journey. But apparently a sunny, dry day in Landry was hard to come by. Ademo dressed quickly, putting on the thick underwear Banon had left for him beneath his bulky outer clothes. Banon had told him he'd be thanking him for the extra layers once they reached the higher elevations.

Ademo found Banon, packed and ready to go, sitting at the kitchen table studying the map that Morin had drawn them.

"So," asked Ademo, "do you know where we're going then?"

Banon nodded, then shook his head. "Yes, I think I know where we're headed. And that's because the good news is that Morin has drawn us a very good map."

"Okay, and the bad news?"

"This hideout of Renata's is farther away than I imagined. No wonder no one ever finds where she lives. No one really ever has need to go that far into the mountains. I don't know how she manages in the dead of winter. It'd be like living on the North Pole."

"The North Pole?"

"The top of the world."

"I take it it's cold at the top of the world then? You've been there?"

Banon laughed. "Been there? Me? No. Not personally. It's kind of a figure of speech. Everybody knows the North Pole is cold. It's kind of the epitome of cold."

"Ah, I see," Ademo said, shaking his head. Knowing a language, technically, was one thing. Understanding all the idioms and cultural references was another thing entirely.

After a hearty breakfast and a mug of steamed milk to warm their insides, the two dawned their backpacks and headed for the hill trail. It was early and only a couple of merchants getting ready to open their stores were out in the streets.

Ademo was glad when they reached the trail – the same one they'd taken to the Cloud Dome overlook. He was glad to be away from the strange culture of the town. It still felt so foreign. And that made him feel foreign to all the others. And after a while, that alien feeling wore on him. Nature seemed much more forgiving of his differences. Even if the nature itself was alien compared to the world he'd grown up in.

He said as much to Banon. And that prompted the Landrite to ask Ademo to describe Kiraboa. And Ademo did, slowly and with as much flourish as he could muster. Storytelling was a prized pastime on the island, so Ademo had no difficulty filling the first couple of hours with his colorful descriptions. The tales left Banon enthralled, marveling at what a colorful, carefree world Ademo must have come from.

Around the time Ademo finished his story, they passed the spot they'd stopped for lunch on their previous hike. Ademo would have been happy to stop there again, but Banon said he wanted to push on farther. So on they walked, winding round the meandering trail until they came to a ridge line. Here they followed a narrow footpath, with steep drop-offs on either side, until it spilled out onto another ridge; a little steeper and higher than the one they'd just ascended.

Banon finally signaled they'd stop for lunch when they came across an open, sloping meadow. By then Ademo was hungrier than he'd been in days, and bone tired, too – though he didn't want to mention that to Banon, who seemed to barely have broken a sweat. To Ademo's chagrin, though, they only stopped for twenty minutes or so, before Banon pulled his backpack on and said they'd better keep moving.

When the sun started setting, Ademo was sure Banon would stop. But he kept on moving, if anything increasing his pace to put as many miles behind them as possible before the light disappeared altogether.

By the time Banon finally stopped and pulled off his backpack, the light was so dim that Ademo was having trouble making out detail in the trail.

"Guess we'll call it a day, if you don't mind," Banon said.

"Mind? No, I don't mind. I wouldn't have minded two hours ago."

Banon caught Ademo's drift, and smiled. "Tell you what, let me get this tent set up and then we can build a fire. A cooked meal would be nice, don't you think?"

Ademo nodded, then happily sat down on a fallen log while Banon went to work.

Even before they finished their meal, Ademo felt his eyelids getting heavy. He was exhausted, and tonight he would be a man of few words. Sure enough, within minutes of hitting his pillow he was fast asleep.

After a light breakfast and a drink of cold water from a nearby stream, the two trekkers dawned their backpacks and prepared to resume the climb.

"Any idea how much farther we have to go?" Ademo asked, hoping Banon would say they were within a few hours of their destination.

"It's difficult to know with any precision. Morin drew a good map, but it was done by hand and memory, so the scale might be off. I'd say, best case scenario, we might get close by the end of the day. If not, hopefully by lunchtime tomorrow. But that partly depends on the conditions along the way. Right now the skies look calm enough. So as long as a storm doesn't roll in we should be okay. But by this time of year the skies can change in a heartbeat, especially at the higher elevations."

Ademo nodded, dropped in step behind Banon as they took to the trail again, not feeling much relieved.

The trail continued to wind up and around a series of hills, and they tread a narrow ridgeline along each one. Ademo kept hoping that, as they reached the summit of a hill, the trail would level off. But it never did. As soon as they'd reach a summit he'd see yet another ridgeline leading to the next, even taller hill.

Soon after they'd finished lunch and resumed

their trek, Ademo noticed something bright and reflective amidst the trees.

"Banon, what's that there?" Ademo asked, pointing.

Banon seemed unsure what Ademo was referring to. Then it dawned on him. "That? That, my friend, is snow."

"Snow? Wow. Strange looking stuff."

Ademo walked over and touched it with his bare hands, his eyes maintaining their expression of surprise.

"You've never seen snow before have you?"

Ademo shook his head.

"Well, friend, we best keep going. Don't worry, you'll be seeing plenty more of that before we're done."

When they stopped to set up camp in an alpine meadow later that day, the temperature had dropped noticeably. Banon suggested they wear an extra layer of clothing overnight, and Ademo was glad to follow the suggestion. It occurred to him that a third set of clothes might have been more appropriate. Even packed in with two layers of clothes and a thick blanket, he'd never felt so cold in his life.

When they awoke the next morning, two things surprised Ademo. For one, for the first time since he'd arrived in Landry, the sky was clear. And that was a very welcome relief. Secondly, he awoke to find he was breathing steam. Or, more specifically, he could see his breath evaporating in the cold, morning air.

Feeling chilled to the bone, Ademo talked Banon into making a quick fire so they could have a hot drink before pushing off for what they hoped was the last leg of their journey.

Once the fire was made and the drinks were in hand, Ademo was content to sit with the warm mug thawing out his cold hands. He sat on a nearby stump and admired the vivid blue expanse of sky that he'd missed so much. Banon took the opportunity to consult the map one more time.

Ademo would have been content to sit for a good while longer, as he felt he was only just beginning to thaw out, when Banon abruptly folded up the map and said they'd better push on.

"So by lunchtime you think?" Ademo asked, slinging the heavy backpack over his shoulders once again.

"Maybe. Give or take a few hours. We'll know soon enough."

And with that they were off, taking to the trail again, seeing patches of snow with some regularity now.

Several hours on, Banon began to slow down, and was glancing left and right with some frequency.

"We're not lost, are we?" Ademo asked.

"I'm just trying to find a landmark Morin drew on the map. We're looking for three large boulders, stacked next to each other, each one larger than the next."

They both stopped for a moment, scanning the

terrain from left to right. There were rocks of various sizes all around. But nothing that quite met the description they were looking for.

"Hmmm. I thought this was where we'd find the landmark. But it appears not. There must be another meadow, farther on – higher up."

"Wonderful. Higher yet. Any higher and I swear we'll be able to reach up and pluck at the stars when they come out later tonight."

Banon smiled slightly, then took to walking again. Apparently he was a man of few words when a task was at hand.

Not long afterward the trail dove back under tree cover. They were in the thick of a forest, and it was difficult to make out the trail amidst the patchy snow and carpet of frozen pine needles and brush.

Neither Ademo nor Banon was fond of the idea of eating lunch under the dark cover of the woods. But it was already mid-afternoon, and it was apparent they weren't going to find Renata's cottage any time soon.

"Can we make another fire?" Ademo asked, eager to cast some light into the darkness of the wood.

"No, we best not. There's something about these woods... I think we'd better leave them undisturbed."

Ademo nodded, but was unsure what Banon meant. He decided perhaps he didn't want to know, and sat eating his cold sandwich in silence.

A couple of hours after they had resumed walking, the surrounding cover of trees grew more sparse. Soon after that they emerged onto another craggy plain, dotted with small, purplish-colored alpine brush. Neither one said anything. They both knew the key was finding the landmark from the map. Surely they must be close now.

The plain stretched out for several miles, still climbing slightly. The snow was all around them now, with only sparse patches of rock and bush rising up out of the white carpet. While Ademo at first found the view beautiful, he was quickly growing tired of the white. With the sun glaring down off the shiny, icy snowscape, he found his head beginning to hurt. He squinted as they walked on.

And then, quite suddenly, the sun dove behind the western peaks and they were shrouded in semi-darkness. When Banon stopped, Ademo realized they wouldn't be finding the landmark today. Without words, Banon began unpacking the tent. Ademo took the opportunity to find what twigs and brush he could to build a fire with. He had felt a chill in his bones all day long, and now shuddered to think about how cold the fast approaching night would prove to be.

When dawn broke over the alpine meadow, cold and clear for the second day in a row, Ademo turned towards the sun, trying to draw some iota of warmth from the distant orb. Somehow Ademo knew Banon wouldn't be interested in another fire, and didn't bother asking. They ate a few scraps of bread and near frozen fruit, filled their flasks with snow that would serve as their water supply for the day, and took to the trail again.

On and on they walked, so far that Ademo began to fear that they would inevitably run into another tree line, only to discover that they still hadn't reached the place they were looking for.

It was around the time when Ademo's stomach was really beginning to plead with him for a hearty lunch that Banon suddenly stopped. He was eyeing something far off in the distance.

"There!" Banon suddenly exclaimed, pointing.

Ademo turned his eyes in that direction, and squinted to make out what Banon was seeing. He found it difficult to see much of anything from that distance.

"Ah hah! Well, better late than never, right?" Banon said, clapping Ademo on the back and resuming the march, with greater pace now.

Ademo fell into step, still straining to see what Banon had seen. Minutes later he did see it. Barely. Several hundred yards ahead: three boulders, stacked next to each other, each one larger than the previous.

When they reached the spot, Ademo suggested it was the perfect place for lunch. A much more enthused Banon heartily agreed, and they dropped their packs to the ground to draw out their now diminishing provisions.

32

Meanwhile, half a world away...

If anyone had been present in those dense woods they would have seen a tall, powerfully-built figure making his way down through the canyon, looping back and forth in a descent towards the gurgling stream below.

Even ignoring his formidable size, it was clear this man was a figure of some significance. He was draped in a crimson and black cloak, one that had a strange sheen to it, making it difficult to determine its material origin. And over his head he wore a closely fitting black skullcap, apparently made of a tough, rubbery material, that extended down the back of his neck, where it was fastened at three points between his should blades. Layered over the cap was a crimson colored, triangular head-piece, that arched over his forehead and came to a point just above the bridge of his nose. The shape of the headpiece seemed to accentuate the angular features of the man's sharp, skeletal face, which made for a daunting impression – which was just how he, Wylen Sciavo, wanted it.

Once he reached water level he walked alongside the stream until it divided in two. Rather than following the faster moving waters that curved to the right, Sciavo turned left, following the lesser stream until it slowed to a near trickle, spilling out into a modest sized pond, green with algae.

Sciavo removed his boots, then unclipped his black, crimson-streaked cloak and let it drop to the shore. After glancing once all about him – though he was quite sure he hadn't been followed to this remote location – he dove into the nearly still waters.

It took him a couple of minutes to reach the other side of the pond, which rested against a chalky cliff face. And then, stopping to take in one deep breath, he dove down into the depths.

Moments later he found what he was looking for, a cave opening, far below the waterline. He used his powerfully built arms to pull himself in sweeping, strong strokes into the cave. On he swam, as one minute became two, and two became three. The narrow channel curved slightly to the left and on he swam, till he felt his lungs would burst.

Finally the channel became wider, and Sciavo knew he'd reached the location he was looking for. He then angled his way upwards, pumping his now nearly exhausted arms and legs in efficient manner.

And then he crested the surface, inhaling the cool, slightly dank air of the interior cave with relief.

After he'd fully recovered, he pulled himself onto the smooth, obsidian shore, and began marching towards a tunnel entrance nearby. The farther he walked the more still and dank the air became. Sciavo found himself breathing the thin air in large gulps, even though he'd nearly fully recovered from the swim.

Eventually the tunnel opened up into a large cavern. Even in the dim light, points of light sparkled all around him, shining like jewels from within the surrounding stalactite columns.

But Sciavo wasn't here to enjoy the scenery. He paused only for a moment, gathering his bearings, before moving to his left. He stopped when he came to a stalactite column so large that it dwarfed his own impressive size. The thick column came down from the cavern ceiling high above, and disappeared into the ground beneath the man's feet, narrowing in girth only slightly in the middle.

He sat down, crossed his legs, closed his eyes.

And then he began to focus his mind, the way his master had taught him.

For several minutes, nothing happened.

And then, a slight hum began to arise, apparently from deep within the crystal column itself.

And then, from the very center of the crystalline depths and gradually spilling outward, a deep indigo light began to grow.

Sciavo, still dripping from his swim – the water cold against his skin in the dark, damp cavern – kept his eyes closed... until he felt the presence.

And then he opened them.

The column before him now danced in shades of purple, indigo, violet. And in the middle of the light was the vague gathering of a shape: a face, obscured, and never quite solidifying completely.

After a moment a voice spoke, echoing strangely as it passed through the thickness of the column.

"What tidings bring you, my lieutenant?"

"Your Preeminence, good news: we have word of the young man."

For a moment the distorted face took in the news, silently, save for a strange hissing sound that seemed to follow the movement of the light.

"But Prigg's ship transgressed from your scope only recently, and has not yet returned," the voice finally said. "I would know if it had. And none of the other ships in the fleet have yet discovered the island's location."

"No, sire. But recently one of the ships docked in Landry, a small city on the western coast of Corselva. And there was news there of a visitor, a boy of the correct age, fitting the description."

"Be that as it may, what proof do you have that this wasn't just some wandering rogue, come from some other place?"

"Your Preeminence, locals in Landry claim he was shipwrecked on the shore. On a simple handmade raft no less; claiming to have come from an island somewhere in the middle of the Emalderine Ocean, even though no such island was known to the locals."

The shifting shape of the face, surrounded by the dancing light, didn't respond, but the man sitting cross-legged in front of the stalactite column could have sworn he saw the eyes open wider, and the light increase. Sciavo felt a swell of pride. He knew his master was pleased.

And now for the encore.

"And sire, most important of all, this young man came bearing a name. They say he goes by the surname of Asterling."

And this time there *was* a distinct increase in the light emanating from the column. And the particles seemed to dance faster, more sporadically, in response to the news Sciavo had shared.

"Excellent!" the voice said, with lustful enthusiasm. "You have pleased your master, Wylen. Well done, indeed. And where is Asterling now?"

Sciavo took a deep breath, knowing this is where his lead ended.

"We're not sure, your Preeminence. Apparently he left Landry some days ago. What are your orders?"

"Have the crew scour the area. If he really did leave, find out where he was headed. And direct the other crews to ports nearby. If he was in this city only days ago, then he couldn't have gotten far."

"Yes, sire. It shall be done as you say."

The blurry face, drawn with dancing violet light, stared forth only a moment longer. And then, almost instantaneously, the light suddenly went out, and with it the slight hum that had reverberated around the cavern chamber.

Sciavo took a moment to let his eyes adjust to the near darkness, and then turned back the way he'd come.

33

"So we turn north from here, till we reach that line of trees. Then east again. From there it shouldn't be too much farther," Banon said, pointing ahead as they began walking.

"Will we reach it by nightfall?" Ademo asked, hoping against hope that Banon would answer in the affirmative.

"We should do, if the scale of the map is at all accurate."

They reached the tree line sometime later, and to Ademo's chagrin, the wood was as dark and mysterious as the one they'd trekked through the day previous. After a while, Ademo realized what was so disturbing about these woods: it was the silence. So unlike the lively environment he was used to in the jungles of his home island.

Despite his strained departure, Ademo now found himself feeling pangs of homesickness for Kiraboa. At first the newness of Landry and the surrounding environs was fascinating. But now he found himself longing for what was familiar, for a habitat that he knew like the back of his hand.

On and on they walked, deeper into those dark woods. The light, already muted, began failing sometime later that afternoon. When the sun dove behind the mountains yet again, they quickly found themselves in near dark. Banon stopped, seemingly unsure what to do.

"Are you planning on camping here?" Ademo asked, his tone betraying concern.

"I'm not sure," Banon replied, looking all about him. "We really must be close by now. I had hoped to find the cottage before dark."

Ademo nodded, glancing around the woods that felt more menacing by the minute.

A few moments later Banon sighed, then said: "Well, let's push on a little farther. Perhaps it's just around the corner."

Ademo certainly hoped so, drawing a deep breath and then following lockstep behind the Landrite.

Only minutes later, Banon suddenly stopped, holding his hand out to indicate Ademo should do the same.

"So this'll be the spot then? We're not going any farther today?" Ademo asked, already wondering if Banon would permit a fire.

Banon turned to Ademo, his finger placed over his lips, his eyes betraying alarm. The Landrite bent down to his knees, and Ademo followed suit. Slowly, silently, Banon pointed ahead of them. Ademo looked but didn't see anything. He certainly couldn't make out anything that would suggest they'd finally found Renata's cottage.

And then he caught the glint of something small and round, deep in the bush. Two of them in fact.

Around the time he realized it was eyeballs he was seeing, staring back at him, he heard a guttural snarl off to their left. Both young men turned their gaze in that direction. And then, this time to their right, they heard another growl.

And then something stepped out from the shadows. And then others did the same, creeping purposefully towards the two men. Ademo didn't have to ask. He knew these must be the creatures Banon had mentioned before: wolves. Grey in color and covered in a thick fur, they didn't look much like hillcats. But they were just as fearsome to behold. With their teeth drawn, the pack crept closer, Banon and Ademo now surrounded.

34

Banon drew his sword, and it glittered in the twilight. The wolves seemed unimpressed. They continued creeping forward, slowly drawing in a circle around the two trekkers. Banon focused on the one to their left. It was the largest of the pack, and he figured it to be the leader. Its eyes glowed an eerie green. Saliva dripped from its mouth, its razor-sharp teeth threatening violence.

The chorus of snarls was like nothing Ademo had ever experienced. Unlike these wolves, hillcats, the only large predators on his island, were solitary hunters. This pack mentality was something far more terrifying. How they would survive this was beyond him.

Ademo reached behind and placed his hand on the edge of a throwing disc. Despite their weapons, Ademo felt completely vulnerable before this pack of vicious predators. How many could they hope to take out before the rest were upon them? Two, three at the most?

The pack drew in closer, the leader a step in front of the others, making his dominance known. Banon was facing him straight on now, eye to eye. Ademo almost forgot to breathe, feeling an attack was imminent.

And then there was a whistle, that sounded loud and clear over the chorus of snarls. The moment the wolves heard it they stopped in their tracks, sat down. They kept their eyes focused on Banon and Ademo, but the snarls had stopped.

A moment later a figure stepped out from the shadows. It was a human figure. As it approached, both Ademo and Banon were surprised to discover it was a woman; no, check that: a girl, who looked to be no older than either of them. Long auburn hair fell well past her shoulders. Her eyes were a sapphire blue, vivid even in the failing light. Like Banon, she was fair-skinned and slender. In her right hand she held a bow, and a quiver of arrows hung from a pack on her back.

When she reached them, she bent down, stroked the lead wolf's neck. It lifted its head to greet her, gazing with its glowing green eyes, seemingly enjoying the attention. Ademo and Banon simply stared, almost too perplexed by this strange turn of events to feel thankful that the apparent danger had passed.

"Who are you and why are you here?" she asked coldly, turning her attention to the trekkers.

"My name's Banon, and I come from Landry," Banon said, somewhat taken aback by the beautiful girl before them.

"And him?" she said, nodding towards Ademo. "He doesn't look like a Landrite."

"No," Banon agreed, "he's from elsewhere. His name is Ademo. We're here because we seek the cottage of the Lady of the High Hills."

"The *Lady of the High Hills*?" she said, her tone a tad sarcastic. "What makes you think she lives here? Or lives at all? She hasn't been heard from in years."

Banon nodded, but remained silent. Ademo looked at his friend, and discerned that he was sizing up the girl, trying to determine her intentions.

"So you live up here by yourself? In these high hills?"

"Where I live is my own concern. I was asking *you* the questions," she said, sternly.

"Fair enough," Banon replied. "You're the one with the wolf pack in tow, so I won't argue."

"So what business would you have with this Lady of the High Hills, anyway?" Again, she used the expression with some degree of condescension.

Ademo decided it was time to speak up.

"If I may, we're looking for her because someone referred us to her. We have a matter we need her council about."

"And the name of this person who referred you to her?" she asked, turning to Ademo.

"Morin," Banon said, studying her for a reaction.

At the sound of that name the girl seemed to take note. Both trekkers were quite sure she'd heard it before.

"*Morin*," she repeated, almost sounding skeptical. Banon nodded.

"And how can I be sure it was Morin who sent you, rather than someone else. Or perhaps you stumbled here by chance, having been sent by no one but yourselves."

Banon stepped forward, then paused when he saw the lead wolf grow suddenly alert.

"It's alright, Grenwyn," the girl said, reaching down to stroke his neck again. "These two wouldn't be so foolish as to attempt something in the position they're in."

"Certainly not," Banon agreed, holding his hands out to help steady the wolf's nerves. He turned his attention to the girl.

"It was Morin who provided us with a map that brought us here. He drew it by hand, from memory. How many people do you know that could do that? If not Morin, then who?" Banon asked, meeting the girl's stare.

"I would see this map," the girl said, matter-of-factly.

"Fair enough," Banon replied. "If you would be so kind as to calm your friend there while I pull the map from my pack."

She nodded, and reached down to whisper something to the wolf. It remained still as Banon pulled off his pack, slowly. He handed the map to the girl. She opened it quickly, glancing from it, to the two strangers, and back again. Ademo wondered how she could make much detail out in the faint light, but after a moment she seemed to relax.

"Alright, it does appear to be an accurate map. And as you say, very few know the way here. So perhaps it was Morin who sent you. But you still haven't told me *why* he sent you."

"Before we do that," Banon said, trying to sound conciliatory, "we would have you name, and your purpose here, please. It seems you have us at a disadvantage."

The girl eyed them both for a minute, then answered Banon's question. "My name is Kyanessa. And I am Renata's great-niece."

Banon's face bore a smile. "Well, Kyanessa, great-niece of the Wise Lady, I would say 'well met', only that might be stretching it a little bit. But I trust that you are now comfortable to count us as friends and not foes?"

"Perhaps foes you are not, but friends certainly is

stretching it, and more than a little bit. Still, my great-aunt has spoken well of Morin on many an occasion. And she would trust his discretion. So I will take you to her, and let her decide what to do with you and your questions."

35

The walk to the cottage wasn't far. The girl led them on a zigzag course through the woods, then up a small hill that quite suddenly spilled out onto a clearing. The cottage was smack dab in the middle, surrounding by the towering forest on all sides. While they walked the wolves padded along silently, never once glancing up at Ademo and Banon.

The wooden cottage was small, and looked very old. The roof tiles were warped and pealing, and even the walls of the structure seemed to lean slightly. Kyanessa opened a door (she had to give it a stiff yank first, further evidence that the foundation had shifted over time), then led them into a small kitchen/sitting area. She told them to take a seat while she went to fetch her aunt. Both Banon and Ademo sat completely still, almost holding their breath, as the wolves lay about the room.

While the others seemed less interested in the

two strangers, the leader, *Grenwyn* she had called him, kept a wary green eye on them. Ademo marveled at the color of those eyes, then grew concerned that perhaps the wolf took his gaze as a challenge, and looked off towards the window instead.

A moment later voices could be heard from the next room. Apparently, in her old age, Renata was a little hard of hearing, as she bellowed out voluminously whenever Kyanessa asked her a question.

"*What?* Visitors, you say? I don't receive visitors! You shoulda sicked the wolves on 'em! They're probably thieves, come to steal what little we have!"

Kyanessa replied in a much more hushed tone, and neither Ademo nor Banon could make it out.

"Morin? That's who sent them, is it? Or *so they say*. Well, how we be knowin' they didn't roast the poor fella for my whereabouts?"

Another hushed response from the niece.

"Why? Cause I'm a senson, that's why. They probably be thinkin' I can help 'em find gold. And I could, too! Bless your heart I could. But I won't! No chance of it, the filthy beggars!"

Ademo and Banon exchanged glances, both thinking the same thing: Renata's response didn't sound promising. Grenwyn followed their eyes, not missing a beat.

There was more mumbling from the other room, but again, neither could make it out. Clearly Kyanessa was doing most of the talking now.

Suddenly there were footsteps in the hall. Kyanessa entered the room, helping an aged Renata as she sauntered slowly along in bed clothes and slippers. The woman looked vaguely familiar to Banon; though clearly older, and far less nimble. Her skin was sallow now, and littered with age spots.

"These are them?" she questioned, loudly.

"Yes, Aunt. These are the two."

When Kyanessa had helped her aunt into a soft chair by the window, she took a seat herself. Renata eyed both Banon and Ademo suspiciously, not even attempting to hide her lowly impression.

"This one's not from anywhere near here!" she said, pointing her cane in the vague direction of Ademo.

Again Banon and Ademo exchanged glances, not sure if they were expected to respond. Kyanessa spoke up instead.

"I suggest you inform my aunt as to your business here. And make it swift. She tires easily."

Banon leaned forward slightly, and Grenwyn's ears immediately perked in attention. Banon noticed, and eased himself back a little.

"Wise Lady, thank you for seeing us. My name is Banon, and I come from Landry, on the coast-"

"I know where Landry is, beanpole. I'm old, not ignorant!"

"Yes, of course," Banon continued. "And this is my friend Ademo. You are correct. He is not from here. Not from anywhere near here. He came to us upon a raft, sailed it across the Emalderine Ocean. His homeland is unknown to most folk. My father, the mayor of Landry, had never heard of it. In fact, he suspected Ademo was perhaps being untruthful as to where he came from-"

"Wise suspicion, no doubt! Most tall tales are just that!" the old woman said, cackling.

Banon cleared his throat, continued.

"Yes, well, as it turns out, someone else attended this meeting... I speak of Morin, whom I think you know well. And after hearing the tale, it was Morin who insisted we come see you. It was he who drew us a map in order to find this cottage. We have traveled these three days to find it."

The old woman turned her head from Banon to Ademo, her stringy grey hair flipping sideways in the process.

"Name this homeland of yours, boy," she bellowed.

"Kiraboa, my Lady. I come from Kiraboa," Ademo replied.

Renata sat absolutely still, but her eyes narrowed.

"Say again?"

"My homeland is called Kiraboa."

The old woman sat still, chewing gums where her teeth used to be. She seemed to be deep in thought. There was silence all about the room for several moments.

Kyanessa, who up until this point had sat quietly, shifted in her seat. She too seemed to have noticed a change in her aunt's demeanor.

"Have you heard of this island, Aunt?" she asked, her curiosity peaked.

"Not too hasty, dear. Not too hasty now," Renata replied, not taking her eyes off Ademo.

"What did you say your name was, boy?" she asked.

"Ademo. Ademo Asterling, my Lady."

"Dropped something along the trail, didn'tcha?" the old lady replied, cryptically.

"Sorry?" Ademo said, not following.

"Tell me your tale, then. Tell me about this island of yours, and how it is you came to Landry."

Neither Ademo or Banon were sure what Renata was thinking, but Kyanessa knew her aunt well. And she knew there was something to this stranger's tale that greatly intrigued the old oracle.

And so Ademo told his tale for a third time, right up until the point that he was forced to flee from Kiraboa's shores. The old woman sat quietly, cane in hand, taking it all in.

When he finished, Renata remained still, as if studying him. Then, quite suddenly, she placed her weight on her cane and began to rise from her chair. Kyanessa jumped to her aid, seemingly fearful the old woman would fall without help.

The old woman shuffled down the hall, the same way she had come. She was halfway to her room when Ademo and Banon heard her say: "Those two probably hungry by now, Kyanessa. Fix 'em some stew, dear.

And then they can bed down in the back room. I've heard enough for one day."

Again Banon and Ademo exchanged glances. Was the old woman just being courteous? Or did she place some value in Ademo's tale? Whatever significance it held for her – if any – she clearly wasn't speaking of it this night.

36

The morning sun greeted Siya like an old friend. She leaned forward, rubbing her arms and legs, still sore from several nights on the unforgiving, wooden hull of the ship.

But almost as soon as she was awake the pressing questions returned: how was it that the marauding ship had returned, apparently against the crew's will (and without their knowledge), to the shores of Kiraboa? And how was it that the villagers seemed to know it was going to happen? So much so that they had seemingly lain in wait?

Above all, though, were the questions revolving around her son's absence. Where was Ademo? Why wasn't he on the island? All the villagers had told her the night before was that he was no longer on the island – but that he was safe the last time they saw him. Had they banished him like they had her before the ship had come? Did she dare hope that he could still be alive if that's what indeed had happened?

She put her hands to her head, rubbing her temples, rocking gently. Ademo's unknown status was almost too much to bear. And if something had happened to him... Well, if that were the case, she'd just as much prefer that the marauders had finished her off when they had the chance.

After a few moments she heard foot falls approaching, and then a voice. It was Simi, Chief Fyoma's second eldest son, saying that if it did her well, the council had convened in the Skytent, and had requested her presence.

It was then that the issue of her own standing with the tribe arose in her mind. Even before she'd been taken prisoner by the marauders, the tribal council had banished her from the island – *forever*. She expected to be reminded of that command as soon as the council saw her; perhaps right after she was scolded for the hateful fate that had befallen the village. A fate the council no doubt attributed to her and Ademo.

Suffice it to say, however, that what she learned in that meeting was nothing she expected.

The meeting began with the council members greeting her warmly. More warmly in fact than she could have hoped. Of course, the council was not as it was before. Several of the former members were no more, killed in the marauders' initial siege of the island. Not the least of these lost, of course, was Chief

Fyoma himself, who had been murdered on the beach along with so many of the brave village brothers.

In his place, at the head of the table, was not Tyaso, Fyoma's rightful heir, but Simi, the next oldest son. This was the very boy, barely sixteen years old, who had fetched her that morning.

And then she saw another face she was surprised to see – and surprise put it lightly. It was Huriso – the village elder; the man who had lain in a comatose state for eleven years. He smiled warmly across the table, wrinkles spiraling into his aged face. Siya well remembered that it had been Huriso who had, more than all of the others, lobbied to allow her and Ademo to remain with the villagers all those years ago; indeed to be accepted as two of their own.

As she remembered this kindness, tears welled up in her eyes. Huriso reached across the table and took her hand in his, patting it gently.

That morning she learned much. She discovered that Ademo had returned from his Placca very soon after the marauding ship had set to sea. The villagers hadn't seen much of him, however, as the accusations hurled against him apparently led him to flee the village.

And then she learned that Tyaso – who very much assumed he would soon be appointed chief – had pursued Ademo with the intent of bringing him back to the village, not as a cherished brother, but as an outsider, to face trial and judgment. Tyaso had apparently been driven by this goal, almost obsessed with it – scheming with Kuio in preparation for Ademo's capture.

But as it turned out that very obsession, so obviously selfishly motivated – after all, Tyaso's jealous contempt of Ademo was well known throughout the village community – was what led to the council's surprising move to block Tyaso's ascent to the chiefdom.

And of course, that was their right – if they were unanimous in this decision. And clearly that had been the case. And, startlingly, that meant that even Tyaso's mother had agreed. That truly *was* something.

Of course, another factor had played a key role in the council's decision: the sudden re-awakening of Huriso. It was Huriso, the eldest of them all, who – when he learned of recent events – lobbied most stridently against Tyaso's appointment as chief. And Huriso's surprising advice went even further. For it was he who had convinced the others that the wrong decision had been made about Siya and Ademo.

The only council member who opposed this was Kuio, who had long since sided with Tyaso. In fact it was Kuio who had been the fly in Tyaso's ear, egging him on in both his bloodthirsty pursuit of Ademo, and in his expectation of his own chiefdom.

But when it became clear to the council that Kuio had shared privileged information with Tyaso, information that was strictly forbidden to be shared with anyone outside the council, Kuio was relieved of his council seat, effective immediately.

Apparently that had been too much for him. He was found the very next morning, dead in his hut, having drunk from the juices of a poison shulunti fruit.

With Huriso's return to the council, and Kuio's departure, the council was soon of one mind: Tyaso would not ascend to his father's post. Rather, in an unusual move, never before made, it was Fyoma's next oldest son, Simi, who would be appointed chief; or more specifically, chief-in-waiting. For the time-being, perhaps several years or longer, the unofficial leadership role was to be given to the remarkably resurrected Huriso.

Now, under different circumstances, Siya would have wept for joy at such news. And truth be told, she did shed many tears that morning. But even despite these miraculous events, there was still the issue of Ademo's unknown whereabouts. And for Siya, that issue stood out above all others.

All the council could tell her was that Ademo had been safe when last they saw him; that being several days after the siege, when he had been spotted making his way out towards the foggy boundary that was the Lord's Shield, on a raft of some sort.

He had not been seen since that day.

The council grew silent after relaying this news. And no doubt they thought the news dire indeed. Because, even after the arrival of the marauding ship from beyond that seemingly impenetrable boundary, several of the council members still didn't really think there was much else out there.

Of course, Siya knew different; because both she and Ademo had *come* from another land, one of many others she knew of. But still, Siya thought that the nearest landmass was, at best, many days away; far across a raging sea.

So what hope was there that her son could have survived such a journey? She dared not hope too much. But, as a mother, she also refused to assume the worst. Her poor heart couldn't bare to do that.

37

In the morning, Ademo and Banon awoke to a room so cold they could see their breath. Ademo's bones were stiff and he felt like he'd barely slept a wink. It was probably already mid-morning, but the sunlight had yet to eclipse the towering tree line surrounding the cottage. Clearly it would be lunchtime before any natural heat crept through these dilapidated walls.

"So..." Ademo began, in a hushed tone, as he rubbed his hands together and stood up, "do you think Renata will have anything useful to say today?"

Banon smirked. "I don't know. To be honest, I guess this is pretty much what I was expecting of her. She seems a lot like I remember her being years ago, just older."

"So then why did Morin send us here? He must

have expected she'd be of some help."

Banon looked at the ceiling, thinking deeply. "True. Yes, I suppose your right. He must have had some reason."

Just then the two heard the floorboards creak by the entrance to their room. They looked over and saw Kyanessa eyeing them. Both Ademo and Banon wondered how long she had been there; how much she'd overheard.

"If you're hungry, there are scones and coffee in the other room," she said, matter-of-factly.

Both of them nodded, following her out into the other room, exchanging a glance along the way.

In the front room Kyanessa leaned down to tend to the old stove, where she had a small fire started. She added some kindling, and then two larger pieces of wood, once the fire had caught well enough. Soon the flames were raging.

Both Banon and Ademo watched, a little entranced, as the light from the fire seemed to bring out the color in her flowing auburn hair. In the dim of the weak morning sun, light from the flames highlighted her striking profile, carving along her high cheekbones. When she turned towards them, quite suddenly, they each picked up a scone, looking a little sheepish.

They brought their mugs of coffee over by the stove. Ademo thought he'd never felt heat so divine. Then again, he'd never *needed* heat like this before. Kyanessa pointed out where the coffee was kept, and said they could brew a second pot on top of the stove, if it suited them. The boys thanked her, and then she disappeared down the hallway, probably to tend to her aunt.

"Do you think she lives up here year-round?" Ademo asked after she'd left.

"Probably. It looks like her aunt needs her help year round now."

"But you don't think she grew up here?"

"No," Banon smirked. "Her accent gives her away. She's from Grantin, clearly."

"Grantin? Is that another city like Landry?"

"Yes. It's really the only other city of size on the western side of the continent. Besides that there are just a few villages here and there. But Grantines have their own way of speaking, their own way of *being* for that matter, and I recognize it in her. She's definitely from there."

Ademo thought he heard some element of condescension in Banon's voice, and was about to inquire further, when they heard shuffling in the hallway. Kyanessa reentered the room, her arm held out to help Renata to her chair.

When the old woman was seated, Kyanessa poured her aunt a cup of coffee and brought it to her with a scone. Renata held the hot beverage up to her mouth with a trembling hand, took a sip, eyeing the boys all the while.

She leaned back in her chair, the springs creaking. The boys weren't sure if it was the chair or the woman making the sound. In the light of day, she looked even more aged than she had the night before; thin too, like she was having difficulty keeping on weight.

"So I 'spose you wonderin' what good an ol' lady like Renata can be to the two of yous; 'special-like as you came all the way here. You probably wonderin' if old Morin was out of his mind. Wonderin' if he's as dumb as he is mute. Am I right?" she said, cackling loudly when she finished.

Banon and Ademo looked to the floor, both feeling like their minds had been read. This made the old woman cackle all the more. And then her cackle turned into a cough. A cough that went on and on, prompting Kyanessa to rise from her chair, and hold the old woman's mug up for her to take a sip.

Ademo looked on with admiration. Kyanessa's nurturing spirit reminded him of his mother. And in that moment he missed her terribly.

For his part, Banon seemed embarrassed by the whole matter, suddenly seeming to take interest in the tall pine trees lined up outside the window.

When Renata seemed to have recovered, she took a bite from her scone, crumbs falling onto her lap and the floor. She seemed unconcerned, taking another sip from her coffee mug.

"Well, it took me some time to make sense of it myself," she finally said, picking up from where she'd left off minutes before. "But this mornin' it dawned on me – if you'll 'scuse the pun." She cackled some more, coughed some more, took another sip from her mug.

Kyanessa was on the edge of her seat again, ready to be of aid if need be. Banon watched her closely this time.

"Maybe you boys were thinkin' Morin sent you to the wise oracle to speak some prophesy over yous, or some such silliness. Come on, you dids, didn'tcha? Tell the truth now," She was smiling again, in a manner that looked half wicked and half mischievous.

Well," she continued, in a more subdued tone, "hate to disappoint yous, considering you came so far and all, but that ain't why he sent you to me. Ain't that at all."

Banon was beginning to grow impatient with the old woman's ranting. For Ademo's part, he thought her entertaining. Banon spoke up.

"But you said it *did* dawn on you: the reason..."

"Ooh, this Landrite is the hasty one, isn't he, Kyanessa," Renata said, speaking to Kyanessa.

Color rushed to Banon's face, but he held his tongue, waiting for the old woman to continue. Kyanessa seemed to notice, and looked amused.

"No, there be only one reason why Morin woulda sent yous here. Well, make that two reasons. For one: he trusts me. For two: he thought yous was in clear danger down there on the coast. So he sent yous as far as he could on short notice."

Banon and Ademo exchanged glances.

"Danger? Danger from what?" Banon asked, sounding as frustrated as he was confused. "There's no danger to Ademo in Landry."

"The marauders," Ademo spoke up, a thought occurring to him. "He thought the same marauders that came to my island would come to Landry."

Banon looked doubtful, but the old woman was nodding.

"This islander is the wiser of these two, that's for certain," Renata said, cackling again when a scowl fell over Banon's face.

Ademo, realizing that the old woman had just stated his background matter-of-factly, felt relief wash over him, like a loosening in his chest. Renata clearly wasn't one to mince words. If she'd had any doubt about his story she would have voiced it, or called him a liar outright. No, she believed him. She didn't just *want* to believe him. She *did* believe him.

"But why? Why would they come to Landry of all places?" Banon asked, still sounding doubtful.

"Boy, you really should think before you speak. If you gave it some thought it'd come to you fast enough. Wait now, now I'm being the hasty one, not thinkin' things through. You said you were Bergador's son, didn'tcha? Well, now that makes plenty o'sense. Surely does! That fool of a bureaucrat tried to throw me out of town the day I got there! He's got no manners and no common sense. Bet he wished he listened to me now, doesn't he?" she said, following it up with another chorus of cackles.

Banon's fair face flushed again, and he wondered what cryptic matter the old hag was speaking of. Whereas Ademo was thinking that perhaps the old woman wasn't quite as mad as Banon and his father had made her out to be.

Kyanessa kept silent, but a smile was spreading across her pretty face, and her eyes seemed to sparkle. She *was* beautiful, Ademo thought. And he knew Banon thought so too; knew that had a lot to do with his friend's embarrassment. Banon wanted to come across as wise and valiant before Renata's niece. And it just wasn't working out that way.

"Forgive my lack of sophistication, my Lady, but would you care to enlighten me?" Banon managed to say, gritting his teeth.

"Well, now that you asked so nice-like, I certainly will. If only your father would'a done the same, things might'a turned out different when all your crops failed 'bout five years back. *Ah!* Now you know what I'm talkin' 'bout!" the old woman said, slapping her knee and cackling yet again.

"To answer your question, Mista Junior Maya, the reason why it makes perfect sense for Morin to guess there'd be danger in Landry, is 'cause it lies east of Kiraboa. And because anybody sailing east 'o there would'a been caught up in the Sirica Current, sooner or later.

"So, you see, it makes perfect sense they'd come lookin' for the boy there, cause there only be so many other places he *could'a* landed. Maybe they went west first, thinking he was headed to Criesca. But if east, then soona or later they'd a-come calling in Landry. It'd be the first or second logical choice."

Banon sat still and quiet, letting Renata's reasoning sink in. Suddenly he felt foolish. Because the words she spoke did make sense. Perfectly. Then he thought of the townsfolk, going about their business in Landry, unaware of the potential danger. He stood straight up.

"Then we must be going! If Landry's in danger then I should be there to help my people."

Renata patted her hands in the air, motioning for Banon to sit back down.

"So hasty, aren't you, Mista Junior Maya? Brave you may be, but not so wise. Now what would be the point of Morin sendin' you all this way, for yours own safety, only to have yous run straight back into the heart of the danger the second you get wind of it? *Huh?* No, it don't make a lick o' sense. You best stay put. Let Morin do what he's gone to do."

"You mean you know what Morin's plan is then?" Ademo asked, sounding hopeful.

"Well, let me guess at somethin'," Renata replied, "I bets Morin left the same morn you did, am I right?"

"The morning before, actually," Ademo replied.

Renata nodded, like it all made perfect sense to her. "Well there you go, then. He's gone for help is what he's done."

"Help from whom?" Banon asked, still sounding confused.

"Well I don't *know* exactly. Someone he trusts can be helpful. Someone who knows what all this means and what should be done about it... Well now, I take

213

that back. Maybe I *do* know who he's gone to find," Renata continued, her gaze wandering to the window and beyond.

The others waited patiently for her to continue. Finally her head turned back to them, but she seemed to have moved on.

"Well, enough o' this spec'lation. For now, as I said, you boys best stay put, as Morin intended yous to. And since yous here, you might as well make youselves useful. There's a whole lotta wood that needs chopped up out back. Winter's long up here. And we'll need plenty of firewood to keep us alive till spring. And my dear Kyanessa's got enough to do as it is. So you best get to it. There's an axe by the door. If yous two take turns you should have the whole lot cut up and stacked by dinner."

With that Renata reached for her cane again, and Kyanessa rose to help her aunt back down the hall. The boys exchanged glances and then looked to the axe that hung on the wall by the door.

38

The towering, powerful figure in crimson and black was in familiar territory; making his way down the meandering canyon trail towards the pond at the bottom. Only this time he was not alone. Following not far behind were three others; two of which were guards, one of which was a prisoner.

The guards were doing their best to keep to the brisk pace set by the First Lieutenant. The prisoner, looking gaunt and only half-conscious, was being dragged as much as he was moving under his own steam.

Finally they came to the shore of the small, algae-covered pond. There they found their leader, the one called Sciavo, waiting impatiently for them.

"Here we dive. Be sure to stay close behind, the clarity of the water leaves something to be desired. We'll be swimming into a cave well below the waterline, over on that cliff-face there," Sciavo said, pointing.

The two guards barely had time to register the instructions before the leader took to the water in one fell swoosh, this time not bothering to remove his cloak.

"Swim with us, or we'll beat you silly," said one of the guards, glaring in the direction of the prisoner.

The captive gave no acknowledgement of the command. Again, he seemed only partially conscious. There was no time to wait, however, and the guards quickly took two steps into the water, till they were thigh deep. And then they dove in simultaneously, the ropes tying them to the prisoner pulling him in after them.

Once below the water it took them several

seconds to make out the shape of the First Lieutenant, moving quickly through the water with powerful strokes. They did their best to move as fluidly as they could; which is to say, not very fluidly at all.

Just when they thought they'd lost all sight of Sciavo, they spotted him, treading water, small bubbles escaping from around his mouth. He pointed upwards towards the surface. Seconds later they emerged from the watery depths, their lungs about to burst. Sciavo only gave them a few seconds to recover, and then he dove again.

They dared not lose him a second time.

Down they swam, angling towards the cliff line. Finally they were through the cave entrance, still churning for all they were worth.

When they finally reached the open air again – this time amidst the dank atmosphere of the hidden, interior cave – they (both guards and prisoner) gasped and vomited up water. Just when they had finally recovered, they heard a simple command from the First Lieutenant.

"Come," he said, already moving towards another tunnel opening ahead of them.

The guards exchanged glances, amazed they'd been privileged to see such a place. For while they greatly feared Wylen Sciavo, they also respected him, in an almost adoring manner.

Their amazement only grew when they entered the larger cavern, the crystalline glitter sparkling all about them. As they approached a large central column, their master sat down cross-legged.

A moment later they heard a humming, and began to see color dance and move from within the semi-transparent column.

And then there was a face; distorted and never fully resolving. And then the voice.

"Bring the prisoner closer," the voice announced.

Sciavo motioned that they do as the voice commanded.

When the prisoner was forced to his knees in front of the column, the light around the face seemed to brighten, and particles could be seen darting to and fro in and around the hazy rendering of the face.

"Ah, the Vaida Morin. I see *you*, Watcher. Do you see me?"

Morin seemed to have revived somewhat, and the scene before him certainly seemed to raise his awareness further. His eyes went wide when he beheld who was speaking. A faint chuckle could be heard emanating from the face beyond.

"So, you have seen this Asterling boy in the flesh, have you not?" the voice asked.

Morin sat silently, swaying slightly in his weakened condition.

"I'm told you were captured while returning hastily from some meeting. So, *Watcher*, who were you meeting with?"

Morin's gaze didn't waver. He stared ahead, but remained silent.

"He hasn't spoken a word since his capture,

Master. Not one. Even after several beatings of increasing intensity," Sciavo reported.

"So he thinks himself a strong one, does he? Not one to betray his friends? Well, no matter. There are other means at my disposal. Yes, indeed. *Other* means..."

If Morin understood the voice's meaning, he gave no indication. He just continued staring, barely blinking before the face that the guards found almost too dazzling to behold for more than a few seconds.

And then suddenly, simultaneously, the light emanating from the column intensified, and Morin's hands rose to clasp either side of his head. And then he screamed – loud and long.

The face had means of more subtlety. But on this occasion, with an audience, even if it was a small one, he preferred a show of force.

After a moment, even as his screams continued, Morin collapsed hard onto the stony ground, and began writhing to and fro. Indistinguishable mumbling sounds could be heard emanating from within the column. It was the sound the phantom specter made as he scoured Morin's mind for evidence of his activities.

Finally, as even the guards began to grow a little sickened by the brute show of force, the interrogation stopped. At the same time as the light dimmed within the column, Morin stopped moving altogether.

It was clear, unequivocally so, that old Vaida was dead.

Daring to look a little closer, one of the guards noticed a deep red, puslike substance trickling from Morin's ear and down his cheek.

"Was the interrogation fruitful, your Preeminence?" Sciavo asked, almost drunk with admiration.

"*Fruitful?*" the voice mocked, as if finding humor in that particular description. "Indeed. Indeed it was. The Watcher didn't know much. But what he did know was enough. So now we will prepare. But before we discuss that matter, we must first deal with another."

"Your Preeminence?" Sciavo said.

"Do you remember what I told you about how to train your men? About how to gain their absolute allegiance?"

"I do, Sire. And as always, your instruction was wise. The men follow me with almost willful abandon. They fear me. And therefore they dare not disobey me."

"Yes, fear is a powerful tool. One of the most potent. But it is not the greatest, my lieutenant. Not by far. Now you are ready for your next lesson."

"Sire, my ear is ever attuned to your voice."

"Worship," the voice hissed. "*Worship!* That is the most powerful tool of all. When those who follow you see you as a god in their midst, then your control is absolute. Men are content enough to die for a cause they believe in. But they will *throw* themselves into the path of swords for one they worship. As an act of adoration! Do you understand?" the swirling face asked.

"I do, Sire. And though the glory is yours alone, I will gladly accept their adoration in honor of your name."

"As you should, my faithful lieutenant. As you should. I have trusted you with my plans because I *do not* doubt your allegiance."

Here Sciavo bowed, surging with pride and purpose.

"With the wonders your men are about to see, they will stand in awe of you. Awe! None will doubt you when they see our plans come to pass."

"Yes, your Preeminence. The wonders will astound."

"Yes. Yes, indeed. Save for these two," the voice announced, matter-of-factly.

The two guards exchanged glances. Something about the way his Preeminence uttered that phrase gave them pause.

"These two would fear you after today, Wylen, but they would not worship you. Not when they have been in my presence. Therefore they are no longer worthy of you. Do you understand, my lieutenant?"

"I do, your Preeminence. I do. As always, your wisdom is complete."

"Good. Now learn. *Remember.*"

Once again the guards exchanged nervous glances, and shifted awkwardly on their feet. Beads of sweat trickled down their foreheads, though the cavern was cool. Their minds were racing, but they had little time to consider further.

Another hum arose, of a higher frequency this time. And simultaneously both guards reached for their ears, where it felt like sandpaper was suddenly grating across their naked ear drums.

Sciavo also felt the pain. But in some sick way he wanted the pain to rack his brain. He reveled in this unabashed display of his master's strength. He drank it in like a sip of fine wine.

In the large scheme of things this was just a drop. But nevertheless, a hint; a promise, of what was to come. A draught that all of Eiasa would one day drink deeply from. Whether they wished to or not.

The guards' fingers were now digging deep into their ears, as if trying to rip at their own ear drums. Anything to make it stop. *Anything.*

Another rumbling chuckle was heard. His Preeminence was enjoying himself.

And then, suddenly, the high frequency hum scaled up several octaves. Both men screamed at the top of their lungs.

Sciavo smiled wide, even as his own eardrums began to bleed.

And then the crystal columns all about them suddenly shot through with cracks, like ice in hot water.

The guards were in too much agony to notice this. But Sciavo did.

And then, all in an instant, the entire crystal cavern shattered into a hundred thousand pieces.

Shards shot in every direction, blasting around the source of the sound: the large stalactite column where the impression of His Preeminence's face danced before them. And then it too shattered into oblivion.

Sciavo unwrapped the cloak he'd drawn around himself only seconds earlier. And, just as his master had promised, it had made him impervious to the barrage of razor-sharp shards. As he shook the cloak, a few pieces of crystal fell to the ground, no more damaging to him than pebbles on a beach.

The guards were not so fortunate.

Their crumpled bodies lay motionless on the ground, shot through with the shrapnel of hundreds of knife-sharp shards.

Sciavo noticed that one of the guards had a sharp blade of crystal protruding directly from his left eye socket. And he laughed. He thought it marvelous. *Glorious.*

And then, after only seconds of silence that had followed the crescendo of noise, Sciavo's near deafened ears began to hear the slightest hum. He looked down at his feet, saw a shard – perhaps ten inches long and two inches thick at the base – begin to radiate in shades of purple.

He reached down, his smile still wide, picked up the shard. And then the voice spoke to him, spoke from within the shard itself. The sound was different, more trebly. But still familiar.

"Now, my lieutenant, take this with you. But keep it safe. Keep it hidden. Only your eyes must behold it.

And you need not return to this cavern again."

"Yes, Your Preeminence. I will guard this shard with my life, and keep it secret."

"See that you do," the voice said. "Now go... this cavern is unstable. When you reach your camp, prepare to leave. For the time has come."

Even as Sciavo swam back through the murky depths, a rumble disturbed the still waters. And then the cavern collapsed in on itself in a thunderous roar.

39

One thing was evident: Banon was frustrated. And the Landrite took it out on the logs they needed to split before dinner. Ademo stepped in to give the axe a few swings now and then, but he was unfamiliar with the tool, and Banon seemed content to swing away all afternoon long. So Ademo stacked while Banon chopped. And that arrangement seemed to work pretty well. By dinnertime an impressive collection of firewood lay stacked against the outside wall.

Apparently Renata wasn't feeling well that evening, and so Kyanessa made some soup and left them to serve themselves. Banon found that arrangement suited him just fine, as he wasn't in the mood for more ridicule from the old oracle. So Ademo did most of the talking, telling the Landrite stories about life in Kiraboa. By the time the moon rose over the tree line, Banon said he was ready to turn in. As Ademo didn't feel like being left alone with the wolves in the sitting area, they both retired to their room for the night.

When Ademo awoke sometime in the pre-dawn hours, there was a strong beam of moonlight streaming into the room. Looking over at Banon, he could see the Landrite was laying wide awake, his eyes open and staring at the ceiling. Ademo pulled the blankets up around him again. He wasn't used to sleeping with so much covering, but the bitter cold made it imperative.

"Trouble sleeping? Too much moonlight?" Ademo asked.

Banon kept staring at the ceiling as he replied: "I've been awake for hours. Long before the moonlight started streaming in."

"Oh? What's the root?" Ademo asked, in a Kiraboan idiom that sounded strange to Banon's ears.

"Hmm? Oh, I don't know. I guess I just don't feel right about this turn of events."

"Being here you mean, when Landry might be in danger from those marauders?"

Banon nodded. "Yes. And I don't see why I have to abide by it, just because old Morin decided it was best. I mean, I hardly know the man, he doesn't speak and he mostly keeps to himself. And yet I'm supposed to abide by this?"

"Didn't you say he used to be a Vaida? Aren't they

well-respected?"

"Well respected by some, yes. Not so much by others. And he might have been a Vaida. But nobody in Landry seems to know that for sure. Besides, as I mentioned before, even if he was a Vaida, he was kicked out of the Order at some point. Who knows why."

The two lay on the floor in silence for a time, before Banon spoke up again. "And there's something else that irks me, too."

"What's that?"

"If Renata is right – and that's a *big* if, if you ask me – and Morin sent us here out of concern for your safety, then that means he didn't tell my father all that he suspected."

"Would that have made a difference? Would you have refused to go if you knew there was a potential that the marauders would show up?"

Banon snapped his head quickly towards Ademo. "I would at least have had the opportunity to weigh the options! But that never happened. Instead, we were sent off with only half the relevant information at our disposal. Morin's not even a native Landrite, who's he to make all these decisions for those of us who are? And again, that's *if* Renata's right about Morin's intention."

Ademo felt the sting of those words: *native* and *non-native*. Those distinctions had recently been used to make him feel like an outsider on the island he'd lived his whole life upon. But he kept his feelings to himself, rolling over and seeking to return to sleep.

Sleep, though, was slow in coming. Because now his mind was racing, replaying events from his final days on the island. His last thoughts before sleep finally took him were again of his mother. Where was she? Was she still alive? He felt so helpless in not knowing the answer to any of these questions.

The next day passed much like the previous one. The young men awoke to find that Renata lay ill in bed; though she was apparently well enough to make up a list of chores they could do to keep themselves occupied. Since they both had plenty on their minds, they were content to do what was asked of them. Before lunch they chopped up more firewood, and in the afternoon they used left over wood to make shingles to replace patchy parts of the cottage roof. Ademo was impressed with Banon's handiwork. On Kiraboa they used much lighter materials for roof-work, as the cold was never a threat. So this kind of carpentry was new to him.

Ademo still found Banon distracted and distant for much of the day, and was relieved when it came time to retire for the night. Both of them were exhausted from a day of physical labor, and sleep came easily.

The next morning Ademo awoke to find Banon fully dressed and standing by the window, staring into the pine forest.

"Been up long?" Ademo asked, sitting up and stretching.

'Hmmm? Oh, an hour or so I guess."

"So I wonder what Renata will have us doing today?" Ademo asked, with a hint of humor.

"She won't have me doing anything," Banon replied, matter-of-factly.

"Yeah, a break would be nice. If only we had a gursa ball around here somewhere."

"I'm leaving," Banon said, sounding resolved.

"Leaving?"

Banon turned from the window to face Ademo. "Yes. I understand if you want to stay here, Ademo. Perhaps that's best even. But if there's any chance there are marauders coming to, or already *in* Landry, then I should be there. I *will* be there," he said, resolutely. "Regardless of what the old hag would have to say about it. I'm tired of waiting around here for God-knows-what."

Ademo just sat there, not knowing what to say. Banon gave the distinct impression that the matter was not up for discussion. Ademo couldn't help but wonder what had happened to the carefree friend he'd met those first days in Landry. Because the young man by the window was all seriousness.

When they walked into the sitting area only Grenwyn was there to greet them. The great wolf lay seated on the floor, but followed them with his eyes as they walked into the small kitchen alcove. As they munched on bread and butter they could hear

Renata's bouts of coughing down the hallway. Then they heard the muffled sound of Kyanessa's gentle voice, urging her aunt to drink some water.

"She doesn't sound well," Ademo said, concerned.

"She's old. It happens," Banon said, in a curt manner that caught Ademo by surprise.

After their breakfast Banon made quick work of packing up his gear, preparing to leave. When Ademo started doing the same, Banon stopped, looked over at him.

"What are you doing?" the Landrite asked.

"What does it *look* like I'm doing. I'm packing. I'm going with you."

"You sure that's a good idea?" Banon asked, looking unsure.

"Are you sure it's not?" Ademo replied, not looking up, still stuffing clothing into his pack.

Banon let it go, continued with his own packing.

When they walked out into the sitting room an hour later, they found Kyanessa sitting by the window, stroking Grenwyn's neck.

"How's your aunt?" Ademo asked.

"Resting," Kyanessa replied, turning from the window.

When she caught site of them with their packs on her eyes grew wide.

"What are you doing?" she asked.

"Going back to Landry," Banon said.

"You know that's not what my aunt recommended. She believes Morin's intent was for you to stay here until-"

"Until what?" Banon said, hastily. "That part's all very vague, isn't it. No, we've stayed still for long enough. I may be needed back in Landry. My place is there."

The wolf, sensing the tension, seemed to change posture slightly. His ears perked up in a way that made both young men nervous, even if they tried not to betray their fear.

"You plan on sicking your wolf on his to keep us here?" Banon asked, only half in jest.

"It's not my place to stop a fool on a fool's errand, Landrite. Go as you like. But where I'm from we're not so quick to dismiss the council of elders."

Banon looked like he wanted to say something snide in reply, but stopped himself. "Thank you for your hospitality, miss. Goodbye to you."

Banon started marching towards the door. Ademo moved over to Kyanessa, bowed slightly and smiled awkwardly. And then he followed Banon out the door.

A few minutes later they came to a place on the trail that they recognized as the spot where they had first encountered Kyanessa and her wolf pack. Banon didn't stop to compare notes though, he marched on, keeping to a brisk pace through the forest of pines.

40

It was clear to Ademo that Banon was focused on getting back to Landry as quickly as possible. The Landrite was short on words for the remainder of that day. On the few occasions when Ademo tried to strike up a conversation, Banon would make it clear he wasn't interested, responding with only a word or two and then resorting to silence again.

As the afternoon sun began to descend towards the western horizon, Ademo noticed Banon looking more frequently to the north, where dark clouds could be seen rising up over distant mountain passes. If Banon was concerned about those clouds he didn't say so; still, his expression betrayed as much to Ademo.

They camped out in an open meadow that night, and the cold was something fierce. Ademo was wrapped in three layers and still found it impossible to chase away the chill. He slept sporadically that night. With little tree cover nearby, the winds would often gust around them, dropping the temperature another ten degrees, and awakening him each time.

When the pale light of dawn crested over the mountain ridge, Banon quickly arose and started packing up. Ademo didn't bother asking about a fire. He knew Banon would refuse the idea outright. With the deep chill in his bones Ademo was content to resume their hike, in order to generate body heat and chase away the persistent chill.

An hour or so into their trek Banon pulled up next to a steeply descending slope. The trail they'd been following continued on in front of them, diving into dense forests ahead. But Banon seemed interested in the steep hill face to their left.

"We'll try this I think," Banon said, stating, not asking. "It should meet up with the trail farther down. It'll save us a good several hours if we play it right."

Ademo didn't feel like it was his place to question the Landrite's opinion. After all, he knew nothing of these lands. Still, as someone somewhat familiar with attempted shortcutting, he knew things didn't always work out as planned.

"Ready then?" Banon asked, glancing over Ademo's head, where the dark clouds from the day before were still hovering.

Ademo nodded and followed Banon as the Landrite began descending through the scree and alpine shrub brush of the steep hillside.

As Banon had hoped, the hillside did eventually meet up with the original trail. And they had certainly saved hours in the process. And that was a good thing, because the clouds that had looked stationary only hours before, now seemed to be scrolling steadily across the sky, headed their way.

After the briefest of lunches they resumed their trek. Not long after, they came to another point in the trail where a steep descent appeared off to their left.

Banon held up his arm to halt their progress, walked over to the steep slope to inspect it.

When Ademo joined him at the edge it was clear this hillside was even steeper than the last one, and mists below made it difficult to know how far down it went.

"You think this meets up with the trail again?" Ademo asked, sounding unsure.

"Should do," Banon said, deliberately avoiding eye contact. "Come on, we better get going."

When they had descended several hundred feet they walked right into a dense fog, and suddenly seeing ahead became difficult. Banon seemed intent on not acknowledging that fact, and continued with a brisk pace, holding onto low shrub brush as an anchor while scampering down the scree slope.

It was hour or more later that they finally emerged from the stubborn mists. What they found with their cleared vision didn't offer much relief, however. Below them the slope continued on and on, growing steeper still. And dark clouds were now rolling above them, fast moving and dense.

Ademo felt something strange on his head. He held out a hand and was surprised to see snowflakes landing there. It was quite the marvel for someone who'd never experienced a snowfall before.

Banon muttered that they must keep moving, and soon resumed his brisk descent, almost leaping down the hillside now.

The snowfall picked up in intensity. Before long it

was coming down heavily, and Ademo realized that any hope of banishing his chill for the day was gone. The fast-moving clouds above also brought brisk winds with them, and soon the flakes were gusting all about them. Visibility was quickly becoming as diminished as it had been in the fog earlier.

To make matters worse, the scrub brush that had served as a handhold up until now, was decidedly more scarce farther down the slope. Slippery rock and loose scree proved treacherous as the two trekkers continued their difficult descent.

As light began fading in the late afternoon hours, Ademo found it difficult to keep Banon in his line of sight; especially because the Landrite was choosing erratic lines of descent. The swirling snow had now reduced visibility to a few feet.

The winds howled all about them, and as Ademo called out, the sound of his voice was quickly swallowed. Still he pushed on, and was relieved when, a few moments later, he found Banon stopped and waiting for him.

His relief was cut short when he saw the look in Banon's eyes. The Landrite looked near-terrified. He leaned in close to Ademo, shouted over the howling wind gusts.

"We can't go on like this, it's too dangerous. We need to cut straight across from here, till we find the tree line."

Ademo nodded, and tried to stay close as Banon started scrambling to his left. He hoped the Landrite was right that the forest could be found in this direction. Amidst the blizzard-like conditions it was impossible to know.

The situation grew even more dire as the minutes ticked by. The slope was now at an even steeper angle. One false move and either one of them could be sent hurtling down the icy rock face. Banon held up his arm to signal to Ademo, then stopped in his tracks. Ademo caught a glimpse of his friend's expression and recognized near panic.

The light was now very faint, and the temperature was dropping quickly, as the sunlight's weak rays retreated over the western horizon.

After a few more moments of glancing frantically in every direction, Banon's shoulders seemed to sag, as he leaned back against the cold rock face, resigned. Banon was saying something, but amidst the swirling fury of the winds and snow, Ademo couldn't make it out.

And then, quite suddenly, something dropped in front of them, dangling from above. Banon reached out, grabbed onto it. Ademo realized it was like vine, though not from a tree. Banon knew what it was: rope, and he held on to it for all he was worth.

Both trekkers turned, carefully, to glance above, but only a few feet up the rope disappeared into the grey swirl of the blizzard. Then Banon felt the rope go taut, and he confirmed this by giving it a few swift tugs.

Banon made sure Ademo was watching him, and

then pointed his finger to his chest once, and then once to Ademo's. Ademo got that: *me first, then you follow.*

Banon pulled on the rope one more time, to ensure it was secure, then trusted his full weight to it. He started climbing the rock wall with his body hanging out at a near ninety degree angle.

He soon disappeared from view and Ademo was alone in the swirling blizzard, keeping his eyes focused on the rope as it jerked left and right every few seconds.

Several minutes later the jerking stopped, and Ademo concluded that Banon had finished climbing. He reached out, tugging gingerly on the thickly chorded rope. It was taut and seemed relatively secure.

The thought of ascending like Banon had, with his body exposed at a right angle like that, terrified Ademo. But he soon realized – after repeated attempts of various other methods – that this was the only way to gain any traction against the slick granite surface.

Ademo looked up one more time, but was greeted with nothing but the nebulous grey and the stinging sensation of snow pelting his nearly numb face.

Realizing that further delay could be deadly, Ademo leaned back, giving his full weight to the rope. His feet, scrambling up against the slippery stone, found firm footing when he was at ninety degrees.

Then he began his ascent – pulling and stepping, pulling and stepping. It was exhausting work, but slowly but surely he began to make progress.

A few minutes into his near vertical ascent, his arms were burning. He tried to relax, trusting the rope with his full weight, but his tense muscles made this difficult. So on he ascended, pulling and stepping, pulling and stepping.

A few more minutes passed and then Ademo finally caught sight of something: *a hand!* Reaching down to help him.

Then he heard a voice. It was Banon, barely audible above the swirling blizzard: "Almost there, Ademo! Keep pulling! You're almost there!"

Finally Ademo felt arms grasp a hold of him. And with that aid Ademo managed to scramble up and over the lip of a ledge. He wiped crusty snow from his eyes and turned to see Banon standing at the foot of a cave that was carved into the near vertical rock face.

Banon was smiling now, clearly relieved. Then Ademo saw movement behind the Landrite. Someone else was there, smiling. Dressed heavily in thick wintry gear was Kyanessa Worthing. And by her side, the wolf Grenwyn, his intensely green eyes penetrating even through the dense snowfall.

41

"Kyanessa!" Ademo shouted, rushing forward to

embrace her. She was thicker than usual, with her layered winter coat, but he hugged her as well as he could, anyway. When he pulled back he saw she was more than a little surprised by his gesture, but he also caught the hint of a smile cross her pretty, fair face.

"You're a lifesaver, girl. Thank you! How ever did you find us?" Ademo asked, still excited by the prospect that they were still alive.

Kyanessa motioned for them to follow her deeper into the cave, and they did so. Soon they were out of the fierceness of the blizzard, though it was still very cold.

"I've been tracking you," Kyanessa said, matter-of-factly, in response to Ademo's question.

Banon looked surprised. "Tracking us, why?"

"For this very reason!" she said, more severely. "Because I knew you were liable to get yourselves killed. You ran off so quickly, you weren't-"

"We weren't thinking straight," Ademo said, completing her thought.

She nodded, her eyes moving to Banon, who turned away to observe the raging storm, looking stung.

"Soon after you left I noticed the clouds moving in from the north. I knew those were harbingers of the season's first winter storm. And I knew you were likely to be caught up in it if you kept to your path. So I came after you. I lost your trail for a time, when you moved off the path that second time. Honestly, I couldn't believe you'd even attempt such a descent!"

she said, again eyeing Banon, who stared back blankly.

"But when I followed the trail into the woods it became clear you hadn't followed it yourselves. So I knew you must have gone off course. Eventually I caught up with you, saw you standing so precariously down there. Luckily I knew about this cave, I found it last summer when I was out trekking."

"Well, we are greatly in your debt, Kyanessa. Aren't we, Banon?" Ademo said, looking towards the Landrite.

"Indeed. It appears we are. Our thanks," Banon said, nodding slightly.

Kyanessa returned the slight nod with a slight one of her own.

"Come on," she said, "there's some firewood stacked back here. I've got some flint. Let's get a fire going."

The three figures sat hunched over the fire, deep within the confines of the cave. Outside, under the cover of darkness, the blizzard continued to rage.

"So who stored wood in here, anyway?" Banon asked, looking towards Kyanessa.

"I don't know. From the look and feel of it, it had been here for a very long time. Long before I found it. Probably long before my aunt came here as well."

"Speaking of Renata," Ademo began, "how is she? Has her cough cleared up?"

Kyanessa suddenly grew quiet, began stoking the fire with a stick. Ademo and Banon exchanged glances. In the dim firelight Ademo thought he saw a tear streaming down her face.

"She passed on, the day you left," Kyanessa finally said, her voice pained.

"Oh," Ademo said, "so sorry, Kyanessa. So sorry to hear that."

Kyanessa nodded, biting her lip as she continued stoking the fire. Grenwyn, seemingly sensing her pain, nuzzled his nose against her leg.

"You were very kind to her," Banon added. "And she lived a full life. Fuller than many, I am sure."

Kyanessa nodded again, but said nothing, tears wetting her porcelain cheeks.

When the light of dawn filled the mouth of the cave the next morning, it was clear the blizzard was raging on. Banon walked to the edge to have a look, but visibility was almost zero, and the cold, swirling winds quickly chased him back inside.

Kyanessa was already piling more wood together, preparing to make another fire. "Here," she said, passing her flint to Banon. "Can you do this? There's something else I need to do."

He nodded, taking the flint from her and bending down to strike a flame. Ademo watched as Kyanessa walked to the mouth of the cave. For a few moments she disappeared from view.

With Kyanessa momentarily out of earshot, Ademo decided to breach a subject he'd been thinking about for some time.

"Banon, help me understand something... you and

Kyanessa look alike – almost like you could be brother and sister. And your two cities are not located very far apart, considering how large the world is – even I realize that now. So how is it that there's so much enmity between you two, and your two cities? Don't you all descend from the same people?"

Banon remained silent for several seconds, continuing to strike the flint in search of an illusive flame. Finally he said: "I suppose that's true. We do come from the same people originally: the Huriq, who settled this land long ago. But that was an age ago. Since then our two cities have grown... different."

"Yeah, that's clear. But different how?"

"We have different views on how to get on with the world. How to prosper. In Grantin they're determined to stay stuck in the past. To continue on even as our ancestors did: resisting outsiders, living off whatever the land will give up, stubborn as she is."

"And in Landry?"

"In Landry we believe in modernizing to welcome outsiders. My father has a vision where we grow to become a major seafaring port; *the* major location on the west side of the continent for trade. We see this as the way forward. The *only* way forward really. Why live in the past when better options present themselves? On Criesca the peoples are more advanced, and more prosperous. And that's no coincidence. We aim to model ourselves off of that growth."

"So in Grantin they actually turn away outsiders

then?"

Here Banon paused before answering, still striking the flint for all he was worth, breathing more heavily now.

"Well, maybe they don't turn them *away* exactly. It's more that they refuse to model themselves off of the expectations of visitors from other lands. And so they end up looking uncivilized. Backwards, even. And so they don't grow."

"Grow... you mean in terms of wisdom? Size? Population?"

"All of the above. Stay rooted in the past and all aspects of growth will elude you."

Ademo nodded, then looked on as Banon finally managed to elicit a flame. As Banon bent over to gently blow on the fledging flame, adding a little bark as fuel, Ademo asked: "So why do they do it then?"

"Do what?"

"Refuse change. Refuse growth, as you put it."

"Don't know. You're better off asking Miss Worthing about that. As far as I can tell it's just about enshrining the past – as if it's better just because it's older. Like I said, backwards."

For a few moments the two sat in silence, waiting for Kyanessa to return. With one more glance to the mouth of the cave – to confirm she wasn't coming – Banon asked a question, without looking Ademo's way.

"So, do you like her?"

"Like who?"

"Miss Worthing."

"Ah, well... she's beautiful and all. But I hardly know her."

Banon nodded, glancing Ademo's way quickly – almost with embarrassment – before turning his gaze back to the fire.

"Do you have a girl back in Kiraboa?" Banon asked.

Ademo's mind went immediately to Jania, remembering their last conversation, brief as it was, on the night before he left for his Placca. Suddenly he felt sadness at not having had the chance to say goodbye to her. He couldn't help but wonder if she was pained at his leaving the island so abruptly. Could she have understood the strain he was under at the time?

"There was a girl I was interested in, for sure."

"And did she like you back?" Banon asked, again, with a hint of embarrassment.

This time both of them looked towards the mouth of the cave, but there was still no sign of Kyanessa.

"I think so, yes," Ademo said, after a moment's hesitation.

Banon nodded, looking thoughtful. He stoked the fire, looked to the cave entrance once more. "How did you know?"

"Know what?"

"Know that she liked you in return."

"Oh, I don't know... I guess just in the way she looked at me sometimes; the way she responded when

I asked her questions. You know how it is," Ademo suggested, feeling a little awkward himself. And while Banon nodded, Ademo, in that moment, had the distinct impression that perhaps Banon didn't know about such things. That perhaps growing up without a mother for much of his life, with a father that wasn't exactly communicative or emotionally available, left Banon with something of a deficit in this area.

Ademo was about to say something else, to ease the awkwardness, when he heard something. He looked up and saw Kyanessa approaching. She was covered in fresh snow. Both he and Banon eyed her a little warily, but she seemed otherwise occupied, seemingly not having overheard their conversation.

After placing a small cylindrical object inside her jacket, she knocked the snow off of her clothes, before sitting down next to them. The flames were now licking around the logs, crackling as they ate up their fuel.

To their great relief, Kyanessa seemed to come and go with preparation always in mind. From within her own pack she pulled out bread, bacon and water, and soon they were sharing a hearty breakfast. Though there wasn't much to go around, Kyanessa made sure to share some of hers with Grenwyn.

"Again, our thanks, Kyanessa. This is wonderful. What do you call this meat? It's very… flavorful," Ademo said, licking his lips.

"It's bacon. The meat comes from a pig."

"A pig?" Ademo said. "Never heard of it."

"You've never heard of a *pig*?" Kyanessa replied, looking surprised. "You *are* from a strange land, Ademo. So what kind of meat are you accustomed to eating then?"

Ademo listed off a few of his favorites, which led to an accounting of several of his less than wildly successful early attempts at hunting.

As he shared, the other two seemed genuinely intrigued by his background. Noticing this, Ademo continued on about Kiraboa for some time. Doing so brought some measure of comfort; even if it was mixed with pain. It was near midday when he finished.

It was then that Kyanessa rose up and stretched. Then, saying she'd be right back, she walked out towards the mouth of the cave again. This time both Banon and Ademo watched as she disappeared into the swirling snowstorm.

"What do you think she's doing out there?" Ademo asked.

"No idea," Banon replied. "I can tell from sitting here that the storm's not letting up. Not sure why she feels the need to step right into it to confirm that."

A few minutes later she re-emerged, placing that same cylinder in her pocket, before brushing the snow off and returning to the fire. Banon was busy adding a log or two to give it plenty of fuel.

"That tool you have," Ademo began, "were you taking a measurement or something?"

Kyanessa looked up from the flames. "Tool?"

"Yes, you put it back in your pocket when you

came in. And you did the same thing this morning."

"And last night," Banon added, making it clear that he was more observant than he first appeared.

"Oh, you mean this?" she replied, taking the object out of her pocket.

"What is that?" Banon asked, leaning forward to get a closer look. "It almost looks like a flute!"

"It *is* a flute," Kyanessa added.

"Playing a tune to sooth your soul?" Banon asked, smiling.

"You think it's funny, do you, Landrite?"

Banon shrugged. "Hey, if you want to blow a flute in the middle of a raging blizzard, go for it. You don't have to be embarrassed, though. We'd be happy to hear you play in here. Wouldn't we, Ademo?"

"Sure," Ademo replied. "A little music would be great. How about a tune right now?"

Kyanessa shook her head, rolling her eyes in the process. "It's not *that* kind of flute," she said, as if this point should be obvious.

"No? A non-musical flute, is it?" Banon said, smiling widely.

"It only plays a single note, you wisard. Difficult to make much of a tune with a single note."

"Only one note?" Banon said. "Now what's the point of that? What a waste of wood!"

"As I said, it's not *that* kind of flute," Kyanessa added, leaning down and petting her wolf's head.

Banon rolled his eyes a little, as he continued stoking the fire.

42

Ademo stood next to Banon, a few feet from the cave entrance. Outside, snow and winds were hurling around as ferociously as ever, for the third day in a row.

"What did you say you called these storms again?" Ademo asked.

"Blizzards," Banon replied.

"Do they usually last this long? For days on end?" Ademo asked, sounding exasperated.

"You're asking the wrong person," Banon said. "I'm from the coast, where the elevation is much lower and the nearness to the ocean makes the temperature milder."

Hearing their conversation, Kyanessa stepped forward, joining them as they gazed outside.

"Yes, blizzards often do last for days. Up here in the high passes one storm can roll in after another. There were times at my aunt's cottage when we wouldn't see a blue sky for a week or more. That's why we always kept our provisions up," she said.

"I don't know how you do it. It's *so* depressing. And so *cold*. Must take years off your lifetimes," Ademo said.

Banon and Kyanessa chuckled. Banon said: "You get used to it, Ademo. In fact, if you're born into it, you never think twice. It's just... normal. We don't get snowstorms like this in Landry, but it can rain for a week straight, no problem."

After munching on a light breakfast (their provisions were dwindling at this point), the three sat quietly around the fire. After a time Ademo spoke up.

"So, this might sound like a stupid question, but how many other lands are there in the world?"

"Other lands? You mean continents?" Banon asked.

"What's the difference?" Ademo asked, feeling even more ignorant.

"Well, a continent is a large landmass, like Corselva. It can contain one, or many kingdoms and countries."

"So how many countries or kingdoms are there in Corselva?" Ademo asked.

"Well, there are also city states. That's what we have here on the western side; two city states, Landry and Grantin. Besides that there are a few villages and estates. And on the eastern side of the continent are two countries: Pordovena and Shinora. And each of them is home to numerous cities the size of Landry, some much larger. Most are located in the central and southern parts. Up north it's so cold that no one lives up there. "

"Some do," Kyanessa interjected.

"What, beyond the Saquin River?"

Kyanessa nodded. "Yes, well north of there, actually."

Banon looked skeptical. "What, are these tales your aunt told you?" he said.

Kyanessa shook her head. "No, some of us have ventured beyond our own cities, Landrite. I've seen them myself."

"You've seen them yourself," Banon repeated, laced with doubt. "You've been on an expedition beyond the Saquin River?"

Kyanessa nodded, seeming to enjoy Banon's reaction.

"Beyond the Plains of Yordash?" Banon asked.

Kyanessa nodded again, a smirk crawling around her mouth.

Banon looked half impressed, half shocked.

"Anyway..." Ademo interjected, "you two were telling me about the lands around the world..."

"Right," Banon said. "Sorry. Well, as I say, there are continents and then people groups within those continents."

"And how many continents are there?" Ademo asked.

"Four," Banon responded.

"Five," Kyanessa corrected.

"Five? How do you... Well, maybe, maybe I missed one. You see, one of the continents, Suderin, is so far south, and thus so cold, that no one lives there. Unless..." Banon added, after a moment, "perhaps our fair Grantine has perchance visited such lands and discovered vast throngs of people?"

"Har har," Kyanessa said, shaking her head.

Banon smiled, enjoying his jest, before adding, "And as far as countries, kingdoms and city-states go, there are probably hundreds of those, spread around the world."

"Hundreds?" Ademo said, surprised by the large number.

Banon nodded, stoked the fire some more.

"But you don't know exactly how many?"

Banon shook his head. "No. There was a time when people knew more about the world. But that was before the Disintegration."

"The Disintegration? What's that?"

"It's when things started to go wrong with the world," Banon replied, somewhat cryptically. Ademo wondered if his Landrite friend was being evasive, or really didn't know any more. Either way, this sounded vaguely similar to the stories of an apocalypse told on Kiraboa.

"It happened when people galloped too far ahead of themselves, disturbing the natural order," Kyanessa added, with a sideways glance at Banon, who seemed to be pretending not to notice. Ademo sensed that same tension around the differing cultures of Landry and Grantin.

"Well... it was a long time ago. We don't know exactly what happened. Guesswork will only get you so far," Banon said, deciding he would add his thought, after all.

"Willfully forgetting will get you even less far," Kyanessa added, her lips drawn in a tight line.

Ademo sat still, taking in the information, as the other two seemed to stew. Banon looked like he was about to say something, but then Kyanessa turned to Ademo.

"Why do you ask?" she asked, seeing concern in Ademo's expression.

"Well, my mother was taken somewhere. I'm just trying to figure out where. I had no idea there would be so many possibilities."

Both Banon and Kyanessa shared a glance, remembering Ademo's plight. And that seemed to curb their disagreement.

Something suddenly occurred to Ademo.

"You know, the ship that came to Kiraboa, it was painted in red, black, and silver. And the flag they flew had a figure of some strange claw, drawn in the middle of a crimson circle. Do you know it?"

Again Banon and Kyanessa exchanged a glance, before both shook their heads.

"Sorry, not familiar with that, 'Demo." Banon said.

Ademo's hopeful look turned sour, and his shoulders sagged.

Kyanessa reached over and rubbed Ademo's back sympathetically. Banon, looking almost embarrassed (or jealous?), continued stoking the fire.

It was mid-afternoon when Banon first noticed that the blizzard seemed to be letting up. Visibility had improved enough that he could step just outside the mouth of the cave and make out the surrounding terrain. Snow continued to fall, but it was lighter now.

And the winds had almost let up entirely. Looking up, Banon could see the shape of the sun, hidden behind a much thinner layer of cloud cover.

Hearing a strange sound to his left, the Landrite caught a peripheral glimpse of a bird flying low overhead. Banon turned his head back towards the interior of the cave, calling to the others.

"Hey, check this: the weather's improved enough that birds are flying again. That's a good sign. Maybe we can get out of here before dinner!"

Suddenly Banon hard a strange voice offer a reply.

"That's probably not advisable. Best wait till morning."

Banon spun around, almost loosing his footing in the process.

"Careful now. That's a long drop-off in front of you," the voice said.

Banon saw a figure walking towards him. He was not as tall as Banon, about Ademo's height, clothed in a thick grey robe. The face was shrouded behind a hood.

Banon reached for his sword, taking a defensive posture.

"I'll have your name, sir," he said, looking stern.

"Muirik!" Kyanessa exclaimed, rushing from the cave and embracing the strange, robed figure.

Ademo and Banon exchanged surprised glances.

"It appears my name has been announced for me," the man said, a smile visible below the shadow of his hood. "It's rather cold out here, though. Do you think we could step inside to continue our conversation?"

Kyanessa, smiling broadly, took the man by the hand and led him inside. Ademo followed. Banon took a moment to glance around, where he noticed one strange fact: there were no footprints in the snow leading away from the place where the man had first appeared. Wearing a perplexed expression, Banon followed the others further into the confines of the cave.

43

The four sat around the warm glow of the fire. The man Kyanessa had called Muirik graciously declined her offer of food, saying he'd eaten not long before. Banon was still almost speechless. From the looks of the man's clothing, it seemed nearly impossible that he could have trekked through the recent weather and survived. The robe was thick, but not thick enough for the blizzard that had been raging only hours before.

When Muirik removed his hood it revealed the bald head and weather-worn face of a middle-aged man. Though his face betrayed the many miles he had traveled, his eyes still seemed youthful and alert.

The man's appearance took Banon somewhat

aback. One moment he saw the unassumingly common face of a man you might see wandering the streets of Landry on any given day, only to, moments later – under a different flickering of the firelight – become a face with a much more complex facade. The effect was almost mesmerizing, and somewhat troubling.

Muirik held Kyanessa's hand as he offered his condolences for the passing of her aunt. From the way he talked about the late Renata, it seemed they had known each other quite well. Muirik remembered her fondly, even with humor, discussing her rather brusque way of addressing those who weren't quick to heed her warnings. When Kyanessa recounted one such experience – a time when Renata had traveled to Grantin to share one of her premonitions several years before, only to end up being locked away in the town jail – Muirik erupted with laughter.

However, while he clearly found Renata's ways amusing, neither Banon nor Ademo got the impression that Muirik doubted the sincerity or legitimacy of her messages.

Eventually Banon's curiosity got the better of him. He interrupted the conversation to ask a question.

"Sir," he asked, "if I may, from what port did you travel from to reach us here?"

Muirik turned from Kyanessa to meet Banon's penetrating gaze.

"A prudent question from a mayor's son, my friend," the man began. "Many ports have led me to you. But most recently I was in Grantin. And not long before that I was in Landry."

The man's response confounded the Landrite in several ways. First, how was it he knew who he was? Had he spoken to his father directly at some point? Secondly, what reason would he have had to be in both major ports so recently? And how on Eiasa had he managed to reach them in this remote location, being dressed as he was? That was what he was hoping to understand. But Banon found that while his initial question had been answered, he was none the wiser.

"Banon, don't you know who this *is*?" Kyanessa asked, her expression looking surprised, near dismayed.

Banon shook his head. "Should I?"

"Muirik Ravencloak. This is *Muirik Ravencloak*," Kyanessa said, motioning as if the fact should be patently obvious.

"Sorry," Banon offered. "I'm not familiar with that name."

But even as he said that, Banon had the passing notion that perhaps he had heard that name once or twice before, though he couldn't remember where or when. And now that he'd had a good look at the man, he thought that perhaps he did look vaguely familiar.

Ademo, who had been quiet up until this point, was next to speak. "Sir, are you what they call... a Vaida?"

The man turned to face Ademo, and seemed to dwell on Ademo's presence for a moment, in a way that made Ademo feel rather strange. Banon and Kyanessa noticed it as well.

"You are an astute learner, Mr. Asterling. And you are correct. I am what they call a Vaida. And I am very pleased to make you acquaintance," he said, smiling broadly.

As soon as Ademo had asked the question Banon wanted to kick himself. Now that the question was out there, the answer was obvious. Of course the man was a Vaida. That was evident not only by his appearance – the grey robe and all – but also by his demeanor. But Vaidas had that uncanny nature about them: both distinctly recognizable in a certain kind of context, and very much unassuming in another.

"Sir, was it Morin who sent you to us?" Banon asked, now putting two and two together.

"Indeed it was, Banon. Morin came to me as soon as he could. And I came here as soon as I could. I was delayed for longer than I had hoped. And when I finally reached Renata's cottage, I was at first distraught to find you gone. I had thought Morin's instruction was for you two to stay put."

At this point Kyanessa gave Banon what could easily pass for a glare. Banon saw it out of the corner of his eye, but pretended not to. Muirik's eyes flickered between them, giving the impression that he knew exactly what had happened.

"Thankfully, your wise friend Kyanessa had left a note for me, saying she had left the cottage to track you down. I knew the general direction you were going. But it was her resont that led me right to you in the end."

"Her resont?" Banon asked, not familiar with the term.

Kyanessa reached into her jacket pocket and pulled out the flutelike object she'd used earlier.

"That? You mean you were sending out a signal with that?" Banon asked.

Kyanessa nodded and Muirik smiled. He seemed to do a lot of that.

"But how on earth could one possibly hear that from so far away, especially above the howling of the blizzard?" Banon asked, looking skeptical.

"Resonance, Banon. Hence the name. You'd be surprised just how far that little instrument can send a sound; especially to one who's accustomed to listening for it," Muirik said, smiling yet again.

Ademo leaned forward, studying the old Vaida. Like Banon, he was intrigued by him. He had a mysterious quality about him that was difficult to pinpoint. But, above all, Ademo had a profound sense of the man's goodness. He felt he was someone to trust. And, when it came to authority figures, that had been something in short supply of late. Muirik's presence represented something else as well – something just as important: the opportunity for answers. Answers to questions that had been with him ever since the island siege.

"Sir," Ademo began.

"Please, call me Muirik," the man said, smiling.

"Muirik, if Morin went to find you, I trust he expected you to have some knowledge about this whole affair. Up until this point I've been rather... confused about everything," Ademo said, deciding to stop there, to see how Muirik would respond.

"Yes, I understand, Ademo. And I do hope to offer you some answers, and some guidance. But before I do that, I would like to hear of your experience first hand. All of it. We have time now, as I would recommend that you wait until first light to move again."

"But how do we know another blizzard won't roll in overnight?" Banon asked, clearly uncomfortable with the idea of staying put when the weather was finally clearer.

"Well, my dear Landrite, you'll just have to take my word for it. I do not think you'll need to worry about a blizzard in the morning. In fact, I suspect there will be clear skies by then. And, even if I'm wrong, and another storm does arise, leaving now – in late afternoon – makes little sense, as you'd only be able to travel for a few hours before nightfall. And then you'd be without shelter if the weather did take a turn for the worse. You're better off waiting till the morn, when you can be sure to make it to your destination by day's end."

Banon still seemed a little discontent with sitting still. And he really knew almost nothing of this Vaida figure. But the man's reasoning was sound. And he could respect that. He nodded and sat back down, noticing Kyanessa glaring at him from the corner of his eye.

All eyes then turned to Ademo, who paused for only a moment, before beginning a telling of his tale for a fourth time. When he got to the point in the narrative when he was atop the Whispering Cliffs, and had his strange dream, Muirik interrupted for the first time, asked him to go slowly and not leave out any detail. Ademo did as asked, doing his best to recount every strange element of the dream. He was also careful to mention that he had the same dream, only slightly different, on his return trip to the village. Muirik nodded slowly, meaningfully, when he heard that. So much so that Ademo asked him if he should stop. Muirik shook his head and said: "No, please continue, Ademo."

When Ademo finally finished his tale, Muirik shifted slightly, looking off towards the dwindling light at the mouth of the cave, seemingly immersed in deep thought. He remained in that same position for several minutes. The others exchanged glances, wondering if and when he would get around to responding. Finally, minutes later, Muirik shifted his posture, leaned back, and looked at them.

"Your tale fills in many details that were unknown to me, Ademo. And yet, as is often the case with these kinds of things, it also begets almost as many new questions. But there is much I can tell you; things that will no doubt bring the larger scope into focus for you. But I warn you, you may not like what you hear."

Ademo didn't know how to respond to that. He gulped involuntarily, nodding slightly, his eyes fixed on the Vaida.

"I would begin by telling you," Muirik said, "that what the elders told you on your island was not far from the truth. The marauders were most definitely looking for you. And you already knew as much, I'm sure, because you already know you're likely the only male islander with a birthmark behind both ears."

"But how would these marauders know that? They'd never been to the island before. No outsiders had," Ademo said.

"Well, it may be true that no boats had arrived at the Kiraboan shoreline in a very, very long time. But that's not the point. Those marauders knew you not because any of them had visited the island before, but because *you* once lived elsewhere."

Muirik paused and let that point sink in. Ademo's jaw dropped slightly, but he remained silent, staring back at the old Vaida, who was smiling again.

"And while this may be news to you, Ademo, something tells me it is not as much of a surprise as it might be. Am I right?"

Ademo swallowed, nodding slightly. "I always knew there was something... *something* different about my past. My mother wouldn't talk about it. But still, I knew. In a thousand little ways I knew."

Banon wore a puzzled expression. "But Muirik, you just said no boats had landed on the island in a very long time. And by that I assume you mean for a much longer time than Ademo's lifetime. So, if he had lived elsewhere, how did he get to the island in the first place? And why doesn't he remember any of this?"

Muirik smiled wide, turning his gaze to the Landrite. "He doesn't remember any of it because he was very young when he came to the island. No more than a babe in fact."

"His *dream*," Kyanessa said, her eyes lit up with revelation. "The dream he had – that was actually a recollection of an earlier time. He was the baby. And that means the woman must have been his mother."

Muirik nodded. "Indeed. You speak truly, Kyanessa."

"So as Kuio and the others claimed, I am not a native Kiraboan then?" Ademo asked, in an almost pained way.

"No. You are not," Muirik replied.

"So where *am* I from then? Originally, I mean? Do you know that, Muirik?" Ademo asked.

"I do have an idea, Mr. Asterling. I'd say you have the look of a native Criescan to you."

Ademo's surprise was evident. And yet he felt, somehow, relieved. Relieved to finally know the answer to a riddle that had been with him for much of his life. While he sat in stunned silence, Banon spoke up.

"Okay, be that as it may, there's still the issue of how he got to the island in the first place. So it turns out one ship did make it through? One carrying

Ademo and his mother?"

Muirik shook his head. "No. Not that way. That way has been barred for a very long time. At least up until very recently. But there are other ways; passages that open up on rare occasions, making possible a connection between two very far away points."

As Muirik finished speaking, both Banon and Kyanessa tilted their heads, trying to understand the meaning of the old Vaida's words.

"The dream?" Ademo said, thinking back. "When I awoke from it that second time, I assumed the baby and his mother had drowned. But if what you're telling me is true, that it was my mother and me in the dream, then, since I didn't die, it must have been during *that* event that this passage was made."

Muirik nodded. "Yes. I think that's true. The memory you had during your Placca was key to who you were before, and how you came to the island. But, just as Chief Fyoma said to you, that Placca experience – even though you aren't a native Kiraboan – was also meant to tell you something of your future. Because where you came from is key to who you are. And, in this case, key to what you will be called upon to do."

"And what would that be?" Banon asked, his curiosity peaking, even if he wasn't really following the Vaida's line of reasoning.

Muirik shook his head, standing up and pacing around the cave. "Alas, that is a question I do not know the answer to. At least not yet. But it is a question we must endeavor to answer. No doubt *much* depends upon it."

"I'm sorry," Banon said, holding up his hand like a child in a classroom. "But who were these marauders then? How do they fit into all of this?"

Muirik was still pacing, but after a moment he stopped, turning to face the fair-skinned Landrite.

"Marauders are marauders, Mr. Kriedar. They usually do the bidding of whoever pays them. They are hired to do unseemly work. And are content to do it, so long as they're paid well enough. The question is... who's giving *them* orders? And I'm afraid I don't know the answer to that question – not at this moment. The black, red, and silver color scheme of the vessel is unfamiliar to me."

A strange expression then fell across Banon's face, regarding something Muirik had just said.

"Wait a minute... Ademo didn't mention the colors of the ship to you. But he did mention it to us yesterday. So how did you know about the red, black and silver?" Banon asked, his eyes narrowing.

Muirik paused for just a moment, before saying: "Because I saw such a ship with my own eyes, just two days ago, in port at Landry."

44

"You tell us this *now*? What game are you playing, old

man? We must tarry no longer! Storms be damned!" shouted Banon, bounding to his feet.

The Landrite seemed almost surprised when Ademo and Kyanessa didn't immediately follow suit. Shaking his head, he said: "Her allegiance being to the Grantines, I can understand why *she* delays, but I don't understand *your* hesitance, Ademo. You saw firsthand what those marauders will do to people! We can't stand idly by and let it happen again!"

Muirik frowned and held his hands in the air, motioning for calm. "Banon, please, *calm down*. Would you not hear what I have to say on this matter before running off?"

"He learns nothing!" Kyanessa said, clearly disgusted with Banon's demeanor. "First, he almost gets himself and Ademo killed – running off when he was told to sit put – and now he would run off again, without even considering the council provided to him!"

"What council do you speak of, Grantine? That which comes from *him*? I don't even know him! Would you have me let my people suffer simply because an old man from a far-off land tells me I should?"

"He is no old man, you blockheaded Landrite. He is a Vaida. He is *Muirik Ravenclouk*! It is to your townsfolk's own folly that you have grown ignorant of the wisdom of the Movadem."

While the shouting between Banon and Kyanessa continued, Ademo jumped to his feet, placing his hand on Banon's shoulder.

"Please, Banon... let us at least hear what Muirik has to say. These matters are far beyond both our understanding. We have no choice but to listen to those who would help us. We have no hope without such council. I sense that, deep in my bones. This is beyond you or me. Beyond your town or my village."

Banon spun around to face Ademo. At first he motioned as if he would swat at Ademo's hand, but stopped short. After a moment of tension – when it was unclear what the Landrite would do – he seemed to relax, just a little bit. Taking a deep breath, he sat down. His tapping foot told them it was taking all of his focus to remain still.

Muirik breathed deep as well.

"Banon, let me make one thing clear: when I saw these marauders in Landry, they were certainly *not* attacking the townsfolk. Their approach seems very different there. They are merely asking questions, making inquiries, and trying to loose people's tongues with coin – of which they seem to have plenty. Furthermore, it's very unlikely to be the same ship that invaded Kiraboa. From the same fleet? Yes. On the same mission? Yes. But not the same ship."

"And what makes you so sure of that?" Banon demanded.

"Well, for one, I spoke with a couple of the crew myself – and there was no word of a female prisoner being held on board. And believe me, even if they'd been sworn to secrecy, these kind of men would have bragged about their bounty the moment they had the chance."

Muirik paused, letting this news sink in. All Ademo could do was hope that Muirik was right, because the alternative thought that flashed through his mind was that his mother was already dead; discarded by the crew when she couldn't, or wouldn't, help them find him.

"And what assurance do we have that they won't change tactics and grow more aggressive when they aren't able to find what they're looking for with questions and coin?" Banon asked.

"None," Muirik said, flatly. "But you must understand, I think their approach is different this time. In Landry they're only making inquiries, not making demands. I expect they will move on to the next place once their investigation turns cold, even if they perhaps learn from the townsfolk that Ademo might have been there not long ago.

"Now, I know a little something of your father, Banon, and if nothing else, he is a cautious, prudent man. I assume therefore that no one in Landry, *besides* your father, knows where Ademo went. So eventually the marauders will go elsewhere to look for him. In fact, if they learn that he *was* in Landry, but is no longer, they will be all the more eager to move on, with hopes of finding him at the next port.

"Besides, Landry is a much larger place than Kiraboa, and better able to defend itself. And no single crew of one marauding boat is going to take that on."

Banon's foot finally stopped tapping on the dirt

floor, as he considered Muirik's words. After a moment he looked towards the others, rather sheepishly. Ademo smiled, and Kyanessa shook her head. But both realized he'd come around.

"Now, we have spoken at some length already," Muirik said, "But there is still more I would tell you – about the grand scope of things; about how Ademo may fit into all of this. But before we discuss such matters, I suggest we take some dinner first. Afterwards, I will tell you what I can – and offer my advice to you in regards to your next steps. Do you find that plan favorable?" Muirik asked, smiling at them all, but most pointedly towards Banon.

Each one responded affirmatively, Banon with a mere nod. As the Landrite rose to tend to the fire, Kyanessa reached into her pack to retrieve the last of her provisions.

Once they'd finished their meal of re-heated salted pork, bread, and water, Muirik surprised them by pulling teabags from his cloak. They boiled water in a clay jar they'd found with several rudimentary mugs near the firewood, and were soon drinking contentedly from steaming mugs of peppermint tea.

The fire spit and crackled in front of them, and outside the mouth of the cave the cover of darkness had fallen, with only a few stars shining through the shallow cloud cover.

"Let me begin by saying that there are ages and there are ages," began the old Vaida. "And by that I mean modern people have some sense of history, but

SHROUD OF THE SCION

the scope of time goes back far beyond that. Humankind itself has roamed Eiasa for a very, very long time. But it is only the most recent age that is known well by most.

"To tell the fullness of this story I must reach back to another age. In that time there arose a group of very privileged men and women who had discovered wonders in the very fabric of nature. They had discovered keys that could unlock the very essence of reality."

"Do you speak of enchanted tools, Muirik? I'm not sure I believe in such things," Banon said, almost defiantly.

"No, no, not enchanted tools in a *literal* sense. You see, the knowledge these people had was of a mathematical sort."

"You mean *numbers*? How could a knowledge of numbers possibly prove powerful? Our town's treasurer is steeped in numbers, and he's a mouse of a man," Banon said, shaking his head.

"Would you keep your mouth shut long enough for Muirik to make his point, Landrite?" Kyanessa asked, sounding exasperated.

Banon glared at her, opening his mouth to say something, then thinking better of it. When his eyes returned to the dancing flames, Muirik took this as his cue to continue.

"I know you will find this very difficult to believe, or even to comprehend, but these people had learned that reality itself is, in a sense, comprised of equations.

They learned that mathematics was key to unwrapping the very essence of nature. And they became very adept at doing so. So much so in fact that they began to realize, some of them anyway, that shortcuts could be found, or diversions interjected – into this fabric of reality, with dizzying results."

Kyanessa looked puzzled. "Excuse me, Muirik, do you speak of Priolancy?"

"Ah, so you've heard that term have you, dear? No doubt from your aunt, of course. Yes, that is one word for it. It's also called the Deep Math, or Lodenics. Whatever one calls it, it is in many ways just a deeper understanding of reality; of the nature of how everything works. It's difficult to understand because that thinking seems so foreign to us now. For we have fallen a long way from that time. Please just take it for what it is, and let me move on to how this all applies to us now."

"Hold on a minute," Banon said, holding his hand up. "What do you mean when you say numbers are behind the very *essence* of reality? See, we're sitting here on cold, hard stone, covered with a thin layer of dirt. Now this stone is real. I can *feel* it. It holds us up. It's what these very mountains are made of. So how can you say that numbers are essentially what reality is made of?"

"As I say, Banon, it's difficult to explain in a few minutes time. But let me just say this: the rock beneath us is not nearly as solid as you think it is. In fact, it's mostly empty space – with vibrational waves coalescing in such a way as to offer the sensation and perception of solidity."

Banon stared wide-eyed at Muirik, not knowing what to say.

"So you're saying," Kyanessa asked, "not only do numbers *represent* real structures, but that they're what's actually *most* real – at a fundamental level?"

"Well put, Kyanessa. That's it exactly."

Kyanessa and Ademo nodded, their attention locked on the Vaida. Banon continued to stare into the fire, shaking his head but keeping silent. He prodded the fire and sent sparks flying toward the roof of the cave.

After a moment Muirik continued.

"However, as these learned ones began to seek these shortcuts, and even to rewrite – as it were – some of the mathematical sequences, grave implications soon came to light. Indeed it turned out that interfering in such ways brought on a host of unintended consequences.

"Before long, the world became unstable. Please understand – reality itself began to behave like a fabric stretched too thin. And that brought on social disorder as well. Many of the less educated cultures of the time assumed it was some dark magic that had come upon them; some demonic manifestation appearing from the netherworld to wreak havoc. But, in reality, it was merely the consequences of the experiments run by these ones steeped in this special knowledge.

"Thankfully, before the situation grew any more dire, this same group of enlightened ones realized they were toying with something far too powerful, something much too beyond their comprehension, to be fiddled with.

"Now, some of them thought they should simply slow down the experiments, study the mathematics more thoroughly to learn what they'd missed, find where they'd gone wrong. But the majority agreed that the only prudent action was to abandon the work altogether. They realized that the very safety of the world was at stake.

"And so they proceeded to destroy all of the knowledge they had gained. Their aim was to destroy it beyond recognition, so that no one else could pick up where they had left off, ever again.

"Even when they had finished erasing any and every record of what they'd discovered, there were still tragic, horrifying consequences that continued to manifest for generations and generations. These consequences wrecked havoc upon the civilizations of the time. Wars broke out over it, as one people group blamed another. When all was said and done, the global population was only half of what it had been before the experiments began.

"Eventually, isolation set in; isolation between the peoples of Eiasa. In a period known as the Cold Peace.

"Unfortunately, not only was this deeper, dangerous knowledge abandoned as a result, but so too was much of the knowledge that *was* useful, that had aided in the cultivation of civilization over hundreds and hundreds of years. In short, the world became much more primitive and superstitious than it had been. It is to this fallen world that each of us was born into."

Here the Vaida paused, letting what he'd said sink in. Kyanessa poured each of them another cup of tea before Muirik continued.

"Now, what I have just told you, this deep history of the world, is known by very few people. But there is a group that has survived with a limited understanding from that earlier age. Indeed, this group is a remnant of the very people who discovered, and later destroyed, this deeper mathematical understanding."

"The *Vaidas*," Ademo said, looking up from the fire as the inspiration struck him.

"Yes, indeed, Ademo. The Vaidas. The Movadem. Or, to use an old title: the *Watchers of the Land*. We are not simply meditatives or desert monks as most assume. We are caretakers, sworn to watch over the world, as a result of what was done by our predecessors long, long ago. It is a calling we have kept to for generations and generations."

"And what of the women that were part of that enlightened group, Muirik? What happened to them? Have they simply died out?" Kyanessa asked.

"No, certainly not. Their descendents roam the world still. They are sisters to the Vaidas. And they are called Sihras."

"But I've never met any of them. And yet I've known several Vaidas in my time," Kyanessa added.

"That's because the Sihras went away, to another land; one that is shrouded in the same way that Kiraboa has been. They are healers in that land."

"And the way that some lands are shrouded from others, that too is a result of these experiments that were run generations ago?" Kyanessa asked.

"The unintended *consequences* of those experiments, yes."

"So how does all of this relate to the marauders, and to me?" Ademo asked, trying not to sound rash, but with curiosity getting the better of him.

"Well, I am afraid to say that the mission of the Movadem has not been entirely successful. We know that because we've recently begun to see... ripples, signatures, in the fabric of the world, that suggest someone, or some group, has somehow resurrected that ancient knowledge and is again applying it.

"This next part is difficult to explain, but trust me when I say that this knowledge even allows for a type of foreknowledge. The mathematics, when played with, allow one to, in effect, look along the curve of time and space to see what is coming. But this practice is imprecise, and only glimpses arise. And even then we're unsure whether these are things that will happen, or only that *may* happen.

"Now, as our predecessors swore to long ago, we Vaidas no longer practice this craft. But... we can observe its effects when it is being practiced by others. And recently we have begun to see things, things we assume pertain to the curve of the future. And, to make a long tale less so, in these incomplete visions, in these glimpses, we have seen you, Ademo."

Muirik paused again, letting the point sink in.

"So that's why these marauders came looking for Ademo? Because of these *visions* of the future?" Banon asked, trying to wrap his brain around the strange tale.

"We think that may be. Whoever it is that's behind this has determined that Ademo plays an important role. And so they're preemptively moving to control that element of the equation."

"So what important part is Ademo to play?" Kyanessa asked.

"That we do not know. And we're not even sure if whoever's behind all of this knows either. Perhaps they do, perhaps they don't. And that's why I was saying earlier that questions beget more questions in this whole affair."

There was silence for a time, as each took a moment to process. Eventually Kyanessa spoke.

"So what council would you give us now, Muirik? What happens next?"

"There is a place, known only to the Movadem, where the effects of that age gone by are still felt more strongly. It is in this same location that we've beheld these visions of the future. There is a kind of potency there, a power if you will. My aim is to escort Ademo there, where Vaidas wiser than me can try and ascertain what role he is to play.

"Once we know that we hope to be better equipped to deal with whoever it is that is instigating all of this. To – *we hope* – be equipped to find them, and stop them, before the consequences become too dire."

"And where is this place you would take me?" Ademo asked.

"Far from here, Ademo. It is located in Criesca. In the continent of your birthplace, no less. You should leave first thing in the morning. But not via Landry or Grantin. It's too dangerous in both of those places, because marauders or spies of the enemy may still be there.

"I have a ship waiting for you almost due south of here, in a location I doubt the enemy would venture to look. You will leave from there, and make sail for Criesca as soon as you can.

"I would ask Banon to accompany you to this location, because I have business elsewhere for a time. I will rendezvous with you later."

"I will go with Ademo as well," Kyanessa said. "I know the way better than any other, for I have walked it myself."

"Was that before or after you ventured north of the Sequin River?" Banon said, with sarcasm and a trace of good-hearted humor.

Kyanessa glared at the fair Landrite, but remained silent. Muirik smiled and laughed.

"Then a band of three it shall be. I had hoped for as much, Ademo. It would seem you have found faithful friends to aid you in your journey."

"But you will be joining us as well, won't you?" Ademo asked, feeling suddenly crushed by the weight of it all.

"I will," Muirik said, nodding, "as soon as I can."

Muirik then suggested they each get some sleep, since the plan was to leave at first light. The three young companions agreed. But as they laid down on the cold, hard ground only minutes later, sleep came slowly for each of them.

45

While Ademo had been awakening cold and stiff for days on end now, he still wasn't really getting used to it. He certainly wasn't growing to like it. As he rose up, his body protesting with every movement, he pined for the days when he could fall asleep without so much as a shirt on his back on the beaches of Kiraboa.

And not only did this particular morning bring him stiff joints, but it also brought back the realization that he had somehow found himself in the midst of a vast, ominous threat.

And then there was the issue of his mother: still gone, unaccounted for. Stolen away by a phantom enemy that even one as wise and knowledgeable as Muirik Ravencloak couldn't identify. Ademo shook his head, tried to put it all aside for the moment.

Standing up, he could see that, while Banon was still asleep, Kyanessa was standing out by the cave entrance. Ademo looked around but couldn't find any sign of Muirik.

"Morning, Kyanessa," Ademo said, as he stood beside her, overlooking the cliff face. As Muirik had predicted, the morning was relatively clear, but still bitterly cold.

"Morning, Ademo," she said, turning to him and smiling.

"Where's Muirik?" he asked.

"Gone already. Left a couple of hours ago. He woke me to tell me which path to hold to, and then said he had to be off. We should be off soon as well, if that Landrite ever gets around to waking up."

Ademo smiled. "What's up with the whole Landrite – Grantine situation, anyway? Why do I get the feeling that it's not only you two who clash, but your two clans as well?"

Kyanessa rolled her eyes as if to say, *you don't know the half of it*, but only said: "That's a long story, Ademo. And might be told differently depending on which one of us you asked. Suffice it to say that our two cities have very different approaches to life; different cultures, different priorities."

"And how long has it been that way?" he asked.

Kyanessa shook her head. "Good question. One I

can't answer. As long as I can remember, that's for sure."

"Banon seems to think it's about embracing the future versus the past."

Kyanessa shook her head, laughing quietly. "He *would* say that."

"So that's not true then? It's not about old versus new?"

"It's definitely not that simple. If I had to pin it on something, I'd say it's about what's sustainable versus what's not."

"So your people see Landry pursuing an unmanageable future?"

"We see them as not even considering the question. And of course, while that might very well be their concern for now, what happens when that growth begins to infringe upon our way of life?"

"You don't think they consider that?"

"I think they think that's a bridge to cross when it's come to. They tend to call that kind of thinking pragmatism. But we pragmatically reply that by then it may very well be too late. Besides, even now, their practices are already affecting us in terms of fishing and timber."

"So your people prefer to follow the practices you always have – that your ancestors did? It was that way in Kiraboa as well. But on Kiraboa, it wasn't so much that change was rejected, it just wasn't really considered. As far as I can tell, the Kiraboan way of life changed very little from generation to generation.

Seems much of that was the result of superstition. Or so my mother thought, anyway."

"Well... sometimes old ways are rooted in superstition alone. But tradition can also be rooted in something true. Something *perpetually* true. The ancients got away from that. And that cost the world dearly. We try and remember that fact. And it *is* a fact, not just a fairytale. But in Landry they somehow think they can begin that same pursuit and end up with different results. We find that kind of enthusiastic abandon... troubling. Foolhardy, even."

"Do your two peoples speak to each other about these things? Perhaps you can learn from each other."

Kyanessa flashed her beautiful, sapphire-blue eyes towards Ademo with a look of.... *disbelief*? Did she consider it too much of a stretch that her people could also learn from Landrites, and not just the other way around?

"We've tried to organize meetings to discuss these things, Ademo. And we used to meet, twice a year in fact. But those meetings broke down several years ago, when the Landrites claimed that talking was fine, but actions that pertained to themselves alone was within their purview alone. Of course, that very premise is what we wanted to talk about – what we thought we *were* talking about."

Ademo nodded, then turned to face into the cave, as he heard Banon finally stirring.

After a meager breakfast of stale bread and cold water, the three dawned their packs and began their descent. Banon wasn't too keen on letting Kyanessa lead, but she clearly knew the way, and, truth be told, she had much more experience in this kind of terrain than he did.

They made good time following Kyanessa's able guiding, and by lunchtime they found the ground begin to flatten, as they entered a dense forest of fir trees. Their food supplies were virtually gone at this point, but thankfully Kyanessa also had experience with the kinds of foodstuffs that the forest itself would avail to them.

After munching on larvae, berries and water (Ademo stuck to the berries and avoided the larvae), they were off again, keeping to a brisk pace as they trekked through the needled floor of the forest. Several hours on from there the trees began to thin out, and eventually spilled out onto a steep, craggy, descending slope. They trekked down this terrain as carefully as they could, though it proved treacherous with loose scree underfoot. Each of them took a turn losing footing at various points along the descent. But scratched and bruised, they eventually found themselves at the bottom.

Then they came to the edge of another steep cliff, this one the steepest of all, so much so that they couldn't even see the slope as they gazed down below. But there was something that was visible: the ocean; its choppy, grey-green waters stretching all the way to the horizon. And something else was within site as well.

"Look!" Banon said, pointing far below.

Tucked behind the curve of the bay, out of view of the open ocean, lay a small vessel, almost indistinguishable from its surroundings from this height.

"So I guess that's our ride," Ademo said. Then, shrugging, he added: "Sure beats a raft."

The other two smiled at that.

"The question is," said Banon, looking all about them, "how on Eiasa do we get down there? This way is impassible, even for our sure-footed Grantine. Wouldn't you agree, Miss Worthing?"

"Clearly. But there's another way down."

"Oh? What's that, on the backs of birds?" Banon said.

Kyanessa seemed to ignore him, started walking off to their left. After a moment Ademo followed, and then Banon soon took up chase.

They walked for another fifteen minutes before Kyanessa abruptly stopped, studying their surroundings more intently.

"We're actually farther from the boat now than when we began. Is there some method to this madness?" Banon said, stopping and dropping his pack at his feet.

Kyanessa ignored him, kept looking around, till something caught her attention.

"There," she said, pointing towards a rock outcrop about three hundred feet away.

When they reached the spot, Kyanessa started

looking for an entrance of some sort. She moved back and forth in front of the outcrop, but found no opening of any kind.

"I guess we go up before we go down," she said, already looking for a handhold and then deftly leaping onto the rock face and quickly ascending.

"What – are you trying to get a better perspective or something?" Banon asked, watching as she scampered up with impressive dexterity.

From the top they heard her exclaim: "Aha!" and point to something that was out of their sight. Once they'd managed to clamber to the top – though not as quickly as she – they beheld a small gap between two blocks of rock that were bumped up against each other. There seemed to be a hidden chamber underneath, leading into darkness.

Kyanessa pointed and then, without further discussion, carefully lowered herself down through the opening. There didn't seem to be much room, but with some shifting and squirming, she managed to make it through. Ademo and Banon knew she'd unstuck herself when she suddenly dropped away from them, disappearing into the darkness of the crevasse-like opening.

"Okay," they heard her call up, her voice sounding strange, "it's safe... come on down."

They did. Banon first, and then Ademo. When Ademo crawled in through the opening it took some degree of body contorting to free himself from the rock around him. Then he looked down and, as his eyes adjusted, he made out the shapes of his friends looking up at him, from about ten feet below.

"Just swing yourself around and drop down, Ademo," Kyanessa said, motioning with her hands.

Ademo did so, dropping down and bending his knees to absorb the landing. When he had brushed himself off, he looked in the direction the others were already staring. In front of them was a series of steps, leading down into a narrow, corrugated tunnel – not quite high enough for Banon to walk upright through. The tunnel disappeared into darkness some fifty feet beyond and below them.

"I'm impressed, Miss Worthing. How ever did you know about this place?" Banon asked.

"I didn't. Muirik did. He told me about it this morning, before he left. Apparently it leads right down to the shoreline; should put us not far from the boat."

Walking down the steps, Ademo reached out and touched the sides of the tunnel walls. They seemed too symmetrically cylindrical to be naturally occurring.

"So how did this tunnel get here?" he asked.

"Looks like something the ancients built," said Banon, feeling it himself. "In fact, it looks almost like a pipeline of some sort. Interesting, I've heard about these kinds of archeological finds, but never come across one before."

"Is there enough light to make it through?" Ademo asked, looking nervously towards an area where the tunnel seemed to go completely dark.

"Only one way to find out," Kyanessa said. "We

best keep moving. The sunlight will be dwindling soon, and then we *will* find ourselves in darkness."

46

They made steady progress descending through the tunnel, even as the light faded. But then they came to a section where rocks and dirt and tree roots protruded from the ceiling, barring them from going any farther.

"Looks like the roof caved in at some point," Banon said, looking up where faint beams of light were coming through from above.

"Can we get through?" Ademo asked, studying the others' expressions.

"We might be able to push our way through the roots and dirt, but..." Banon began.

"But what?" Ademo asked.

"But we might just cause a more massive cave-in in the process," Kyanessa replied.

"Burying ourselves alive," Banon said, agreeing with Kyanessa's assessment.

"So what now? We go *back*? We've come a good way already," Ademo said, looking back in the direction they'd come.

"Tell you what," Kyanessa said, gently parting one of the thick tree roots that hung down from the rounded ceiling. "I'll give it a go first. I'd suggest you two stand back in case it does cave in. And if it does, *run*."

"Kyanessa, no. You should let me go first," Banon

announced, firmly.

She looked at him with a smirk. "Why? Because I'm a girl and you're a boy? *Please*," she said. "I should go first because I'm the smallest. I'll test it, see if it's passable."

Banon opened his mouth to say something, then thought better of it. He glanced at Ademo, who shrugged.

Kyanessa pushed a root to the side, then slid into a small opening between the rocks and dirt. As she pushed through, gingerly, bits of soil and rock crumbled around her.

"Careful..." Ademo said, looking nervous.

Soon Kyanessa disappeared behind the debris. They could hear her voice faintly for a time – then nothing.

"Kyanessa?" Ademo called. "You alright in there?"

Her voice, sounding more distant now, came back to them: "I'm fine. My clothes are filthy, but I'm fine. The larger rocks seem to be holding everything in place pretty well. Seems relatively stable. Hold on a minute, I think-" she said, stopping mid-sentence.

"Kyanessa?" Banon called. "What is it? You see something?"

Again, with her voice sounding muffled, she replied: "Yes, I think I've come to the end of the debris field. Looks clear ahead of me and – *ahhhhhhh!*"

As Kyanessa cried out, they heard what sounded like rocks falling, clattering on the tunnel floor ahead.

"Kyanessa!" Ademo called out. "*Kyanessa!* Are you

alright?"

Banon reached out, placed a firm palm on Ademo's shoulder, signaling for silence.

There was no sound.

"Kyanessa? Kyanessa, can you hear us?" Banon finally shouted, after several seconds had passed.

They could hear the faint sound of dust and debris settling, but nothing else.

"She's trapped!" Ademo said. "We need to go in after her!"

"Yes, but let me go first. I'll call back when it's safe to come in after me... *if* it's safe," Banon said, already parting the dangling tree roots and stepping forward.

Ademo was about to say something about being the next smallest, but, seeing Banon's determined look, thought better of it.

It took some effort for Banon to fit his larger frame into the opening, but eventually he managed. Moments went by and Ademo heard nothing.

"Banon?" Ademo called out. "Banon, do you see her? Is she alright?"

Again, only a faint echo of his own voice returned to him.

"Oh, come *on*!" Ademo said, suddenly feeling very alone in the dim light of the cylindrical tunnel. He called out again, a second time. Then a third time. But no reply came back to him. He sighed, turning around to look back in the direction they'd already come. Was he better off climbing back out? Trying to find his way back to this location from above ground? No, there was no guarantee he'd be able to do that, or reach them even if he could. He had no choice but to go in after them.

He took a deep breath then, parting the tree roots like the others had done, he pushed through. The debris field seemed relatively stable, but Ademo spat when his mouth filled with dust and pebbles that tumbled down from above him. Then he noticed a tingling on his arm. He glanced down and, in the dim light, watched as a spider crawled towards his wrist. He swiped it away, only to see other ones, just like it, crawling all around him. They were everywhere.

Ademo wasn't a fan of such beasts, even if they were small compared to the tarantulas found on Kiraboa. He swallowed hard, focused on pushing ahead, weaving a path between root and rock.

Then he felt something... air, against his face. It was a welcome change in this claustrophobic, stagnant environment. He called out for the others again; waited... but no sound returned to him, save for his own voice, echoing slightly off the tunnel walls. He pushed forward some more, feeling more of the fresh air coming towards him. Had the others found a way out? Maybe they were waiting for him above ground?

He pushed on, a little more hopeful. But it was really difficult to see now, because what little light had been bleeding through from above was now almost completely blocked by the debris. As he pulled himself around one particularly large tree root, packed full of dirt, he saw that the area directly in front of him was clear of debris. It was mostly dark, but the path seemed unencumbered.

He called out again, then listened.

Nothing.

He leaned out, holding onto the root, and looked down. To his surprise, he could just make out the floor, and saw that it started sloping down at a steep angle, just in front of him.

That's when he realized what had happened to the others. They probably had taken a step too far, only to find themselves slipping and falling down that steep slide. It looked as if the pipe material here was metallic. Ademo could also hear water trickling. Clear of other debris because of the steep angle, that no doubt only made the cylinder all the more slippery.

Ademo turned around, looking for a place to stand, so he could lean farther out to have a better look.

And just then the ground shifted beneath his feet. He tried to clutch to the tree root but his hands slipped right through. Dirt and debris fell all around him, and suddenly Ademo felt himself falling.

He hit the surface of the steep, wet pipe and started sliding, quickly.

Ademo let out a screech, and clutched for the sides of the cylinder. But it was no good. He was simply moving too fast. He could feel water underneath him, making it impossible to find traction. So he hurtled along at an alarming pace, rushing down into the darkness of the steep shaft. It wasn't quite freefall, but it felt like it. Ademo grasped in vain at the slick, muddy material around him.

The seconds felt like minutes. Ademo braced himself for the inevitable crunch that was about to happen, his thoughts turning to his mother.

Then, quite suddenly, there was an opening of light, far below. The light grew closer, very quickly. And then Ademo found himself flying out of the opening at enormous speed, hurtling into the open air, blinded by the glare of the bright sunshine.

Ademo's legs churned, as he sought to slow his speed. He looked down and saw a surface of water rushing up at him.

A second later he splashed, feet first, into the ocean.

He plunged deep underwater before finally slowing. He was in shock, but found himself churning towards the surface. It was like his leap from the Whispering Cliffs all over again!

His head popped up above the waterline and he gasped for air.

"Ademo! Over here – *Ademo!*" a voice called out.

He looked in that direction, and saw his two friends, looking unharmed but dripping wet. They were standing on an outcropping of rock, waving their hands over their heads.

Ademo swam over to them, felt them reaching down and helping him climb up onto the rock.

"Quite the ride, wasn't it?!" Banon said, smiling wide.

"Ademo, are you alright?" Kyanessa said, looking concerned.

"I'm fine," Ademo replied, shaking his water-soaked, wavy head of dark hair.

Kyanessa laughed, and Banon held his hands to his face, as water sprayed in their direction.

"You're as bad as a wet dog on a rainy day!" Banon said, still smiling.

Ademo smiled as well, then turned to take in his surroundings. Looking up at the chalky cliff, he could just make out the circular opening he had plummeted out from only seconds before.

All about them, the water was littered with little outcroppings of rock, just like the one they were standing on now. It was then that he realized they were very lucky to have been deposited in the ocean, and not right onto one of those rocky outcroppings.

Just then they were sprayed with salty surf, as a wave crashed in on the small bay.

"Come on," Kyanessa said, "we'd better move closer into shore before one of those waves knocks us over."

The other two followed, Ademo still shaking out his wet hair.

47

The mayor ambled through the rain-soaked streets of Landry feeling ill at ease. As he passed by *the Thicket* he couldn't help but notice the raucous laughter coming from inside. The pub had been that way for several days now, ever since the boat full of outsiders had arrived.

When he was first told of the ship's arrival he thought it unlikely to be a coincidence. And then, when the foreign crew began asking around about a young man of an olive-skinned, wavy-haired variety, he knew for a fact that they were looking for Ademo.

The mayor wasn't feeling very self-congratulatory, even if the concerns he'd raised with Banon – who was still too innocent to know any better – had proven correct. As he feared, the foreigner who'd washed up on their shores *was* wanted by others. So much so that they had come looking for him; which is exactly what the mayor had been worried about all along.

As the mayor rounded the street corner and shuffled towards his office, he noticed a man – tall, lean, wearing three days gruff of beard – leaning against a storefront, not far away. It was one of the foreign crew. He'd noticed this same man before, in that very same location. This, amongst other clues, gave the mayor the distinct impression he was being watched.

He'd told the foreign crew – in a friendly, as-a-matter-of-fact kind of way – that Landry had served as a temporary port of call for the young man fitting the description they gave. But, alas, he'd moved on several days previous. *Where to? Sorry, no idea – he seemed the quiet sort, kept to himself mostly.*

The one who'd been asking most of the questions – a rotund, thick-bearded man named Sorenson – had said the young man they sought was a deserter, wanted by a foreign power. When the mayor had finished explaining that the young man had pushed on, and that his whereabouts were now unknown, the supposedly jovial Sorenson had suddenly grown stern, for a only a few seconds, as he studied the mayor with an intensity that likely would have brought many a man to his knees. Mayor Kriedar had returned the stare with his smile in tact, not even blinking. Then the tone shifted again, just as quickly – Sorenson smiling wide and thanking him all the same.

The mayor had hoped that would be the last of them, that they'd move on to another port by morning. But alas, no… they had decided to stay for a few days longer. They claimed they'd been at sea for a very long time, and that they were eager to rest their weary bones in a town as hospitable as Landry. The mayor responded amicably enough. And he knew the townsfolk certainly were appreciative – because this crew was passing out coin like it was going out of style. Still, the mayor would be happy to find them gone, sooner than later. He knew they were ultimately up to no good.

The mayor nodded towards the man standing by the street corner, and offered him the briefest of smiles. The lean man winked and nodded back. The mayor supposed the gesture might look friendly to the casual observer, but he sensed something more sinister beneath the surface.

The mayor unlocked his office door and walked inside. After hanging up his overcoat and hat, he sat down in front of his massive mahogany desk. Next he began shuffling through papers. He always seemed to have a stack waiting for him. And truth be told, he kind of liked it that way – because others always noticed, too. And a busy mayor was generally thought to be a productive mayor. It did no good to appear idle. *Ever.* He'd been elected four times over. And he had no intention of giving up the mayorship anytime soon.

Besides, he preferred staying busy. Because his spare time was never that – never spare. It was taken up with flashbacks from the night his wife died; died walking the cold, frozen streets of Landry, looking for him. On a night – like so many others in those years – when he was out on the town, drunk as a skunk.

The mayor froze in his chair, his eyes staring into empty space, as a familiar vision flashed before his eyes: his wife's scarf, dangling over the precipice, half of it blowing in the wind, the other half frozen to the black ice of the pavement.

It was a vision that had haunted him for the better part of a decade. And even when he did his best to keep busy, it would sneak up on him, just like this; letting him know that, try as he might, he would never be free.

After a moment the mayor snapped back to reality, sighing deeply. He turned his attention back to the task at hand. As that was all he could *ever* do.

When he found the paper he was looking for – a request from the merchant association – he reached for his pen to sign off on it. Only, his pen wasn't where he expected it to be. That was odd. He almost always left it in the same location: on the left corner of his desk, by the lamp.

He opened his top drawer and looked for it in there, to no avail. Then he tried the next drawer down, though he knew it wasn't a place he usually kept his pen. Sure enough, it wasn't there. But something else was. Something he didn't remember putting there. It was an envelope, with his name written neatly on the front. What caught him by surprise was that it listed his full name, including his given name of Bergador. Very few people knew his given name; he chose to go by his middle name, Anders, as he thought it more noble-sounding.

He pulled out the envelope, flipped it over. There was nothing else noted, no address or name on the back. Taking a quick peek towards his windows, which were typically rain-streaked and misty, he used his letter opener to tear the edge of the envelope. Inside was a single sheet of paper. He pulled it out. The note was a short one, and to the point:

10PM – The Saltyard

The mayor read the short note over three times, waiting for inspiration to strike. But it didn't. He'd no idea who'd written the note.

Could it have been from one of the foreign crew? Perhaps someone who planned to tip him off as to their true motives?

Or… was it a setup? Was he heading into a trap, set by Sorenson and his gang? Still, if they planned to kidnap him – or worse – they'd already had a dozen opportunities to do so. So that seemed rather unlikely.

The mayor went over to the fireplace, lit it, put his hands out to warm them. After a few moments he went back to his desk. Just before doing so he dropped the envelope with the note into the flames, not stopping long enough to see it catch fire and quickly turn to ash.

In the third drawer down he located his pen. He knew *he* hadn't put it there, and had no idea who did. But for now he thought it best to get on with the work he'd usually do at this time of night. So he looked over the petition from the shopkeepers one more time, then scribbled his signature at the bottom: *Mayor Anders Kriedar.*

Before moving on to the next order of business he stole a quick look outside, then to the clock on the wall; its hands told him it was nearly half past eight.

When another hour's time had passed, the mayor reshuffled his papers into a neat stack, put his pen back in its usual location, and walked over to retrieve his overcoat and hat. Turning out the lamp, he walked out into the damp night air, being sure to lock the door behind him.

He began ambling in the general direction of the town square. From the corner of his eye he saw the man from earlier, still leaning against the brick wall down the street. This time the mayor didn't acknowledge him. He just shuffled along as a gentle drizzle began to fall.

Having keys to numerous town-owned buildings was handy on this particular evening, because it allowed the mayor to enter through one door, and exit through another, often at the back. Mayor Kriedar did this several times, each time with the premise that he had something legitimate to check on. And often he *did* do this before returning home at night. Though it usually was just one or two stops, not several.

When he was quite sure that he wasn't being followed, the mayor shuffled down a back alley that led him to the Saltyard. This was where they kept the salt for the rare occasions when the Landry streets would line with snow; even though, more often than not, the wet, white stuff melted the moment it hit the ground, being that the temperatures rarely dropped below zero this close to the ocean.

The mayor used his keys to unlock the gate and swung it open, cringing when it made a groaning sound. He walked into the near pitch darkness of the large shed, his footsteps echoing on the paved floor.

When he reached the center, he stopped, spun around, not sure what he was waiting for. Only a pale sliver of moonlight fell across the south wall. The large building served up silence, making the darkness all the more ominous.

He didn't know exactly what time it was, but assumed it was close to 10pm, give or take a few minutes.

In that cold, quiet, near-darkness, the mayor began second guessing his initial assumption that this wasn't a setup perpetuated by the boat crew. Perhaps they had lured him here to take him quietly, outside the purview of the rest of the townsfolk. Perhaps they planned for a convenient accident to befall the town's leader, with not a single witness present to testify that anything more sinister had taken place.

Suddenly the whole idea of coming here alone, in the dark, seemed preposterously foolish. The mayor turned to leave – when a voice broke the silence.

"Hello, Bergador."

48

The mayor spun in the direction of the unfamiliar voice, but saw nothing but shadows.

"Who's there?" he said, trying to sound more resolute than he was.

A figure stepped quietly out from the shadows.

"My name is Muirik. And you have nothing to fear. I am a friend, bringing news."

The mayor eyed the grey-cloaked man warily. "I don't know you. How do you know me? And how do you know that name? I haven't used it since I was a boy."

"I knew your father. And the last time I saw you, you were but a boy, not even fifteen years old if I recall."

"And what business did you have with my father?"

"It's not really important now. I just wanted you to know that I'm not with the crew who are loitering about your town."

"Uh huh," the mayor uttered, still not sure about the man he was speaking to. "And why do you call me out here into the darkness? And what business did you have breaking into my office? We have laws against that round here, you know."

The man stepped closer, revealing piercing, yet kind eyes.

"My apologies, Mayor," Muirik said, smiling, "it was rather difficult to get a note to you without any of that crew noticing."

"I will accept your explanation, sir – for now. But what of this news you have for me?"

"First, I would have you know that your son is safe. As is the friend he accompanied," Muirik said.

The mayor stood silently for a moment, weighing

DARREN BRETT KING

the words. "You've seen them, then? If so, where?" he asked, his curiosity peaking, but still finding himself wary of the stranger.

"Not at Renata's cottage, if that's what you're expecting me to say," Muirik said, smiling as the mayor reacted to the name.

"And how do you know about that?"

"Morin came to me, soon after he left you with a map and council to send them there."

"Do you mean to say you're a Vaida?"

"I am. Morin came to me so it could be arranged for me to rendezvous with your son and his friend."

"And were you able to do that?"

"Not at the cottage, they'd already left, as it turns out. But I did meet with them soon after."

"And where are they now then?"

"Safe, but headed elsewhere as we speak."

"Elsewhere? *Where* elsewhere? I didn't expect this to be a drawn out affair. I had expected Banon would be back home within a week or so."

"As it turns out, that's not possible. You see, Banon's offered to help his friend with a task. And that will take them away for a time."

"Yes, but away *where*?" the mayor asked, growing frustrated with the stranger's vagueness.

"If you don't mind I'd suggest we not discuss that at present. I simply wanted to let you know that they're both alright. And that I will do what I can to help them."

"That's it, then? That's the news you've come to

bring?"

Here Muirik paused, letting the silent dark stew for a few moments before speaking. "There is another reason I came to see you. I wanted to remind you of something."

"To *remind* me of something? Again, sir, I'm afraid I don't remember any previous conversations you and I have had. You yourself said I was just a boy the last time you were here."

"What I came to remind you of was not something I said to you. Truth be told, I myself don't even know what it is you need to remember."

"Sir," the Mayor began, shaking his head, "you're speaking in riddles. How can you possibly remind me of something you yourself don't even remember?"

"Because it is not I that spoke it to you. It was Renata."

"Renata Worthing? Well... she spoke many things to me over the years – most of it nonsense if you ask me. So, I'm not sure what you're referring to, but-"

"You do a disservice to Renata's memory, Bergador. She was more right than wrong, most of the time. And I think a part of you knows that. Even though it unnerves you.

"Now, what you need to remember is something Renata spoke to you in regards to Banon. Again, I know no more than that. But she mentioned that the two of you had had this conversation at some point. It would behoove you to remember the details of that conversation."

The mayor tilted his head, as if doubting he'd heard Muirik correctly. If he knew what conversation Muirik was referring to, he certainly didn't say so. After a moment he straightened.

"Anything else, Mr. Muirik?"

"No. Other than to say that what Ademo and Banon are doing is very important. But it must remain a secret."

The mayor nodded, remaining silent for a moment.

"So this young man, Ademo... he was telling the truth then?" the mayor asked.

"Indeed he was," Muirik replied.

"Well, I certainly don't plan on telling this boat crew anything. And I don't think any of the townsfolk have anything to offer, other than to confirm that the boy was here. I just wish they'd shove off and go looking elsewhere."

"Between you and I, Bergador, I think you can be fairly certain they will do so – sooner than later."

"Oh? And how would you know that, Mr. Muirik?" the mayor asked, now looking more baffled than wary.

"They are men under someone's command. And when it becomes clear that Ademo's no longer here, they will no doubt be ordered elsewhere."

Bergador nodded, then asked: "And when can I expect Morin to return to Landry, or has he been called elsewhere?"

Muirik froze in place, just for a moment, and Bergador recognized then that this news had caught the Vaida by surprise.

"Morin hasn't returned?"

"No. I haven't seen him since the night he spoke to me about Ademo and recommended the boys go see Renata."

Muirik nodded, looking off into the distance, trying to make sense of the news. This was troubling, because the plan had been for Morin to return to Landry. And Muirik couldn't think of any legitimate reason to explain his old friend's absence. But, whatever the case, there was nothing more he could learn now. He turned to meet Bergador's gaze one more time in the dim light.

"You best be getting back to town, Mr. Mayor, before anyone notices your absence. I should be going as well."

The mayor nodded, and turned to leave. When he reached the doorway, he turned to ask Muirik to deliver a message to his son. But only shadows remained in the now empty shed.

49

The moon was bright and nearly full. But sometime after midnight a lonesome cloud wandered across the sky and shrouded the orb. It was then that the raven, black as the night, took flight. The bird landed high on the mast of the large ship, where it could see everything below. It moved its head about in sharp turns, its eyes taking everything in with laser focus.

The ship was mostly silent. One man, drinking rum from a flask, was doing a half-hearted job of guarding the gangplank. Only two others were above deck, slurring their speech and laughing amongst themselves. The rest of the crew was either asleep below, or still out on the town – though that would have been against the captain's orders.

The raven took to flight again, this time gliding noiselessly down to deck-level. The bird remained unseen. The man guarding the dock was singing at the top of his lungs, his eyes closed as he reached for a high note.

Muirik pushed his way through the swinging door that led below deck, being careful to catch it before it creaked when it swung back. Inside were two sets of stairs, one to the right, and one to the left. The old Vaida was familiar enough with these kinds of ships to know that the captain's cabin was likely located at the foot of the left side staircase.

He stepped as quietly as he could, taking the steps one at a time. He expected a guard to be posted at the door to the captain's cabin, but the area was empty. There was no doubt that someone was behind the door, however, as a loud, wheezing snore spilled out into the hallway.

Muirik tried the door handle, cautiously. As he expected, it was locked from inside. The Vaida closed his eyes, his hand millimeters from the wooden handle. He imagined what kind of lock apparatus was located on the other side. Soon he could picture it in his mind's eye. And in his inner sight the lock turned and disengaged. Gently taking hold of the door handle, he gave it a turn. This time it obliged.

He pushed the door open, slowly, listening for a creak. When it was open wide enough, he slipped through, quiet as a mouse.

A thin stream of pale moonlight shone into the room, illuminating the port side wall. Muirik could see the bed on the other side of the room. The captain's snores continued unabated, wheezing in and out.

Muirik moved stealthily over to the captain's lectern. Right on top was what he was looking for: a large, rolled up piece of papyrus leaf paper; the kind used for maps. The Vaida carefully unwound the thread-bound map, rolling it out, slowly – cringing when he heard the inevitable sound of paper rustling.

Just then the captain coughed, and rolled over in his bed.

Muirik held his breath. For a moment he thought the man had awakened. But seconds later – even as he was searching to see if open eyes were glancing his way – the snoring ensued, louder now, which told the Vaida that the captain was now turned towards him.

The light was very dim, too dark for the average person to read by. But the old Vaida had no ordinary eyesight. He looked on and saw every detail. It was a map of the Emalderine Ocean, as he had expected. And in the middle lay a small island; no doubt Kiraboa, with a circle of grey around the perimeter: the fog line; the Lord's Shield, as the islanders called it.

It was just as the Vaida had expected – and feared. The attack on Ademo's island had been no random happenstance. Someone knew exactly how to locate it; had even drawn up an accurate map for others to navigate by. There was only way to have this kind of knowledge: the Deep Mathematics. Considering the myriad of factors that contributed to the island's precise location at any given time, only the Deep Math could deliver this kind of specificity,

Still, even then, some degree of luck was necessary, because random activity was part of the equation. And that explained why this phantom enemy had sent out more than one ship. If you covered enough of the general vicinity, with enough ships, one was likely to eventually find the Bomine Fault, and transit into the space Kiraboa inhabited. This captain hadn't been the one to do it. But one of his colleagues clearly had.

Suddenly footsteps thundered overhead. Muirik could hear the laughing pair from above deck, bellowing out in uproarious conversation. He bent down even lower, as the captain coughed again, turning over once more, even lifting his head, half-consciously, to straighten his pillow.

The Vaida remained absolutely still, not moving a muscle, until relative silence ensured. He studied the details of the map for a few moments more, then carefully rolled it up again, retying the thread and placing it back atop the captain's lectern.

Moments later he closed the door, carefully, envisioning the lock engaging – until he heard a click. He strode carefully up the stairs, grimacing at the sound of the creaking floorboards.

As he reached the top of the stairway the door suddenly flew open, almost knocking him over. It was the two from earlier, barreling in from outside in a drunken stupor. They were still laughing heartily about some matter, clearly unconcerned with their substantial volume.

Only once they'd clambered down the other stairway did Muirik let himself breath again. He then rounded the corner and pushed carefully through the swinging door.

Seconds later the jet black raven took to the sky. The man drinking by the gangplank noticed, went silent for a moment as he beheld it, for it was a handsome thing. Then he took another swig of rum, and returned to his pitch-challenged singing.

50

As the three rounded the corner of the cove they spotted the boat, which looked to be a small fishing vessel, sitting in shallow waters. All three were watching closely as they approached, but couldn't spot any movement aboard.

"Wonder where the captain is?" Kyanessa said aloud. "I don't see anyone, do you?" she asked, to no one in particular.

Banon, with his hawk-like eyesight, had spotted something, and presently pointed towards the beach. There was something – or someone – there, but it was difficult to make it out from that distance.

As they rounded a moss-covered outcrop they almost stumbled over the man. He was lying on his back on the sand, his arms perched behind his head. His eyes appeared to be closed.

"Uh, hello?" Banon said, not expecting to catch the man so unawares.

The man remained still, and Ademo wondered for a moment if he was even alive. Upon closer inspection the man's chest could be seen rising up and down at regular intervals.

"HELLO?" Banon said, louder this time.

The man snorted, and jolted into a sitting position, looking all about him.

"Oh, hello there. You must be Muirik's friends. Nice to meet you," the man said, standing up and brushing sand off of himself.

He was a smallish, slender man, with a tangled mop of grey hair. His rather substantial, bushy grey mustache arched over the edges of his mouth. With his small, beady eyes (which were a color not dissimilar to his hair), he gazed upon each of them for a moment.

"Ah, you are Muirik's friends, right?" he said, suddenly sounding not so sure.

"We are," Banon said, putting him at ease and offering his hand. "My name's Banon, and this is Ademo and Kyanessa."

The man shook each of their hands, smiling through his bush of a mustache.

"A pleasure to make your acquaintance, to be sure. My name's Grinnig."

After pleasantries had been exchanged they all remained standing where they were. The three companions were waiting for Grinnig to welcome them aboard, but he seemed to be waiting on them for something. Eventually Banon spoke.

"Ah, should we be getting aboard, then?"

"What?.. Oh, yes! Yes, indeed. Time is of the essence," he said, turning and moving towards the boat. "That *is* what Muirik said, isn't it. Speaking of which, where is the old Vaida, anyway?"

"He had business elsewhere today. We had hoped we'd be meeting him here this afternoon," Kyanessa said, as they waded through the shallow water out to the boat. "You've seen no sign of him?"

"No. No, ma'm. That Vaida's difficult to keep track of at the best of times though, isn't he," he said, turning and smiling, his face full of mustache.

An hour later the three sat on the stern of the ship, eyeing the beach line and the chalky cliffs beyond, searching for some sign of Muirik. The sun had set only moments before, and darkness was quickly setting in.

"Do you think he's alright?" Ademo asked.

"I'm sure he's fine, Ademo. Muirik's a very clever and capable man. He's just been delayed is all," Kyanessa said, though her searching eyes suggested that perhaps she said this as much to comfort her own nerves as Ademo's.

"All I know is it feels a little strange putting all our eggs in one basket here," Banon said. "I just hope he's to be trusted. I mean, I don't even know that man."

"Well that's your own folly, Banon Kriedar," Kyanessa said, shaking her head. "Muirik's widely known as a trusted advisor. I can't believe you Landrites are so ignorant of the wider ways of the world. It pays to know who can and can't be trusted beyond your own city streets, you know."

"*Be that as it may*, Miss Worthing, some of what Muirik told us just doesn't hold water. Now, I understand that the world may have fallen from where it was – the result of wars and such. But that still doesn't explain how these ancient Vaidas – the ones who ran these supposed experiments, that supposedly brought on the Disintegration – arrived at that level of knowledge to begin with. I mean, the kind of knowledge Muirik was speaking of was nothing your or my ancestors could have even comprehended. Surely not! No more than you or I can now. Mathematics as root to reality? Does that make sense to you? Honestly?"

Kyanessa stood rooted in place, glaring; her

silence betraying that she didn't completely disagree with what Banon was saying. The truth was, she *had* given thought to what Muirik had told them, and some parts of Muirik's history lesson did seem difficult to square with what she'd always been taught, what she'd always believed. Even if Muirik's account was true, it did seem evident there were missing pieces of the puzzle.

Ademo, eager to avoid another argument, decided to step into the silence. "I, for one, trust Muirik. Sometimes you just have to go with your instincts. And mine say he's here to help us. Besides, if Kyanessa says he's trustworthy, then that's good enough for me."

"If my father were here listening to you talk about instincts, he'd set you straight in a heartbeat. Facts are what we need here, not guesses," Banon offered, in a slightly scolding tone.

"And yet, you helped me when you found me washed up on the beach, Banon. Wasn't that instinctual? Aren't you glad you followed those instincts, even though your father later questioned them?" Ademo asked.

Banon returned Ademo's glance, but only shrugged. Kyanessa rolled her eyes, thinking the Landrite too proud to concede the point.

"Well, my friends, it's time we be off," Grinnig announced, from behind them. "If you'd like to come inside the cabin you'll have some shelter from the wind – which can be pretty fierce once we're out in the deeper water."

The three turned to face him.

"We can't leave yet," Ademo said. "Muirik hasn't arrived."

Grinnig shrugged and threw his hands up in the air in animated fashion. "Like I said, the old Vaida comes and goes as he pleases; and doesn't follow much to a schedule. Either way, he told me to leave by sunset, even if he wasn't here by then."

"He did?" Kyanessa said, glancing back and forth from Grinnig to the beach, still scanning up and down the shore for some sign of Muirik.

"Indeed, he did. But not to worry. After all, he has both the manner and means to find us, doesn't he?" Grinnig said, laughing like a hyena.

It appeared there was little room for debate, as the small sailor was already lifting up the anchor in preparation for their departure. The three friends remained on deck, searching the shoreline in vain, even as the boat moved into the channel that would lead them back into the open ocean waters.

51

Their first night on the open seas was a rough one for Ademo. While Grinnig's boat was a vast improvement over the raft he'd journeyed to Landry with – this time around he didn't get wet, and they weren't in imminent danger of being overturned – unfortunately, the seesawing action of the boat posed its own challenge.

Ademo had no idea what seasickness was – which was ironic considering he'd grown up by the ocean. But on this first night aboard Grinnig's boat, being that they were stuck in the dry but cramped confines of the cabin, he felt it full force. By midnight he was throwing up everything he'd eaten for dinner, and then some.

Kyanessa stayed up with him for a good while, but eventually Ademo insisted she get some rest, as it was likely to be a long night no matter what. From then on he sat awake at the stern of the boat – where the swaying motion seemed slightly less severe – and gave the dwindling contents of his stomach to the ocean in regular intervals.

By the time dawn rolled around, crisp and clear, with the waters tamer, the others awoke to find Ademo in a deep sleep. Kyanessa placed a blanket over him and they let him slumber on.

Soon after breakfast, as Banon and Kyanessa were in the middle of speaking with Grinnig about their course, Banon spotted something far off in the distance.

"What's that?" he asked, pointing up and away from the boat, to the east of them.

"I don't see anything," Kyanessa said, straining to look, her hand raised above her brow to cut down on the glare.

"There's something up there to be sure," Banon said. "Birds I think."

Kyanessa and Grinnig kept looking, but it wasn't until several minutes later that they began to make out the vague shapes. As they grew closer, neither Banon nor Kyanessa could identify the strange winged creatures. They were dark grey in color, with long curved beaks, and wingspans probably as wide as Banon was tall. There were a half dozen of them swirling high above the ship now.

"What strange beasts they are, I've never seen anything like them," Kyanessa said, still shielding her eyes to get a better look.

"Nor I," Banon agreed.

"They're shaklens," Grinnig said, almost with distaste. "Come on, you two, we best get inside."

Banon and Kyanessa exchanged glances, then followed Grinnig inside the small cabin.

"Are you worried they'll attack us?" Banon asked.

"Attack? No. Not likely. They're spy birds generally," Grinnig said, holding the ship's wheel and looking ahead.

"*Spy* birds..." Kyanessa repeated. "Spying for whom?"

Grinnig turned to her. "Now that, young lass, is a question for old Muirik."

"Speaking of Muirik," Banon said, "do you have any idea how we'll meet up with him, Grinnig? Will he catch another boat and meet us in Criesca?"

Grinnig turned and eyed Banon strangely, almost

as if he was looking for some kind of recognition. When he saw none, he turned his attention to the window, bending down to observe the birds high overhead.

"Don't worry, my good fellow. Muirik'll show up sooner or later, if he can. Look: the shaklens are moving off eastward again," Grinnig said, pointing in the direction of the retreating flock.

"Good," Kyanessa said, shaking her head, "those things gave me shivers. Such ugly creatures."

Grinnig eyed her, knowingly. "Aye, miss. That they are. That they are."

52

Ademo's second night aboard Grinnig's boat passed much more smoothly than the first. He awoke before his two companions the next morning, and was thankful for a full night's rest; and for an evening meal that had decided to stay put.

Standing up and stretching, he heard voices from above deck. It occurred to Ademo that this should not be. Not far from where he stood lay the sleeping figures of Banon and Kyanessa. And yet, above deck he could clearly hear *two* voices.

"What in the name of the sky?" he said, out loud.

Just then the sleeping figure of Banon moved, and

he opened his eyes. Then Kyanessa stirred as well. Both looked up with sleepy eyes towards Ademo. Banon immediately recognized the surprised look written across his friend's features.

"What is it, Ademo? You look like you've seen a ghost," Banon said.

Ademo remained silent but pointed above. Then all three of them heard it: not one, but two voices, erupting in laughter.

"What's going on?" Banon exclaimed. "Who's Grinnig talking to?"

"Come on," said Ademo, already moving towards the flight of stairs that would take them above deck.

When they rounded the corner, above deck, they all stood in muted surprise. Sitting next to Grinnig, Muirik smiled back at them.

"Well, good morning, my young friends!" he said, in a friendly tone.

Kyanessa smiled and moved to the old Vaida, embracing him. Banon stayed rooted in place, not believing his eyes. No longer content with Muirik's mysterious mode of travel, he spoke up.

"What on Eiasa am I missing here?" he asked. "Muirik, how is it that you're able to join us in the middle of the ocean? I don't see any boats nearby."

The Vaida turned to Banon, smiling. "Well, my good Landrite, an old Vaida has other means, when necessary."

Banon stood still, his mouth still hanging open. "When you met us in the mountain cave, I wondered how on earth you trekked there in the gear you were wearing. And I didn't see any footprints in the snow, as I should have."

"No, all true. But what *did* you notice, Banon?"

Banon shook his head, was about to say "nothing", when a memory came to him. "I saw a bird, or what I thought was a bird."

"Indeed you did."

"What are you saying? That you can... take the form of a *bird*? What kind of fool do you think I am?" Banon said, sounding almost angry.

Muirik merely stared back, still smiling.

"Banon," Ademo said, "you said it yourself: how does one appear in a boat in the middle of the ocean?"

Banon looked incredulous. "Ademo, perhaps where you're from people are known to turn into animals whenever they feel like it. But where I come from that's considered impossible. A man's a man. And a bird's a bird."

"That is most certainly the almost certain truth, all over the world, Banon. Both in Kiraboa and in Landry; and anywhere else for that matter," Muirik said.

"The *almost* certain truth?" Banon echoed, picking up on the Vaida's strange turn of phrase.

"As I tried to explain in our time together in the cave," Muirik said, "there are mysteries in the mathematics that encode our reality, that, when manipulated in certain ways, can bring about very real results that – to the unknowing eye – would appear impossible."

"That's *it*?" Banon said, sounding skeptical to say the least. "You're trying to tell me this is all about numbers again?"

"Well, in the case of my ravencloak, there's a little more to it. But that's a long story."

Banon stood dumbfounded. He looked towards Kyanessa, realizing she hadn't even batted an eye over the old Vaida's sudden appearance. Muirik's secret was apparently not so secret to her. Nor to Grinnig. Suddenly Banon felt very confused, and more than a little ignorant.

Kyanessa reached for Muirik's hand, took hold of it. She seemed eager to move on, growing tired of Banon's incessant doubts. "Muirik, what delayed you? Do you have news?"

"I do. As it turns out, I've been in both your fair cities the last couple of days, trying to ascertain what I could about these marauders," Muirik said.

"They were in Grantin as well?" Kyanessa asked, concerned.

"No. As it turns out they weren't. But I needed to check to make sure. I wasn't sure how large a fleet we were up against."

"And what of news from Landry?" Banon asked.

"That same group of marauders were still there. But I believe they've moved on by now. They were preparing to leave when last I saw them."

"And the city... the people – are they alright?" Banon asked.

The Vaida met the young Landrite's gaze and smiled. "Yes, indeed, Banon. All is well, relatively speaking, anyway."

Banon's eyebrows furrowed. "What do you mean: 'relatively speaking'?"

"I mean that there was no immediate damage done to life and limb in your fair city. But understand: there is a growing danger, for all of us; from Landry to the far corners of the world. And it will not do for any of us to turn a blind eye when our own homelands are temporarily spared immediate danger. Whatever threat is arising, it will soon imperil all of us, if not dealt with."

"Speaking of which, were you able to find out anything more about who's behind all of this?" Ademo asked.

"No, I'm afraid not. Though, as I expected was the case, I do know now that whoever's behind this is well versed in the ways of the Deep Mathematics. It was no chance encounter between these marauders and the people of Kiraboa. The crew had a map that led them straight there. And only Priolancy could produce that."

"And you know this how?" Banon asked.

"I saw it with my own eyes. And it was no ordinary map. It included probability tables," Muirik replied.

While the others pondered how Muirik had managed to see the map, Kyanessa spoke up.

"Muirik," she began, looking thoughtful, "I thought it was only the Vaidas who had such knowledge. I hate to ask this... but, is it possible one of your brethren may be responsible for all of this?"

Muirik looked pensive, staring off into the distance. "That is a logical inference. And you are correct, Kyanessa. As far as we know it is only those trained in the ways of the Movadem who have access to such knowledge. We've carefully guarded it for generations and generations now, lest it fall into the hands of those with the wrong intentions.

"But, you see, Vaidas all belong to various houses, which we call monats – and all Vaidas must give an account of themselves, on a regular basis, to each monat leader, whom we call the prida. We have made inquiries, and there are no Vaidas unaccounted for. Hence, the mystery. Unfortunately, I am no closer to knowing who's responsible now than I was the last time we spoke."

"But isn't it possible that one of the Vaidas could be acting behind his prida's back?" Banon asked.

"Possible? Yes. But unlikely. A prida takes that responsibility very seriously. And there would be signs if a Vaida were delving into Priolancy like this."

There was a pause in the conversation as each member of the group considered Muirik's words. Then Banon asked a question.

"So where will the marauders be heading next? Grantin? Or farther east?"

"I can't know for sure, but it may very well be that they make their way to Criesca, even as we are," Muirik replied.

Seeing Ademo's dismay, the old Vaida added. "Don't worry, Ademo. Criesca is a large continent. It's very unlikely that we'll cross paths with them; especially considering the place I have in mind for us to make landing."

"What makes you think they're headed for Criesca?" Banon asked, still with a tinge of skepticism.

"I can't know for sure, but I assume that may be the case because, according to the map I saw, that was where they began their journey to Kiraboa. They left from the eastern seaport of Trintell. I doubt they will sail very far east. More likely they will return to receive orders from whomever sent them in the first place."

"Are you saying that whoever's behind this is also somewhere in Criesca?" Banon asked.

"Quite possible, yes," Muirik replied.

"Well then, isn't it foolishness to head there ourselves? Aren't we headed into the lion's den, as it were?" Banon asked.

"Again, Criesca is a large continent. So I wouldn't fear that too much. Besides, more importantly, we really do need to get Ademo to Monat Wisterlac, which is the monat I belong to. There is council for us there that could greatly aid us in this matter," Muirik replied, sounding resolved. "Now, if you don't mind," he added, "I would like some breakfast. That was a rather long journey for me."

53

Later that day Ademo drifted up from below deck to gaze out over the ocean. It was a mostly clear afternoon, with only a few wispy clouds rolling overhead. The environment reminded him of Kiraboa, even if it was colder than he was used to. He had missed the ocean while they were in the mountains, and it brought him some comfort to look upon it now. After a few moments he was joined by Muirik. The old Vaida smiled as he stood next to him.

"Ademo, how are you holding up?" the Vaida asked.

"Well enough, thank you, Muirik."

"Glad to hear it. You are a brave man to be handling this the way you are."

Ademo looked over at the Vaida with questioning eyes. He certainly didn't feel brave.

"Ademo, I meant to ask you: have you by chance had any more dreams like the ones you shared from your Placca?"

Ademo shook his head. "No, nothing like that. Just nightmares from the invasion of the island."

Muirik nodded, a sympathetic expression written across his features. "Well, if you do have any dreams that seem... *revelatory* in that way, be sure to share them. They may be important."

Ademo nodded in agreement. "Muirik, I had a question about the Lord's Shield, the fogbank that encircles Kiraboa... Now that it's been breached, is that way still barred? Or can others find it now?"

"A good question, Ademo. I'm afraid I'm not sure of the answer, though. The implications of recent events are... unpredictable. No one really knows what will happen until after the fact. That's why we Vaidas are so careful with the knowledge. It's dangerous."

"So the fog, and the hiddenness of the island... is that all related to what happened before, with the ancients and their – what did you call them?"

"Experiments?"

"Yes, that was it. Experiments."

"Most certainly. You see, it's more than just a fogbank that kept the island hidden. After all, fog can be penetrated if you simply sail through it. No, there was more than that behind the mysterious location of Kiraboa. When boats used to sail that way, strange things would happen."

"Strange how?" Ademo asked, intrigued.

"Well, sometimes the ship's navigation would reverse itself, so that a boat would find it was heading west when it had been heading east. Sometimes violent storms would rise up at just the moment a ship entered the fog, almost as if there were some sort of interaction going on between the vessel and the fog."

"Are you saying the fog itself was... was aware somehow?" Ademo asked, straining his brain to make sense of what he was being told.

"No, not like that exactly. Think of it like this: you know what happens when you pour water on hot rocks, don't you?"

Ademo nodded. "Sure. Steam."

"Exactly, the mixture of the two elements creates a reaction. I'm saying something similar happens when boats enter the fogbank around Kiraboa. At least... that's what used to happen. As I say, now that the marauders have found a way through, via the Deep Math, who knows what the implications will be. Could be the same as before, could be vastly different."

Ademo took in what Muirik said, ruminated on it for a few moments. Then his thoughts turned to a familiar – though maddening – question: where was his mother? And what was her condition? The not knowing was tormenting indeed.

Seeing the troubled look come over Ademo, Muirik asked: "What is it, Ademo?"

Ademo shook his head. "Just thinking about my mother again. Wondering where she is. And trying not to..."

"Think the worst?" Muirik said, completing what Ademo didn't really even want to voice.

Ademo nodded, his damp eyes focused on some random point out on the water.

Muirik sighed, drew breath. "Not knowing the fate of someone you care deeply about is indeed difficult to deal with. I am not immune to that experience myself. But we must take solace that there is still hope."

"After seeing how callous those marauders were with the villagers... how easily they killed..."

"I know. That kind of flippancy is hard to deal with. But, in your mother's case, they may be much more cautious. After all, she is their greatest link to you."

"You're saying they'd keep her alive as... what, as bait?"

Muirik shrugged. "Perhaps. Or as a bargaining chip. Or simply because, while you still roam about Eiasa, she is worth much more to them alive than not. So don't lose hope, Ademo. Not while hope still exists."

54

The next morning brought overcast skies. Ademo walked above deck with Banon, to find Grinnig speaking with Kyanessa and Muirik. Ademo drew a blanket about his shoulders and commented on the cooler, grey environ they found themselves in. Grinnig explained that they had turned further north, late the previous evening, according to Muirik's instruction.

Ademo was about to follow Kyanessa below deck to help prepare breakfast, when Banon called out from the back of the boat. The others, sensing alarm in the Landrite's voice, quickly moved to join him.

"What is it?" Grinnig asked. "Are those shaklens

back?"

"Shaklens? No one mentioned you'd seen shaklens," Muirik said, with some gravity.

"No. It's a ship. A large one, heading straight towards us," Banon said, pointing at a speck on the horizon.

"How can you be sure of that from this distance?" Kyanessa asked, straining to see.

"He's right," Muirik concurred, with his equally adept eyesight. "And not just any ship. It's one of the marauding warships."

Even Banon was impressed with this, as he couldn't make out quite that detail from this distance.

"Are you sure?" Ademo asked, realizing the question sounded silly the moment he uttered it.

"Unmistakably, I'm afraid," Muirik said. "Grinnig, I suggest we turn due north. Perhaps they haven't seen us yet, and we can hide behind the low-hanging cloud that is gathering over there."

The captain nodded his head, his mustache shaking in agreement, as he shuffled off to make the adjustment in their course.

There was a stiff breeze that morning, blowing from behind them, and once the sails were fully extended, Grinnig's small fishing vessel darted across the water with speed.

Ademo looked to where they were headed, and saw that Muirik was right: it did look like it was about to rain there, if it wasn't already. The question was whether or not the trailing marauders had seen them already, and whether or not the cloud cover would suffice to hide them if they hadn't yet been spotted.

Hopes were quickly dashed, however. They were barely two minutes into their new course when Banon pointed and said the marauders' vessel was turning to follow. Not only that, but the trailing vessel was gaining on them, quickly. Ten minutes later and even those on board with less keen eyesight could make out the shape of the ship, as it chased them in dogged pursuit.

Banon rushed to where Muirik and Grinnig stood on the bow. "Do you think we'll be able to lose them in the weather ahead?" he asked, pointing northward, where sheets of rain could now be seen falling.

"I don't know," Grinnig responded, looking behind as the trailing vessel continued to close on them. "We'll soon find out."

Minutes passed and the marauding vessel was even closer, with details clearly visible to the naked eye. Ademo felt a flood of horror when he recognized the black flag with its crimson and silver insignia, snapping in the brisk wind.

"It's no good," Grinnig called out, "the weather ahead is moving northward as well. We'll not catch it before that trailing ship catches us. Any other ideas, Muirik? Anyone?"

The fact that a seasoned fisherman was asking them for advice didn't exactly lend confidence to the younger members of the crew. All three exchanged nervous glances.

Suddenly there was a loud, concussive bang that erupted from behind them, followed by a strange whining sound. Everyone turned to look. Seconds later a sphere the size of a man's head splashed into the water a hundred feet behind them.

All eyes were on the marauding ship now. Just then there was another bang, as smoke exploded off the marauding ship's bow. Another one of those spherical projectiles tore into the water just behind them, only moments later.

"What kind of devilry is this? What weapons are they using?" Banon asked, as smoke ambled towards the sky from the deck of the marauding ship.

"They're called canons," Muirik said, looking more stern than troubled.

"But what in the world causes the explosions that propel those iron balls like that? The force must be immense!"

"Indeed it is, Banon. No doubt a kind of dynamite is at work."

"Dynamite?" Banon said, almost as if he hadn't heard the Vaida quite right. "But that kind of thing hasn't existed in the world since..."

"Since the Disintegration," Kyanessa said, finishing his thought.

"Exactly. So how..."

"Apparently new days are upon us, Banon," Muirik said. "No doubt the handiwork of our enemy."

Just then another explosion concussed across the waters, and only seconds later a cannonball splashed just off of their port side, sending water across the bow.

Ducking, Banon shouted: "Those shots are getting closer to us all the time. We'll be dead in the water even before they catch us!"

Another canon boom and its accompanying whine rang out to testify to this fact. By now the sound was beginning to give Kyanessa shivers. She stood close to Ademo, both of them with their mouths hanging half open in shock and dismay. The cannonball splashed into the surface of the water to their starboard side this time.

"We must do something!" Banon shouted, running to where Grinnig stood by the wheel.

The small, wiry captain threw up his hands and said: "I'm open to suggestions!"

Just then Muirik moved to the rear of the boat, and stepped up onto the very edge of the rail, balancing on the precarious ledge with what appeared to be relative ease. The others watched as he drew his arms apart, until they were at ninety degrees from his side, at shoulder height. The position looked almost prayerful. That's exactly what Banon assumed Muirik was up to.

"Is that all that there's left to do? To call upon the mercy of the gods?" Banon exclaimed, sounding desperate.

No one responded to Banon's rhetorical question. They merely stared at the figure of Muirik, who was standing completely still, his arms held out, palms facing the trailing vessel.

Just then yet another thunderclap was heard, and a cannonball crashed down just *in front* of them. The marauders were now overshooting them. Not a good sign. They all knew it was only a matter of time before the marauders got the distance right.

Even as they prepared themselves for another firing of the canon, a strange phenomena began to occur. Ademo noticed it first, and silently pointed towards the water between them and the trailing vessel.

The waters there had begun to circle around, and a depression was forming on the surface. Muirik continued to stand completely still, seemingly deep in concentration. All eyes were glued to the water now, as the depression grew deeper, and the waters seemed to churn faster around it, spiraling inward.

Soon Grinnig's boat began to feel the tug of the whirlpool, and the drag slowed their progress. The circumstances were much more dire for the marauding vessel. The whirlpool was now spinning wildly, a deep depression forming immediately in the path of the warship.

Whether or not the marauding crew tried evasive maneuvers was difficult to tell. Either way, there was so little time. Their momentum carried them straight into the path of the churning whirlpool. Aboard Grinnig's boat, the younger companions watched in speechless awe as the whirlpool opened even wider, seemingly swallowing the marauding ship whole.

Seconds later it had disappeared entirely from view.

With the others gazing in wonderment, Grinnig was desperately trying to fight the pull of the whirlpool. All of their forward progress had been neutralized, and they were beginning to be sucked backward.

The captain was about to call out to Muirik, who was still standing in the same motionless position at the edge of the boat, when he noticed the whirlpool's grip began to lessen. Soon the depression in the water was more shallow. And seconds after that the once swirling waters were nearly calm, almost as if the strange phenomena in the water had never occurred.

55

Awaking before his two companions, Ademo quietly climbed the stairs to the deck and stepped into the cold, misty morning, where the sun was only palely penetrating the murky darkness. He found Muirik staring out into the featureless waters, seemingly deep in thought. Hearing Ademo approach, the Vaida turned to greet him.

The two stood for several minutes, almost like old friends, leaning over the rails, letting thoughts crystallize. Eventually Ademo got around to asking a question he'd been pondering since the day before, when Muirik had worked his seeming magic in sinking the enemy ship.

"Muirik, can I ask you a question?"

"Of course, my friend," the Vaida responded.

"I'm trying to understand how the Deep Math works. And I'm wondering: if you're able to manipulate reality to the point when you can sink a full size enemy warship like you did yesterday, then..."

"Then why don't I use such tactics more often?"

"Yes. The Deep Math: it's such a powerful force. And I'm guessing if you can do that, that you can do other things to help us on our journey as well."

"Well, there are limits to my capabilities, Ademo. But your point is well taken. There is certainly more I *could* do. But, as I mentioned in passing before, you must understand that these kinds of actions are not without cost. For one, every time you do something like that you disturb the fabric of reality's structure, creating unintended consequences. That alone is enough to prevent one from doing such things, unless the most dire circumstances require it."

"Circumstances like yesterday, when we were all in mortal danger."

"Precisely. But there is a second reason as well: our enemy, who still remains unknown, is most likely much more adept in these matters than me. And my guess is that he or she can read the traces of my actions, like you or I can observe ripples in a disturbed pool of water."

"You mean he could see the whirlpool you created yesterday?"

Muirik grinned. "No, I didn't mean that literally. I meant it as an analogy. You see, there are traces left, traces in the numbers. And those can be discerned, if one knows what to look for. Do you understand what I mean?"

Ademo shrugged. "I think so. Sort of. The whole affair seems otherworldly. But that's nothing new for me these days."

Muirik smiled kindly, reached out to put his hand on Ademo's shoulder. "I suppose not," Muirik agreed. "And yet, you have handled all these revelations remarkably well."

"One thing I definitely don't understand in all of this, though, is what possible role I am to play. To be honest, I've felt quite useless most of the time. And I rely almost completely on you, and on Banon and Kyanessa. Without any of you I wouldn't have even gotten this far. So, if this enemy you speak of is as powerful as you say, what possible importance can I hold to him? And what possible help can I offer any of you who would resist him?"

Muirik smiled again, sympathetically. "I can understand how you must feel, Ademo. But know this: the numbers don't lie. And if our enemy is convinced of your significance, then so am I. And hopefully, once we reach Monat Wisterlac, we'll be able to understand a little more of why."

"Muirik, you mentioned that Vaidas also have

leaders, those you called pridas. Does that mean you also report to a prida?"

"Indeed," Muirik said, nodding his head up and down demonstrably. " Indeed I do. My prida has been the head of Monat Wisterlac for longer than I've been alive. He is considered by many, including me, to be one of the wisest of all the Vaidas. His aid will be invaluable to us, I am sure."

That thought seemed to cheer Ademo some. "It's hard to imagine someone wiser than you, Muirik."

"Oh, don't be fooled, my young friend. Wisdom is like a disappearing sun on the horizon. It travels farther than any of us can see with our eyes alone. Trust me when I say that my prida's knowledge and wisdom greatly exceed my own."

"If it is you that says so, Muirik, then I will believe it. But only because it's you who says it."

Muirik smiled again, chuckled lightly, as they both gazed out on the endless waters.

56

The next two days passed without incident. It was on the morn of the day after that when Banon, he with his eagle eyes, called out to the others from the bow of the ship. His one spoken word was a relief to all of them.

"Land!"

As the ship drew closer to shore, it was clear they were headed for a cove lined with a pebbly shoreline; one that butted up against a sloping, moss-covered hill, populated by strange, half-tall trees. These trees seemed permanently bent backward by the wind that often swept over them. The tree cover carried on up the hill, where it disappeared into mist.

Ademo felt his spirits sink a little. This land, though different, looked almost as wet and foggy as Landry. And it made him yearn for the clear, warm mornings of Kiraboa.

They each thanked Grinnig, who smiled back at them through his bushy mustache. As Ademo and his two younger companions stepped through knee deep water that led to the shore, Muirik turned to speak one more time with Muirik, apparently giving him instructions. Grinnig nodded and the two men embraced. By the time they each stepped onto the pale, pebbly sands, Grinnig had already turned his boat around and was headed out to sea. He waved his arms widely above his head and the others waved back.

Without speaking, Muirik led them onto a narrow trail that wound through the tree cover and up the hillside. Before long the tops of even these half-tall trees were disappearing into the clouds that swirled just overhead, almost within reach. Though it wasn't raining, Ademo felt himself quickly becoming damp as they stepped through the cold, moist air.

It was past lunchtime when they at last felt the

ground flatten out, and soon afterwards the half-tall trees, that Muirik called mittlespur, began to thin out. An hour later they found themselves emerging from the low hanging cloud cover. Ademo smiled when he beheld a vista of rolling green hills stretching out before them. The sky was bright and blue, the hillside littered with a scattering of lime-green, broad-leafed trees.

When Muirik signaled they would stop to eat, each opened his or her pack to retrieve provisions. It was a meager meal of bread, dried meat, and water, but the pleasant vista made the food go down pleasantly. As they sat looking out over the rolling hills, Banon pointed off in the distance.

"Are those horses over there, Muirik?"

"Over where?" Kyanessa asked, glancing in the direction Banon had pointed.

"Indeed they are, my young friend. And not just any breed of horses, either. Those are the wild Faring; a hearty breed that can run as swiftly as a derecho, for days on end if need be."

"Too bad they couldn't bear us for a while," Banon said, "we'd make it to your monat in double-time."

"Double-time?" Muirik said. "More like fourfold time, I'd say. Believe me, those majestic four-legged friends make it seem as if the ground were flying by below you. And as far as your wish goes, Banon, that is precisely my aim. And perhaps these noble Farings will do just that, if we ask them just so."

With that the Vaida stood up, put his fingers to his

mouth, and let out a loud whistle. The sound was impressively loud, though not painfully so. But Ademo thought it unlikely that these beasts, so far away that he couldn't even quite see them, would be able to hear the call.

Muirik only whistled once, content then to sit back down and drink some more of his water. The three younger companions exchanged glances but didn't say anything.

It was only a few minutes later that Ademo began to feel a rhythmic thumping in the grassy ground beneath him. And then, soon after, four majestic steeds came thundering into view over the crest of a neighboring hill. Each of the companions rose to greet the approaching horses.

Each was a different color. One, whose bronzed hide almost appeared metallic in the sunlight, immediately trotted up to Kyanessa. Kyanessa, apparently familiar with such beasts, smiled and stroked the neck of the giant, thick legged horse. Another, as black as night, nuzzled up next to Muirik, and the Vaida greeted him almost like an old friend.

The two remaining horses were hazel brown and white, respectively. Banon, apparently also familiar with such animals, strode up to the white one, reached up to stroke its noble mane.

Ademo stood with his mouth agape. He'd never in his life beheld such majestic beasts. But as immense and impressive as they appeared, Ademo thought it highly unlikely they would permit any other being to ride on their backs.

But no sooner had Ademo thought this than both Muirik and Kyanessa limberly leapt onto the backs of the beasts beside them. Both horses neighed and stomped their feet a little, but seemed content enough.

Banon decided to follow his friends lead, and began to pull himself up onto the back of the white steed. The Faring, however, seemed to have other ideas, stepping sideways and bowing its had in such a way as to elude Banon's grasp. As a result the lean, lanky blonde crashed hard onto the grassy hillside, which thankfully, was rather forgiving.

Kyanessa put her hand to her mouth and laughed out loud. Ademo saw that Muirik was smiling too, but managing to muffle any laughter. Banon pulled himself to his feet, brushing mud and grass from his pants, glaring towards Kyanessa, who was still trying mightily to stop laughing, though clearly loosing the battle.

"Perhaps our hazel-colored friend will bear you better, Banon," Muirik commented, in a friendly but knowing tone.

The frustrated Landrite looked at Muirik, realizing it was a suggestion as much as a comment, and moved silently over to the brown horse. As he placed his hand on the animal it seemed content to stand still. Banon placed his other hand over its back, and still the horse stood its ground.

Banon then pulled himself up, in one fell swoop, perhaps fearful that if he did so too nonchalantly, he would face the prospect of being spilled a second time. But this brown beast seemed prepared to bear him without protest, only neighing slightly once Banon was comfortably seated on its back.

Then the others turned to look towards Ademo. His expression betrayed his fear and discomfort.

"Ah, sorry to say, but we weren't blessed with such fair beasts in Kiraboa. So if you think I'm going to be able to ride one, well..."

Muirik smiled and gently nudged at his horse's side, unctioning the beast over towards Ademo.

"Fear not, Ademo. For now, because time is precious, I will bear you with me. But perhaps, before our journey is through, you will learn to ride one of these wonderful steeds. It is quite a thrill, I assure you."

Ademo didn't think that likely, but was happy that such a task wasn't being required of him for the time-being. He held up his hand to grasp Muirik's forearm, and the Vaida pulled him up with one swift tug, proving stronger than he looked. Ademo, feeling a little sheepish, dug his feet into the sides of his horse, and hung onto Muirik as if they were already galloping at great speed.

Muirik smiled again, encouraging Ademo to grip a little less firmly. "Once we're moving you'll find it's actually easier if you just let momentum hold you in place, Ademo. But enough talk, such tasks are best learned in full flight."

And with that the old Vaida shouted out an

enthusiastic whooping sound.

In what felt to Ademo like half a heartbeat, the great black steed suddenly leapt into full gallop. The other horses, including the riderless white steed, almost immediately leapt into pursuit, neighing loudly in the process.

As they chased over the hillside, the ground blurring beneath his feet, a startled Ademo glanced over to see his two young friends galloping beside them, with broad smiles upon their faces.

57

With the aid of their steeds' swift feet the companions galloped over leagues of Criescan ground that day. The rolling hills spilled out onto a fertile plain, filled with apple orchards, and eventually they came to a wide river, which Muirik announced as the Realmwinder. They followed this westward until dark began to gather around them.

Off to the still distant west, Ademo could see another set of hills rising up, these were the slopes that lay at the feet of the famed Jasperius Mountains. Ademo could just make out a few of those towering peaks, snow-capped in the very hazy distance. According to Muirik, Monat Wisterlac lay hidden somewhere in the deep folds of that impressive range.

As they sat around a campfire later that evening, munching on a rabbit caught by Kyanessa, Banon asked Muirik if there were no towns on this eastern side of Criesca.

"Indeed there are," the Vaida responded. "To the south of us, just beyond that rise over there, lies Hueron. And to the north, less than half a day's ride, is Filamor. Both are good sized cities. But I've deliberately chosen a route that keeps us out of the eyesight of others."

"Why?" Kyanessa asked. "You think there are those that serve our enemy in such places?"

"Perhaps. I really don't know. He has us at a disadvantage that way. I don't know how far his reach is, or how many serve his evil cause. Better to be safe than sorry, however. So I think we best keep to this course."

"So do people in these neighboring towns know of Monat Wisterlac's location?" Ademo asked.

"No. It's location is secret, to all but the Vaidas and a few trusted others," Muirik said.

"But how is that possible? Surely someone would stumble upon its location sooner or later," Banon said.

"If that were left to its natural course, then yes, I suppose you're right, Banon. Someone would inevitably stumble upon it. After all, it's no small structure. But because the Monat's location is a closely guarded secret, we Vaidas employ a few... techniques, to keep it that way."

"Magic you mean?" Banon said, sounding half

skeptical and half intrigued.

"Some call it that, yes. But as I've said before, it is really a manipulation of the Deep Math."

"So there is nothing supernatural about it?" Banon asked.

"Well... let's just say that what one *calls* it is relative to one's understanding of the complexity of the natural order. What some would no doubt call *supernatural* is, in this case, a purely natural phenomenon. Even if it is 'magical' to behold," Muirik said, smiling and winking.

Banon found himself nodding, but felt no clearer for the effort of his question.

They awoke the next morning to crisp, clear air. Ademo sat up from the cold, hard ground to see Muirik, already awake, standing next to the white horse. It appeared almost as if the Vaida was speaking with the majestic animal. He stroked the long main while leaning close by the steed's ear. Ademo couldn't confirm this, however, as he was out of hearing distance. As he sat up further still, Muirik turned to him.

"Ah, Ademo. Good morning. My friend and I have been waiting for you to arise. Why don't you come here for a moment?" the old Vaida said, smiling in the pale morning light.

Ademo lifted himself up, did his best to work his cold, stiff limbs, and moved over to where Muirik was standing next to the horse.

"Now, Ademo, I think it's high time we name our noble friend here, don't you agree?" Muirik asked, smiling.

Ademo nodded, still a little sleepy, though he'd slumbered long and hard.

"Excellent," Muirik added, "why don't you do the honors, then. What shall we name him?"

Muirik's eyes fell on Ademo. And in that moment the horse turned to look towards Ademo as well. Ademo sat there dumbfounded for a moment, glancing back and forth between the horse and the Vaida.

"Ummm, a name... Okay..."

"Take your time," Muirik added. "Think of the nature of this majestic steed. What names come to mind when you do that?"

Ademo turned his gaze to the animal, thought of some words that would describe it well: *white*; *large*; *dangerous*... These just wouldn't do. He knew Muirik had something more essential in mind.

"Pearlsand," Ademo said, after a moment's thought. "It's a kind of sand we see in Kiraboa, in our inland pools. It's a very pure shade of white. Kiraboans have jars of it on our eating tables. It's thought to represent essence and focus."

"Ah, *Pearlsand*. Yes, a very fitting name, Ademo. Very fitting indeed. Well, why don't you go ahead and swing up on Pearlsand's back then?"

"Sorry, do what?" Ademo asked, hesitantly.

"Go ahead now. Don't be afraid. This horse won't resist you like it resisted Banon."

"And why's that?" Ademo asked, feeling his breath becoming more labored. Somehow he knew Muirik really did intend for him to mount the back of this massive animal.

"Because the noble Faring aren't only chosen by their riders, they choose their riders as well. And from the time he pranced up to us yesterday, I knew this was to be the horse that would bear you. That's why he's been patiently galloping alongside us all this time. He's been waiting for you."

"Waiting for me..." Ademo parroted, not sure what else to say.

Muirik nodded, smiling wide. "Go on then, don't worry, he'll sit still as a stone. I promise."

If this were anyone but Muirik, Ademo would have found some excuse to return to bed. But somehow he knew that the Vaida wasn't one to refuse, not when his mind was really set on something. Besides, he didn't want to burden the rest of them unnecessarily. If they were riding, then perhaps he should try the same.

He took a deep breath, reached out to put his arm around the beast's massive neck. Then, awkwardly, he swung himself up. To his great surprise, even though Muirik had promised as much, the horse stood unmovingly beneath him. Only after a few seconds went by did Ademo finally let himself breath again.

"Now, let's take a stroll, shall we?" Muirik said, suddenly moving forward, without touching the horse. Pearlsand followed, and Ademo gasped, groping about the beast's neck for a better hold.

"Remember Ademo, just like yesterday, this is more about positioning yourself and letting the momentum of the horse's movement carry you. If you hang on too tight you'll just make it more uncomfortable for yourself, and for Pearlsand."

Ademo wasn't at all sure that he'd be more comfortable assuming a looser posture, but he took to heart Muirik's comment that doing so would be more comfortable for the horse. After seeing the horse eject Banon yesterday, he had no desire to provoke him in any manner whatsoever. So Ademo tried to sit high, only gripping the sides of the horse gently with his legs, as he'd seen the others do so deftly the day before.

No sooner had he done this than Muirik started jogging beside him. The horse, almost immediately, fell into step with the Vaida, now twisting and turning as Muirik moved around in every which way. Muirik was laughing now, and the horse seemed to contentedly follow his senseless dance. But Ademo's expression was not far from horror.

Only when Muirik finally relented and stopped – with the horse following suit – did Ademo notice that both Banon and Kyanessa were now sitting up, looking over at him with broad smiles. With the aid of Muirik's arm, Ademo swung awkwardly off the horse's back.

"Well done, Ademo. Well done. Enjoyable, wasn't it?" Muirik asked.

Ademo only nodded, in a non-committal fashion. As he walked over to the others he stole a glance back towards the horse, and noticed that it was looking his way as well. Banon and Kyanessa greeted him warmly, but Ademo didn't say much, still feeling a little faint.

After they finished their hasty breakfast, Ademo feared Muirik would ask him to ride Pearlsand for the remainder of the day. But, to his great relief, no such request came. When it was time to saddle up, Muirik held an arm out for Ademo to climb up behind him. Soon they were off, galloping over the open plain, Pearlsand content to run riderless beside them.

58

It was with foothills visible on the horizon that they began their journey that day. But by the time they stopped for the night, just after sundown, Ademo was surprised by how little closer those hills seemed. He was still having difficulty adjusting to the vast sense of scale here in Criesca. It was such a different world, by leagues, than his home on Kiraboa.

And then, as he thought about it, an even stranger fact occurred to him. The truth was that *this* land was apparently his native one; the one of his birth and descent anyway, not Kiraboa. And yet it seemed so unfamiliar, so foreign.

The next morning began the same way as the previous one. Only this time it was Muirik who awoke Ademo, before ushering him over to where Pearlsand stood, munching on dew-covered grass.

As Ademo stood next to the horse, preparing to leap on its back, he felt the massive snow white horse shift a little bit, so that he was nuzzling his long, handsome face against Ademo's. For whatever reason, it did seem Muirik was correct about one thing: this majestic beast did seem somewhat taken with him. Ademo reached out and began stroking along the horse's mane, did so for several moments, before hopping on its back.

As with the day before, Muirik led the horse around in circles, letting Ademo grow accustomed to the feel of it. Ademo could feel it working, too. He soon found himself enjoying the experience. And then, all of a sudden, Muirik said: "Hang on, Ademo!"

"What do you mean?" Ademo blurted.

Muirik then clapped his hands together, before shouting something unintelligible – to Ademo, anyway. Pearlsand seemed to understand the command perfectly, breaking out into a speedy gallop in less than a heartbeat.

At first Ademo felt every muscle in his body contract, as he used all his might in an effort to stay aboard the massive, galloping beast. But then, from a distance, Ademo heard Banon's voice call out.

"Just go with it, 'Demo. Don't fight it!"

Ademo tried putting that into practice. Though he

felt he was then using every muscle in concentration just to say loose. The horse, seeming to sense his discomfort, kept to a straight line, galloping at impressive speeds over the open plain, shrub brush and oak trees rushing past them in a blur.

As they chased over those plains Ademo began to feel himself finally relax. As it turned out, riding with Muirik *had* taught him something. And, although riding solo brought its own challenges (control being the chief one!), Ademo began to feel as if he was getting the hang of it. Pearlsand – still seeming to sense that this was all new to Ademo – began to lean slightly, before taking a long, sweeping turn back towards the others.

Soon they were back where the ride had begun. Pulling up next to Muirik, Ademo felt as if he'd passed a threshold. Sure enough, as long as he let himself go with the movement of the horse – and didn't fight it – staying aloft was manageable after all.

Ademo looked over at his young companions, saw them sitting munching on their breakfast. Kyanessa waved, and Banon smiled. Ademo nodded back before turning to look down at Muirik.

"Can we do that again?" Ademo asked, a gleam in his eye.

"Again?" Muirik said, feigning surprise. "Well, if that's what you want, Ademo, then you'll have to be the one to give the command."

Ademo nodded, thought for a moment about what Muirik had done. Then he clapped his hands together and called out a command that sounded something like – "Hiyar!"

The problem was that Ademo did these two things almost simultaneously. And as the mighty steed took off below him, Ademo found himself leaning back, his hands still in the middle of the clapping gesture. As a result he flew backwards as Pearlsand shot out like an arrow beneath him. Ademo did a backwards summersault in the air and landed in a heap on the cold, hard plain.

Feeling blood rush to his face in embarrassment, Ademo quickly jumped to his feet, knocking dirt off his pants. Off to the right Banon laughed out loud, and Kyanessa clapped him on the back in protest, feeling sorry for Ademo.

The horse had only gone a few paces it turns out, and had turned back once it felt Ademo slip out from beneath him. Ademo felt the horse nuzzle against him, as he continued to brush himself off.

Without looking over towards the others, Ademo deftly leapt onto the horse's back. This time he called out the command again, but kept his hands at his sides, holding to the horse's flanks.

Horse and rider shot off like arrows in tandem, dust rising like a cloud beneath them as they raced over the plain.

"Well, well, I do believe the islander is getting the hang of it, after all," Banon said, as he and Kyanessa watched Ademo and his steed disappear into the distance.

So it was each rider to his own steed that day, as Ademo was now confident enough riding solo beside the others.

The plains rolled on and on beneath them for most of the day. But when they emerged from a field of oaks, later that afternoon, Ademo was pleasantly surprised to see the hills were finally looking much closer.

By the time they pulled up for the night the ground beneath them was gently sloping upwards. Looking around, Ademo saw that hills now filled their vision on three sides. As the setting sun cast its purplish-orange glow over them, towering pine trees were silhouetted in the distance, where the Jasperius Mountains lay like sleeping giants.

59

Under an overcast sky the landscape was draped in almost complete darkness. Only the palest moonlight shone the way for the three Vaidas as they made their way towards Wisterlac. They had been summoned to the monat two days before, and had been on the march ever since, making the southward trek from the small hamlet of Trewin.

As they crested a small hill they saw trees encroaching upon the narrow, dirt path before them.

Normally they would have thought nothing of this. But on *this* night such a sight brought on near-claustrophobic anxiety. Nothing was said between them, though they each felt it; that nagging feeling that told them that they, the Watchers, were being watched.

The same feeling had come upon them only hours before, when the trail had led them through a wooded valley. But that was at twilight. Now the darkness pressed in around them like an oppressive force. And that made the feeling all the more intense.

Still, they walked on, willing the fear from their minds – as much as was possible. As they descended the hill the trees pressed in all the more. At the bottom was a small creek bed that gurgled with water. As they took turns crossing the narrow, wooden beam that led them to the other side of the creek, they each noticed – though made no mention of the fact – that the gurgling noise made them all the more vulnerable. Because now sound as well as sight were robbed from them; their awareness compromised by their immediate surroundings.

Normally they would not travel this way, under these conditions. Not when there was some rumored threat in the land. But, of course, it was that very threat that had them on the march. And they knew the prida would not have summoned them thusly unless that threat truly was formidable.

Such was their predicament.

Two of the brothers crossed successfully, and

turned to watch as the third navigated the beam.

Once across, that third Vaida pointed forward to the trail before them, which climbed back up yet another hill. Both of the others understood the thought behind the gesture: *Let's keep moving; this particular place doesn't at all feel safe.*

And so on they marched, pushing their pace even more, hoping that the crest of the next hill would reveal a flatter, more wide open landscape once again.

Unfortunately, they never got the chance to discover whether or not this was the case.

Nearly a hundred yards from the top of the hill, marching in close tandem, the three suddenly felt the solid ground beneath them fall way. They each flailed for purchase, but the trail, covered in leaves and brush, had hidden a large hole, dug out since last they had come this way months earlier.

And so they fell... into darkness.

When finally the ground rushed up to meet them a dozen feet below, the youngest of the three – a Vaida named Costac – cried out in agony when his ankle snapped like a twig.

The other two rushed to help him, feeling themselves bruised but otherwise unharmed. They could tell Costac was doing his best to control his volume, but even in the dim light, it was clear from the acute angle at which his foot was contorted that the break was significant.

And then they heard movement and what sounded unmistakably like laughter, coming from up above.

They each peered up and out of the narrow hole. There they saw a crowd of men, gazing down at them, smirks draped across their satisfied faces.

"Well, well..." one of them said, "what have we here? Three Vaidas in a hole? How quaint. And it looks like one of them has taken a nasty spill. Little sloppy for a supposedly surefooted Watcher, don't you think, boys? But not to worry, gents. We'll get you out of there soon enough. There's someone who's very eager to make your acquaintance."

The three Vaidas were hauled up from the hole and forced to march in an eastwardly direction, into the thick of the wood. Their captors had little sympathy for Costac's injury, and forced the other two to share the load of their injured brother the entire way.

Eventually they came to a camp. Cistern, the eldest and most experienced of the three Vaidas, did his best to assess the enemy's habitat as they came to it. But when one of their captor's caught him looking a little too closely, a swift slap to his ear forced his view forward again.

The light was low, with only a few dying campfires to light the area. Still, Cistern thought he could make out dozens of figures, moving between the various tents of the encampment. Of those tents, a few were dimly lit from within.

Presently Cistern and his two brethren were marched into what seemed to be the largest tent of all.

Inside it was high enough to stand in, and could hold two dozen men, if need be. Each corner was lit by a torch, and the shadows danced like ghosts all about them, as they were forced to their knees.

Though it had been difficult to make out much detail in the diminished light of the camp, Cistern couldn't help but notice that they'd been allowed to enter without blindfolds. From his experience, with these kinds of men, that wasn't a good sign. It suggested they weren't too worried about what details you might relay to others upon your release.

Cistern wondered if the same realization had occurred to the other two. Probably not to young Costac. And Cistern saw no reason to tell him.

The three soon found themselves alone, with what appeared to be only a single guard stationed by the entrance of the tent. Cistern thought that perhaps this might leave open the possibility for escape.

Their hands were bound behind their backs, the stiff rope already cutting deep into their wrists. But while they had been ordered to their knees, they weren't bound that way. And so perhaps they could rise, and storm the entrance – if they moved fast enough.

But then Cistern sensed a hint of movement, from directly behind them. And suddenly it occurred to him that they weren't alone, after all.

The shadows shifted ever so slightly. And then a voice, deep and cold as the night, spoke out.

"Three noble members of the Movadem, in our

very midst. Well, isn't that something... I suppose we should feel privileged."

The figure stepped out from behind them, walked around in front, shadows now casting strangely across his formidable frame.

He was a large man. One of the largest Cistern had ever seen. Tall and thickly framed. While the three of them were presently on their knees, this man would have towered over them even if they'd been standing. Dressed in crimson and black regalia, Cistern had little doubt they were kneeling before the enemy army's commander.

The man reached behind him, pulled forward a wooden chair and faced it backwards. Then he sat down, his chest pressing against the chair's back. He stared them down with a penetrating gaze.

"Now, perhaps you are expecting rough treatment, brothers. Well, fear not, that need not be the case. All I seek is one morsel of information – just one!" he said, pointing a single, long finger skyward.

And then he paused, as if for dramatic effect.

"What is the energy signature that makes it possible to cross the putrid waters of Wisterlac and enter your monat?"

Cistern remained absolutely still, though internally his heart skipped a beat. Neither of his two brothers were quite so discrete. They were both visibly taken aback by the question. And that's because, as far as they knew, besides members of the Movadem, no one else knew about the energy signatures that were at the root of Wisterlac's defenses.

Who was this enemy? And how did he know so much about Wisterlac – one of the most closely guarded secrets of the Vaidas?

Cistern swallowed deeply, but stared silently ahead, not saying a word. Costac, his young companion, was not so quiet. The young Vaida was now breathing heavily. And Cistern knew a broken ankle wasn't to blame. It was fear. Pure and simple.

Inwardly, Cistern began his meditations. Because he knew inner fortitude would soon be required like never before in his life.

"You know," the man began, leaning back further in his chair, cracking his knuckles one by one while speaking, "perhaps you're expecting me to pull out a knife at this point... Or perhaps a burning hot iron? Because surely you know I am aware of the famous resolve of the Vaidas – so determined never to share the secrets of the Movademic Order? Well... you needn't worry about that. I have no such tools. In fact, all I have is this," he said, holding out a small crystal shard.

It didn't look particularly menacing. Didn't even appear sharp enough to draw blood.

The formidable figure then leaned forward and drove the shard hard into the pliant ground, only a few feet in front of them. Their captor chuckled, noticing that Costac had reared backwards, no doubt fearing the stake would be driven into his skull.

"I know history suggests I could spend all night torturing you three to my heart's delight, and still you wouldn't reveal your secrets. I must say, part of me is very curious to put this legend to the test – especially with this one," he said, nodding in Costac's direction. "He looks as green as he is young... But, alas, time is short. So I must resort to more direct methods."

Cistern's mind was searching for the meaning behind the man's words. What method was more direct than torture? All Cistern received for his questioning was a sinister smile from the man seated in front of them. The man seemed to know that Cistern's mind was spinning, and enjoyed every moment of it.

And then, without warning, the crystal shard before them began to glow, ever so slightly. And then the glow grew brighter, and a hum began to fill the tent, rising in pitch and rippling the cloth walls all about them. And unless Costac was mistaken, he would have sworn he'd seen the vague tracings of a face in the dancing light of the shard.

And then, all three Vaidas felt their heads snap back forcefully, as some strange presence began to penetrate their skulls; reaching, grasping, groping... into the very recesses of their minds.

Cistern's chief concern had been for Costac, so new to the Movadem. He knew Costac's mind would be the first to give up the information this enemy sought. But as his own mind began to tremble under the strain, he soon realized that none of them would be able to guard their long held secret for long.

The men outside the tent turned their heads towards it when the horrid screams began to fill the night. And they smiled. This was the work of the man they served. A man apparently even Vaidas were helpless to resist.

60

Banon and Kyanessa awoke to find Ademo and Muirik nowhere in sight. Looking around the camp, Banon noticed that only three of the horses were grazing nearby. And no sooner had he noticed this than they began to hear a rhythmic thumping beneath them. Moments later the blurred figure of Ademo, riding high on a galloping Pearlsand, came thundering into view.

As Ademo pulled up only feet from them, he smiled down broadly. "Morning, friends!" he said, leaping off his horse in one quick motion.

"See, Ademo, you ride like a native Criescan already!" Kyanessa said, encouragingly.

"Careful," said Banon, "keep that up and his head won't fit within the city gates."

"City? What city?" Ademo said, tilting his head, as if trying to understand Banon's meaning.

"It's a figure of speech," Banon said, waving

dismissively.

Ademo winked at Kyanessa, having clearly understood more than what he was letting on to Banon.

"Where's Muirik?" Ademo asked.

"You haven't seen him?" Kyanessa asked Ademo.

"No, he was still asleep when I went riding."

"And how long ago was that?" she asked.

"I don't know, half an hour ago maybe."

Just then they began to hear a shuffling and what sounded like a twig snapping. Presently an oak tree off to their left began swaying.

"What the..." Banon said, reaching for his sword, his mouth hanging agape.

Then, quite suddenly, the figure of Muirik dropped from above and landed deftly on the grassy ground.

"What's he doing climbing trees?" Banon asked, resheathing his sword.

As Muirik strode over to them, he bore a more intense expression than usual.

"Good morning, friends. Have you broken fast yet?"

"No, not yet," Kyanessa replied. "Everything alright, Muirik?"

"No, I fear not. Everything is not as it should be. I suggest we make our breakfast a quick one. Today we must make haste."

"What is it? What's wrong?" Ademo asked.

"That is difficult to explain. And I don't know the

specifics myself. But the Movademic Harmony is broken. And that generally only happens when something is seriously amiss. Quick now, eat something and then let's be gone – time is of the essence."

Kyanessa was now passing around a loaf of bread and a canteen, and each one of them tore off a piece and chased it down with a quick drink. Ademo kept watching Muirik, disturbed by the solemn expression written on the Vaida's face. He hadn't seen him like this before. And things were already quite "amiss". So what omen could this foretell? Ademo shivered at the thought.

All three of the younger companions had questions unanswered. None of them knew what the Movademic Harmony referred to. But they also sensed that now was not the time to trouble the Vaida with queries; though this bothered Banon more than the other two.

They soon resumed their journey. They rode for several hours, the hills growing steeper as pine tress replaced oaks. Finally Muirik pulled up and dismounted when they reached the top of a steep ridge.

"Go ahead and take some refreshment, friends. I'll be right back," he said.

With that he walked over to one of the tallest and thickest of the pine trees, and began scampering up it, showing surprising dexterity.

The other three began munching on dried fruit as

the Vaida disappeared into the higher branches.

"Do you have any idea what he's up to?" Banon asked, looking over towards Kyanessa.

"None. Though the Vaidas have many mysterious ways," she answered.

"But you're quite sure he's in his right mind?" Banon asked.

Kyanessa glared at the lanky Landrite, dismay written over her pretty features. "His mind is more right than you could ever hope to understand, Banon. Why can't you just accept that there are many things that are simply beyond your experience; beyond your understanding. Just because you're unaware of them doesn't make them less real."

"Come on, what does he expect to see from up there? We're in the middle of a pine forest!"

"Don't you listen? Muirik said the Movademic *Harmony* was broken. Last time I checked, *harmony* refers to sound, not sight."

Banon offered her an incredulous look. "Are you trying to tell me he's climbing the tree to *listen* for something?"

"*Harmony... Sound... Listening...* Yes, it all follows, if you think about it. But what am I saying? Look who I'm talking to. Listening is clearly something you're challenged by."

Banon was about to offer some sort of retort when the branches of the tree began to shake again. A moment later Muirik dropped to the ground, as deftly as earlier.

"Any news?" Ademo asked.

"No, nothing new. But the Harmony is still incomplete. Something is definitely wrong. If you'll pass me a few morsels of food and some drink, we should be off again as soon as possible. If we keep to a swift pace we should be able to reach Monat Wisterlac by sundown."

61

The company of four took to their steeds again and rode higher into the mountains, the air growing noticeably cooler as they went. The riding soon become more difficult, as the terrain grew treacherous.

Some time later they came to a winding path of switchbacks that led them over frozen ground and patches of icy snow. Eventually they came to a point where Muirik signaled they should dismount.

"From here we will go on foot, friends."

At this news Ademo found himself sad to leave the company of his faithful steed. Pearlsand nuzzled against him as Ademo stroked his face. The others also said a brief goodbye to their horses; Kyanessa clearly just as sad as Ademo to leave behind her bronze steed.

They didn't linger too long, however. Because each of them recognized that Muirik had a spirit of haste about him. And by now even Banon was recognizing this was something to take seriously.

They fell into step as Muirik led them onto a narrow trail, bordered by tall, lavender-colored brush plants. The pines were sparse now, as they'd reached an elevation where less could grow. As they trekked along, Ademo noticed himself breathing differently, the air noticeably thinner.

The path was barely wide enough for a person to pass by, and thorny branches reminded them of that fact if they veered too far to the left or right. None of the three younger companions managed to make it through without a scratch or two. Only Muirik, with his precise steps, seemed to manage that.

After following silently for a long time, Ademo spoke up to ask why they seemed to have left the snow and ice behind them, even though they were continuing to climb.

"Yes, that's because here the ground is heated from underneath," Muirik said. "The heat comes from volcanic vents that keep the summit of Wister snow and ice free for much of the year. The snow that falls tends to melt quickly."

Eventually they came to a spot where even the narrow path seemed overgrown with a thorny shrub, standing nearly six feet tall. At this point Muirik dropped down low and, in one fluid motion, slipped into an opening of the shrub, barely two feet high. Each of the three younger companions shared a curious glance before attempting to follow.

They continued to follow their guide, now forced to crawl along the ground in order to avoid being pricked; the sharp, barbed thorns protruding every which way above and around them. It occurred to Ademo that without knowledge of this low tunnel path (if you could call it that), the prickly shrub would be virtually impassible.

Before long the way became even more treacherous, as the steep slope suddenly fell away beneath them. Realizing they had likely crested the summit – though they couldn't see beyond the lavender canopy of shrub to confirm this – they continued following Muirik, their skin now scraping uncomfortably against the nearly naked volcanic basalt beneath them.

This went on for nearly an hour, to the point where each of the three was near exhaustion. And the claustrophobic nature of their descent only added to their discomfort. While they knew the sun and sky were still there, high above the gnarled mass of prickling shrub brush, it felt like too long since they'd actually gazed upon them with their own eyes.

Then, quite suddenly, the ground leveled out and the prickly canopy came to an abrupt end. The companions rose to their feet, brushing themselves off and carefully picking at the nasty barbs that lay buried throughout their clothes.

They had emerged onto the shoreline of a lake of some sort. However, the putrid smell that rose up from the surface betrayed the fact that it didn't consist primarily of water. The liquid bore a sickly greenish-yellow hue, and a steam of some foreign gas drifted along its surface. In the very center of the steamy, sickly stew, lay a shallow island, hosting not a single living thing. Ademo found the scene thoroughly depressing.

A steep rim rose up all around the shore of the circular, acidic lake. Both Banon and Kyanessa recognized this place as the crater dome of a volcano.

"Oh, what is that smell? It's horrible!" Kyanessa asked, pinching her nose.

"A steaming acid, my dear. And it is as dangerous as it is repulsive," Muirik replied. "Be advised: if your skin were to come into contact with it, it would dissolve to the bone. I bid you welcome to Wisterlac."

"Lovely," Banon commented. "But no worries, Muirik, I don't think any of us is planning to get too close. The odor takes care of that."

"I'm sure you have no natural inclination to get too close, Banon. But, you see, our path takes us directly across this lake, to that island in the center," Muirik said, pointing.

"What?" Banon said, incredulously.

"Yes. Now if you'll each follow me, it's important that we stay close together. The path will be narrow and will only extend a few feet in either direction. So it's important that we stick together until we reach the island."

With that Muirik moved towards the shore. Ademo thought, just for a moment, that perhaps their faithful guide had – quite suddenly and unexpectedly – gone mad. He gasped as Muirik didn't slow his stride, but moved to step directly into the murky Wisterlac stew.

But then, surprisingly (to say the least), when Muirik's foot fell it landed on a narrow patch of land that suddenly extended from the shore, a few feet out into the acidic lake. Muirik walked another two steps, and a little more path suddenly appeared in front of him.

At this point the old Vaida turned and smiled. "Come, my friends. As you can see, there is a way, though it is a bit of a tricky one. So stay close behind me. Come on, Kyanessa, you next. Then Ademo. And then Banon. Quickly now, if you will, time is of the essence," Muirik said, waving them forward.

Each of the three younger companions shared an *are you serious?* glance amongst themselves. And then Kyanessa did as Muirik asked, stepping out onto the path, the stench from the steamy, acidic stew nearly overwhelming.

"Now, as we walk on, you two fellows will need to fall into line directly behind us. Just a warning: the path will not linger long," Muirik said.

With that the Vaida waved them forward again, as he stepped farther out into the lake – a new segment of path suddenly manifesting just a moment before his foot would have plunged into the acidic stew.

Ademo followed next, with Banon close behind.

Then Muirik said: "On we go then. Remember,

stay close!"

Banon, taking up the rear, couldn't believe what he was seeing. But he forced himself not to think too much about it, as staying on the narrow path demanded all of his concentration. When he glanced behind him he saw the path disappearing into nothingness again. The lanky Landrite gulped and turned his gaze forward, promising himself he wouldn't look back until they'd reached the island in the middle of the putrid, steaming, cesspool of a lake.

As they followed close behind Muirik, Ademo glanced towards the island ahead, wondering what feat of bravery would be demanded of them next. As he searched along the rocky surface of the island he couldn't make out anything of import; no structure, no trail – nothing. It was just a flat piece of rock rising only a few feet above the surface of the yellowy-green lake.

But then, something quite extraordinary happened. Even as he kept his gaze on the flat island, he began to notice a faint outline appear. At first it was a hazy sight, as if he was seeing a structure through a thick fog. As they got even closer to the middle of the lake, the hazy picture continued to solidify. And it was no small structure he was seeing materialize before his very eyes. It was a large dome, rising up and sloping over the surface of the island. His mouth hung open as they walked on, the impressive structure now seeming so solid that it was hard to believe that only moments before it had been nearly invisible.

Ademo caught a glimpse of Kyanessa's profile and saw the look of astonishment written upon it. He also heard a gasp of surprise come from the Landrite behind him.

Just that moment Muirik turned his head around, a knowing smile draped across his face. He winked once towards Ademo, before turning to face forward again.

As the company marched the last few paces and stepped foot onto the hard, rocky ground of the island, an arched door, made of a material that looked simultaneously natural and not, slid aside with relative ease, and out stepped two grey robed men, one small and slender, the other tall and broad-shouldered.

"Tiamoc; Crion," Muirik said, embracing each of them, "may I introduce my band of friends: this is Kyanessa, Ademo, and Banon," Muirik said, gesturing towards each as he said their names.

The two men stepped forward and shook hands with the three younger companions. Ademo couldn't help but notice how they seemed to regard him strangely, almost as if they were shaking hands with a ghost. Kyanessa and Banon noticed it too, and exchanged a glance.

"My brethren, what news? The harmony is broken. What ill sign is this?" Muirik asked, a concerned look cast across his face.

Both of Muirik's colleagues sagged a little, dropping their heads when Muirik asked the question.

Then Tiamoc, the smaller of the two, looked up and said: "Ill news indeed. Three of our brothers are dead. Murdered."

"*What?*" Muirik said, his mouth hanging open and his eyes pained. "Which brothers?"

"Cistern, Georn, and Costac," Tiamoc replied, solemnly.

Muirik took this in silently, though his face betrayed heartache. News of Cistern's passing was of particular grief for him; for the two had been friends since they were young men.

After taking a moment to compose himself, he asked in a quiet voice: "Do we know who is responsible?"

Both shook their heads, then Tiamoc added: "Their... bodies... were discovered by Hadlan and Birnce, as they made their way here. The bodies were lain out on the path, for all to see – almost as if whoever did this meant for us to find them; as if they knew Vaidas were trekking to Wisterlac, and would stumble across the fallen."

"But who could know our movements, our plans, so well?"

"Who indeed," Tiamoc added, solemnly. Then after a moment he added: "The prida has convened a meeting for this evening, and will be greatly relieved to know you have arrived safely and will join us, Muirik. But let us show you friends to their rooms. They are no doubt fatigued from the long journey you've all made."

62

Later that evening Ademo, Banon and Kyanessa were sitting around a table in Ademo's arched, windowless room, silent and deep in thought. They hadn't seen Muirik for several hours, as he had left earlier to meet with the rest of the Vaidan council. The mood in the minimally decorated room was somber, it being clear that whoever had been hunting down Ademo was likely also responsible for the deaths of the three Vaidas.

Eventually the silence was broken by a knock at the door. Ademo looked to the others, then rose to answer it. It was Tiamoc, the diminutive Vaida they'd met earlier. He bowed slightly and Ademo, awkwardly, tried to mimic the gesture.

"Muirik asked me to pass on a message to the three of you. The council is still meeting, and will likely do so well into the night. So he bids you a good night's rest, and says he will come for you in the morning, when you will have the opportunity to speak before the rest of the council."

"Oh, okay. Thank you, Tiamoc," Ademo replied.

The Vaida bowed and retreated back into the corridor. Ademo closed the door and turned to the others.

"We'll speak before the council of Vaidas? What will we say?" Ademo asked.

"Not 'we'. *You*." Banon said, pointing towards Ademo. "Whether you like it or not, Ademo, he meant you, and you alone, will address the council."

Ademo thumped Banon on the back, playfully, trying to downplay the Landrite's comment. "Come on, get off it. I'm sure he meant all of us," Ademo said.

Kyanessa leaned forward, gave a reassuring smile, sensing Ademo's unease. "Banon's right, 'Demo. It's you they mean to hear from. You saw how Tiamoc and Crion looked at you when we three were introduced. It was like you were a character from a story or something. They could hardly believe their eyes."

"Well, truth be told," Ademo said, "I did notice that. Which makes me all the more positive I'm bound to disappoint them. I mean, what do I possibly have to offer? I don't know any more than the two of you, less even!"

"Just tell them what you *do* know, 'Demo. Muirik probably just wants them to hear your tale first-hand," Kyanessa said, touching his shoulder reassuringly.

"She's right, 'Demo. Don't sweat it. If these Vaidas really are as wise as they claim to be, then they'll know the situation. And they won't expect the unreasonable."

Ademo looked into both his friends eyes, did his best to draw strength from their words and their support, though the feeling of mistaken identity stayed with him well into the night.

While the three companions were talking amongst themselves, the Vaidan council was taking place in the Centrarium. The Centrarium was a large, elliptic paraboloid-shaped chamber located at the very center of the Wisterlac dome. The architecture was simple, and clean. The chamber was largely without detail except for the Movademic insignia stenciled high above them in the very center of the roof.

The Vaidas, all dressed in their traditional grey, hooded robes, were gathered together, seated in raked, circular rows. The mood in the large room was tense, and confusion abounded.

After other formalities had been dealt with, a tall, slender brother named Mossic, who's bald head made his thick, black eyebrows seem all the more pronounced, spoke a question that was on all their minds.

"It would seem the most pertinent question for us to answer is: who is ultimately behind this? Who could possibly be entertaining such expansionist tendencies?"

"Expansionist tendencies?" Lensing, a brother with golden brown skin and bronze hair mimicked, with clear skepticism. "Do we know that's what this is really about – a leader somewhere with *expansionist tendencies*?"

"Doesn't it seem evident that this is the ultimate

desire?" Mossic continued. "To remove us as a factor in order to grow in power, perhaps unchecked?"

Then a lean and muscular Vaida named Jian chimed in: "But what leader would even see us as such a threat? We have been discrete in our dealings with the outer world. They would have no reason to assume we would be a major obstacle to their aims. In fact, getting involved in political disagreements and border skirmishes is not even within our Movademic purview."

"*Border skirmishes*? I think this is a little more than that!" Mossic called out, sounding tense.

"Fair enough. But please see my point, and it is twofold. One: who would have enough knowledge of our ways to see us as a threat? And two: even if they did know of our potential strength, surely they would also know then that politics are something we steer clear of."

"The present emperor of Junderland might very well have such intentions," said another of the Vaidas, a thick-set man named Brellwick. "He and his people have long held us in contempt, often banning us from their lands when identified. And only last year he started a war with their neighbors in Truatia. What's to say he doesn't plan to trump his success with the domination of other lands and peoples?"

"First of all, there has long been a land dispute between the Junderlanders and the Truatians," Jian replied. "As you well know, this goes back generations, ever since the Truatians first declared independence from Junderland four decades ago. I don't believe their particular war is indicative of "*expansionist tendencies*". And it's not only the Vaidas the Junderlanders are prejudiced against. They would prefer to have their lands free of all foreigners, period. That prejudice, of course, goes all the way back to the Disintegration."

Then a voice that would have been familiar to Ademo and his friends entered the fray. It was the calm, clear voice of Muirik.

"I believe Jian is right. The emperor of Junderland is not the enemy we seek. The enemy who has brought war to us has knowledge that no king or emperor alone could hope to obtain.

"Besides, we keep close tabs on the leaders of various lands, and no warning signs on this scale have come to us. So I would suggest that whoever this ultimate enemy is, he has existed in shadow up until recently. He has trodden lightly, so as not to expose his identity, waiting for this particular time, this particular moment in history, to make his move."

"It does seem that whoever this enemy is, he has knowledge on the Movademic level," Lensing added.

"And yet, as per our code of conduct, all Vaidas in the world are asonded for," said yet another brother, a man named Oria, who's penetrating, sky-blue eyes contrasted starkly with his nearly translucent skin. "So who – besides a Vaida – could possibly obtain this kind of knowledge? All remnants of Priolancy have been destroyed outside our shared community trust."

"Or so we thought..." said Lensing, ominously.

63

Ademo was in the middle of a deep, dreamless sleep when the knock came at his door. At first he dreamed it was a bird pecking at his skull. He tried to brush it away, to no avail. When it persisted he slowly came to the realization that he wasn't dreaming, but that there was someone at the door.

Ademo sat up, rubbed his eyes, then rushed over to the door. When he opened it he found Tiamoc, smiling back at him in a friendly but apologetic way.

"Hello, Ademo. So sorry to wake you in the middle of the night like this, but you've been summoned."

"Summoned? By whom?" Ademo asked, still feeling groggy.

"By the prida; our leader. I think Muirik mentioned that he would want to speak with you."

"Ah, yes, yes he did. But now? In the middle of the night?"

"Afraid so, yes. You see the council's been meeting most of the night. And now's the first occasion the prida's had to speak with you."

Ademo thought about asking why the morning wouldn't serve equally well. But somehow he knew these Vaidas probably had their reasons.

"Oh, okay. Just give me a moment."

"Certainly," Tiamoc said, bowing slightly and retreating into the hallway.

Tiamoc led Ademo along the gently winding corridor. The lamps along the wall were dimmed so that there was just enough light to see by. Without windows, Ademo assumed variable lighting was the only way these Vaidas could maintain a sense of the time of day.

"Is there any particular reason why there are no windows here at Monat Wisterlac?" Ademo asked, as they came upon a major artery that met the main corridor at a right angle, leading them inward towards the center of the massive structure.

"Oh yes, certainly. Every aspect of the building's design has a reason. The lack of windows has to do with the stealth nature of the structure."

"Stealth structure?" Ademo repeated, unfamiliar with the expression.

"The invisibility of the dome is what I'm referring to. If windows were included the light wouldn't look natural when people were viewing the island from afar. And that might draw unwanted attention."

Ademo nodded, wondering how the Vaidas had attained so much secret knowledge that was shrouded from the rest of the world. His curiosity getting the better of him, Ademo asked: "So how does it work?"

"How does what work?"

"The invisibility of the dome... How is that accomplished?"

Tiamoc chuckled awkwardly, then shrugged. He gave Ademo a backward glance, pausing as if considering how – or if? – he should elaborate.

"Well," the Vaida finally began, "that's complicated. And, truthfully, the dome is something we inherited from our predecessors. I don't think any of us now fully understand how it works."

Ademo was still taking in this strange revelation, when Tiamoc stopped abruptly before another arched door. He motioned towards it as he turned to face Ademo.

"If you'll go ahead and enter, the prida should be joining you soon enough. He's still occupied at present, but shouldn't be detained too much longer."

Ademo nodded his understanding, and Tiamoc turned to walk back the way they had come.

As soon as Ademo passed through the doorway he noticed a distinct change in environment. The air inside the chamber was warm and humid; so much so that it immediately reminded him of Kiraboa. The chamber was brighter than the corridor, with organgish orbs providing an almost natural light from high above. The area was filled with dense, tropical shrubbery – and again, the plants were of varieties that reminded him of the jungles of Kiraboa.

Ademo reached out and touched one of the leafy shrubs, letting its glossy texture pass along his hand. Even the smells were familiar. He breathed deep and closed his eyes. For a moment he could almost believe he was back home.

He then noticed what sounded like the trickling of water, coming from somewhere farther ahead. He followed a pebbly path as it spiraled towards the center of the room. Just then Ademo heard a fluttering above him, and looked up in time to see a bright colored bird fly across his field of vision. Ademo smiled. This *was* a pleasant environment. If he'd known of it earlier he would have asked to visit it sooner.

He rounded the corner and came to a center circle, where a large ornamental fountain stood, with springs of water bubbling up at the top. Just then Ademo noticed someone not far from the fountain. The stranger was tending to one of the plants, pouring water into the soil around it. As Ademo approached, the caretaker – who was a tall, slender, dark-skinned man, with a smooth bald head, and wiry grayish-white beard – looked up and smiled.

"Oh hello," he said pleasantly. "Don't mind me. I'm just here to make sure these plants stay healthy and green. Lovely, aren't they?" he said, turning and admiring the environment.

"Yes, they are. You've done a wonderful job. It all looks so... so natural."

"Well, thank you, sir. I do my best. It is a labor of love," the man said, smiling, before turning to tend to another of the plants.

"If you'd like to sit down for a while, there is a chair right over there," the man said, pointing to a lounge chair off to the side.

"Oh, I'm supposed to be meeting someone here."

"Well, I'm sure he'll be along soon. But until then, wouldn't you like to relax a little? The Vaidas do it all the time. Helps them find clarity."

"Thank you," Ademo replied, moving over to the chair and sitting down.

The chair was set in a reclining position, so that Ademo felt that he was almost lying down as he leaned back. As he relaxed he could hear the man whistling softly as he moved about, watering various plants.

Ademo found the environment almost perfectly tranquil. He breathed deep, closed his eyes, let himself remember an earlier time, when he was carefree in his island home. He could almost hear his mother's laughter, feel the warmth of the sun's rays, hear the sound of the surf gently lapping on the shore...

The next thing Ademo remembered feeling was a weighty warmth above his eyebrows. He let his eyes flutter open, with the sense that some duration of time had passed, and saw that a hand lay on his forehead. Presently the man sitting next to him removed his hand, smiled down at him, as Ademo shook his head and sat up. It took him a moment to gather his thoughts, as he felt very drowsy, as if he'd been woken from a long, deep slumber.

When Ademo looked over to the man again, he recognized it was the smiling, kind face of the caretaker he'd spoken with earlier.

"I must have drifted off to sleep," Ademo said,

gradually feeling the sleepiness lift off of him. "How long have I been lying here? Didn't the prida ever arrive?"

"Indeed he did, though I should tell you, he prefers to be called by his first name," the man said, smiling and handing Ademo a cold beverage.

Ademo drank deep from it and found some of the weariness lift off of him. Then he looked around, not seeing anyone else in the room (if you could call it a room).

"What is the prida's name? I don't think Muirik or Tiamoc ever told me," Ademo said.

"Rumillion."

"Rumillion," Ademo repeated, "Well, I'm embarrassed that he came and left after finding me asleep. I didn't intend to fall asleep. It's just that..."

"The Solarium is very relaxing," the caretaker said, finishing Ademo's thought.

"Exactly."

"Not to mention, they led you in here in the middle of the night, after waking you in the middle of a deep sleep."

"Yes, there's that, too," Ademo agreed, meeting the caretaker's smile with his own.

"Sorry," Ademo said, swinging his legs over the side of the chair, "I don't think I ever got your name. I'm Ademo," he said, offering his hand.

"Good to meet you, Ademo," the man replied, shaking his hand warmly. "I'm Rumillion."

Ademo stopped shaking the hand the moment he

heard the man announce his name.

"Rumillion? You mean, you're..."

"Yes. I am what some call the prida. But like I said, I prefer to go by Rumillion," he said, still smiling wide.

"Oh, again, let me apologize. I didn't realize-"

The man waved a hand in a carefree gesture.

"Not to worry, Ademo. It should be I apologizing to you. After all, I didn't introduce myself properly when first we met. But you see, there was a reason for that."

"There was?"

"Indeed. My intention was actually that you would remain relaxed, and that you would lie down here and fall asleep."

"It was?"

"Yes."

"But why?"

"Because I needed to interact with you in a dream state."

"Oh, well sorry, I don't remember dreaming at all. Did I pull a blank?"

"Oh no. Not at all. You did dream. In fact you dreamt the dream you experienced on your Placca."

"I did? I don't remember that. Not at all."

"No, you wouldn't remember anything. It was I who was directing things. And it was I who actually received the vision of the experience."

"Do you mean..." Ademo began, trying to make sense of what the prida was telling him, "that my dream was being passed over to you?"

"Exactly correct. And not just passed on in its normal state. You see, I'm able to change the course of the dream, repeat certain sections, even backtrack if need be."

"Backtrack?" Ademo said, a quizzical look written across his face.

"Yes, and that's what I did in this case. I searched in and around the events of your dream, in order to learn what I could. To learn more than perhaps you were able to ascertain on your own."

The prida's explanation was bizarre, and yet Ademo felt he had no reason to doubt it. Rumillion seemed a thoroughly trustworthy sort of fellow. It was very much the same way he'd felt about Muirik when first he met him.

"Did you learn anything of value from my dream? Anything that might help us identify the enemy? Or my background, or... anything?"

Rumillion smiled thinly, shaking his head almost apologetically. "Hard to say. Perhaps. Perhaps not. Time will tell."

Ademo nodded, yawning wide, feeling too tired to read too much into the prida's response.

"Again, my apologies for this unorthodox experience, Ademo. Why don't you go back to your room to sleep. We'll talk more tomorrow."

Ademo was curious, but he was also very tired. So he found himself eager to agree, and exited the Solarium the same way he had come.

Only moments later the figure of Muirik stepped

into the Solarium, joining Rumillion by the waterfall.

Muirik immediately recognized that the prida was deep in thought- *troubled* thought, if Muirik had it right. He waited patiently for a moment before Rumillion spoke.

"You did well to bring Ademo here, Muirik. There is much I have yet to understand. But I saw enough to surmise that our earlier suppositions may have been correct."

"The prophecy?" Muirik said, his eyebrows arching skywards.

"Yes, the prophecy. There were signs. Perhaps even unmistakable signs, if taken in context."

"Such as?"

"I saw the castle from which Ademo and his mother were escaping, the architecture was unmistakable; it was Deridian."

"*In the forests of Derida, the divided branch did seed,*" Muirik said, repeating the fragment from the prophecy.

Rumillion nodded, still looking lost in thought.

"Anything else?" Muirik asked, eager to hear more of the prida's revelation.

"Not much. But again, in context it might mean something... At the top of the hill, looking down with eyes ablaze, was another woman; a babe in her arms. It seemed clear to me that what she felt towards Ademo's mother was pure hatred. It seems likely that it was she who had ordered them hunted down."

"That fits with the Anquiline interpretation of the

prophecy. Surely it *must* be then. Ademo is the one foretold."

"So it would seem, yes," Rumillion said, nodding his head almost sadly. "That which we were warned of, so long ago, seems finally to be happening. And yet, we are so ill-prepared."

"Some will still doubt all of this; consider it superstition, even now. Even after what you've learned," Muirik said, realizing the challenge ahead.

Rumillion turned to Muirik, nodding slowly. "I fear you are right. Even amongst some of our brothers this notion will seem beyond the realm of possibility. Time has made us deaf to history. Deaf to its warning. And now, despite our foreknowledge, it seems we are caught unawares. Let us hope that this revelation has not come in vain. Not come too late to be of use."

64

Ademo woke to the sound of voices not far from his bed. Upon sitting up he realized the sounds were coming from the room adjacent to his, which was where Banon was staying. Quickly putting some clothes on, even though he was still a little groggy from his interrupted sleep, Ademo walked over to Banon's door, knocked and opened it slightly.

Inside he found Banon and Kyanessa, sitting

around the table with Muirik and Rumillion. Ademo smiled a little sheepishly, not expecting such a large gathering, and was in the middle of apologizing for interrupting, when Muirik stood up quickly, smiling, and came over to greet him.

"Come in, Ademo, come in. Rumillion was just getting to know your friends a little. And we were just talking about the plans for this morning."

"This morning? Is there another council meeting planned?" Ademo said, taking a seat.

"That comes later, Ademo," said Rumillion, leaning back his long frame in the chair and smiling over at him. "First we have something we'd like to do, with just the group of us here at the table."

"Oh, okay," Ademo said, his curiosity growing.

"But why don't you have some breakfast first. And then we'll go for a little walk, all of us, when you're done."

The five of them were standing at the center of the Solarium, the waterfall gently lapping over its sides in front of them. Kyanessa was looking skyward, with a smile, as colorful birds the likes she'd never seen before darted back and forth over their heads.

"So..." Rumillion began, "what we're about to share with you three is privileged information. Very few people know about what we're about to share with you – not even all of the Vaidas here at Wisterlac are aware of it."

Ademo, Banon and Kyanessa exchanged glances,

wondering what this news could portend.

"Now, this particular monat was built in this particular location for a very special reason. You see, below us here, at the very center of this dormant volcanic lake, is a pocket of energy. A pocket of energy containing very peculiarly charged particles."

Banon's face took on a strange expression, and even Kyanessa looked a little lost. Muirik noticed this and broke in.

"Prida, I'm not sure they're quite aware of the nature of charged particles."

"Oh right, sorry. Suffice it to say that there lies, directly below us, a chamber with very mysterious capabilities. And these capabilities may grant us insight, or so we hope, into the identity of our enemy; and even into the nature of Ademo's background, and his role in this whole matter."

Ademo's mouth was hanging open a little, and a quick glance towards his friends suggested they were just as lost as he was. Muirik caught Ademo's attention out of the corner of his eye, and tried to smile reassuringly.

The prida removed a small vial from his front cloak pocket and took a step towards the fountain. He opened the end of the vial and proceeded to empty the crystallized contents into the trickling water. Apparently done with whatever he was doing, Rumillion then backed away to stand next to the others.

The three younger companions each exchanged

glances (again), but no words were spoken. Then Rumillion, catching their expressions, added: "This will just take a moment."

At first nothing happened. The water kept gurgling up near the top of the fountain, before trickling back down to the bottom, in what they assumed was a continuous loop of some kind.

But then something *did* happen. At first it was hardly noticeable. But because they were each staring so intently towards the fountain, they each began noticing as the water began to fizz.

And then, just as the sound of the fizzing water was reaching a crescendo – tiny bubbles darting to and fro – something much more dramatic happened. The lip of the stone fountain directly in front of them began sliding backwards, the sound of stone scraping on stone echoing throughout the chamber.

As the echoing sound faded, they noticed a four foot section of the lip wall had retreated several feet, revealing a series of stone steps that led down into darkness.

"Now, if you'll just follow me, each of you, one at a time, we'll make our way down," Rumillion said, already moving forward.

They each got a little wet as they made their way down the spirally descending steps, water trickling from the fountain now directly above them. Placing their hands on the wet, moss-laden wall face for support, they wound their way down into the growing darkness.

If it weren't for the fact that they were being led by Rumillion at the front, with Muirik taking up the rear, it occurred to Ademo that this experience would have been rather terrifying. Soon the darkness below was nearly complete – with the light penetrating from above growing dimmer by the step.

And so they descended, on and on, for what felt like nearly half an hour. For a time the air temperature grew cooler. And then, as they descended further, it began to warm up again. And just when the darkness was at its deepest point, Ademo thought he could make out a faint orangey glow from far below. As they descended farther, this suspicion was confirmed, the light growing again.

Finally they stepped off of the stone staircase and onto a damp, chalky floor.

Ademo looked around and saw they that were in a rounded chamber, that ran about fifty feet across. In the dim light he could see vines and purply colored moss running up the chamber walls. The chamber appeared to grow narrower as it rose up; no doubt narrowest of all at the fountain top from which they'd originally come. The air here at the bottom of the cavernous chamber was noticeably warmer than above, and beads of sweat now ran down their faces.

Ademo followed Rumillion to the foot of a small pool, ten feet across, from which the orangey light source he'd first noticed earlier was emanating.

And then a peculiar thing happened.

The moment Rumillion reached the edge and

looked down into the steaming waters, the light source seemed to dim somewhat, even as the water seemed to calm. Rumillion's reflection could now be seen upon the surface of the still water.

Ademo wanted to ask his friends if they'd seen the same thing he had, but they were only now reaching the pool edge, and likely hadn't seen anything.

"Now, here is where we hope to answer a question," Rumillion said, turning to face the others in the dim light. "I will ask each of you to walk to the edge of the pool, and to look into it," Rumillion said. "Banon, why don't you go next. But be careful: close, but not too close – the water's very hot."

Looking left and right, and feeling a little strange, Banon stepped forward until he was at the edge. He looked down, and as he did so it was almost as if the steam rising off the surface of the water cleared, so that he too could see his reflection.

"Okay, and you next, Kyanessa," Rumillion said, motioning to her.

Banon gave Ademo a *whatever* look, and stepped aside as Kyanessa took his place. She also beheld her reflection.

After her came Muirik, and he too saw his own likeness upon the water.

"Now," Rumillion began, turning to Ademo, "would you step towards the edge here, Ademo, and look into the water?"

Ademo nodded, not understanding, but with his

curiosity growing.

When he first looked down into the water the steam obscured any reflection. But then, as it cleared, his profile came into view.

Except... it wasn't *his* profile.

The male figure reflecting back at him seemed to share his general features, but it clearly wasn't him. Ademo's eyes grew wide and his jaw dropped. And remarkably, the face upon the waters – the face that was not his own – did the same.

"*What on Eiasa...*" Banon began, stepping a little closer, to make sure his eyes weren't betraying him. Kyanessa gasped when she too saw what the others were seeing.

For their part, Rumillion and Muirik remained calm, but exchanged a knowing glance, almost as if this was precisely what they were expecting.

Ademo leaned down, till he was kneeling, and stared into those eyes; the eyes so much like his own, yet not his own.

"Careful," Muirik said, "that's volcanically heated water, Ademo. It would melt your skin if you were to fall in."

Ademo nodded, but kept staring, transfixed.

It was remarkable how much detail was visible in the still water. The olive complexion of the face was similar to his own. And the hair too was comparable – curly and dark, but with hints of grey. But the eyes... the eyes were different; chestnut brown in color and sitting farther apart. There were faint age lines around those eyes as well. He recognized the jaw as his own, but the lips were thinner, the mouth smaller.

Ademo had had enough, quickly standing up and stepping back, his breath coming rapidly. "What does it *mean*?" he said, looking from Muirik to Rumillion and back again.

"It means that our suspicions are confirmed, Ademo. For this is what Muirik and I expected we might see. It fits with the puzzle placed before us. But let us go back up, we'll speak of this soon enough."

Ademo was still in such a state of shock that he hardly heard what Rumillion had said. But when Muirik gently prompted him, gesturing towards the stony, spiral stairs that the prida was now ascending, Ademo managed to nod and move his feet.

As he ascended, Ademo glanced backwards once more, towards the pool that was again covered in a thin layer of rising steam.

65

Answers or explanations weren't quick in coming for Ademo. Because no sooner had they made their ascent to fountain level, than word of a surprise visitor to the monat reached their ears. Muirik and Rumillion excused themselves, promising they would speak more with Ademo and his friends as soon as circumstance allowed.

The next day the three companions were back in Ademo's room, sitting around the table. They hadn't yet seen or heard from Muirik or Rumillion. The evening before they'd been told by Tiamoc that the council had convened under emergency circumstances, after a messenger from one of the other monats had arrived, bearing news of import for the council.

All three of them were eager to know more of the situation, but found the daytime hours drifting slowly by, with no news. One of the Vaidas brought them some food in the early afternoon, but had nothing further in terms of information.

In these windowless quarters they really had no way of discerning the time of day. But eventually their stomachs told them it was probably dinner time, at the earliest. None of them felt particularly hungry, but eventually Kyanessa stood up and began putting out dishes with food and drink. With nothing else to do, the three sat around nibbling at their food, and afterwards sipping from coffee cups as the evening hours dragged on.

Just when Ademo thought the day would pass completely by without news, there was a rap at the door. Ademo glanced at the others and then jumped up to open it. He was both relieved and surprised to find Muirik there, dressed, as ever, in his grey robe. Muirik smiled, but behind the greeting Ademo sensed unease.

Minutes later they were all sitting around the table again. The Vaida took a few moments to gather his thoughts before speaking.

"Friends, I apologize in being delayed from seeing you. Recently a Vaida named Yersa arrived, bearing very ill news from Corpazon."

"Corpazon?" Ademo said, repeating the unfamiliar name.

"Monat Corpazon is located in a territory west and north of here. Some four of five days travel by horse. He has traveled day and night to reach us with this news."

"What news?" Kyanessa asked, finding the anticipation difficult to bear.

Muirik sighed, bowing his head slightly. "A tragedy, I am afraid. Monat Corpazon has been destroyed."

The three companions gasped as they took in the news. Kyanessa especially seemed surprised and distraught. She was not used to such a fate befalling the Movadem. She knew it was grave news indeed.

"*Destroyed?*" she said. "And what news of the Vaidas there?"

Muirik sighed again, and his head seemed to slump even further. "We're not entirely sure. Yersa escaped even as the monat was being burned to the ground. But we fear that he may be the only survivor."

More gasps around the table. For his part, Ademo stared at the ground, not knowing how to respond. This was ill news indeed. But with everything so new to him, he felt as bewildered as he did sad and fearful.

"Was that other monat as seemingly impenetrable and difficult to discover as this one?" Banon asked.

"It didn't have quite the defenses we have here," Muirik replied, "but it *was* cloaked though. So it's location should have been secret. Clearly, that's no longer the case."

"So what does this mean? Will each of the monats come under attack now? And does this mean this illusive enemy now means to kill not only Ademo, but also every Vaida who walks the earth?" Kyanessa asked, a hint of desperation in her voice.

"We don't know the aims of the enemy, dear. But it stands to reason that he is killing Vaidas because we are perhaps the only ones capable of stopping him."

"Capable of stopping him from doing what?" Banon piped in.

"Again, we can't know for certain. But pride seldom produces anything original... Power; domination; those are the usual aims. And so perhaps this enemy is removing anyone that might be an obstacle to his succeeding in that goal... But I'm afraid the news I've shared might not even be the worst of it."

"What?" Ademo exclaimed, his eyes wide. The others shared similar expressions.

"As you three know, I knew something was wrong on our way here, because the Movademic Harmony was broken. Three of our brothers had fallen, and so their tones were removed from the constant communication we Vaidas all share. However, even as we speak, the tones from Monat Corpazon still ring true."

"But how can that be? You said it was destroyed, and the Vaidas there killed," Kyanessa said.

"All we can surmise is that this enemy has somehow found a way to mimic those tones. Which poses another problem for us: the possibility that other monats have fallen under attack, without us being aware of it. This has caught us all by surprise. I'm afraid we Vaidas have been too slow to respond to this growing threat. We can only hope it is not already too late. This enemy is powerful beyond our imagining. And he has us at a grave disadvantage, to be sure."

After a moment's silence, as each of the young companions let the dire news sink in, Ademo asked: "So what happens next?"

"Well, first thing's first: we must do our very best to take away this enemy's greatest advantage: his anonymity."

"And how will you do that?" Banon asked.

"By spreading our collective wings; by gathering evidence. Vaidas have already left Wisterlac to gather news from north, south, east and west. And after our meeting here, I must do the same."

"You're leaving?" Ademo asked, distraught.

"I'm afraid I must. And since we no longer know for certain that this monat is secure, you three must leave as well. But you won't be going with me, as speed demands that I dawn the ravencloak. Instead, Tiamoc will take you to a friend, who will hide you some place secret and secure. I hope to return to you when more is known to us."

"You don't sound very certain!" Ademo said, sounding desperate.

Muirik sighed, reached out a hand to grasp Ademo's shoulder.

"Certitude has only led to folly thus far, Ademo. So I won't pretend to know more than I do. But try not to despair too much. Let us hope that now that we are working together on this one task, that we can quickly reduce the enemy's advantage, and yet find a way to oppose him."

66

Ademo slept fretfully that night, dreaming that the monat fell under attack from the skies as they slept, fire reigning down upon them and trapping them inside to burn alive. He awoke to learn the others had slept just as restlessly, if not as vividly. So the three companions, tired and anxious, ate their breakfast with very few words passing between them.

Soon afterwards Tiamoc came for them. They learned, not to their surprise, that Muirik had already departed from Wisterlac. He and most of the other remaining Vaidas had left well before first light, for fear that perhaps spies were watching the monat. Only a handful would remain in the dome after the companions departed.

After breakfast they gathered their provisions and left with Tiamoc. The small Vaida, light on his feet, took to a brisk pace that the three companions were hard-pressed to keep up with. He led them across the opposite side of the lake from which they'd arrived, again making the crossing on a suddenly appearing (and then disappearing) pathway. Scouts had earlier that day scanned the area and deemed it safe. Still, it was with trepidation and some degree of anxiety that they made headway.

Ademo had hoped that perhaps this way would prove less arduous. But, alas, they were forced to crawl under the thorny scrub brush yet again to escape the volcanic rim, this time scrambling upwards.

When they finally emerged from the dense, prickly growth, they again found themselves in a thick pine forest. The four marched on with only the sounds of the forest to accompany them. When Banon finally broke the silence to ask where they were headed, Tiamoc only held his finger to his lips. He had mentioned that they would do their best to march quietly. And now the three companions understood this to mean conversation was forbidden altogether. Banon looked pleadingly to Ademo, who shrugged.

So on they marched, down the westward slope of

the mountain. Eventually the terrain flattened out to become rolling, yellowed hills, dotted with patches of black oaks. They followed a westward course until sometime after lunchtime, when they came to the banks of a wide river. The swollen river's waters were rushing, and Tiamoc decided it was a location safe to converse, with the roar of the river keeping their words safe from spies of any sort.

"This is the Goliden River, and it runs southward all the way to the very southern coast of Criesca, in the territory of Sorafin. We won't follow it that far though. We're to follow it for a day or so more, and then we bear west again. We should arrive at our destination before sundown tomorrow if we play it right."

"And that destination would be..." Banon asked, his eyebrows raised.

"Ah, well, somewhere safe. In the company of a friend of the Vaidas. Let's just leave it at that."

Banon nodded, then turned away from Tiamoc to roll his eyes in clear sight of both Ademo and Kyanessa.

"I don't suppose there are any horses nearby? Perhaps the noble Faring to carry us more swiftly?" Ademo asked, sounding hopeful.

"The *Faring*..." Tiamoc said, as if he were surprised to hear the name. "No, I'm afraid not, Ademo. The Faring are rarely seen at all. And when they are it's usually out in the green hills closer to the coast. That's where some have apparently seen them anyway. I myself have never beheld one with my own eyes," he said, turning to resume the march.

All three of the young companions shared a smile as they turned to follow. Clearly Muirik hadn't had the opportunity to tell Tiamoc *all* the details of their trek to Mt. Wister.

They moved southward, walking under the cover of weeping willows that lined the banks of the river. Even with the roar of the river to their left, Tiamoc kept silent. Banon began to wonder if it really was necessity that demanded the silence, or if Tiamoc just preferred it that way, regardless. Either way, on they walked, until the sun began to set behind the western horizon.

The banks were covered with several layers of leaves that made for relatively soft bedding. Three of the four sojourners rested well that night, their tired legs sending them quickly to deep, dreamless sleep.

Ademo, however, had a different experience. He was plagued with frightening dreams. He saw Monat Wisterlac falling under fiery attack from the sky, a full moon present to brightly illuminate the horrifying scene. Those Vaidas left behind at the dome were burned alive, their bloodcurdling screams sending panic and adrenaline through his system.

Sometime before dawn Ademo sat bolt upright, his breathing coming in gasps. He looked around and saw a hint of pale light to the east. The others lay motionless around him, looking almost tranquil.

Ademo sat in silence, watching the sun make its gradual ascent. Eventually the others stirred and awoke. Ademo kept his nightmare to himself, eating a meager breakfast in silence. Tiamoc was soon ready for them to resume their journey. Ademo fell into step at the rear of the group, as they marched silently along the river that gently meandered on its southern journey to the sea.

Sometime before lunchtime, when their stomachs were beginning to growl for a meal, Ademo saw something flash before his mind's eye. And it was just a flash. No sooner had he seen it than it was gone, replaced by the familiar scene of his friends marching single-file in front of him.

Ademo shook his head, willing the mental scene from his mind. It had come and gone so quickly that he'd hardly had a chance to register it, or discern what it was exactly. But it left him with a feeling of dread and foreboding. *What was it he had seen?* Something had flashed before his field of vision... a hand?

Then, later that afternoon, Ademo had the same vision. Again his sight was replaced by some otherworldly scene; the bright of day instantaneously replaced by darkness. No, not darkness... but dim lighting to be sure. He saw something – an arm, flashing out in front of him, *grasping*... Somehow Ademo knew this latest vision, and the earlier nightmare, were connected.

But then, almost as soon as it had begun, the vision was gone. And all Ademo now beheld was Banon's back, as they continued along the trail.

Ademo must have gasped because, just then,

Banon turned around.

"You alright, 'Demo?" he asked.

"We have to go back," Ademo said, with conviction, stopping in his tracks.

"What? Go back? Go back where?" Banon asked, wondering what had come over his friend.

"We have to go back. The others. At Wisterlac. They're in danger."

By this time the conversation had attracted the attention of Tiamoc and Kyanessa. Presently the Vaida turned around.

"Is something wrong?" Tiamoc asked, seeing the dazed, concerned look on Ademo's face.

"We have to back. To Wisterlac," Ademo repeated again.

"Back to Wisterlac?" Tiamoc parroted. "Why would we do that?"

"They're in danger."

"Well, yes, they are. That's why we left as quickly as we could. Believe me, Ademo, the Vaidas left behind at the monat are well aware of their situation. They have accepted their role because it's important that some stay behind to watch and guard," Tiamoc said.

"No, I mean they *will* face attack. It's coming. I've seen it twice now."

"Seen what twice?" Banon asked, stepping forward to get closer to Ademo.

Ademo looked up at his lanky friend, his eyes betraying a kind of startled revelation. "I've had dreams of an attack on Wisterlac. From the sky. Only it wasn't just a dream. It was a vision of what's about to happen."

"Ademo, one shouldn't confuse a nightmare for a premonition," Tiamoc offered. "We're all under pressure, and these are frightening times. But you..."

"It *wasn't* a nightmare!" Ademo said, almost shouting now.

Kyanessa and Banon shared a glance, concerned about the demeanor that had come over their normally calm, easygoing friend.

"I mean, it *was*... But not *just* a nightmare. It *is* going to happen, under a full moon," Ademo said, firmly.

Tiamoc shook his head. "Ademo, you said you *envisioned* an attack from the sky. But that's impossible. Generally we don't talk about these things, but the entire dome is protected by a shield of energy."

"A shield of energy?" Banon repeated, his eyebrows raised. His tone, as usual, betraying both surprise and a little disbelief. "More of that Deep Math?"

"Yes. But we don't need to get into the details. Rest assured that the dome is quite safe from... from an attack from the sky. Besides, again, Rumillion's wishes were clear: we are to get as far away from Wisterlac as we possibly can under short notice; to take cover elsewhere, while other Vaidas gather recognizance about this enemy. It's precisely *because* there is danger there that we were advised to leave. So why would we now turn around to go back?"

Ademo met Tiamoc's gaze, taking in what he was saying. What Ademo wanted to say was that he should return because he thought he could make a difference; be of aid to the Vaidas there somehow. But he felt silly thinking such a thought, let alone voicing it. What exactly *could* he offer in such a situation – even if his dreams really were premonitions?

Ademo paused, looking at the others, before letting his eyes fall to the ground. Tiamoc stepped forward, placing his hand on Ademo's arm.

"I understand and appreciate your concern for my brothers, Ademo. But we really must carry on to our destination, as Rumillion wished. There will be a time to gather again, once we know more."

Ademo looked up, noticing the concerned look written on his friends' features. "Okay. Sorry," he said, offering a weak smile.

"Think nothing of it," Tiamoc said, before giving Ademo a reassuring pat on the back.

They resumed their march, Kyanessa and Banon flashing Ademo encouraging smiles before they started walking again. Ademo returned their smiles and fell into step.

They continued following the river as it wound southward, growing narrower. They carried on in silence, with only the flow of the river to fill their ears.

It was some time later that day that Ademo had another vision. And again, it was the briefest of flashes. Ademo's perspective was replaced, just for a second, with a vision of a dimly lit room, and that familiar form, grasping at something. This time Ademo felt more certain of what he was seeing: a hand, stabbing forward to grasp at something. Something, or... *someone*?

The nature of the vision was uncanny. And the sense of resolve that accompanied it was alarming. It was almost like some other kind of consciousness; some other kind of knowing.

But Ademo knew such thinking would only sound like foolishness to the others, so he kept it to himself. So on they walked, following the path of the Goliden River, Ademo plagued with the thought that he was in two places (and two times?) simultaneously.

67

As the afternoon was growing long, the sun dipping towards the west, Tiamoc turned to face them.

"Friends, here we turn westward. We will have to travel out on an open plain for a time, but that route will take us into a forest, where we will have cover for the remainder of the journey. I urge you to walk quickly and quietly while out on the plain, for we do not know where spies may be watching and listening."

"Have you spotted any sign of spies while we've journeyed this far?" Banon asked, wondering if the fear of watching eyes was really warranted.

"No," said Tiamoc, even now looking to and fro, "but that's almost as troubling as if we had."

Banon wasn't quite sure what the Vaida meant, but the serious expression on Kyanessa's face suggested she did. Banon looked to Ademo, but his friend seemed preoccupied and didn't make eye contact.

As Tiamoc had described, the tree cover next to the river quickly dissipated, and the terrain gave way to an open plain, where only a knee-high yellow grass grew. They all felt rather vulnerable out in the open terrain, and so they were relieved when Banon, ever with the keen eyes, pointed to an obscure tree line somewhere ahead of them, some time later. It was only a slight blur on the horizon for the others, but they knew by now to trust the Landrite's remarkable vision. And sure enough, as the day gave way to sundown, the tree line came into view for all of them.

Soon they were marching through a shadowy wood filled with tall, narrow, white-barked trees that Tiamoc called mepikas. As Ademo looked high above, he saw that the broad leaves of the mepikas were a bluish color, and grew only at the very tops of the trees, joining to form an almost impenetrable forest canopy.

Tiamoc led then downhill through a shallow valley, until they came to a small creek that ran in a generally southwesterly direction. Here the tree cover was the thickest, and they followed this trail for some time, until the light gave way to near darkness. Finally, when each of their legs felt as if they would fall off, Tiamoc signaled they would stop to rest for the night.

"How much farther do we need to travel tomorrow?" Banon asked, as he let his pack fall to the ground next to him, before collapsing in a heap beside it.

"One would hope we'll arrive by early afternoon. Perhaps even in time for lunch if we start our trek early enough," Tiamoc replied.

Kyanessa let herself fall to the ground as well. "Please, no more talk of walking. Even the thought tires me further."

"What? Even you, miss? You who've trekked to the far northern reaches of Vaselhelm? Where even battle-hardened warriors fear to tread?" Banon said, a smirk on his face.

Kyanessa ignored him, only rolling her eyes and turning to Ademo. It was then that she noticed the olive-skinned Kiraboan didn't seem quite himself. He was sitting on a log, staring off into the distance.

"You see something, Ademo?" Kyanessa asked, innocently enough.

Ademo seemed jarred back into reality. "What? What do you mean?"

"You're staring off into the forest," Kyanessa added. "I was just wondering if you saw something out there... Maybe dinner?"

"Oh," Ademo said, sounding relieved. "No, I was just thinking is all. Thinking about the warm, sandy beaches of Kiraboa."

"Can't say I've ever been somewhere quite like that. But it certainly sounds wonderful," Kyanessa added.

Ademo smiled and nodded and then, without really realizing it, turned to stare off into the distance again. Kyanessa noticed Ademo's absent expression but was distracted when Tiamoc wandered over towards her.

"Lady, I hear you are adept with bow and arrow. Do you think there's any hope we might have something 'special' for dinner? I don't know about all of you, but for me the thought of bread, dried fruit and water has lost a little of its luster."

Kyanessa smiled and nodded. "I'll see what I can do," she said, already drawing an arrow and moving off into the trees.

Ademo bolted upright, his heart heaving in his chest. He placed his hand over his mouth to muffle the breath that was coming in gasps. He looked around him, saw that the others were fast asleep, apparently unaware of his recurring nightmare.

He'd dreamt again of the attack on Monat Wisterlac; the screams of the Vaidas still echoing in his ears. He remembered the full moon bearing painful witness as fire rained down from above. The terrifying memory kept his adrenaline pumping throughout his body.

Ademo slowly got up, quietly tiptoeing away from

the location where the others slept, panic still gripping his heart. Why was it that this particular nightmare seemed so different? So... *real*? He didn't really have any answers. But everything about him was reacting as if these nighttime visions were real, not imaginary. And that's why he was having such a hard time calming down, even now that he was wide awake.

He wandered off some distance from the others, finally sitting down on an old stump of a tree, letting his gaze drift upwards where a 3/4 moon shone through the forest canopy, casting sheets of light over the forest floor.

Then a thought struck him: that moon. That *3/4* moon. It would be full two nights from now. What if... What if the nightmare he'd had *was* actually a premonition? A warning: foretelling that Monat Wisterlac would be attacked two nights from now?

On the one hand the thought seemed preposterous. Who'd ever heard of such a thing? Nighttime premonitions? But, at the very same time, something told Ademo that this is exactly what this was. Monat Wisterlac was going to be raided, from the sky, two nights from now, under the illumination of a full moon.

But why was he being made aware of this? What could he hope to do about it?

Perhaps it was enough to tell Tiamoc. The Vaida would know what to do. After all, he was the one leading them. Certainly the responsibility was his. Wasn't it?

But then... what if the Vaida didn't take the warning seriously? After all, Ademo knew this would be difficult to believe. Even he would find it difficult to believe if it weren't for... if it weren't for his own intuition; this inward knowing that seemed to be growing on him, day by day. It told him to take the warning seriously, that the events he saw in his dream were as inevitable as the sun's rise the very next morning.

Ademo shook his head, rubbing his eyes with clenched fists, trying to think clearly.

And yet, he was clear. Somehow he knew that thinking this through from a merely rational frame of mind would fail him. No, this time he needed to trust his intuition.

Besides, people's lives were at stake. Even if he did turn out to be wrong, he'd rather act on this knowledge than stand idly by, fleeing to safety himself, while the Vaidas at Wisterlac were left to die a horrible death that could have been prevented.

But could it be prevented? Maybe it could be. Maybe that's why he was having these premonitions. There had to be a reason, didn't there? To know, and not be able to do anything about it, now that *would* be torture.

No, he had to act on this – act on the notion that he *could* make a difference. Help somehow, in a way he was never able to when horror befell his village on Kiraboa.

Ademo stood up again, suddenly feeling very

resolved. He thought about his pack, which lay on the ground next to the sleeping bodies of the others. Should he go and retrieve it?

No. He couldn't risk it. He might very well wake one or all of them in the process. And what then? What if they refused to let him go? What if they tried to reason with him, saying that acting on nightmare visions was foolishness?

Well, they had a point, from one perspective, anyway. But it wasn't the perspective he was planning on relying on. Not this time. No, he would leave now, under the cover of dark, hours before dawn would wake the others. And by then it would be too late for them to come after him.

Ademo listened for the sound of the creek, moved over towards it, stepping carefully over twigs and brush. Soon he was wandering back along the course of the creek bed, marching back the way they had come.

68

The tall, brown-robed figure pulled himself those last few yards from underneath a canopy of thorny vines, before standing to quickly brush off. For a moment he gazed towards the center of the Wisterlac, where only a flat, rocky island was visible. It was nothing much to look at for the casual observer. But he knew differently.

Lining up with the landmarks he'd been advised of, he made his way down the pebbly shoreline and out into the stew of the acidic lake, a small peninsula of land suddenly appearing a moment before his feet would have plunged into the poisonous waters.

From within Monat Wisterlac, a Vaida named Doven, who was posted at the entrance, noticed the acoustic signs indicating someone was nearing the dome. As the brown-robed figure covered those last few yards over the surface of the lake, the Vaida opened the door.

"Greetings!" the brown-robed figure called out.

The two Vaidas, one brown-robed, and one in grey, shook hands in Vaidan fashion.

"Brother, you come from Corpazon?" Doven asked, knowing that the color of robe was associated with that monat.

The other brother nodded. "I do."

"That's welcome news, brother. We thought Yersa was the only one to escape the destruction there. Such horrible news! Such trying times!"

"Yersa?"

"Yes, you're not the only one to escape the assault there. Thankfully your brother from Corpazon also survived, by the skin of his teeth. He came to us not long ago now."

The brown-robed Vaida stood absolutely still for a moment, as if stunned by the news.

"I can see that's caught you by surprise, brother. But fear not, I will send him to see you once we get you settled inside. I would send our prida to meet with you as well, but alas, he is presently occupied elsewhere."

"Thank you, brother," the newcomer announced. "The news about Yersa is welcome indeed!"

As the Wisterlac Vaida led his brother from Corpazon along the perimeter corridor, he called over his shoulder.

"And what name shall I give to your brother when I tell him you've arrived safe and sound?"

"Rodero. My name is Rodero."

"Good to meet you, Brother Rodero. Please, make yourself comfortable," he said, opening the door to the guest room and motioning him inside. "I'll have Yersa come to see you before long."

"Thank you, brother," the man replied, smiling kindly and gripping the other's arm.

As Doven marched down the hall, with a spring in his step, the brown-robed figure leaned his back against the closed door, letting himself breathe deeply for the first time since he'd entered the dome. The prida was away from the monat, that he already well knew. Sentinels had informed him of this fact the moment Wisterlac's leader had made the lake crossing in the dead of night. Of course, the prida was off pursuing a false lead. That part of the plan had worked to a tee.

But the news of the survivor from Corpazon was

unexpected – and troubling. *What had he seen?* What had he shared with the Vaidas here at Wisterlac? And most importantly, were the plans that had been laid out so carefully now in jeopardy as a result?

69

By mid-morning of the next day Ademo was already drenched, sweat clinging to him and matting his greasy, black hair, when the rains began. At first the rainfall was sporadic, but before long a full-on downpour was underway. Even under the cover of the willow trees that lined the river, he was getting drenched.

Ademo no longer really noticed the wetness. What he *did* notice was the nagging fatigue in his bones. He'd been trekking for hours on end now, nearly jogging much of the time. From time to time he would look behind, fearful that his friends had come after him, but would see nothing.

Eventually, when midday came, he almost wished he *would* catch a glimpse of them. Because by this time he was definitely harboring second thoughts about his decision to return to Wisterlac.

And his concerns weren't limited to the decision to turn back; he also wondered about the timeline. Even if he was supposed to return to Wisterlac, had he waited too long to do so? After all, it was only after he'd had that horrific dream more than once that he'd finally turned around. And now, with less than two days to go before the invasion was due to start – if his dream was to be believed – he had many leagues yet to cover.

Even at this pace, he wondered if it was possible for him to make it back in time to warn the others. Surely, at some point, he would need to rest. Could willpower alone make him jog the whole way – without sleep? He doubted it, despite his intense resolve.

For now he willed himself not to think about such things. For now it was enough to put one foot in front of the other, even as the rains turned the already soft banks of the river to mud.

70

Banon and Tiamoc sat silently on a fallen tree, waiting for Kyanessa to return. She'd left them almost an hour before, gone to look for Ademo's trail. They'd all looked for him when first they awoke that morning, but no trace was found. At some point they realized their own searching was marring whatever clues may have been available. It was then that Kyanessa suggested she look alone – since she was the most adept at tracking. The other two had agreed, Banon with reservations – and since then they'd sat without talking, waiting for her to return.

Presently they heard rustling in the bushes, and both men turned to look as Kyanessa emerged, still alone.

"So, any sign of him?" Banon asked, before she'd even reached them.

Kyanessa, clearly tired, sat down herself. "Well, I can't be sure, because this rain is making tracking much more difficult, but I think he may have returned the same way we came."

"What?" Banon asked. "You mean... he did it, didn't he – he decided to return to Wisterlac. And since he couldn't convince us, he decided to go alone. That Kiraboan boar!"

"Any idea how long ago he left?" Tiamoc asked, standing.

"Again, hard to tell with the rains, but I'd say hours ago, probably well before first light."

"And not one of us awoke? " Banon said, shaking his head. "This is inexcusable! We should have posted watch. Then we'd-"

"What? We'd what? What good would that have served if it were Ademo's turn to stay awake? He would have snuck off just the same," Kyanessa said, sounding frustrated.

"The lady's right, Banon. There's no use blaming ourselves here. That only wastes time and energy. We best focus on what we'll do now."

Banon opened his mouth to say something, but thought better of it, slowly shaking his head instead.

"From the look of the footprints it appears Ademo was running. If that's true, then it seems unlikely we'll catch up with him, not when he's hours ahead of us," Kyanessa added.

"Running? And how on Eiasa can you tell from a footprint that someone is running?" Banon asked, sounding incredulous.

Kyanessa rolled her eyes before answering. "My word, don't you learn anything useful in Landry? *Because*, when one runs, one falls on the balls of the feet, leaning forward. Whereas, when one *walks,* the whole footprint shows up, evenly. These footprints looked like someone running. Got it?"

In truth Banon wanted to protest. But he had difficulty knowing how to dispute Kyanessa's logic. In fact, he was a little embarrassed the footprint clue hadn't occurred to him already. It was pretty common-sensical after all. He decided to switch gears.

"But what good is it if we go on, without Ademo? He's the whole reason we're here. We're supposed to help him. To help keep him safe from this enemy..."

Seeing Banon's clear concern for Ademo, Kyanessa felt a change of heart, and regretted speaking so rashly to the Landrite – even if his comment was foolish.

"Banon's right about that. It seems pointless to seek cover for ourselves when Ademo's out there all alone," she said.

Banon looked towards her and nodded his thanks, if a little sheepishly. Then both turned to look Tiamoc's way. The diminutive Vaida was looking skyward, his eyes closed, as if deep in thought.

"You speak true, both of you. But sometimes, in trying to help, one can actually make a situation worse. Rumillion and Muirik and the others expected us to go on to our destination. And when they send word about our next steps, they'll send it there. So to turn back now, and possibly miss that signal, might very well make things worse. If it's true that we can't hope to catch up with Ademo, then I say we must push on for our destination, and hope that he makes it back to Wisterlac safely."

"And hope that Wisterlac isn't attacked as Ademo fears?" Kyanessa asked.

"Yes, that too. I know it seems much to hope for. But at least this plan stands some chance of success. Rashly turning around to pursue someone we can't hope to catch up with would simply be foolishness, even if foolishness born of a pure heart."

Banon, who towered over the Vaida, stared down at him, doing his best to think of a curt response. But as with just a moment ago, none came to mind. He hated to admit it, but the Vaida's reasoning was sound. Glancing over towards Kyanessa, Banon could tell she had decided the same.

"So we keep to our present path, then," Tiamoc said, when neither offered a rebuttal. "With luck, we may reach our destination by nightfall, even though we have already been long delayed today. And perhaps there will be a message waiting for us when we arrive. One can hope for as much."

Banon and Kyanessa said nothing, but began gathering their belongings. Banon slung Ademo's abandoned pack over his free shoulder, and then fell into line behind the others as they resumed their westward march.

71

Yersa knew it would not appear very Vaida-like to run down the hallway like an excited schoolboy; especially in a place as revered as Monat Wisterlac. Still, he found himself rushing to the point of a near jog as he headed towards the quarters where Rodero, a brother from Corpazon, was waiting and resting.

When the news had been spoken to him he could scarcely believe it. He was almost certain he had been the only brother to escape the devastation at Corpazon. When he had crawled to freedom, singed and coughing, the castle-like structure of Corpazon had been an inferno, hardly even recognizable through the hundred-foot tall flames and churning plumes of black smoke.

And yet, now he had learned that he was *not* the

only one to survive the massacre that day. He was eager to speak with Rodero, whom he didn't know intimately, but whom he had seen and interacted with in Movademic gatherings throughout the years.

Yersa made note of the room numbers as he rounded the perimeter of the dome. Finally he came to the one he was looking for. He walked up to the door and gave three quick raps. At first he didn't hear anything in reply, and so he rapped again. This time he heard a muffled reply. Then he heard the doorknob turn and the door swung slightly ajar.

"Come in," a voice from inside said, even as it trailed away.

Yersa smiled wide, pushing the door inward and walking in. "Brother Rodero, I was so pleased to learn about your arrival... Rodero?"

Inside he found the room empty. He said the name again, and heard a muffled reply. Then he noticed the door to the bathroom slightly ajar.

"Have a seat, brother," Yersa heard the man say, from behind the bathroom door. Yersa smiled again, sat down on one of the chairs facing the wall.

"Brother," Yersa began, "I was so relieved to find I wasn't the only one to make it out alive from Corpazon. I would have stayed behind longer, continued searching, only I feared no one could possibly have survived that inferno.

"I'm eager to learn of the manner of your escape. I expected you would have been gathering with the brothers in the main chamber, since it was the hour of the morning sonir, when... when it all happened."

"It is amazing," a voice from within the bathroom called out, still sounding muffled. "Tell me, brother, how did *you* manage to escape the inferno?"

"Sheer, stupid luck, as it turns out," Yersa said, the guilt of survival rushing over him again. "I was gathering molicar leaves from the forest, and fully intended on being back in time for the sonir. But, as it turns out, I twisted my ankle when jumping down from one of the trees. Clumsy of me, I know.

"So I began hobbling back, but soon realized I wouldn't make it in time. So, knowing that it wouldn't be wise to enter half way though the sonir gathering, I decided to take my time and gather more of the leaves that I saw on the way. Plus, I needed to rest my ankle, as best I could.

"It was on my way back that I heard the strangest sound. I don't know how to describe it. Perhaps it was an animal of some sort, I don't know. But it was a *horrific* screech.

"Then I did my best to move as fast as I could, since the sound seemed to be coming from the general direction of the monat. But by the time I emerged from the forest the monat was already engulfed in flame.

"I rushed inside to look for the others... but the flames; the smoke... it was overwhelming. And I could hardly even see in front of me... And then the walls around me began collapsing. So I fled before the smoke overcame me."

There was a pause as Yersa considered, yet again,

what he could have done differently. Perhaps if he'd only pushed a little farther into the monat, maybe he could have helped others escape. Knowing that Rodero had survived only drove home the point that there may have been others struggling, in desperate need of his help.

After a moment, Yersa collected himself, cleared his throat: "Brother, enough about my clumsiness, what about you? Where were you when it happened? And did you hear that sound as well? Do you have any idea what it could possibly have been?"

As Yersa finished speaking, he turned around, hearing footsteps approach from behind. He saw Rodero emerge from the bathroom, dressed in their common brown robe, his head hung low and shrouded in its hood. Such manner – the wearing of a hood indoors – was actually common at times of mourning, and for a moment Yersa thought that perhaps he should have shown the same respect.

As Rodero approached him, Yersa thought he looked rather taller than he remembered.

Just then the man lifted his head, and from within the hood two piercing eyes looked forth. The eyes were stern, and beneath them was a wide mouth, carved in a crooked smile.

"Oh yes, I heard the sound. For I was there. And I know exactly what the source of that bloodthirsty screech was. Glorious, wasn't it?" he said, with that crooked smile.

"But that's not important," he continued. "What *is*

important is that *you* didn't see anything. And thus, while you have surprised me with your survival, you've shared nothing of import with the Vaidas here. And that is welcome news indeed.

"You see, we have prepared so meticulously, for so long; waiting, patiently… It would have been such a shame for it all to have ended before it even began. After all, where's the show in that?

"But the harm is less than I had feared. It almost makes me grateful. You see, now I'm able to make good on a promise I made that day. *No survivors*, I said. And now, there won't be. Aren't second chances wonderful?"

Yersa felt the breath catch in his throat. One thing was clear: this robed figure was not his brother Rodero.

In fear, Yersa tried to step backwards – but found his foot catch on the edge of the throw rug. And then, like lightning, the arm of the man standing across from flashed out. Long, bony fingers gripped Yersa's neck, immediately cutting off his windpipe. The brown-robed figure stood watching as Yersa's eyes dilated, and then grew glossy. Yersa's skin color turned white, and then a pale shade of blue. The figure leaned in, his eyes penetratingly intense, even as Yersa's field of vision went blurry and began to fade.

And then the skeletal fingers clamped shut, and there was a snapping sound, like that of a twig stepped on in the dead of winter.

When the brown-robed figure let go, Yersa's

lifeless body slumped to the ground in a heap.

72

As afternoon gave way to a drenching, grey dusk, the group of three trekked on, as the terrain grew muddier and the mood decidedly more somber. It seemed as if the longer they walked the heavier the rains became.

Soon the soft but relatively dry ground along the creek-bed gave way to muddier terrain, as Tiamoc lead them on a weaving path between ponds that looked more like swamps, with strange blue-green algae growing over the entire surface of the water.

"Are we almost there yet?" Banon broke the silence to ask, feeling like a child almost as soon as the words were out of his mouth.

Tiamoc glanced backwards, eyed the taller Landrite for a moment, and then said: "It's not far now. Maybe an hour more. Maybe two."

Banon's eyes rolled as he glanced towards Kyanessa. She chose to ignore the complaining gesture, though inwardly she felt just as exhausted and uncomfortable as Banon. They were both cold, drenched, and covered in mud up to their waists. Even though they'd been trying to carefully choose their steps, often – without warning – they would sink deep into the pliant ground. Tiamoc seemed to be having a little more luck. But with his diminutive height, when he did sink, he would do so up to his chest.

Eventually they came to a row of tall thorny brush, that, though of a different variety (more colorful and dense), looked just as impenetrable as the shrub leading up to Wisterlac. Tiamoc turned right and marched along for a hundred yards or so, before turning abruptly to the left, and making his way through a small, door-like gap in the shrub wall. He followed this new direction for half that distance, before turning to enter through yet another gap in the wall, and turning abruptly the other direction again.

As Banon and Kyanessa followed Tiamoc's seemingly haphazard course, they noticed other gaps in the shrub walls that Tiamoc ignored. Peeking through these openings, they spotted yet more rows of shrub on the other side.

This twisting and turning went on and on, and before long, neither Banon nor Kyanessa needed to ask Tiamoc to confirm, because it was clear that the small Vaida was leading them through a man-sized maze.

"So who tends to these rows? Seems like these shrubs would grow up in no time," Banon said.

"That's true," Tiamoc called over his shoulder, not slowing even an iota. "In fact, in less than a season these openings grow over unless cut away again."

"So who is it that tends to it, then?" Banon asked, hoping this time to get an answer that might offer some insight as to where they were headed.

Just then Tiamoc abruptly stopped, so much so that Banon almost walked into him. The Landrite thought perhaps he'd offended the Vaida with his question, which made him rather annoyed. What was wrong with a little information at this point? Banon thought to himself. Surely Tiamoc didn't think spies were still about, in this storm... in this muck?

But Tiamoc hadn't turned to face Banon. Rather, the Vaida's eyes were staring straight ahead, to where a wall of shrub rose up before them.

"Oh," Tiamoc said. "I guess we took a wrong turn back there somewhere."

"A wrong turn?" Banon exclaimed. "You mean we have to *backtrack*?"

"Afraid so, my friend. Afraid so. That's the thing with mazes, they're rather unforgiving that way," Tiamoc said, offering Banon a wry smile before passing by him and marching back the other way.

Banon glanced over towards Kyanessa, offering a look of dismay. Choosing not to make eye contact, she strode quickly by, to catch up with the Vaida who was already some way down the trail.

One wrong turn would have been bad enough, in this weather, under these circumstances. But as it turns out they came to a dead end twice more that evening. Dark had fallen almost completely by the time Tiamoc made one more abrupt right turn, before leading them down a trail where a small stone cabin came into view through the fading light, smoke trailing out of its small, slightly crooked chimney.

As they approached the cabin Tiamoc surprised them again, with yet another abrupt stop. He stood still for a moment, staring ahead.

Banon wondered what on earth the issue was this time. Clearly they hadn't made a wrong turn; surely their destination was just ahead of them. So why were they stopping now? When dry, warm, welcoming quarters were within sight?

"What's wrong?" Banon asked. "Isn't the cabin our destination?"

Tiamoc didn't look over at Banon when he replied. "Oh, it's our destination alright, but..."

"But what?" Banon asked, his patience worn beyond thin.

"I fear something's wrong," Tiamoc said, almost in a whisper.

Just then the Vaida turned his head to look to his left, where a cleanly cut shrub wall rose nearly fifty feet into the air. Above the wall, the tangled branches of a neighboring tree could just be made out in the growing darkness.

Tiamoc's head then darted to the right – to the opposite shrub border wall; his eyes roaming, as if searching for something.

"What is it?" Kyanessa finally asked, Tiamoc's concern clearly contagious.

"The cabin... it's lit from both the back and the front," he said, cryptically.

"Yes, so...?" Banon asked, not seeing the

connection.

"So... I was told to expect only one light, coming from the back, unless..."

"Unless what?" Kyanessa asked, her anxiety building.

"Unless there was trouble," Tiamoc replied. "Quick: we must turn back. It's not safe here," he said, already pushing past Banon to retreat the same way they'd come.

"Wait!" Banon said, frustration draped across his features. "How can you be sure? You mean we've come all this way only to-"

Just then there was a rustling sound from overhead. All three turned to the skies just as something draped over them. They clawed forward, only to find themselves drawn in tighter to each other, caught in a net that had dropped from the tangled branches high above.

Suddenly several voices erupted from around them. And in the near dark several hooded figures dropped adeptly from the branches high above.

Banon looked from figure to figure, but found their faces obscured in the near darkness. Then he caught sight of Kyanessa's expression, as one of their captors leaned in close to her. Whatever she was seeing, it had clearly terrified her – for her bright, blue eyes were drawn wide with fear.

73

Once the net had bound them tightly together the hooded figures moved in, quickly disarming Banon of his sword and Kyanessa of her bow and quill of arrows.

"Move!" one of the figures demanded, pointing in the direction of the cabin down the narrow path.

The three of them found it difficult to move in one direction with their limbs entangled. But with a combination of shoves from their captors, and the chaotic stepping of their tangled legs, they eventually made it. As they approached the now open door, Banon beheld the cobble-stone walls and the warm, yellow lighting that poured through the thick-rimmed windows, and thought it ironic that such a welcoming place would serve as their apparent prison.

Once inside the three were separated and tied to posts, with their hands behind their backs. Kyanessa cried out in pain when the rope was drawn so tight that it cut into her skin.

"Get off of her, you brute!" Banon shouted, trying to free himself, but only managing to tighten his own bonds.

One of the figures stepped forward, and backhand slapped Banon across the face. "*Silence!*"

Banon looked into his assailant's eyes, noticed they were almost completely black. The eyes stared back, unblinkingly, for the eyelids had been cut away. The ghoul's skin was pale, to the point of almost appearing translucent. The left cheek, from the half-missing ear down to the jaw, looked disfigured, as if burned to a crisp.

Banon leaned back, repulsed. The figure's eyes seemed to swim with an oily substance as it fixed its glare on the dismayed Landrite.

"What *are* you?" Banon said aloud.

The ghoul smiled, as if enjoying Banon's revulsion.

As the night wore on, Banon, Kyanessa, and Tiamoc tried to ignore the pain they all felt, bound uncomfortably on the hard floor. Across the room the group of hooded figures, all dressed in black, were gathered and talking quietly amongst themselves.

Though they hadn't removed their hoods, Banon caught sight of several of their faces, and saw that they each shared that same strangely pale, scarred skin. And the horrifyingly dark, pupilless eyes.

Banon looked over to Kyanessa, who's back looked slightly contorted in the position she was in.

"Kyanessa, you alright?" Banon asked with concern.

She nodded, biting her lower lip to fight off the pain.

When Banon looked over to Tiamoc he registered shock on the usually steadfast Vaida's face. Banon sensed something had dawned on the small Vaida. Probably nothing good.

"Tiamoc? What is it?" Banon asked, trying to whisper, so as not to encourage more retribution from their captors.

The diminutive Vaida didn't look over towards him, but kept staring straight ahead, in the direction of their captors.

"I know them," he finally said, quietly.

"You *know* them? Who are they, then?" Banon asked, eyeing the group across the room warily.

Just then one of the captors turned in their direction. As the figure strode purposefully over towards them, it pulled something from its belt.

It was a whip, which it unwound quickly.

"Silence!" the figure said, before quickly, almost effortlessly, letting fly with the whip. The chord lashed out and struck Banon hard on the shoulder, ripping open a wide gash.

Banon let loose a muffled cry, one laced with both frustration and pain. Then his eyes flared wide as he stared up at his assailant. This was not the same ghoul who'd addressed him before, though strangely, grotesquely similar.

This hooded figure seemed to almost enjoy Banon's resistance; as if egging him on, looking for the slightest reason to strike again.

The tension broke when an interior door opened from across the room. Another of the ghastly figures then came striding in, with what looked like another prisoner in tow.

The man, who appeared to be close to

unconsciousness, was thrown down on the floor next to Tiamoc, and tied up like the rest of them.

This new captive was a tall, wiry man, with long, wavy black hair, sprinkled with grey – and a matching goatee. In the position he was in, leaning forward with his hands tied behind his back, his long grey-black locks fell forward, obscuring his face from the others.

Banon looked over towards Tiamoc, searching for a sign that the Vaida knew the identity of their new cellmate. Tiamoc's face was written with concern, and some degree of shock. Banon wondered: was this man the owner of the cabin? Was he the one who was to provide them shelter? If so, clearly he hadn't betrayed them, but had been ambushed like the rest of them.

Then the man suddenly shifted his weight, and, in an exhausted way, blew the hair from his face, leaning back against the wall. As he did so his face became visible.

"Dianvolo!" Kyanessa exclaimed softly, looking with startled concern towards the new captive.

Banon watched the ghouls, fearing more retribution. But, mercifully, they seemed not to have heard her. They were again engaged in conversation; of a heated kind – if he had it right.

Banon was astonished that Kyanessa knew the identity of the prisoner. *How could that be?* Had they not grown up in the same region of the world – on a continent that lay on the other side of the Emalderine Ocean?

Of course, he knew the answer... Part of it,

anyway. Grantine culture had kept abreast of the ways of the Movadem, whereas Landrite culture had not. Now, seeing matters spinning out of control before them, Banon was beginning to question the wisdom of his own people's decisions, of his own father's governing perspective; not that he would admit that to anyone if asked.

"Sirs, would you bid a lady a moment to let nature take its course?" Kyanessa called out, suddenly, catching them all by surprise.

The same ghastly figure as before spun around and marched over towards them, fixing its oily eyes upon the slight figure of Kyanessa.

"Bite your tongue, woman!" it barked, unfurling the whip to send a message.

"But sir, a lady cannot but help if nature calls. All I ask for is a moment to empty my bladder. *Please*..."

Banon regarded Kyanessa with amazement. How calm she appeared!

The guard seemed equally surprised by her demeanor, and continued silently staring, as if searching for an ulterior motive.

"Rise," the ghoul finally said, moving forward to untie the bonds that held her to the poll. Then he called to one of his comrades, who came lumbering over. "Take her outside. Let her empty her bladder. But watch her closely."

The other reached out and grasped Kyanessa by the arm, almost fiercely. Kyanessa grimaced but didn't say anything, quietly letting herself be carted away.

Outside, her black-robed captor stopped once they'd moved a few dozen yards from the cabin. He pointed to the hollowed out trunk of a large, half fallen tree.

"You can do your business in there," the ghoul said, pointing. "But, I warn you: if you try and run, I will lash you so deeply you'll be scarred for the rest of your life, short as it may be."

Kyanessa nodded, moving into the shadow of the hollowed-out trunk.

After a few moments, the ghoul watching the others inside began growing restless. Several times he glanced towards the door, wondering where the other ghoul and the woman had got to.

"Move and I'll whip you to shreds," the ghoul said, pointing a gnarled finger at Banon, before moving over to the door.

From the corner of his eye Banon could see the ghoul looking out the window, searching for sign of the other two. Dianvolo took the opportunity to speak, but he did so under his breath, and managed to do it almost without letting his mouth move at all.

"Tiamoc, what of the seer? He's not with you?"

"No, he turned back while we slept. Back to Wisterlac we think," Tiamoc whispered in reply.

Banon's heart was racing. He wondered if it was wise for them to speak when the whip-happy guard was almost within earshot.

"Back to Wisterlac?" Dianvolo repeated. "But why?"

"A vision. He believes Wisterlac will be attacked."

"Attacked? By wh-"

Just then their guard, who'd apparently caught sight of the two he was looking for, turned and walked back over to them. Banon held his breath for a moment, but it seemed evident the guard hadn't overheard Tiamoc and Dianvolo's conversation.

The front door swung open, and Kyanessa returned to her place against the wall, next to the others. Her bonds were then refastened, as tightly as ever. Banon couldn't help but notice Kyanessa turn her head towards Tiamoc, who seemed to smile knowingly in return.

74

Ademo opened his eyes. There was near darkness all around him. *How long had he been asleep for?*

Looking up to the moon – the *nearly full* moon that both lit the landscape and served as a harbinger of evil tidings to come – Ademo guessed several hours had passed since he'd finally collapsed to the ground, exhausted from a day of endless trekking.

He sat up, rubbing the aching muscles in his legs. To his chagrin, they seemed even more sore now than when he'd first stopped. Though he didn't want to admit it to himself, the idea of pushing on again now seemed almost preposterous. He was still *so* tired. He half wondered if his legs might just collapse under him, even if he were to mentally summon the fortitude to continue.

Perhaps... But either way, he had to try.

Still, time seemed as if it were passing like the rushing river. If he had it right, he had twenty-four hours, maybe even less, to make it back to Wisterlac. Was that even possible? It was difficult for him to know exactly how much farther he had to go. But he hadn't even left the banks of the Goliden yet. So the pine forests and the hike back up to the crater summit of Mt. Wister still lay ahead of him.

Truth be told, there was much ground yet to tread, he was already exhausted, and much of the journey ahead would be made at a steep incline. Still, he had to try. He *had* to try. At least until his body simply collapsed under its own weight.

He gripped onto a handful of nearby reeds, to garner support, and pulled himself up – almost every muscle in his body screaming in protest.

And, just then, Ademo heard something shuffle from behind him. He spun around, again feeling his muscles protest.

He was greeted with nothing but the dark and the sound of the rushing river.

And then he heard it again: a shuffle, the sound of bushes being rustled. Ademo tensed, wondering what lay on the other side of those bushes.

Were there hillcats in these lands? Something

similar? A hungry predator eager for a meal?

Or had the enemy's forces finally found him?

Ademo breathed deep, trying to summon strength, even though he knew adrenaline alone could only carry his exhausted muscles so far.

Then he heard it again, louder this time. Something... Something large... was pushing its way through the brush that lined the riverbank.

Ademo's eyes drew wide, and he backed up a few paces, until he was only feet from the rushing waters.

As the bushes were pushed aside, a startling shape began to emerge. Ademo gasped, his eyes betraying surprise.

"Pearlsand!" he exclaimed, his fear turning to a cocktail of joy and relief. He stepped forward, even as the majestic, white steed managed to fully free himself of the brush. Horse and rider shared a warm greeting, Pearlsand nuzzling up next to Ademo and snorting a hello.

"How ever did you find me, you wonder of a beast?" Ademo asked, stroking the long mane. "Your timing couldn't be better, my friend. You've given me a chance to help. To help those at Wisterlac. They're in trouble. You must carry me across the distance at a speed like the lini wind. Can you do that, dear Pearlsand?"

The horse neighed, digging one of its front hooves into the soft ground.

"Right then," Ademo said, leaping atop the horse's back in one swift movement, "let's do it then,

Pearlsand. *Hiyaar!*"

Ademo held tight as Pearlsand neighed loudly in excitement, rearing back on his hind legs, before darting off along the river trail at breakneck speed.

75

Banon, Kyanessa, and Tiamoc were all stiff and uncomfortable. The hardwood floor and knobby, round poles they were tied to proved less than forgiving. And by now they were all dealing with kinks in their backs and legs.

Even worse than their immediate discomfort was the daunting question of what these horrific captors planned to do with them. They had been told nothing, and hours had now passed since they first were captured along the cabin trail.

Eventually, despite the unpleasant circumstances, fatigue from their long day's march overcame them. They all fell into a restless sleep.

When Kyanessa opened her eyes for what felt like the sixth or seventh time, she saw a faint light dawning outside. She had been awoken when two of their captors had started conversing from across the room. When Kyanessa realized they might be saying something they'd rather her not hear, she closed her eyes and feigned sleep, straining to make out their words.

"The others have gone looking for the one that's missing."

"Missing?"

"Yes. We were told there would be three with the Watcher. One's missing."

"No one told me about that! If I would have known that we would have questioned them hours ago!" the ghoul replied, in a distressed tone. Then after a moment he asked: "What does he want them for, anyway?"

"No idea. All I know is I don't want to disappoint him. You know what he'll do if he thinks we let one escape."

"But we didn't let one escape! There were only three of them to begin with!"

"You think he'll concern himself with that small detail? He'll burn us anyway. Just like he burned us before. You know that as well as I do."

The other one grunted his assent.

Could these monsters really feel fear? Kyanessa gathered that they could.

"How long do we have before he arrives?" the second one asked the first.

"Don't know for sure. But he was sent for as soon as we captured them."

The second one grunted again, with what sounded like trepidation. Kyanessa wondered: what kind of person, or thing, could provoke such fear in these unfeeling brutes?

Just then she heard shuffling, and she let her eyes open just a crack. The two figures were now marching purposefully over to them. One of them drew his whip, then let it fly, snapping it against the hard wood floor. Kyanessa's companions were all jolted awake, now staring with eyes wide as the ghouls approached.

"Wake up, you fools! Where's your friend, huh? *Where is he*?" he barked, letting fly with the whip again, lashing it against the wall behind them, missing Banon by inches.

When none of them replied to the question, Kyanessa gasped when their captor curled his whip again, ready to strike.

"I asked you a question! Where is your miserable friend? Tell me now, or I'll whip you till your skin hangs from your bones!"

When none replied, the captor gritted his rotting, stumped teeth, lifting his arm behind his head to wind up the whip.

"Your intelligence was wrong!" Dianvolo suddenly blurted out, only a moment before the whip would have ripped into Banon's flesh.

"I asked *them*, not you, reject!" the ghoul shouted, before lashing the whip against Dianvolo's leg.

Dianvolo grunted and drew his leg back in pain. Kyanessa looked on with concern, seeing the deep slash and blood oozing from the fresh wound.

After a moment Dianvolo gathered himself, stared back up at their captor, his injured leg trembling slightly. "Why do you care who answers the question

437

as long as you get your answer! I'm telling you this because I want *better* treatment, not worse. And for that you lash me?"

With blackened, unblinking eyes, their captor studied Dianvolo, as if searching for hints of deception. Once again an oily substance seemed to be swimming behind that gaze.

"And why should we believe you, reject?" the captor demanded.

"Because, like I said, I want better treatment. So if you'll promise not to strike me again with that blasted whip, and if you'll let me stretch my legs a couple of times before the day is through, then I'll tell you what you want to know."

"Tell me first, and *then* I'll decide if your information is worth leniency!" the captor barked, drawing the whip back in threat.

When Dianvolo took a moment too long to comply, their captor again let fly with the whip, this time drawing fresh blood from Dianvolo's right arm. Dianvolo yelped in pain, and his body seemed to spasm.

"Leave him alone!" Kyanessa shouted out.

Their captor turned, strode over, and leaned in close to Kyanessa; the slick, oily eyes now swimming inches from her face.

"Silence, woman! You want some of the same?" the ghoul threatened, putrid spittle spraying over Kyanessa's face.

"Don't bother with her. She won't tell you what

you need to know. But I will, so deal with me," Dianvolo said, with that same determined look.

The captor stared for a moment longer into Kyanessa's eyes, as if deciding whether or not to strike her, just for the sport of it. But then the ghoul turned again, facing Dianvolo.

"Speak then! And make it quick. Or I'll lash you till you're more red than pink!"

"Let me tell you outside, in the fresh air. Like I said, I need to stretch my legs," Dianvolo said.

The guard stood silently for a moment, a slight hissing sound emanating from his thin, almost lipless mouth. Then he turned to the one who'd escorted Kyanessa outside the day before.

"Watch these three. If any of them even as much as breathes too loudly, let 'em have it. Twice for good measure. Got it?"

When the other nodded, the ghoul reached down and quickly untied Dianvolo's bonds. He then grabbed Dianvolo's arm and pulled him up in one brisk motion.

"Easy," Dianvolo said, wincing and rubbing his wrists where the ropes had bitten into the skin. "Remember: I'm the one with the information."

"We'll see about that," the ghoul said, pushing Dianvolo towards the door.

When the door slammed shut, silence ensued. Banon strained to hear the conversation outside, but couldn't make anything out. He then looked over towards Tiamoc, who was sitting with his head leaning back against the pole, his eyes closed.

Banon shook his head in disbelief. He'd heard Tiamoc tell the long-haired stranger about Ademo's whereabouts. And now that same man was outside with one of their captors, quite likely about to give Ademo up.

The lanky Landrite let his head sink. Because suddenly everything they'd done to help Ademo reach safety and wise counsel seemed in vain.

76

By the time the sun was high in the sky Ademo was much closer to his destination, riding atop the swift-footed Pearlsand. Hours earlier they'd left the banks of the Goliden River and had turned east to climb the slope towards Mt. Wister, which could now be seen peaking above the foothills.

Ademo knew they were making good time, but was still hesitant to halt, even once. But by now he was suffering from hunger pains, not having eaten a proper meal in a very long time.

Eventually they came upon a row of bushes and, seeing something that caught his eye, Ademo drew Pearland to a stop. He leapt from the horse's back and strode over to the bush. He could see why he'd spotted these particular berries, even while galloping by at top speed: they were huge. Plump and of a rich, cherry red.

Ademo leaned in, plucked one from the bush. It came off easily enough, and felt substantive in his palm. By now Ademo's stomach was cramping and his mouth was watering. Enough with the waiting, it was time to take some sustenance. He raised his hand to plop the berry in his mouth, whole.

But just then Pearland neighed loudly from behind. Ademo turned to see the horse dig his hoof into the ground. The majestic white steed then snorted, before striding over to Ademo and brushing his long face against Ademo's arm.

"What?" Ademo said. "What is it, Pearlsand? One has to eat once in a while, you know. Don't worry, we'll be away again in just a moment. Just let me-"

The horse swung its head, knocking the plump berry from Ademo's hand.

"*Pearlsand!* What'd you do that for? That was a perfectly good berry!"

The horse neighed in protest. Ademo stared into those kind but fierce eyes and sensed something: warning?

"Unless..." Ademo said, looking from the horse to the ground where the berry had fallen. "Are you trying to tell me something about that berry? That it's no good or something?"

Pearlsand neighed and stomped his hoof, for good measure.

Ademo bent down and picked up the berry, tentatively. He drew it near his lips. Pearlsand's eyes drew wide and he neighed again.

"Don't worry, boy," Ademo said, stroking the horse's mane, "I get the point. You're saying it's no good. Maybe poisonous?"

With that he let his tongue touch the very edge of the berry.

He didn't notice anything at first, and was about to toss a frown Pearlsand's way. But then he did feel it: a rush of prickly sourness at the edge of his tongue. He'd only barely let it touch and yet half of his mouth now began to take on the uncomfortable, prickly sensation. Ademo spat and spat some more, until all the saliva in his mouth was gone.

"I see your point!" he said, wiping his lips and trying to spit again, even though his mouth was now bone dry.

Pearlsand turned and trotted down the path, stopping before an opening in the bushes. Ademo cocked his head and gave the horse a quizzical look. Then, figuring that Pearlsand had more than earned his trust, he followed.

Almost immediately behind the large bush with the colorful berries was another row of bushes, small and low to the ground.

"What?" Ademo said. "What is it?"

Pearlsand bent his large head towards the ground, brushing his nose up against the small plants. Ademo moved forward, bent down to look more closely.

"Well, I'll be darned... this one has berries, too.

Not nearly as impressive. But a berry's a berry, right?"

Pearlsand huffed.

Ademo, still looking up into the horse's eyes, plucked one of the small, turquoise-colored berries from the plant, and held it up – as if in toast to Pearlsand – before plopping it whole into his mouth. This time Pearlsand didn't offer any objection.

To Ademo's surprise, the berry was quite flavorful; tasting something like a cross between a raspberry and a kiwi.

"Mmm, not bad. My thanks, my friend," Ademo said, smiling and patting Pearlsand's impressive, thick neck.

Then Ademo reached down for more. And before long he'd plucked the entire row almost bare. It wasn't much of a meal, but he felt more replenished, nevertheless.

"Okay," Ademo said, "onward then. Let's hope that was our last stop. We're headed for the top of that peak over there. Are you ready to run some more Pearlsand?"

The horse neighed enthusiastically, and reared back on his hind legs. Ademo smiled and leapt onto the steed's back.

A moment later horse and rider were racing between the pines.

77

"So... *speak!*" the ghoulish captor barked, standing across from Dianvolo outside the cabin.

"Certainly. Would be glad to. As you say, I owe no allegiance to the Vaidas. After all, it was they who threw me out of their order."

"I don't care about your feelings, reject. I just want the information. Where is the other member of their traveling party? Where is the seer?"

"*Seer*? You really believe that stuff? That the islander can see the future? And, as some say, even change it? Seriously? That doesn't seem a little farfetched to you? Cause you seem like a reasonable-"

"Stop stalling!" the ghoul shouted. "We're not having a conversation here. You're merely telling me where the missing member of their group is. We know there were four that set out from Wisterlac. And now there are only three. So one is missing. Now, if you know where he is, speak up. Otherwise, I may have to resort to other... *enticements*."

With that the ghoul drew his whip once more, played with it in his hand, before snapping it against a nearby tree.

"Alright! Fine! I'll tell you. Just put that thing away, would you?" Dianvolo said, shrinking away from the glare of the ghoul, whose foul breath saturated the clean, forest air.

"Now!" the ghoul shouted, raising an arm into striking motion.

When Dianvolo took a moment too long to speak, the ghoul let fly with the whip; this time not only in warning.

The hard, rubbery chord struck Dianvolo where his neck met his shoulder, tearing a gaping wound there. Dianvolo let loose with a guttural screech and collapsed to the ground, his body convulsing in waves of pain and nausea.

In all of the commotion, several birds nesting nearby took to the sky; flapping their wings and cackling in protest. Only one particular bird seemed more resilient than the rest. When the others took to the skies, it landed and proceeded to hop closer, watching the scene with piercing vision from the branches above.

"I'm going to give you one more chance," the ghoul said. "And then I think I may just finish you off, because I'm tiring of you. You speak too much, while saying nothing. So make it quick: what do you know of the seer? Where is he?"

Dianvolo rolled over, holding his hands up in front of him in protection, even as the ghoul wound the whip once more.

"I don't think you're going to hit me again," Dianvolo said, lowering his hands just slightly.

The ghoul, perplexed by Dianvolo's reaction, seemed to be taken by surprise.

"*What?* And why would you say that? I've already struck you several times!"

"Because," Dianvolo began, looking almost tranquil, "you're in the presence of a Vaida. And you know how much Vaidas detest violence; especially the needless kind – just won't stomach it."

At this bold pronouncement the ghoul smiled – if you could call the crooked grin that grew over that ashen, scarred face a smile. Lowering the whip, the ghoul leaned in towards Dianvolo.

"You know as well as I do, reject, that *you're* no Vaida. You said yourself: they threw you out of their order. Found you too weak!"

"Me? Well, no argument there. But what makes you think I was talking about me?"

The ghoul cocked its head to the side, sizing up the peculiar response offered by the bleeding man lying on the ground. Then it cursed itself for even letting the fool speak. It wound the whip once again, high above its head, ready to deal a death blow.

And then there was a shuffle from behind.

Spinning around, the ghoul found a grey-robed man standing there.

An oily rage surged through the veins where untainted blood used to pump. The ghoul raised the whip above its head and, in one lightning quick motion, let it fly.

The movement appeared as if in slow motion to the man standing there. His eyes followed the journey of the whip, watching as it corked back, and then kicked forward with force.

A hundredth of a second before the whip came slashing down over his left shoulder, the man turned and kneeled on one leg, grasping the chord as it arched over his shoulder.

Before the ghoul had even a moment to recognize what had happened, the man quickly wound the whip in loops, shortening its length, and then pulled hard. The ghoul, still holding tightly to the other end, came flying forwards.

The grey-robed man stepped deftly to the right, letting the ghoul fly by him. And using the ghoul's own inertia, the man spun the whip several times around the ghoul's neck, until the chord formed a tight choke hold.

The man leaned in, whispered something to the ghoul, and then pulled hard – in one crisp movement. There was a snapping sound, and a cloud of some strange grey-white powder exploded the from the ghoul's neck. The oily mixture behind the ghoul's lidless eyes swam no more.

As he was helped to his feet, Dianvolo shared a grateful smile with an old friend. Then, pointing towards the cabin, Dianvolo motioned for silence with a single finger to his mouth.

"The others are still being held inside. Are these things what I think they are?" Dianvolo whispered, pointing to the grotesque corpse that lay on the ground.

"Yes. Eilodens. Hard to believe, I know. How many

are there?" the man asked.

"Just one inside the room here. But there may be others nearby. It seems most of them have gone searching for the seer."

"Ademo? You mean he's not here?"

Dianvolo shook his head, registering the concern on the other's face. "No. But the others seem to think he's alright. He was the last time they saw him, anyway."

Inside the cabin, the ghoul guarding the others seemed almost nonchalant. But as the minutes ticked by with no word from the other, concern began to register, even though emotion didn't seem to show on these faces like they would on those of normal men.

Finally, his anxiety getting the better of him, the ghoul walked over to the window. The others heard him grunt with relief when he saw his black-cloaked comrade marching back towards the door, the other prisoner in tow.

"Looks like your friend took quite a whipping. Silly man. Should have fessed up earlier, if he knew what was good for him," the ghoul said, sneering.

The door swung open and the two marched in. Dianvolo was shoved to the ground next to the others. The ghoul who'd waited inside smiled when he beheld the bleeding gash on the prisoner's neck. Just as he had thought; *quite* the whipping.

The ghoul turned to comment to his colleague, even as Dianvolo groaned in pain. And in that moment, as the one he thought was his colleague raised a black-hooded head, the ghoul's ghastly breath caught somewhere in his throat.

Who was this?

With blinding speed the man struck directly at the ghoul's mid-section. As the ghoul doubled over, the man grabbed it by the head, twisted one time, hard to the right. There was a snapping sound, another explosion of powdery material, and the ghoul collapsed in a heap on the floor.

While the man was dealing with the ghoul, Dianvolo stood and rushed over to the doorway. No sooner had he got there than he heard footsteps rushing from the other room. Seconds later, two more ghouls rushed through the doorway. They stopped momentarily, seeing one of their own collapsed on the floor.

Then they turned to the other ghoul, who presently had his hooded head turned away from them.

"What happened?" one of them called out. "And where's the long haired one who–"

Before the ghoul could finish his question Dianvolo's hands reached from behind the door, wrapped around the head, twisted hard to the left. Again there was a snap, a cloud of powdery grey-white material exploding into the air, and a ghoulish body falling to the ground.

As the one remaining ghoul turned to register Dianvolo, the temporarily black-cloaked figure they had mistaken for one of their own turned and lunged, making quick work with the same technique: an iron grip around the neck and a swift twist. Snap, puff, and another ghoulish body collapsed to the floor.

It was only then, the immediate danger passed, that the man – who had temporarily dawned the black cloak of the ghoul who lay outside – removed his hood, turning towards the others.

"Muirik!" Kyanessa exclaimed, with a mixture of joy and profound relief.

Banon wanted to shout out as well, but was too taken by surprise to say anything. He just sat there motionless, his jaw hanging open.

Muirik rushed forward and began untying Kyanessa's bound hands. The second she was free she used them to embrace him. He smiled and returned the hug gladly.

"Well done, Kyanessa. Well done."

Then Banon found his vocal chords again, even as Dianvolo was leaning in to untie him.

"Well done? I don't understand. What did Kyanessa do?" he said, feeling perplexed and a little out of the loop. Looking around, he noticed knowing smiles draped across the others' faces.

Then Kyanessa turned towards him, and when she had finished rubbing her sore wrists, she placed her hand between her breasts, drew something out.

Banon stared at the small, flutelike object in her hand, and let the contagious smile of the others overcome him.

Muirik clapped him on the back and drew him in

for an embrace. "Well met, my faithful Landrite," the Vaida said, smiling.

78

Once horse and rider reached the notorious shrub brush near the summit of Mt. Wister, the two parted with a friendly embrace; Ademo less sad than the last time they parted – because he knew now that Pearlsand had an uncanny way of finding him. Somehow he felt that, if he could survive the night that was to follow, they would see each other again; that they would again have a chance to race the wind together.

It was a big *if*, but it brought comfort, nonetheless.

Not surprisingly, the thorny shrub brush was not at all passable, even when crawling; not unless one found the actual tunnels that had been dug. Ademo spent another twenty anxious minutes searching for the path Muirik had led them on.

When finally he found the almost imperceptible opening, he immediately dove down and started scurrying for all he was worth. And by the time he emerged on the pebbly shore of Wisterlac, he was scratched and bleeding like a battle victim.

Considering a Vaida had led him across the lake each time, Ademo wasn't exactly sure how the crossing worked. Were there only certain locations where the path formed? Ademo assumed so. So, going by memory alone, he did his best to step out into the acidic stew at the same location as before.

Ademo's heart stopped as he made that first step. But when a patch of path suddenly formed in front of him, he breathed an immense sigh of relief. Soon he was chasing across the acidic, yellow-green waters, ignoring the putrid smells as he pushed towards the dome that was now appearing before his very eyes.

Ademo stole a glance towards the western side of the crater rim, and saw that the sunlight was quickly fading. How much time did they have? Not much. Here at Wisterlac it would be dark within a couple of hours. And the attack that he had foreseen could happen any time after that. Again, this thought didn't feel like conjecture. Somehow Ademo simply knew it as fact. The challenge, of course, lay in convincing the Vaidas inside the dome of that.

As he neared the dome it was Crion, the tall, broad-shouldered Vaida whom they'd met when they had first arrived, who was there to greet him.

"Ademo!" he exclaimed, surprised. "What are you doing here? Where are the others? And how did you cross the lake? Only -"

"Crion, well met, friend. Unfortunately, there's no time for me to explain everything right now. I'm here because the monat is in danger. It's about to be attacked."

"Attacked? But how? By whom? And how do you

know-"

"Again, there's little time. It'll happen sometime after nightfall, I'm sure of that. What we need to do is gather the Vaidas so I can tell you all at once. We're going to need to act quickly!"

Crion took only a moment longer to absorb the news, then he stood aside and motioned for Ademo to enter.

Moments later they were both rushing down the perimeter hallway towards the Centrarium.

79

When Ademo finished briefing the hastily gathered council of Vaidas who had remained at Wisterlac, silence ensued. The Vaidas sitting around him seemed to be ruminating in stunned silence. Ademo swallowed hard, waiting to hear how they would respond. He already feared from their expressions that they likely considered him foolhardy, if not insane.

Eventually Rumillion, sitting in the first row, broke the tension when he moved ever so slightly from his meditative posture.

"Ademo, do you remember anything else? Any other details? Do you remember the position of the full moon in the sky, for instance?"

"Umm..." Ademo thought out loud, surprised by Rumillion's response, "not really. There was so much turmoil in the dream that I can't say I really noticed."

Rumillion nodded, leaning forward, resting his elbows on his knees and holding his hands in front of him in teepeed fashion.

"You have done us a great service, Ademo. And I thank you. *We* thank you," Rumillion said, with appreciation in his eyes.

Ademo felt a surge of relief pulse though him. Rumillion *believed* him. That meant a lot. It was much like the relief he had felt when Renata had shown a similar confidence.

But no sooner had Ademo registered this feeling than one of the other Vaidas spoke up. It was the tall, slender brother named Mossic.

"Prida, I also am thankful that Ademo has risked so much to return to us, to... warn us. But, if I may, how can we be sure of this... premonition? Do we have any other information to suggest an attack is imminent?"

Crion replied: "We know that Corpazon was attacked. So there is recent precedence for this kind of thing."

"Yes," replied Mossic, "but, if I may say, Ademo was also aware of that information. So how do know that his mind wasn't merely piecing together two disconnected recollections? Perhaps this premonition was, after all, just-"

"Just a dream?" Rumillion said, finishing the

other's thought.

"Yes, that's what I'm wondering. No offense meant towards Ademo. But sometimes a dream is just a dream; isn't it?"

"Most certainly," Rumillion began. "But in my experience a seer can tell the difference between a true premonition and a run of the mill dream."

When Ademo heard Rumillion's statement, his mind caught on that word: *seer*. Was that how Rumillion saw him? As a seer? The word was only vaguely familiar, but he'd heard it a few times when his mother used to read to him. What was it that seers could do again? See the future? Did that mean that this was some sort of... gift? One that wasn't isolated to this one event?

Before Ademo could think further on this one of the other Vaidas spoke up.

"If the prida has declared Ademo a seer, then we should take it on faith," said Lensing, the golden-skinned, bronze-haired brother. "And that means that we must take this warning seriously. So, that being said, what will do about it? How can we best prepare ourselves, with so little time left? Debating the validity of the threat seems a poor use of our time."

Nods and mumbles of ascent reverberated throughout the chamber. Ademo noticed that even the Vaida who'd first raised the question seemed to recognize the wisdom of this course. And it made sense. After all, if he turned out to be wrong they could deal with that luxury later. If he was right, however, then time was of the essence.

"But if an attack were to happen, how would this enemy negate our shield signature?" Mossic asked.

More mumbles of ascent and concern rumbled throughout the chamber. The Vaidas trusted the shield that protected the monat, having never had reason to doubt its reliability. Eventually it was Rumillion who spoke again.

"In all my years I have never heard even a hint of the possibility of negating an energy shield if the signature is secure. Therefore, I think we can draw only one conclusion: the signature is *not* secure."

This time Ademo heard gasps of surprise rise up around him.

"But if that's true, that means our security has been breached!" one of the Vaidas offered, with dismay.

"And that we have a traitor in our midst," said another of the brothers.

Ademo's jaw dropped as near chaos ensued around him.

That same Vaida added, over the rising chorus of voices around him: "I am sorry to voice such a thought, but we must consider the possibility! How else could we explain such a breach?"

Then another of the Vaidas chimed in, nearly shouting to be heard: "What about our murdered brothers? Clearly their deaths were the work of this enemy. What if he gained the information from them – through torture?"

Rumillion held up his hands, motioning for calm. Eventually he had it. "As your prida, I am responsible for each and every one of you. It is I who asonds to the purity of heart and vision for each of you. And I am firm in my endorsement of each man in this room today, and of each of our Wisterlac brethren currently afield; including our fallen brothers. If I am wrong in this assertion, then may any blood be on *my* hands."

Rumillion's statement seemed to bring some measure of calm to the chamber. Eventually another brother spoke.

"Prida, if I may, what of Yersa, our brother from Corpazon? Have you also had opportunity to meet with him, and can you asond for his standing?"

"Yes," Rumillion replied, "I know Yersa well. And I did meet with him personally. I can asond for him as well."

"I am sorry to speak of this," said Mossic, "but, if I may be so bold – considering the circumstances – what of the companions of Ademo? The tall one and the girl? What do we know of them? Could they have ascertained the signature while here at Wisterlac?"

Ademo frowned at the suggestion. He knew there was no way in the world that either of his friends were responsible. He'd bet his life on it if need be.

"If either of them was serving this phantom enemy," Rumillion stated, without condescension, "then Ademo – I dare say – would no longer be with us. They would have killed him the first chance they had. After all, he is a piece more important to this enemy than even Monat Wisterlac. No, we need not concern ourselves with them. They are trusted allies."

Just then, a rather disturbed voice spoke up from the third row. It was Doven, who had been assigned the watch of the east entrance. "There *has* been one additional visitor to Wisterlac," he said, almost sheepishly.

"You mean the other brother from Corpazon? Rodero was his name, wasn't it?" another added.

Rumillion turned to these two. "What is this you speak of? I wasn't told of the arrival of any such visitor," he said, in a tone of some seriousness.

Doven cast a nervous glance towards the prida. "Forgive me, Prida. When first he arrived you were still away."

"And where is he now?" Rumillion asked, his eyes blazing with intensity.

"He is in one of the guest quarters, I believe. The last I knew he was meeting with Yersa," the Vaida replied.

"Crion, Hurson, please go and check on our two guests. Bring them back here, please," Rumillion said, still eyeing the sheepish Vaida whose eyes were now firmly fixed on the floor in front of him.

In the moments that ensued the Vaidas discussed various points of strategy that were mostly lost on Ademo. Once again, he felt naïve as to the scope of the challenges they faced. Still, they *were* responding to a threat he had brought to their attention. So, after all, perhaps he wasn't so out of place. He did his best to piece together the threads of conversation around him.

But then Ademo noticed something: while the others continued to debate, Rumillion sat silently, staring into empty space; looking detached and preoccupied.

And then the voices in the chamber slowly died out, as footfalls were heard thudding down the hallway. Crion charged into the double-wide Centrarium entrance, his breath coming in heaving gasps.

"Brothers!" he said, sucking in air. "Yersa is dead! We found his body stuffed in one of the guest closets."

Gasps of astonishment erupted all around and echoed throughout the tall, circular chamber. The usually calm Vaidas were now on their feet.

"And what of the other? This Brother Rodero?" Rumillion asked, storming up to the doorway.

"Nowhere to be found!" Crion exclaimed. "We searched each of the guest quarters thoroughly, and Hurson is still looking elsewhere throughout the monat, but I fear he has already fled the dome!"

80

Knowing there were other ghouls in the area – those Muirik had called eilodens, searching for Ademo – the group at Dianvolo's cabin wasted no time in taking to the trail. They marched steadily and silently, their bodies sore after being bound for so long.

Dianvolo, being the most familiar with the area, led them through a shortcut in the maze. Before long they took to a narrow trail that led them almost straight up a steep hillside. Near the top of the hill the trees thinned out and they came to an even steeper section, where boulders and prickly plants littered the otherwise open landscape. Dianvolo led them past several of these boulders before coming to a flat, roughly rounded rock, that lay almost vertically against the hillside.

Dianvolo motioned for them to help him, and they were soon able to roll the large, but shallow rock away, revealing a small cave entrance.

Once safely inside, with the stone again covering the entrance, they finally let their tired bodies collapse onto the damp, dark earth of the cave's interior, where only slivers of light penetrated.

This was definitely no random cave, but one that Dianvolo had stored with provisions. Once they had a fire going, Banon and Kyanessa took to the task of cooking a meal. While the food was being prepared, Muirik spoke quietly with Tiamoc and Dianvolo, and was briefed on all that had transpired since he last saw them at Wisterlac.

When Muirik learned of Ademo's decision to turn back to Wisterlac, alone, he shook his head, his face betraying both fear and respect. "I knew that young man was a fierce one. And in days such as these, that kind of determination is exactly what's needed."

Overhearing Muirik's comment, Kyanessa spoke up while stirring a stew over the fire pit. "Muirik, do you think Ademo made it back to Wisterlac in time? The full moon is tonight. Is it possible he's there now, even as we speak?"

"I don't know, dear. That would have been quite some distance to cover, especially on foot. And there are other agents of the enemy roaming these lands now."

"There are? But we didn't come across any. Not until we got to Dianvolo's cabin, anyway," Banon said.

Muirik raised an eyebrow. "You may not have seen them, my trusted Landrite, but you can trust that they saw you. They just had no reason to intervene. After all, they had already sprung a trap for you at the cabin."

Banon nodded slowly, as his face grew darker, Ademo's journey back to Wisterlac now seeming all the more treacherous.

Seeing concerned expressions on the faces of Ademo's young companions, Muirik walked over to the fire and placed a hand on each of their shoulders.

"But Ademo is both brave and intuitive. And it sounds like he was doubly determined because of the nature of his visions, as is often the case with seers; though we have not seen their like in quite some time. So we can hope that Ademo did indeed arrive safely at Wisterlac. It wouldn't surprise me if he did. And I speak truthfully to that."

"And what about what he expects will happen this evening, under the full moon?" Kyanessa asked. "Will the monat be attacked? Are Ademo and the Vaidas there in mortal danger?"

Muirik paused for a moment before responding. "Yes, I fear that Ademo was right about that," he began, and then, noticing Tiamoc's downcast expression, added: "though *none* of you could have know that at the time. You see, it is only recently that I've discovered more about Ademo's past, and that's changed my view of him a great deal."

"What do you mean?" Kyanessa asked. "What of his past? What did you learn?"

"Well, that's a tale for another time. Rumillion saw something when he sealed minds with Ademo, and that gave us a few threads to pursue. And I've learned even more since we last saw each other. But I think that's best shared at a later time, and perhaps only after Ademo has heard himself what I have to say."

Kyanessa couldn't help but wonder if Muirik had already suspected as much about Ademo, but was breaking the news gently for Tiamoc's sake. Regardless, it certainly seemed that Tiamoc knew a great deal less about Ademo than either Rumillion or Muirik.

"But I assume these... threads you're pursuing, they're also related to what Ademo saw in the water," Banon added, and then turned to look Tiamoc's way, realizing they'd been told that the underground chamber was not common monat knowledge.

Muirik kept a steady eye on the fire. "Perhaps. Time will tell."

"But, do you think Ademo will be able to help the Vaidas when the attack comes? He seemed to think he could when he first shared his vision with us," Kyanessa asked, hoping against hope.

"I believe he can help, Kyanessa; in some way, yes. I don't think he would have had the vision if there weren't some way he could. The two tend to go hand in hand."

"You mean he was given the vision because he *will* help? It was the future he saw, then?" Banon asked.

"No, this kind of vision is more like a collage of images from a trajectory of probabilities, or so I understand. But it's not an exact impression of the future as it *will* be."

"I don't understand. Why not?" Banon asked, his brow furrowed.

"Because, my friend, there is more than one possible future that awaits us all. At this point the future is more like a range of possibilities. Seers have a unique ability to perceive those possibilities. It's not entirely unlike your ability to see a distant vista, Banon, when the details are still blurry. Think of it as something like that."

Banon nodded, but didn't honestly feel much the wiser. These concepts were so fanciful. He couldn't help but wonder what his ultra-pragmatic father would do with all he'd heard and seen lately.

As Kyanessa passed around plates of steaming stew, Banon asked another question.

"Muirik, I noticed you seemed to whisper something to those ghouls you killed. And the last one you actually kneeled over. Were you praying over it?"

"I was saying a word of passing, Banon. Because, you see, those were no random fiends of the enemy."

"What were they then? You've seen their like before?" Banon asked, noting now that Tiamoc and Dianvolo both held their heads low, as if in a kind of grief, which perplexed the tall Landrite all the more.

"Well, before they were 'ghouls', as you put it, they were human beings, no different than you or me."

"Human?" Banon repeated, bewildered. "In what sense?"

"They were men. Human in every sense. Before they were ravaged by a chemical compound called Venink."

"Venink? I've never heard of it."

"You wouldn't have. It hasn't been seen in a long time. It is one of the dark tools developed by a man named Loden, long ago. It is a drug. Loden used it to enslave people. They became known as eilodens, which means 'slaves of Loden' in Old Cremic. And now it appears this phantom enemy is using it to do the same in our own time."

"A drug?" Kyanessa said. "They are injected with it somehow, then? Kidnapped and injected?"

"Perhaps. But in the old days many people took it willingly – at first. It creates temporarily positive experiences for those who take it. But it quickly becomes very addictive. And when someone is a full-blown addict the drug ravages their system. It burns their skin from the inside out; induces horrifying hallucinations; deteriorates the eyes."

"Their eyes," Banon began, remembering with horror, "they were lidless – and black!"

"They were blackened with Venink-saturated blood, which explains why it is often referred to as 'ink' – for short; because of the effect it creates in the eyes. The dark fluid builds up there, and when it leaks from the eyes and contacts the open air it turns toxic, melting away the eyelids and eyebrows entirely."

"That's horrible!" Kyanessa said, shaking her head. "And what would happen if they were to stop taking it? Could they recover?"

"Some can, if weaned from it very early on. But, unfortunately, the damage sets in very quickly, and is largely irreversible. The ones that held you at the cabin were beyond human really; beyond hope. Their wills were fully enslaved to the drug; a drug that had reengineered their brains. If they were to be weaned of it they would merely die, not return to life as it once was."

"But how would this enemy even know how to produce this Venink stuff? It's not naturally occurring, I take it?" Kyanessa asked.

"No, definitely not. It must be concocted. I don't

know exactly how. There are rumors that various Lodenic methodologies were recorded in a book of sorts; though no Vaida has ever found proof of its existence. But with this most recent, dark turn of events, one must wonder if perhaps the book does exist, and that this phantom enemy is now practicing much of the dark science within. The coincidences almost seem too great for any other explanation."

As a silent somberness came over the group, Muirik shook his head, staring into the fire pit as it continued to spit and crackle.

"It is a dire turn, to be sure. But let us hope, rather than despair. Desperation is a signpost on a doomed road, as we Vaidas like to say. It does us no good to go there."

"Speaking of this phantom enemy, do we know anything else yet?" Banon asked. "It would be much easier to plan a defense if we knew who, or what, we're up against."

"Indeed it would, Banon. And the other Vaidas who left Wisterlac the same morning I did are busy trying to learn just that. But we won't know what they've managed to discover, if anything, until we all meet again in council."

"And when will that be?" Banon questioned.

Muirik shook his head slowly from side to side. "That I don't know, either. Much will depend on what transpires this evening under the full moon at Wisterlac."

81

Ademo wound his way around the perimeter of the dome until he came to the correct door. Upon knocking, he was quickly ushered inside by Rumillion's familiar voice. As Ademo strolled into a room, only minimally decorated, save for piles of books, Rumillion pointed to a chair and asked Ademo to have a seat.

"Ademo, I asked you here because I want to share something with you; something that may help to explain our enemy's motivation in attacking Wisterlac."

"Oh?" Ademo said, intrigued, and a little scared.

"Yes. You see, while many of the Vaidas here find the prospect of an attack at Wisterlac unlikely, to say the least, I am far less skeptical."

"Why are the others so doubtful of the possibility?" Ademo asked, not understanding.

"Well, the Wisterlac defenses – though invisible to the naked eye – are rather formidable. In fact, I'd say this structure is perhaps the most well protected building on the entire planet."

"Really? Why's that? Just for the safety of the Vaidas here?"

"No, not primarily. The reason, actually, has to do with what lies *beneath* the monat."

"*Beneath*? You mean the underground chamber?" Ademo asked.

"It's connected to that, yes. But, you see, the pool you and your friends gazed into isn't possessed by any strange water, as some might presume."

"It's not?"

"No. The water is normal enough. Garden variety, actually. The uniqueness has to do with the energy source below there, that comes from deep within the mountain."

"What kind of energy source?" Ademo asked, his curiosity growing.

"Well, it's difficult to describe," Rumillion said, pausing to gather his thoughts. "Suffice it to say that far beneath the pool there emanates a reverberation; a frequency. That's as good a way as any other to describe it. And think of that as a part of a chord that makes up the organizational fabric of our reality."

"You mean, like a sound?"

"Not audible to us, you must understand, but very real, nonetheless."

"Does this have to do with numbers, with the Deep Math Muirik told us about?"

"Yes, certainly. Tones; vibrations; frequencies; numbers... they are all part in parcel of each other."

Ademo was doing his best to make sense of the prida's words, but they seemed almost incomprehensible. And he knew this wasn't just because he'd grown up on a remote island. No, he knew this revelation would sound just as outlandish to

Banon and Kyanessa. He remembered their reactions when the reflection in the water was not his own. They were just as shocked as he. Perhaps even more so.

"You see," Rumillion continued, "that's partly why the other Vaidas find the idea of an attack so unlikely. It's not just that Wisterlac is so well defended, but also that they don't fully comprehend the significance of Wisterlac's location, and why it would be such a prime target."

"But why don't the other Vaidas know about this energy source?" Ademo asked.

"Well," Rumillion said, his face betraying complexity, "there are several reasons for that. Reasons that are difficult to elucidate in the short time we have now. I hope that I'll be able to explain more of this to you later. But for now we must attend to more pressing matters."

"Does Muirik know – about Wisterlac's special location?"

"He does. But he is the only Vaida here besides me who possesses this knowledge."

Rumillion let that sink in for a moment, before continuing.

"The thing is, I believe this secret is not as secret as we would have liked. I am convinced that our enemy has also come into this knowledge. It is really the only plausible explanation as to why he'd try to attack the monat directly, as opposed to targeting Vaidas outside in the wider world, where he could – to put it crudely – pick us off one by one."

"But what of the attack at Monat Corpazon? Was its location just as significant?"

"No. I suspect that may have been a preparation for the attack here. A dry run, as it were."

"But, wouldn't the enemy be tipping us off by attacking Corpazon first?"

"Well, remember, because this enemy can also mimic the Movademic harmony, we wouldn't even have *known* about that attack on Corpazon if it weren't for Yersa escaping. And, even so, Wisterlac's energy shield would make the Vaidas here would feel we had impenetrable protection. I myself would feel relatively safe, were it not for your premonition – which I take very seriously."

"But surely part of this is about targeting Vaidas as well. Why would this enemy hate the Vaidas so much?"

"I don't know. But, as of now, that is a helpful thread we must pursue. Hate usually leaves traces – because it is often the poisoned fruit of a grudge."

"So, find out who has a grudge against the Vaidas and we may just find this enemy?"

"Precisely."

Ademo took a moment to consider the prida's words, and then asked: "And what if this enemy succeeds in destroying Wisterlac? What will happen then?"

The prida let out a long breath, leaned back in his chair.

"That is a complicated matter. Suffice it to say that the fabric of the world will weaken. There will be various consequences, destabilizing reality as we know it. In truth, I don't know *exactly* what it would do. None of us now alive does. But it will be dire, no doubt."

"Do you think we can stop this enemy? Stop him from destroying Wisterlac?"

Rumillion's lips drew together in a forced attempt at a reassuring smile. "Well, whatever chances we have, they are considerably better because of your bravery in coming here, Ademo. And for that I thank you. We all do."

Ademo nodded, feeling strange taking a compliment from a man as wise and powerful as Rumillion. Then a thought came to him. One that had plagued him ever since they'd descended to the pool chamber below the monat.

"Rumillion, that man... that *face*... the face in the pool... We never got a chance to discuss what it meant. I'm just wondering..."

"Yes?" Rumillion said, already sensing where Ademo was going with this.

"Well, he looked like me. I mean... not exactly. He was older, and there were some differences. But still, he looked like me, don't you think?"

"Yes, I noticed that as well, Ademo. As did Muirik."

Ademo nodded, looking up to meet the prida's gaze. "So what does that *mean*? Is he – whoever he is – somehow connected to this enemy we face? Is he – I mean, could he be the enemy himself?"

Rumillion paused, offering Ademo a compassionate, if less than full, smile. "He may be. He very well may be. But I do not know for certain."

"But if he looks like me... what does that mean? Is he a relative of mine?"

"That chance does exist, yes," Rumillion said, in a voice that suggested to Ademo that perhaps the prida was more sure than he was letting on.

"But, according to my mother," Ademo began, shaking his head, "I have no older male relatives left alive. I myself am an only child. And my father died when I was young, and he was an only child; as was my mother. And my grandfathers have both passed on as well, long ago."

Rumillion nodded, meeting Ademo's searching gaze with a silent gravity. "Ademo, I wish I could tell you more. But we need to gather more information before we can guess at what all of this means, and then what we should do about it."

"But you clearly have some idea... yes?"

"Yes," Rumillion said, nodding slowly up and down, as if unsure what to say. "But there is much we don't know. Please trust me when I say there will come a time when we can discuss this more. But for now there are more pressing matters to attend to. We must do all we can with the time we have now to prepare for this attack. Because, I have little doubt it *will* happen. Tonight. In only a few short hours time."

Ademo nodded, quickly being reminded of the

precariousness of their present situation.

He rose with the prida, ready to help in any way he could. Still, as they strolled quickly back towards the Centrarium together, Ademo couldn't help but ruminate on the prida's words: *"I wish I could tell you more..."*

Did that mean Rumillion didn't know anything more? Or that what he *did* know was information he wasn't – for whatever reason – yet prepared to share with Ademo?

82

As darkness swallowed the cave, Banon built up a fire for himself, Kyanessa and Muirik to gather around. Not long before, Tiamoc had accompanied Dianvolo back into the surrounding woods, to scout the area under the cover of dark.

As the fire grew, each of their faces lit up with a warm glow, they sat in silence, each of their thoughts with Ademo and the Vaidas at Wisterlac. Eventually Banon decided to break the silence.

"Kyanessa, how do you know Dianvolo?"

"He traveled through Grantin years ago. I was just a girl then. Still, I remember him well. He stood out."

"How so?"

"Well, it might be a little difficult for a Landrite to

understand, Banon."

Muirik looked up from the fire, a sly grin wrapped across his face. He wondered if these two were about to resurrect the long-standing feud between their two cities.

"Try me," Banon said, in a surprisingly cordial tone.

Kyanessa turned to him, searching his expression for signs of contempt. Finding none, she turned back to the fire.

"Well, as you well know, we in Grantin have our own traditions, our own way of life, our own language. Most foreigners who come to our shore are put off by these differences. Or, at best, they ignore them; and usually move on to more familiar pastures as soon as chance allows.

"But Dianvolo was different. He actually showed an interest in our people and our ways. He stayed with us for half a year or more – if I remember it right. And during that time he did his best to familiarize himself with our history. He was like a sponge. Always asking questions. He and my father grew to be close, because my father knew more of our cultural heritage than almost anyone else."

"Any idea why he was so interested in Grantin specifically?" Banon asked, treading carefully.

"Not really. He just said he found it fascinating. He used that word a lot. I still remember that. But maybe Muirik knows more. After all, Dianvolo was a Vaida once."

"He was? And is no longer? How did that happen? I didn't know Vaidas could leave the fold," Banon said, all the more perplexed.

Muirik looked up, smiled in such a way as to say, *there's more to that than meets the eye.*

"Vaidas certainly *can* leave the fold, Banon. But you're right that they usually don't. But in certain circumstances, rare as they may be, a Vaida can be granted leave."

"Temporarily, or permanently?"

"Either one. But usually the former."

"Muirik, if I remember it correctly, Dianvolo didn't choose to leave, he was banished from his monat. Isn't that right?" Kyanessa asked.

Muirik breathed in deeply and slowly, then nodded his head. "That is true, yes. Though *banished* is probably too strong a word for it. Suffice it to say that Dianvolo's former prida found him – while diligent and capable, and of the highest character – somewhat... *distracted* by other pursuits."

"What pursuits would those be?" Banon asked.

"Well, *one* pursuit is more precise. But perhaps you'd better ask Dianvolo about that himself. I can't offer many details, nor is it really my place to. History was his interest, let's just leave it at that."

"History? And Grantine history specifically? Why would a Vaida be interested in Grantine history?" Banon said, and then seeing Kyanessa turn to him suddenly, he added: "No offense intended. I just mean – why Grantin specifically?"

475

"Well, I don't think it was Grantine history alone that Dianvolo was interested in. I suspect he was doing research, and that his work eventually brought him to Grantin; though he likely visited many places before that, and many after," Muirik said.

"Because he was interested in history?" Banon said, trying to make sense of it.

"Yes," Muirik said, "Movademic history more precisely."

"Ah. So was *that* it then?" Kyanessa said, a light suddenly coming on. "Was Dianvolo asked to leave the Order because he was investigating the history of the Vaidas – the very subject the Vaidas had sworn to leave alone?"

"Yes, though, to be clear, I don't think for a second that Dianvolo was trying to uncover the old, destructive ways of Priolancy. I think he was more interested in origins."

"Origins? Origins of what?" Kyanessa asked.

Muirik shifted, looking uncomfortable, which was unusual for a man so usually unflappable.

"The origins of the Order itself. That's what he was researching when... when things came to a head."

"But it's not like he was sent away in disgrace or anything like that, right?" Banon said, not quite content to the let the matter rest yet.

"No. Though he and Prida Greshim didn't exactly part in the best of terms, either. I think, more than anything else, it was a misunderstanding.

"I have come to know Dianvolo quite well since he

took up residence in these parts. And I know that while his interests, at first glance, fly in the face of Movademic principles, that he may very well have good reason for his pursuits. I myself am certainly sure that he has only the best of intentions."

"What do you mean when you say *it flies in the face of Movademic principles*? How so? After all, Dianvolo wasn't seeking to regain a knowledge of Priolancy, right?" Kyanessa asked.

"No. Certainly not. But... well, it's difficult to describe exactly. Let's just say that we Vaidas are hesitant to peer too deeply into our past altogether. And perhaps there's even a kind of superstition there. It's just that we take very seriously our commitment to keep that part of our past buried where we left it."

"Perhaps Dianvolo is looking into Movademic history because something doesn't quite square. Maybe there's more than Priolancy to find there," Banon said, eyeing Kyanessa from across the fire, purposefully.

"So you agree with Dianvolo's point of view, then, over his former prida's?" Kyanessa asked, ignoring Banon.

"Well, that's really not for me to say one way or the other. But I trust the man, to the core. And I trust that he believes that what he's doing is for the best interests of everyone involved."

"Who's 'everyone' in this case?" Banon asked.

"Friends, let's leave it there for now. If you wish, you can ask Dianvolo himself when chance allows. He certainly won't shy away from discussing it with you. Now, how about some more tea? I know I could certainly use a cup," Muirik said, already rising up to make it plain that the present line of conversation was over.

83

Three of the Vaidas were posted as sentinels on the roof of the dome. It was their task to give first notice of any kind of enemy approach. Rumillion and Ademo were stationed below in the Centrarium. And a few other Vaidas were positioned at various points around the perimeter of the dome.

The atmosphere was both tense and slightly confused. The truth was, several of the Vaidas just didn't know what to do with the idea of Ademo being a seer. They knew those kinds of people had existed in the past, or at least had been rumored to. But it was another thing entirely to meet one in the flesh. What struck them most of all was Ademo's unassuming nature. He just didn't fit with their preconceptions of a seer. Perhaps they were expecting someone more like Renata Worthing.

What did help galvanize the group at Wisterlac was the command of Rumillion. He was their prida.

They trusted him explicitly. And if he said Ademo's vision was to be taken seriously, then taken seriously it was.

Still, some of them had their doubts, though they kept these to themselves.

Adding to the general sense of confusion was the fact that this experience was so new to all of them. The Movadem had existed for generations and generations. But there hadn't been a true threat like this in a very long time. So, to say the Vaidas waiting for a supposedly inevitable attack that evening at Wisterlac felt unprepared – would be an understatement. The truth was that many of the brothers there had come to believe, through the sheer repetition of their day to day experience, that their lives would be lived out in relatively quiet study, travel, and meditation.

Suddenly it was becoming quite apparent that those expectations needed some adjustment.

Ademo stood near Rumillion in the very center circle of the Centrarium. High above them was an open skylight. The moment there was any hint of trouble one of the sentinels would call down from the roof, hopefully providing some sense of warning. That was the plan, anyway.

"Should we call up to them?" Ademo asked. "See if they've seen anything suspicious yet?"

Rumillion turned to Ademo, his expression both kind and surprisingly calm.

"Would that help quench the silence, Ademo?"

"Well, I–" Ademo's words caught in his throat.

Rumillion had exposed his fear. He knew full well that if trouble was spotted, the sentinels would call down. It was the silence, stretching for hours now, that was driving him mad. His body was shot through with adrenaline that had nowhere to go. It was an unnatural sensation to say the least.

Rumillion put a hand on Ademo's shoulder, leaned in. "Ademo, place your attention in this present moment, as much as you can. Worrying about what is to come five minutes, or five hours from now, will do you no good. We have prepared as best we could. Now we must be still, be present in this moment. Our strength is in our focus; in our ability to be here; now. And nowhere else."

Ademo nodded, swallowing involuntarily. On the one hand, such advice seemed almost preposterous. How could he *not* think about what was about to happen? And yet, on the other hand, he sensed that the prida was right. Worrying did nothing to prepare him. In fact, it only served to sap his energy.

"Breathe, Ademo. *Breathe*. It all begins and ends with breathing; remember that," Rumillion added.

Ademo nodded, not understanding, but choosing to follow the advice anyway. And as he took in a long, deep breath – letting the air fill his lungs entirely, before breathing out again, slowly, fully – he *did* feel better; as if some of the nervous, negative energy exited his system as he exhaled.

On the rooftop of the dome Crion sat perfectly

still, facing in a generally westward direction. He let his eyes wander across the sky; a sky that was now filled with stars. The bright, full moon was lazily climbing behind him, its light casting a bright, if diffused, reflection on the acidic, still waters of Wisterlac.

And then suddenly something caught his attention. From the tree line, not far from the edge of the western shore, something shot upwards with great speed. The fiery bolt began to arc inward and turned towards the dome.

Crion watched with rapt attention. But he wasn't too concerned. He could still feel the steady vibration of the dome's energy field deep in his bones. It would protect them from such a projectile.

And sure enough, seconds later, as the thing angled down towards the dome, it fizzled into pieces as it passed through the invisible energy field.

Only at the last moment had Crion realized what it was: an arrow, its point lit with fire. But again, not even a flit of ash touched the rooftop. The energy field had eliminated the arrow entirely.

That was too easy, wasn't it? *Was this it?* Was this what they had prepared for? If this was all the enemy had to combat them with, it would be a walk in the proverbial park.

And then the deep hum Crion could feel more than hear, suddenly quit. All at once. Entirely.

The energy field was down. Just like that. And every Vaida at Wisterlac knew it the moment it happened.

And now feared gripped their hearts like never before.

Crion and his brothers on the roof hardly had a moment to acknowledge this change in events, as suddenly four more arrows, this time from west, east, and south of the dome, shot skyward, arching inevitably towards them.

As part of their standard training, they each were well versed in the skills of oblitication. And they each used those skills now, concentrating with a degree of focus almost unfathomable to the average person. And as they did, each of those arrows fizzled into nothingness.

This time something *did* rain down on the dome roof. But it was only ashes.

Crion and his brethren breathed deeply, refocusing themselves. That was quite an experience. It was one thing to learn the skill of oblitication. Quite another to use it against an actual, imminent threat.

And then, before they'd even had the chance to fully reflect on the difference between practice and reality, several more arrows launched from the tree line around the lake. And then several more. And suddenly the sky looked to be lit up by these flaming arrows.

Each of the four focused all of their concentration on the incoming arrows. And they were able to deal with many of them.

But not all.

Despite their best efforts, several of the arrows did find their way to the roof of the now unshielded dome. Little fires lit up at various points around the structure. Now there was shouting, and fear, as a whole host of new arrows were launched towards them, the night sky aflame with hurtling projectiles.

Crion ran to the open skylight, called down to those gathered below: "We're under fire from flaming arrows coming from all directions. There are too many for us to obliticate from here! They're coming in ten at a time!"

Then there was more shouting from the rooftop. Crion turned and covered his head with his hands, as one of the flaming arrows came slicing down, only narrowly missing him. A small fire immediately started spreading nearby.

Word quickly spread throughout the monat that they were under attack from bowmen stationed around the shoreline. Several of the Vaidas decided the only way to effectively combat this barrage was to engage the enemy directly. And only a few minutes later they could be seen chasing across the lake towards the shoreline.

Inside the Centrarium, Mossic – he with his bald head and thick, black brows – appeared beneath the arched doorway and announced that several Vaidas had moved to engage the enemy directly. When Rumillion heard this he spun around quickly. Ademo noticed the strange expression written across the prida's face. And it unnerved him, because he hadn't seen it before.

"No!" Rumillion said sternly. "My orders were for us to stay united here at the monat! What if the enemy's very intention is to divide our numbers, and thus our strength, by drawing us out?"

Ademo was astonished to see the man he'd first encountered as a tranquil gardener grow so fierce. Suddenly the prida's strength of will and personality were on clear display. Ademo would almost have been terrified if he weren't so confident in Rumillion's intentions.

"No one else is to leave the dome! Make sure everyone understands that. Our stand is to be here and here alone!" Rumillion called out to Mossic, who nodded – his expression also one of surprise – before running off to convey the prida's orders.

From his rooftop view, Crion was relieved when – under the illuminating light of the moon – he saw several of his brethren running towards the general location of the enemy bowmen. Soon the barrage of flaming arrows lessened, as their enemies were forced to deal with the Vaidas on the shoreline.

Before long several fires erupted at various points within the shrub brush. Distance shouts could be heard as the enemy seemed confused by the unexpected turn of events.

Crion took a moment to lean back over the skylight opening, and called down to those below. "It's working! The brothers who crossed the lake are engaging the enemy with skillwill, and it's thwarting them! We may be able to fend off the arrows that make it through now!"

"No!" Rumillion called from below, tilting his head far back to look up at Crion's overhanging face. "That's exactly what they want us to believe! We need to stay together! We may be able to restore the shield with a collective mindfield. But we need as many of us as possible to do that!"

Ademo thought he saw confusion cross Crion's features, and then the large Vaida turned away, as one of his rooftop brothers called out to him. Ademo couldn't make out the words, but suddenly Crion was gone from the skylight.

What Crion had heard at that very moment was the voice of the thick-trunked Brellwick, booming out to say: "To the East! What *is* that?"

Crion followed Brellwick's outstretched arm, looking in an eastwardly direction. At first he didn't see anything, just a few dark clouds obscuring a mostly clear, star-dotted sky.

And then he saw a shadow cross in front of one of those clouds. He saw it just for a moment, and then it was gone again.

Then he caught sight of movement – a line in the sky moving up and down. It occurred to Crion that the motion almost looked like the flapping of bird wings, seen from a great distance. But if these were birds then – judging from the considerable distance – they would have to be massive. It just couldn't be, could it?

And then a flurry of color, streaming red and

yellow, bolted out against the distant skyline, where those same lines were moving methodically up and down.

"What in the *world?*" Crion said out loud, to no one in particular.

Whatever these things were, they were closing in fast. A nearby cloud was suddenly lit up with some of that same yellow and red flush of color.

And then some great, flapping beast emerged from the edge of the cloud.

Suddenly a horrifying, piercing screech tore across the sky. Crion's eyes went wide and his mouth hung open, speechless.

Then Brellwick shouted the word that was on all their minds; a word they thought belonged solely to the world of myth: *"Dragons!"*

84

To the east there were four of these massive beasts of prey closing in on them fast. Their screeching calls sent chills through the hearts of the Vaidas in and around the monat. The brothers inside could only imagine what creatures were responsible for such a horrifying sound, whereas the Vaidas on the rooftop and along the shore were seeing first hand. And for a moment they all stood in a stunned stupor.

This just couldn't be happening!

And yet, their eyes did not betray them.

As the quartet of dragons neared the monat the first of the beasts dipped its wing and swooped down over them, fire suddenly erupting from its mouth. The flame caught and in a split second that corner of the roof was on fire; black, choking smoke soon billowing skyward.

Before the Vaidas had had more than a few seconds to react, the second beast dove from the north, bearing down at them with blazing speed. It let loose with one of those blood-curdling screeches, before scorching the opposite side of the dome. This time Crion looked on in horror, as his brother Beiron disappeared beneath the engulfing flames, never to be seen again.

"Inside! We must get inside!" Crion yelled, motioning to Brellwick.

From the floor of the Centrarium, Ademo and Rumillion looked up with dazed expressions. All they could perceive was the sound of those horrifying screeches, and the low, whooping sound of the dragon wings as they flew directly over the dome.

Then came a scream from above.

And then Crion was at the skylight again, quickly descending the ladder. Not far behind him was the stocky figure of Brellwick. And then came another one of those screeches, like a scream of vengeance. Flame erupted on the roof yet again, as a third dragon breathed fire down upon them. Brellwick scrambled for the ladder as fast as he could, but then the flame engulfed him.

Ademo and Rumillion stared upward with horror as Brellwick lost his footing and fell through the skylight. On fire, falling like some cursed star, he crashed into the second raked row of the Centrarium, denting the solid floor and sending debris flying.

At first those below were too shocked to react. But then the flame spread from the fallen Vaida's body and began burning through the second row.

Rumillion called out: "Crion! Quick: the fire tarps!"

Awaking from his daze, Crion turned and reached behind him, pulling a lightweight tarp from a compartment along the wall. With the help of Ademo he was able to toss the tarp over the flames, and they quickly subsided.

While the fire was being dealt with, Rumillion ran to the other side of the chamber and began to wind a wheel that was connected to the skylight, which quickly closed.

Outside of the dome, the Vaidas who'd crossed the lake to engage the enemy bowmen stood in horror as the waters of the acidic lake took to flame before their very eyes. Soon the entire lake was one massive, roaring blaze. Mesmerized, they looked on as the light from the inferno glinted against the near-metallic scales of the circling dragons.

In that moment, transfixed by the surreal horror enfolding around them, they realized they were cut off from ever returning to the monat.

Seconds later the enemy bowmen emerged and began firing at the greatly outnumbered Vaidas. As the Vaidas' bodies fell, one by one, onto the now hot sands of the shoreline, the enemy forces shouted and danced with crazed expressions, as the dragons continued raining fire.

85

Ademo, Rumillion and Crion stood in the very center of the Centrarium, the last of the survivors at Wisterlac. Overhead the dragons were still circling, diving in turns and scorching the roof of the monat. The structure was built to withstand fire, but only to a degree. This kind of constant, fiery barrage was wearing down the structure, strong as it was.

To make matters worse, Rumillion was convinced these beasts were actually a variety called terasagons, with accelerant-laced breath that made the fire they breathed all the more potent. Once lit it proved very difficult to douse.

Very few Vaidas even knew of such beasts. The prida himself only knew of them from lore, because they were rumored to be mentioned in a certain, infamous book penned by Loden; a book that, up until recently, many doubted existed at all.

The fact that these beasts were here, in the scaly flesh, in the process of destroying a supposedly fireproof structure that had stood for hundreds of years, only served to prove that the book was no myth. It existed. And, like Muirik had deduced after his encounter with the eilodens, Rumillion knew now that the book must be in the possession of this phantom enemy.

And as normally unshakeable as the prida was, that thought sent shivers down his spine.

There was silence among them. As Ademo looked into their faces he was awed by the calm he saw there. He, for one, was anything but. His blood pulsed – almost pounded – through his veins, and his breath was coming in gasps. Then he remembered what Rumillion had told him earlier: *it all begins and ends with breathing*. He tried putting that advice into practice, with limited success.

When the shrieks of the dragons rocked him back to reality, Ademo finally spoke up. "Is there nothing that can be done? No way of escape?" he asked, his eyes wide.

"The lake itself is on fire, Ademo. And its acidic content will burn for days," Crion said, shaking his head slowly.

"But... surely there must be something? Are there no tunnels underneath the monat? Surely there must be *something* we can do!"

"What we can do," Crion said, breathing deeply, "is prepare ourselves for the transition that awaits us.

Our bodies will die, but our energy signatures will not. We will transmute."

As Crion was answering Ademo, Rumillion turned towards the frightened Kiraboan. And in that moment he caught sight of something. Just the hint of something, actually. A faint blue haze that seemed to glow about Ademo's head. And in the very next instant a thought occurred to Rumillion, one that made his resolute jaw drop.

Both Ademo and Crion noticed this. Ademo thought perhaps he'd disappointed Rumillion. And, despite the imminent danger facing them, he suddenly regretted saying what he had. He wished he could be braver; more resolved – like these courageous Vaidas at his side.

"I'm sorry..." Ademo said, forcing himself to breath again. "It's just that–"

Suddenly the entire monat structure shook as a loud booming sound erupted from high above.

"They've landed on the roof now," Crion said, in a tone that seemed prepared to succumb to the inevitable. "They're impervious to the fire."

And in that moment, as Crion seemed to relent, Ademo's desire to escape only increased.

When Ademo turned to Rumillion he saw something strange in the prida's expression.

"Crion," Rumillion began, while still staring directly at Ademo, "listen to me closely, because time is very short now. We're going to try to form a vortelix."

Crion eyes quickly darted left and right, as if he were trying to understand something that perplexed him greatly. "A vortelix? But how? That's impossible without the presence of two pridas. And besides you, Rumillion, the nearest prida is over seven hundred miles from here. *Assuming* Eraquin is still there at Feldinwall."

In that moment, Ademo gathered that a prida was not only a title, but also a function; a calling, with abilities attached.

"True. Two pridas can do it. But there is another way," Rumillion said, finally turning to look Crion's way.

"Another way? I don't understand..."

"It's not so much two pridas that are necessary, but two who are gifted with the Empulse."

Crion's furrowed brow only creased further.

And just then there was a thunderous crash, and a large section of the domed roof above them tore open, as a giant clawed foot pierced the structure. Debris fell all around them and smoke began to billow in.

"Yes, but who other than a prida is empulsic like that?" Crion asked, his voice rising to a shout amidst the surrounding noise.

"A sone," Rumillion said.

"A *sone*? Well, yes, theoretically... but who-"

"Ademo," The prida said, matter-of-factly.

"Ademo?" Crion said, sounding surprised.

"*Me?*" Ademo added, pointing to his chest.

"Ademo, listen to me – we don't have much time.

A sone is rare. But you are one. I know it. Do you understand me, Ademo? I don't just *believe* it, I *know* it. I can see the energy signature around you."

"But you didn't mention this before..." Ademo said, still perplexed.

"No, but that's because I didn't see it before. The signs are only arising in you now because you have such singular focus. Now listen to me: two pridas, or a prida and a sone, can form a vortelix."

"A vortelix?"

"Yes. It lets us transport to another place, instantaneously. But for that to happen, *both* parties must focus together to form the energy field. And that means both must believe in what they're doing. Believe that they *can* do it. Do you believe you can do it, Ademo? With me?"

"Well I–"

"We must hurry, the structure is about to collapse!" Crion called out.

"Try not to think about it intellectually," Rumillion continued, his focus solely on Ademo, "just try and *feel* it. In that energy that pulses through you right now, seeking refuge from this inferno. Just focus on that. Can you do that?"

"Okay..."

Rumillion held out a hand to each of them, as they stood together in a tight circle. Everything around them was now shaking.

"Remember, Ademo, we're not *thinking* about doing this, we're just letting that feeling arise in us.

That force of will. Can you feel it?"

"Yes, I–"

"Can you *feel* it, Ademo?" Rumillion said, squeezing his hand.

"Yes," Ademo said, more confidently now.

"Good. Now, just let that feeling grow. Let it ooze from every pore of your body. And let your thinking mind be still. Don't think. *Feel*."

Ademo closed his eyes and did just that. And soon the feeling grew to a crescendo in him. He could feel something akin to a buzzing of electricity against his skin. Though his eyes were closed, in his mind's eye Ademo saw something: a room... somehow familiar. And in that moment he knew he was sharing this vision with Rumillion. They were mindsealed.

Just then there was a crash from high above them, as a second taloned claw tore into the roof of the dome. This time the weakened structure could no longer hold. The roof began to implode, falling inward in large pieces, as a choking cloud of debris rained down.

86

Dawn shone its pale light on the scene of death and destruction atop Mt. Wister. The First Lieutenant, the man called Wylen Sciavo, looked on with satisfaction at the smoldering ruin of the monat. His skeletal face was drawn in hard lines, as usual. But this morning, in the timid first light of the day, a crooked smile could be seen curving out towards his chiseled cheekbone.

The terasagons had accomplished their task brilliantly, just as his master had hoped. Their self-accelerated fire-breath had made quick work of the domed structure once the energy field was down. And as his Preeminence had ordered, the flying beasts had scorched the ground beneath the structure as well, eventually revealing the deep underground chamber.

Not only had the energy signature his Preeminence had gleaned via the shard been sufficient to neutralize the defense shield, but even their plan to draw out the Vaidas had worked perfectly. Once they had them on the shore, Sciavo knew they would be prevented from ever returning. At that point it was checkmate.

Sciavo recalled seeing the expression on the face of one of the Vaidas when the lake itself first took to flame. The man's expression was one of horror and panic; a seductive concoction the First Lieutenant had found intoxicating.

And how many Vaidas had that left inside, to perish amongst the choking smoke and scorching flames? Perhaps a handful? He would soon find out. His men were already scouring the ruins for bodies.

The realization that the remains of both Rumillion and young Asterling were soon to be discovered served as the perfect opening to a new day.

The boy had thrown them for a time, when he'd decided to separate from his companions. Brave and foolish he was, as only the young can be. But when their scouts had spotted him heading east again, towards the summit of Wister, it was clear to Sciavo what the young seer's plans were. And those plans suited him just fine. Asterling would burn alongside Wisterlac's prida. How fitting: like two sticks in a single flame.

The First Lieutenant let himself imagine the praise his master would soon heap upon him, and smiled.

With one more sweeping glance over the intoxicating scene, he turned back towards the shrub line. Walking briskly, with a spring in his step, Sciavo made his way along the narrow path that his men had painstakingly hewn through the prickly shrub brush.

It was early afternoon, and the First Lieutenant was drinking spiced tea in the confines of his tent, when he heard footsteps approaching. A moment later his personal guard, a muscular beast of a man named Horath, flipped open the tent door, bent his large frame in, and announced that one of his men, Forlan, approached.

Forlan had been tasked with gathering the evidence the master would want. Of course, to Forlan and the others, the First Lieutenant was the master. They knew almost nothing of his Preeminence. And that went exactly to plan. Anonymity was his

Preeminence's desired course. And Sciavo, ever the one to please this man of glory, was only too eager to serve. The men feared and revered *him*. And that was enough. His Preeminence's time of revealing would come. Oh, certainly it would. And soon even. But not yet. Not quite yet.

"Come," Sciavo said, loud enough for those outside the tent to hear.

Forlan bent down and entered the tent. Over his shoulder he carried a sack of some size. When the First Lieutenant saw what Forlan had brought in with him, he erupted in anger, cuffing the man across the ear viciously.

"Forlan, you idiot! I don't want that filth in here!"

Forlan – his ear now blazing red – cringed. "Sorry, First Lieutenant, I thought you told me not to let this out of my sight, not even for a moment."

"Yes, you imbecile. But you could have simply told Horath what you had with you! Now take that outside immediately!"

Forlan bowed, and then beat a hasty retreat. Outside, Horath, who'd overheard the exchange, gave him a fierce look, suggesting he might add to the punishment the First Lieutenant had just administered.

A moment later, after taking the time to finish his tea, Sciavo emerged from the tent. "Right then, Forlan, what do you have?"

"Sir, we scourged the premises in every direction. And, in addition to the bodies of the Vaidas killed on the shore, we recovered an additional four skulls amongst the monat debris. I collected them and have them here, sir, as you asked."

"Four?"

"Yes, sir."

"I would have thought there would have been more. Are you sure you searched thoroughly, Forlan?"

Forlan, feeling the legendary gaze of Sciavo bearing down upon him, took a deep breath, and resisted the urge to step back a pace before replying.

"Yes, First Lieutenant. We searched up and down, multiple times. I offer you my assurance, as ever your faithful servant, that these four were all there was to be found."

Sciavo glared at him a moment longer, unblinkingly, before finally nodding and pointing to a cage nearby. "Fine. Put the sack in there and lock it up. Horath will watch you throughout. When you're done, give him the key."

Forlan, thankful that what had felt like an interrogation was now over, nodded. "Yes, sir."

As the First Lieutenant turned to re-enter his tent, Forlan's curiosity got the better of him.

"Sir, if I may, I'm just curious, what is it we want these skulls for?"

Sciavo paused beneath the tent flap Horath held open for him. He only half turned his head towards Forlan.

"Forlan, you are a bold one, aren't you? *Too* bold. But this time I'll let it pass. For today is a glorious one.

As to your question, let's just say we're looking for a family resemblance," Sciavo said, with a sinister chuckle.

Forlan stood still for a moment, trying to make sense of the First Lieutenant's reply. But then, seeing Horath's eyes bearing down upon him, he decided to make quick work of securing the skulls in the cage.

87

There was a deafening, tearing sound, as a second taloned claw tore into the roof of the dome. This time the roof just couldn't handle the strain, and the dome began to implode, falling inward in a choking cloud of structural debris.

Ademo gasped and opened his eyes, prepared for the inevitable, already feeling the cold chill of death upon him.

But when he opened his eyes he saw exactly what he had just envisioned with them fully closed: a room, *so* familiar.

One thing was clear, they were no longer in the monat. Ademo gasped, amazed by what he was seeing. He turned towards a crooked window and saw snow falling outside, landing softly upon a pure white, alpine meadow. And beyond the meadow was a hazy scene of powder-covered pine trees.

And in that moment, Ademo's mind swam in disorientation, as he tried to understand how it was that he was standing with Rumillion and Crion in Renata's cottage.

Crion seemed as amazed as Ademo, and that made Ademo feel relieved. As much as these Vaidas were capable of some astounding feats, apparently this particular trick wasn't of the garden variety.

"It worked!" Crion cried out, a hand covering his mouth, as his eyes looked about almost frantically, taking in their new environment. "But where *are* we?"

Rumillion, smiling, reached over and gripped Crion's powerful shoulder. "Why don't you ask Ademo that, Brother Crion? After all, it was he who determined our destination."

"He did?" Crion said, surprised.

"I did?" Ademo said, almost in unison.

Rumillion nodded, before moving over towards the window to admire the winter wonderland. "Yes, indeed."

"Let me guess," Ademo said, a thought striking him, "you perused my memory and chose a location you found there. In other words, you had to choose somewhere I'd been before. You know, if that's the case, I'd rather have preferred the beachfront on Kiraboa. It's a tad more pleasant this time of year."

"Oh, come on, Ademo," Rumillion said, playfully, still looking out the window as snowflakes continued to fall, "this land is a paradise."

"Oh," Ademo said, shrugging. "To each his own, I

guess."

"But you're partially right," Rumillion continued, "I did scour your mind for a location. But, in actuality, it couldn't just be *any* location. In fact, based on your history, this is likely the only one we could have chosen. But that... is a long story," Rumillion said, smiling and turning to gaze outdoors again.

Crion slapped Ademo on the back. "Alright, Ademo, if you've been here before, perhaps you know where we can find some firewood. I don't know if you noticed, but it's freezing in here. *Literally*."

Ademo rubbed his arms and nodded emphatically. "I did. And I do. In fact, Banon and I chopped most of it ourselves. Come on, follow me."

As they exited, Rumillion looked on, smiling thinly. This Ademo really *was* quite something. They had just vortelixed only seconds before being crushed to death, and here he was, ready to get on with the demands of the next moment. That kind of resilience was something Rumillion truly admired.

And then the prida's smile faded, as reality hit home. They had escaped their sure demise by the skin of their teeth. And the cost had been so great. So many brothers lost. How many of those who'd engaged the enemy on the shore could have survived? Rumillion held out some hope that perhaps some had escaped. But still, *such* a slaughter. And under his watch. It was both heartbreaking and daunting.

This enemy was formidable. Of this there was no longer a shred of doubt. In addition to dabbling in

Loden's lore, this enemy was clearly also empulsic. Rumillion knew, even if the other Vaidas didn't, that empulsic sensing was the only way to fully ascertain and interrupt the monat energy shield. So clearly Ademo wasn't the *only* sone to emerge of late. And of course, that too fit with what was foretold in the prophecy.

Truth be told, as harrowing as their escape had been, the challenge had only just begun. And Ademo, most of all, would need every ounce of that resiliency, and then some, to deal with what was yet to come.

And that next chapter would begin with what Rumillion had to tell the young seer about his background, about his very lineage. And dealing with that would perhaps prove most challenging of all. Because it would call into question, for a young man like Ademo, the very content of his person; the very cloth he was cut from, so to speak.

As the front door flung open, and Crion and Ademo came piling back in, a dusting of snow on their shoulders, each with a stack of firewood stowed between their arms, Rumillion moved over to help. Perhaps that conversation could wait, for a while. This evening there more pressing matters to attend to. And that began with a blazing fire to stave off the cold, and a warm meal to appease their hunger.

88

As always with these kinds of missions for his Preeminence, Sciavo made sure he was completely alone. The rest of the camp had already packed up and were headed toward their next destination. And as they marched north, he made his way in the opposite direction, back to the charred remains of what had been the monat.

All that remained of the former structure was a blackened, hollowed out crater in the center of the island. The acidic lake was now non-existent, leaving behind a cracked, grey-green lakebed. The acidic waters that hadn't burned off in the fire had poured into the underground chamber at the center of the island, eventually seeping through cracks to disappear altogether.

The powerful figure in crimson and black marched across the cracked and poisoned earth where the lake had once been. Reaching the center, he climbed down into the blackened crater.

He took a few moments to search for exactly what his Preeminence had described. And then, he found it – a narrow but deep fissure. He peered into the crack and could see a faint yellowish light arising from somewhere deep below. Also rising up was a sound; a hum, that sent shivers through his body.

Sciavo looked around him, and found a stone of about the right size and shape. He dropped the stone into the fissure, then leaned his ear in close to hear it touch bottom. He heard nothing. That told him what he needed to know. The chamber below reached deep into the magnetic core.

Lying down, Sciavo reached into his thick cloak, retrieving the crystal shard from the compartment he had sown to keep it safe. He took one more last, long look at it, feeling somewhat attached, knowing it had connected him to his Preeminence directly.

Still, his Preeminence had said, coming soon was a time when no such tool would be necessary. For soon they would see each other face to face. Sciavo smiled at the prospect, then turned back towards the fissure and dropped the shard through the narrow opening. As with the stone, he didn't hear it strike bottom.

Following his master's orders, Sciavo made quick work of traipsing back across the dry lakebed, and then turned north to catch up with his marching camp.

It was hours later, after he had moved far away from the cratered summit of Wister, that the explosion shook the very ground beneath his feet. Not long after, an invisible – but powerful – wave of energy came sweeping over the tall trees that surrounded him, bending them forward like twigs.

Sciavo closed his eyes, letting the strange wavewind rush over him, feeling heat and a strange tingling sensation crawl over his skin, even as he was pressed into the ground by the concussive force. It was only the cloak his master had given him that prevented Sciavo from being decimated like the disintegrating timber all around him.

Thousands of miles away, Siya sat within her newly constructed hut, weaving a basket from rintu weeds, when a strange rumbling shook everything around her. Gasping, Siya put the half-finished basket aside and rushed outside. There she let her attention move in the direction where other villagers were now looking.

And then she understood the sounds of fear and expressions of concern written on all of their faces. For high above the tree line of guia palms, a thick, climbing column of grey-black smoke was pouring forth from the peak of Mt. Uduri, even as the ground beneath her continued to rumble.

DARREN BRETT KING

www.ingramcontent.com/pod-product-compliance
Lightning Source LLC
Chambersburg PA
CBHW061030030726
47504CB00002B/318